THE
DIAMOND SPHINX

THE LOST ANCIENTS: BOOK SIX

MARIE ANDREAS

DEDICATION

*To my sister—these books
wouldn't have happened without you.*

*And to everyone who ever wanted
a drunken faery of their own.*

ACKNOWLEDGEMENTS

Writing this series has been a labor of love, joy, and tears (mostly mine, sometimes the characters). I could never have done it without the love, support, and kindness from family, friends, and readers.

I'd like to thank Jessa Slade for editing magic—she continues to make sure I don't go following too many wild thoughts. For my most awesome team of beta readers who plowed through the entire book and helped tighten it up: Lisa Andreas, Patti Huber, Lynne Mayfield, Sharon Rivest, and Ilana Schoonover. Any remaining errors are mine alone.

My cover artist, Aleta Rafton, creating yet another awesome work of art. And to The Killion Group for formatting of the entire book and print cover.

And to every one of you who has followed me on this wild journey!

OTHER BOOKS BY
MARIE ANDREAS

THE LOST ANCIENTS SERIES
Book One: The Glass Gargoyle
Book Two: The Obsidian Chimera
Book Three: The Emerald Dragon
Book Four: The Sapphire Manticore
Book Five: The Golden Basilisk
Book Six: The Diamond Sphinx

THE ASARLAÍ WARS TRILOGY
Book One: Warrior Wench
Book Two: Victorious Dead
Book Three: Defiant Ruin

THE ADVENTURES OF SMITH AND JONES
A Curious Invasion
The Mayhem of Mermaids

CHAPTER ONE

HERE WAS ALWAYS A BOOM. Sometimes a big one filled with yells—mostly mine—sometimes a small one, followed by faery cursing. But there was *always* a boom. That had become my reality this past month. If I was honest with myself, that had been my reality since three little drunken faeries invaded my life over fifteen years ago.

Today's boom was a small one, mostly followed by faeries laughing rather than cursing. And it was just them discussing prior booms. Now, "boom" had never been clearly defined by the faeries. Ever. No matter how many times I asked, begged, pleaded, or how much ale I gave them. Boom was a catchall word in their world that could mean something big, bad, and world-destroying, or just a little thing that should have happened but didn't...or vice versa.

I rolled over on my pile of leaves and blankets that I pretended was a bed. It was too early to be up and I wanted to get in a few more hours of rest before we hit the trail again. But Garbage Blossom, Leaf Grub, and Crusty Bucket were having none of that. They were squatting around the fire, drawing something in the dirt, giggling, and talking maniacally about booms. The empty ale bottles next to them pointed out that they weren't up early, they'd not gone to bed yet. I thought about asking them to shut up, but I knew that would just make them louder, so I rolled over and crammed my cloak over my ears.

We'd been on the run for a month now. Just those three, my two constructs, Bunky, my chimera construct, and Irving—my newly named gargoyle construct—and myself. We were hiding from Nivinal, a nasty, unnaturally powerful bastard bent on destroying the world as I knew it. That he apparently needed me to be a part of his plans had made me run away even faster.

We were also running from the people I cared about and loved. Something had happened to me during the battle at the Spheres—I'd changed. Into what exactly, I wasn't sure. But it had been huge. And scaly. It had helped destroy the attackers and save my friends, but I could have easily crushed them. I had never been so terrified in my life. So I took off.

Garbage, Leaf, and Crusty hadn't let me go without them—and that they seemed to know what was happening to me, and were sad about it, wasn't good. Then Bunky and Irving had shown up as well. I'd had the remaining twenty faeries promise to watch over my friends and the love of my life, Alric, and explain I had to go for their safety.

I knew my friends; but more importantly, I knew my elf boyfriend tracker, and so I was surprised I'd made it this long without being found. They'd seen me when I changed; maybe if they'd known what I had become they weren't really trying to find me.

There was one more quasi-member of my group who might have been keeping them from finding me—if they were, in fact, looking. A minkie. It could be *the* minkie, but the faeries always referred to them as plural, so I assumed there was more than one. But the faeries always forgot him immediately after seeing him, and whenever I saw him, they didn't. Even Bunky and Irving gronked at me oddly when I asked if they'd seen the tiny white creature. They would be staring right at it, but apparently see nothing.

Visual mirage or not, I had a feeling the minkie was

somehow masking our trail.

A particularly high-pitched squeal of laughter stabbed through the cloak over my head and I gave up even trying to pretend to sleep. I rolled out of my makeshift bed and stretched. The woods around us were dark and the sounds of night hunts were echoing around. Wolves hunted here. Probably other creatures as well. We'd run into the wolves our second night in these mountains—they'd started circling us, until Crusty flew up to the lead wolf, smacked her on the nose, and chittered at her.

The wolf pulled back in surprise, but stopped snarling and tilted her head. After a few tense moments of faery-wolf silent communication, the pack faded back into the forest. Well, I thought it was tense. The girls just started laughing hysterically. Of course, they wouldn't share what was so funny, nor what Crusty told the she-wolf. But all of the animals had left us alone after that.

There were times I realized that I really should be scared about what my faeries could do.

The mountains we were going through were higher than anything I was used to and the forest was dense and untamed. Unlike many of the areas around the kingdom, there was no sign of prior habitation. If it weren't for the situation, I might enjoy being here. Well, if there was a cabin of some sort. And food. And a real bed.

I dug out some of the last of the travel bread and jerky that had been in my pack when I ran away. I needed to see if the faeries had any foodstuffs in those magic bags of theirs. So far all I'd seen had been ale. As long as they let me have one every once in a while, that was fine. But hopefully they could also get some food. They seemed to eat whatever they found, but I was a bit pickier.

The food supply was alarmingly low—two more days of dry travel bread and maybe three of the jerky. There were plenty of fresh streams, so water wasn't an issue.

I held up the food. "Girls? We need something else to

eat—and do not bring back leaves."

I'd found that I had to be clear of what I wanted or they just brought in leaves. LOTS of leaves. Now that we were higher in the mountains, they also dragged in tons of pine needles, whether I asked for them or not.

"Food good!" Crusty yelled and tipped over backwards.

The other two didn't look much better. I wasn't going to get anything from them until they slept it off. I ripped off a chunk of the dry bread and a slice of the jerky and bit in. Then I reached over and grabbed an ale bottle they hadn't gotten to yet.

"Is mine!" Garbage stretched for the unopened bottle, but only succeeded in falling over sideways. She started snoring a moment later.

I shook my head and opened the bottle. When I ran away from my friends, I had no plan beyond getting away from people I might hurt. Now that it had been a month of not turning into whatever it was, and hiking through these mountains, I was rethinking that logic.

Covey, Padraig, and Lorcan were three of the smartest people I knew. Alric wasn't a slouch in that department either, even though he had a tendency to act first and think second. They might have been able to help me figure out what had happened—and how to make sure it never happened again. Sadly, it only took me running out of food and being sick of camping for that thought to be given serious consideration.

A rustling of footsteps through leaves came from behind me. I'd been around enough sneaky folks in the last year that I knew what to do. I kept my breathing steady, didn't physically react, and slowly reached for a stick that hadn't made it to the fire yet. I used it to poke at the fire, as if lost in my own thoughts, and glanced to the faeries—all three were sound asleep.

After the wolf pack encounter, we'd had no more interactions with any animals. But there could be animals out there who hadn't heard of the faeries yet. Not to mention, Alric wasn't the only excellent tracker in the world. I didn't look like I had much, but it appeared that I was traveling alone—a prime victim if someone was desperate.

Another rustle. They were quiet, but Alric had taught me what to listen for.

I took a slow breath, tightened my hold on my flaming stick, and spun.

To face a tiny old lady in a badly mismatched dress and a ragged shawl, squinting at me with a stick of her own.

"You're not him." She lowered her stick and peered around my fire. "Did you see some scallywag run through here? Maybe a day or so ago. Took my prime bottle of nectar and fled."

She was shorter than I recalled, and skinnier. Her face was hard to see clearly in the firelight. But something about her voice was familiar.

"Mathilda?"

"What did you call me?" The stick came back up and the very pointy end was aimed at my gut.

"I used to know someone and you reminded me of her. Mathilda. Although her sister called her something else."

The woman took a step closer, looked past me to the left of the fire, and started laughing. "You still have the damn faeries! I figured you'd have ditched them long ago." She squinted at me. "But why are you alone in the mountains, Taryn?"

Her voice had resumed the tone I recalled, the one she used before she and her house ran off on me. Mathilda had found me after I'd been left for dead fifteen years ago. She'd nursed me back to health. After a few months, she sent me to go find some berries for one of her tinctures, took her house, and ran off. Leaving me with Garbage, Crusty, and Leaf as my wards.

"Where is your house, Mathilda?"

"Now, I asked first."

"I like the mountains, they are refreshing, and the girls and I often come up here to relax."

Mathilda opened her mouth to speak, but my two constructs dropped from the sky and hovered between us. Bunky was making a low growl and Irving was trying to mimic it. Irving carried the basilisk relic somewhere inside him, but it no longer appeared in his mouth. I'd been debating how to glue a construct's mouth shut until I realized that.

"Oh now, aren't these cute?" She held out her hand, but both flew back out of range. "And trained as well! Have no fear, my stalwart guardians, I mean your ward no harm. Tell them we are friends, Taryn."

I looked at the two constructs—had they been living creatures, and not made of magical metal, their hackles would have been up. I dropped my stick into the fire. "Are we friends? You did trick me into being responsible for those faeries, and then abandoned us in the middle of a forest."

The laughing cackle was the same as it had always been. "Eh, I had places to go and you needed to grow." She nodded down to the sleeping faeries. "So did they. Queen Mungoosey has kept the faeries alive during extremely dark times, but they need to remember who they were— who they *are*. Going with you helped them."

"Bunky, Irving, stand down," I finally said. "But keep an eye on her."

They both flew up a few feet over our heads.

I folded my arms. "Now, what do you really look like?" Her sister, Siabiane, had indicated that Mathilda loved disguises.

Again the cackling laugh. "You really have met Siabiane. Very well." She waved her hand and her glamour dropped. She was still short, just not as tiny as she had appeared before. Just a few inches shorter than I. Her face was unlined and ageless, like that of her sister. Her ears had been rounded before, but now had the slight point of an elf breed. I'd never figured out if Siabiane was an abnormal pure breed elf or a mixed breed. The odds were looking toward both of them being mixed breeds.

"Or we're just so old our ears have lost their points." Mathilda's cackle was more disturbing coming from someone who looked like she did now. The rags and mismatched clothing definitely didn't fit the delicate elegance of her face.

"You're reading my mind?"

"No, just following your reaction. You hesitated on my ears. Siabiane and I are elves, but from a long vanished line." She shrugged. "I think we're the only two left in this land—we came from over the sea. Both of us have our reasons for sticking around. I'm not done here yet." She looked me over slowly. "Clearly."

"I'd offer you some breakfast, but I'm a bit low on rations at the moment. You're welcome to sit by my fire. Unless you need to go chase whoever stole your nectar."

She peered closer into my face for a few moments, her expression serious. Then she smiled. "There is far more to you now than when I found you—you were empty then. But it would make more sense for you and your entourage to come join me in my cottage. It's just over the next hill." She squinted over the fire toward the dark woods beyond. "And that thief is probably long gone. Had he taken off this way, he would have stumbled into you all. You're being here threw off my sense of his location." She shrugged. "I am annoyed, and I will catch him eventually, but I have more nectar." She looked around expectantly. "Well? Pick those little drunkards up, gather your things, and follow me. Unless you truly prefer the outdoors?"

I still wasn't happy about her abandoning me fifteen years ago, but I was less annoyed at her than I was tired of roughing it. I said nothing but grabbed my bedroll, shoved the faeries into my pack, and was back at her side a few minutes later. Bunky and Irving kept diving low over her in what I called their sniffing mode. They were deciding on whether they liked her or not. Which was fair—so was I.

CHAPTER TWO

MATHILDA'S COTTAGE LOOKED PRETTY MUCH the same as I remembered. Since it was a bit before true dawn, the warm glow of lit candles and a fire made it brighter. It was also a bit leafier than before; there were now vines growing around it making it blend in with the surroundings. But the walls underneath were brightly colored with splashes of purple, orange, and vibrant blue.

"Wouldn't it work better if you painted the house more natural colors?" I lifted my pack toward her cottage. "You'd blend in better."

Mathilda clucked and shook her head, but continued to the front door. "I like my colors. And my vines." She patted one strand that hung near the door and I saw it curl around her hand.

I shrugged and nodded to the constructs to follow as I went inside.

The inside was small and crowded with furniture, books, and baskets. I was struck by how different she and her sister were.

"So how was Siabiane the last you saw her?" Mathilda asked as she puttered over and took a kettle off the stove.

"Seriously, stop reading my mind." I'd been about to drop my pack and take a seat, but not if she'd started reading minds.

"I'm not. But you really need to school your face. Everything you think is displayed to those of us who are old and wise. My sister and I are different in many ways. We each want to help the world get back on track—I just take a distant, long-range approach. She prefers to be more hands on. And I like clutter."

I dropped my pack and sat. Bunky and Irving hovered for a bit, before flying up to the rafters and settling down. A peek in my pack told me the faeries were still out. "Back on track?" Somehow Mathilda's ability to combine house-keeping styles and world changing events into a single thought didn't surprise me.

"Yes, yes. Things went off track when the Ancients were lost. Hasn't been right since. That was why my sister and I came here, you know." She came over and handed me a cup of tea.

One I almost dropped. I knew Siabiane was old, even older than the other elves I'd met. "Older than the Ancients?"

She was stirring some honey into her tea and looked up with a grin. "Older than their demise anyway. We came to this land when a massive disturbance was felt by our seers back in our homeland. Unfortunately, we got here after the Ancients had vanished and the syclarions had been severely diminished. We've done what we can, but I fear things are coming back that never should have existed and history might repeat itself. But in an even more cata-strophic manner."

The tea was perfect; something I'd always admired Mathilda for being able to do. The flavor faded at her words. "Worse than the Ancients being destroyed?"

"Yes. And you've felt it too, or you wouldn't be running away with two of the cursed relics." She looked to me, and then up to Irving.

"I didn't have much of a choice." The sapphire manti-core was trapped inside of me. It would only come out upon my death. Or when I turned into whatever monster I'd become at the Spheres. It didn't help that it jumped back inside me right when I returned to myself.

The basilisk had been alive—at least in the sense it had been able to move around and go after victims. Irving had swallowed it. Twice.

"But you would have, regardless," she said. "I know you, probably better than you know yourself. You know those pieces are deadly. They were with someone with a good heart originally, yet they caused one species to disappear and another to regress hundreds of years. You know what would happen if they were wielded by someone evil with an agenda."

"You've used the word disappear now twice. Don't you mean killed?"

"I always use the right word, even when it makes people unhappy. I believe we do not know for certain what happened to the Ancients, beyond that they are gone. It would be foolish to assume that the only avenue for their being gone was being killed." She nodded then looked pointedly to my pack. "Hello, ladies."

My pack was flopping around as three pairs of tiny hands tried to find the way out. I finally undid the tie and the faeries stumbled out.

An orange head popped up first, and Garbage yelled and ran to Mathilda. The other two scrambled to their feet and did the same.

"They sometimes forget they can fly," I said as Mathilda watched them run. "Not sure exactly why."

Garbage hit first and flew up to hover in front of Mathilda's face, the other two followed suit.

"Is good. Fix. Good. Stay safe." Garbage was positively rambling and was pointing to me and nodding furiously.

The other two landed and started jumping around on Mathilda. There was so much genuine affection for her that I was almost starting to feel left out.

"I know, girls, you have done well. But your task isn't over."

Garbage flew to me and patted the side of my face. "Fix. Save. Is good."

At first I thought she meant that since they had fixed and saved me, they were good and done with their task. Then the other two flew back to me as well.

"Is ours." Leaf said.

Crusty was silent but kissed my cheek.

"Good. They know this isn't over and they honestly adore you. I wasn't sure you wouldn't have dumped them—they can be difficult."

I started laughing, that was an understatement. "I made a promise to be their guardian. And even though you left, that promise stood. Although it looks like it was the other way around as well." There had clearly been some deal between the faeries and Mathilda as well as the one between her and me.

Mathilda's face stilled and a line crept between her brows. "If I were to say the promise is done, that none of you have to watch for the others. Would you leave?" She wasn't just watching me, although I was her primary focus. Her eyes darted to the faeries as they flew and bounced between us.

I didn't even hesitate. "They're my family now. I wouldn't leave them—ever." Had she asked me that a year ago, my answer might have been different. However, the past year had changed many things—one of them was how I felt about the faeries.

"Ours," the faeries said in unison.

Mathilda nodded with a smile. "Good. The road ahead of you all is far too difficult to leave to the powers of a promise or even a geas. Geas can be broken with sacrifice. Love can't be broken." She looked to the window and true dawn appeared as if waiting for her. "Now, how about some breakfast? We have a few years to catch up on. And I do want to hear about my sister."

By the time the girls and I had polished off a mountain of scrambled eggs, toast, sausage, and more tea, she was caught up. More or less.

"I feel this Alric person is of far more importance than you are letting on."

The girls were in food stupors, so it was just Mathilda and me. There was no reason I should feel odd telling her about Alric, but I skirted as much information about him as I could. Obviously not enough, judging by the look on her face.

"Fine. He and I are involved." As I spoke, I realized why I hadn't wanted to say it. I'd run away from the love of my life. Not something normal people did.

Garbage was barely awake but managed to make a rude noise. Soon all three were making kissy noises.

"Yes, thank you for the sound effects," I said. "I'm in love with him." It felt odd to say, but good too.

Mathilda laughed and tilted her head. "And he feels the same." Her smile dropped. "But you fled all of them—even him."

I set my teacup down with a sigh. I couldn't really explain what I'd felt when I'd changed. I had no idea what I changed into, or why it happened. How could I explain it to her?

"There was a battle. You're right, an evil mage is trying to gain the relics. He wanted something at the Spheres. I thought it was the basilisk, and it probably was part of it since he's trying to gather all of the relics. But he was trying to raise an army of undead. Victims of the basilisk relic over the past thousand years or so. I was able to stop that. But there was something more…something else." I shook my head as that moment of my change flooded over me. The Sphere exploding. The pain as my body tore itself apart as it changed.

"The Spheres." Mathilda's face went a few shades paler. "What happened to the Spheres?"

"One was destroyed. That explosion seemed to be his focus for the spell he used in raising the undead out of the sand. And part of how I changed." I'd not gotten to that part in my tale yet, but her fear scared me almost worse than that battle had.

"You changed." Her eyes were sad. "I wasn't sure it would happen. It was hard to really tell when I first found you. You were so lost." She seemed to be talking to herself more than to me. "What did you change into?"

I pulled back at that. I figured if she knew I might turn into something she'd at least know what. "I have no idea. What did you think I was going to turn into and why didn't you warn me? Was it something in the exploding Sphere that changed me?"

"I didn't *know* you'd turn into anything. I just knew there was a lot missing from the person I'd found. You had physically recovered, not your memories, but you were you when I left." She shook her head. "I believed you were someone who'd gone through a brutal attack and needed the time to recover. I left when I believed you had recovered, but maybe there was still more. I am sorry."

I reached for some more tea, but it was cold. Refilling the cup gave me a chance to sort things out. "So, the Sphere wasn't the cause? That thing I turned into was the real me?" I was proud that I didn't scream, nor cry, nor run out of the cottage. I did almost spill hot tea on myself before I set the cup back down.

"I have no answers; not yet at any rate. I'd say the shattering of the Sphere was somehow related. But it didn't change you." She reached over and lifted my chin. "This is who you are. But whatever you became might be you as well. That doesn't mean it's a bad thing."

I kept thinking of how pleased Nivinal looked when the Sphere shattered and my change began. He'd expected something to happen, something beyond his undead minions and finding the basilisk. In addition, if an evil mage was pleased with my transformation, there couldn't be anything good about it.

CHAPTER THREE

MATHILDA SHOOK HER HEAD. "THERE are dark things afoot, there's no denying that. But right now, I need help with my garden, and that takes precedence."

I wasn't sure exactly how to process that, but I also didn't think I was ready to find out what I'd turned into—providing she even knew. And manual labor was a good way to forget things.

Except for forgetting that I'd been sleeping badly on the ground for a month.

After a few hours of pulling weeds and vegetables from her wild garden patches, I just wanted to curl up in a pile of leaves and sleep. Parts I didn't even know existed were finding ways to hurt.

"There, I think we've done what we can," Mathilda said. She dusted off her hands on her skirts, grabbed the basket of vegetables, and headed toward the cottage. "And my guest bed is far more comfortable than leaves." She held up her hand. "No, again, still not mind reading, you stared at the pile of leaves near that oak for a full two minutes."

I paused for a moment, and then followed her in.

The faeries had been napping the entire time we were out there but flew up when we entered. It was hard to tell, but they looked guilty.

"Go out. Back later," Garbage said as they flew for the door.

I nodded to Bunky and Irving. "Follow them. Keep them

out of trouble, and one of you come back if it gets ugly."

The constructs both bobbed in their version of a nod and flew out after the faeries. That had been our standard operating procedure during the past month—so far they hadn't needed to send one of them back.

"You really have a good group." Mathilda put the kettle on for more tea and started gathering cheese, meat, and bread for lunch. "Both those five, and the ones following you."

I almost spit out my tea. "The ones following me?" I would have loved to spend more time with Mathilda, for the food and bed if nothing else. But I wasn't ready to deal with what I'd become and trying to explain that to my nearest and dearest—even if I'd thought about it briefly.

She nodded but seemed to be carefully ignoring my panic. "Your friends have been on your trail for a bit. But, since they didn't find it for quite a while, they are a few days from finding you. They love you, you know. I can feel their energy."

I trusted Mathilda, but I wasn't sure about that. My biggest issue was that I might hurt them, but there was a tiny worm of doubt that they were upset at what I'd become. "Can this cottage still move? Could we just keep staying ahead of them?" Maybe there was a way I could have both comfort and seclusion. And I could put off dealing with everything a bit longer.

"Yes, it does, but no, we aren't moving. Whatever you became is a part of you and so are those people. You can't keep hiding."

I sat back in the chair and mindlessly ate the food she'd placed before me. I was well and truly trapped. If Mathilda decided I needed to be reunited with them, that's what would happen. Another check box in the similarities between her and her sister.

"What if I change again and hurt someone? I really wasn't in control when it happened. I could have killed all of them and not noticed." I put down the bit of cheese I'd been nibbling.

"Yet you didn't." She came closer and peered intently into my eyes. "I don't for one moment believe you are evil. I never would have left the faeries with you if I had even a doubt. You might not have been aware of them as your friends when you transformed, but I'd warrant that you did avoid them with a purpose. You will not hurt them. I sense that things are happening too fast now. I can't explain more than it's a feeling. You can't hide anymore."

I sighed. I hated it when a voice outside of my head agreed with the logical side inside my head. "So do we wait? Go find them?"

Mathilda nodded to herself. "We wait. However, I have a feeling you've been betrayed by the faeries. I think they went to go help the rest of your friends find you."

That would explain the slightly guilty looks they'd given. Even when they were raining destruction over entire towns, they never looked guilty. And most likely the minkie interference was gone too. I ran my fingers through my hair. "Do you think I have time for a nap?"

"Aye. They continue to feel far enough away that it should be a while before they find us. The faeries can help direct them, but won't speed them up. Go rest, I'll wake you when the faeries return."

I stumbled down the short hall and collapsed into the guest room I'd used long ago. I was out the minute my head hit the pillow.

———◆———

My dreams were scattered. Images of a life in Beccia, the one I'd had before this entire thing started. Working as a digger. Hanging out at the Shimmering Dewdrop. Going home to an empty house. They merged with images of my friends and me on the run, fighting, getting hurt, never relaxing. I woke up with a start. I knew which path

I needed to be on. My old life was gone, something I thought I'd come to terms with a while ago—but now knew for certain.

"Is awake!"The voice came a second before three bodies bounced on my gut. Three tiny bodies that managed to hit with way more force than their size would indicate.

"We good!" Crusty yelled as she leapt higher.

I rolled to my side, dislodging the tiny faery projectiles. "Yes, I'm awake. What were you three doing?" I noticed that Bunky and Irving were hovering above us, but neither seemed upset.

"We find them!" Crusty yelled again. I was groggy enough that her yelling was worse than usual. Unfortunately, I couldn't grab her and make her shut up.

Garbage noticed my reaction though and walked up from my belly to wave a tiny finger in my face. "Is time. No more hiding." She tilted her chin up as if daring me to contradict her. "We right."

I wasn't sure if Mathilda had influenced the faeries or if they'd decided this on their own, but I had run out of options. Especially when even my own mind was working against me. I had run away with just the thought of saving my friends. And fear at what I'd become. But I'd found no answers on my journey. And enough of my friends were magic users that hopefully they could take me out if things went bad.

"No bad thoughts." Leaf shook her head. They could only hear my thoughts if I focused and sent directly to them—supposedly. I wasn't sure how true that was.

"Are you inside my head?" I narrowed my eyes.

All three tiny faces looked as innocent as possible.

Mathilda stuck her head in the open doorway. "Well, your sleep will be off. But you needed that nap. Have some dinner; tell me more about Siabiane, then back to sleep."

I pushed the faeries off of me; Crusty tumbled a bit before joining the other two in the air. I did feel better, but wasn't sure I could sleep again that soon. Who was I kidding, if Mathilda wanted me to sleep, I'd be lucky if I made it to the bed.

She had set a nice dinner with places for her and me and a single large plate for the faeries. Thinking about her knocking me out brought up another change since I'd last seen her—I was no longer a magic sink.

"Did you notice anything else about me?"

She took a long sip of tea. "Like your magic? Aye. But it's an odd magic and I didn't even know how aware of it you were."

"Odd? How? Can you teach me to use it like you do? Alric's tried to teach me, but it's going slowly."

"And?" She nodded. "There's something else there."

I'd just taken a mouthful of stew, so I had a few moments to compose my thoughts. Not that it would do much good to lie to her. "I think he might be deliberately going slowly. Maybe because my magic is odd?"

"The magic you carry is closer to that of the elves than human or other species. I doubt that is the reason. However, I agree with his caution. You were a complete magic sink when I met you." She narrowed her eyes, as if trying to see inside my head. "That does not simply change." After a few intense moments, she pulled back. "Which means that one of the states was false. Either you were not truly a magic sink, but were spelled, or drained so heavily that even I couldn't tell the truth, or your current magic is simply a spell. One that I also can't pick through. One way or another, a powerful spellcaster was involved."

"So you can't teach me?"

"Now, I didn't say that. I can, but I agree with your young swain's thoughts—slowly is best. And more of the organic magic, I think. Working with natural impulses."

I thought of the one spell I did well, push. "Agreed, I seem to do best with those."

"There, now that's settled, I need to hear all about your

adventures. I would have asked you while we were working, but that nectar thief is lurking and he doesn't need
to hear this." She put the tea and two cups on a tray and
carried it over to the small fire.

"Is he dangerous?"

"Only to my supply," she said. "But the faeries will be on
watch for him tonight, won't you?" She waved a hand to
where the girls were just rising from the table. "My nectar
still is behind the cottage, and I have promised them a bit
if they keep the thief away."

"We guard!" Crusty zipped too high and barely pulled
back before she smacked into the ceiling. The other two
also flew around the room but refrained from slamming
into things.

"You sleep." Garbage stopped in front of me and gave me
a stern look. Once she decided I was sufficiently cowed,
she led her troop out.

Mathilda watched them go through a small gap in her
window with a thoughtful expression. "You have more
who have joined you?"

"Another twenty, but I left them to watch the others."

She continued to stare out the window. "You're going to
need more, many more. But that will come. Now, I want
you to tell me everything from when you met this Alric."

It took a while to tell the story. Things I didn't think
were important, such as how many goras had been in jail
with me when I got locked up in Beccia, would be vital to
Mathilda. But she never responded when I asked her what
difference these tiny details made. She'd just nod, sip her
tea, and then gesture for me to continue.

I was definitely ready for sleep three hours later when
I finally got to the battle of the Spheres. She held up her
hand when my tale of the basilisk ending up destroying the
rakasa was interrupted by three yawns on my end.

"I think that's enough. The more recent events are clearer
for me to see and you need more rest." She didn't get up.

"I'll see you in the morning."

I'd washed, and then tumbled into bed. I'd not even slipped into any dreams I was aware of before the world around me exploded in light and sound.

CHAPTER FOUR

I THREW MYSELF OUT OF BED; glad I had kept my nightclothes with me and was at least wearing something. The explosions that woke me settled down enough that I could tell they were coming from outside the cottage and it had been the thin walls that made them feel like they were in the room with me.

I slowly opened the door, just in case I was wrong and there was a problem inside, but the hall and living room were dark and quiet. The front door was ajar and a strange glow was coming from the garden.

I reached to pull the front door open completely when two black shapes dove at me. Bunky's gronking was enough to make me jump a foot in the air.

"Guys, I need to see what's happened," I said, then waved them off as both Bunky and Irving dipped down trying to push me back as well as bump the door closed.

The glow started dimming outside, but I could hear Mathilda's low chanting. "Guys, what's that coming in from the kitchen?" It was mean, and they'd both be annoyed with me, but it worked. Both constructs looked away long enough for me to get the door open and run outside.

The glows I'd been seeing were faeries. A lot of faeries. And they were all glowing like the glow bugs that came out in the summer in Beccia. Only unlike those bugs, each faery glowed a different color. Most likely whatever color they were but it was too dark to see more than outlines.

I caught the tail end of whatever they'd been doing, but it mostly looked like they'd been zipping around like my girls on tea. They were bright enough that I could see Mathilda off on the edge of her gardens. She was hunched over something and chanting.

I moved forward before Bunky and Irving could try pushing me back again.

Aside from the chanting, things were eerily silent. I couldn't see anything that caused the explosions that woke me up, but I knew I'd felt them.

"Anything I can help with?" I kept my voice low, but had been torn about speaking. Sneaking up on a spell-chanting magic user was a good way to get fried.

"Ah, there you are, Taryn," Mathilda said. She poked at something on the ground in front of her. "I believe we have our culprit."

I peered around her, but all I could see was a man-shape curled up in a ball. I doubted Mathilda would have been actually beating him with her stick, so his position was probably a result of her spell chanting. I was more interested in the dimming faeries. Glancing around, there had to be hundreds of them. But they were not only losing their glow, but vanishing altogether.

"Who are they and why are they glowing?"

"Hmmm?" She finally looked up from the prone form of her nectar thief. "Oh, them. Yes, well, our own faeries gave out a cry when they bravely cornered this hooligan. A pack of locals dove in for an assist." She tilted her head, watching as the lights vanished. "As for the glowing…well, I have to say that is new. Not that I see much of the local faeries, at least not in a large group." She held up her hand, palm up to the night sky. "Garbage Blossom, if you would please?"

I tamped down the bit of jealousy at the quickness with which Garbage flew to land in Mathilda's hand. I was glad they loved me, but that kind of response would have been handy in the past year.

Garbage stood at attention on the palm of her hand. She looked riled up. She wasn't wearing her war feathers, but her well-used war stick was in her hand. She noticeably wasn't glowing.

"Why are these other faeries glowing?" Mathilda waggled her staff at the prone shape on the ground without taking her eyes from the tiny orange faery.

Garbage stuck her lower lip out. "They show off. Was could do. Then no. Now some." She forgot she had her staff in her hand and almost whacked herself in the head as she crossed her arms in an enhancement of her scowl.

Over the past year, the faeries had been demonstrating new tricks. Hearing me when I mentally called them, the ability to go through solid objects, and briefly the ability to transport beings much larger than themselves far distances. Sadly, that trick hadn't stuck around. Unless one counted them picking me up and flying off with me. I shuddered at the memory.

The glowing must be something like those. It really wasn't new, but it was something old and lost that was coming back. The faeries were dangerous enough as they were when I first got them; I wasn't sure their returning old skills were a good idea.

Mathilda nodded slowly and smiled at Garbage. "Never fear, wee one, all that was once will be returned. Now, many thanks to you and the other ladies for catching my thief." The tip of her staff glowed. "Shall we have a look?"

Most of the wild faeries were gone, but the ones remaining joined in as my three yelled, "Is not finished!"

"A male faery?" I could see him a bit better now with her staff light, but he was too curled up to see well. The most noticeably missing things were the wings. I'd seen the mythical male faeries twice. Once a few months ago when we ended up in Null, the second when we were in the sands near the Spheres and a few had poked through to our world to eat some nasty tiny creatures called glough-strikes. In both cases, my faeries expressed their complete annoyance of them.

Maybe the girls were just jealous that the boys were human sized and they weren't.

"Male faery?" Mathilda nudged the form with her foot. "Now those haven't been around since far before my time. Ladies? You are certain?" She released Garbage but all three hovered nearby, glaring at the male faery.

"Is yes. No finished. Go back!"

"Is cute?"

"Yum!"

Garbage, Leaf, and Crusty all spoke as if they said one sentence together. One with different meanings.

I realized that in my conversation with Mathilda last night, I'd forgotten a few things—the male faeries being one item. But it was damn hard to keep track of over a year's worth of weird happenings. "I'll explain more later, but yes, male faeries, yet this one doesn't have—"

The word 'wings' was swallowed as the male faery jumped to his feet, unfurled wings I'd not seen, then vanished. Bunky and Irving had been hovering overhead and both dropped to where the faery had last been, but from their movements, there were no clues as to where it had gone.

"Good! Stay gone!" Garbage glared at the empty space.

Mathilda picked up the small jug the faery had been curled around, put it in her shed, and then placed a few layers of spells over the shed. "I'd actually been keeping the spells low; I wanted to catch my thief. But for now, I think I don't want to contribute to the drunkenness of a mythological being who may or may not be finished."

"Not finished. No be back here." Garbage was annoyed, but even more disturbing was the fact that she looked worried. That wasn't a common look for any of the faeries.

"What's wrong?" I tried holding up my hand, but I

wasn't too surprised when she didn't land on it.

"Not is time."

Leaf and Crusty flew up behind her shaking their heads. Even though both of them had been more interested in the male faery, neither looked happy now.

"Can you be clearer?"

"Not. Is. Time." Garbage just slowed down her words, but didn't change them.

Mathilda peered into the now extremely dark woods around us. The wild faeries, and their odd light, had vanished. "I think we might want to take this inside."

We trooped in and with a wave of her hand Mathilda re-lit the fire in the hearth and about half of the candles in the front room. I rubbed my shoulders as a chill left me. I hadn't even realized I'd had it.

The faeries flew in as well and landed on the sofa near each other in a circle. They were chittering in native faery and didn't look happy. Bunky and Irving flew directly to the rafters and settled in.

"I don't suppose you speak faery?" I nodded to the three.

"Sadly, no. I'd hoped you might have picked it up over the years. It's an odd language and I think they change it regularly. The few words I'd ever been able to pick up, changed context the next time I heard them. Now tell me about the times you've seen these male faeries?"

I quickly started filling her in on the rest of the events.

"Gloughstrikes? You're certain?" She interrupted me. "Those are also something from the distant past. And something no one would ever want to return. They are deceptively slow moving, but can take out anything they touch. Your friends would never have woken up."

I shrugged. "That's what Padraig and Lorcan called them. They were guessing at first, but they seemed sure once they tracked them down in their books."

She busied herself fixing tea. "I know Lorcan, and it is tragic what hardship has befallen young Padraig. I will get a full description of the creatures when your friends arrive."

Every time she mentioned them coming I got a chill and a flood of happiness. I missed them all, with the exception of Flarinen. That elven knight had come down a few notches in his own opinion of himself during our trip, but he was still annoying. Yet I had no idea how any of them were going to feel about me abandoning them. And there was always that issue of me turning into a rampaging monster and possibly stomping on them.

Mathilda didn't comment on what was going on in my head. She claimed she hadn't been reading my mind, but if she'd read my face before, it was probably clear now. She stayed busy finishing the tea.

"Ladies? Do you have something you want to share?" She handed me a cup but was watching the faeries.

"No." Garbage folded her arms and glared at the other two.

"Yes." Both Leaf and Crusty nodded enthusiastically, and they'd both moved out of arm's reach of Garbage. If my little orange faery wasn't careful, there was going to be a coup.

"Now, Garbage Blossom, you know you need to tell us important things." Mathilda patted the chair next to her and Garbage reluctantly flew over.

"They not right."

Even I could hear the lie and Garbage knew she'd flubbed.

"Fine." She waved to Leaf and Crusty before sitting down with a scowl on the chair next to Mathilda. Apparently, she wasn't going to stop the others, but she wasn't going to participate.

Leaf and Crusty stayed on the sofa. "The boys bad," Crusty finally said after a few moments of silence.

"Not done. Not ready. Means bad side." Leaf solemnly nodded. Considering I knew she'd been attracted to more than one of the male faeries, I was surprised.

"Girls, just because they aren't finished doesn't mean they're bad. They saved us more than once."

Crusty's response was lost in the sound of people running through the forest entirely too close to this cottage. I looked to Mathilda, the alarm on her face was enough to bring me to my feet. My on again, off again sword was in the spare bedroom I'd slept in, but in an instant it appeared in my hand.

Mathilda was already to the door, but nodded at the flash of steel in the firelight. "I understand now what you meant. That is an extremely unpredictable weapon. But it might be warranted now." She held her staff in her left hand as she opened the door with her right.

The faeries regrouped in the air, flying a bit above Mathilda. I was right behind, with Bunky and Irving bumping into me as they tried to get out.

Darkness engulfed the forest, but the shapes of a dozen people running were lit by the torches they carried.

Once I realized that they were running past us, not to us, I lowered the tip of my sword.

"Who's out there? Where are you going?" Mathilda had also relaxed her stance, but her staff was held firmly.

"We mean no harm to anyone. We're from the Halin farm and syclarions are attacking and burning everything around." A tall, rangy man slowed down and stepped closer to the clearing in front of the cottage. "They're heading to Beccia to destroy it."

CHAPTER FIVE

I CLENCHED THE GRIP OF MY sword tighter. I knew where the Halin farm was, or rather the massive con-glomeration of farms that joined to create the Halin farm collective. There were at least a hundred people who worked and lived there—it wasn't good if the ones moving past us were the only ones left.

"Why are they attacking?" I told myself they must have misunderstood. Beccia was a quiet, drunken, digger town; there was no one who would be attacking it. But a tiny part of my mind twitched in fear. The few friends I had, who I hadn't left behind at the Spheres, still lived in Beccia.

The man looked over his shoulder, but the flow of escaping people had mostly slowed down. None of them were stopping to talk to us or ask for help. "They came through three hours ago; our farm is the main source of food for this region. They destroyed everything. They told us Beccia was going to pay." He shook his head. "We're too close. We're not stopping for a few more hours. If you were smart, you'd run too." With that, he ran to join the stragglers.

"How close are we to Beccia?" In the past month I'd been vaguely following a low mountain chain. Honestly, I didn't care where I was going as long as it was away from my friends. And Alric.

Mathilda stayed silent for a few moments, watching as the last lights from the torches shrank to tiny specks.

"We are about a two-hour walk, an hour at the pace they were keeping. Why would syclarions attack Beccia? Or a farm?"

"They are trying to cut Beccia off from supplies, but Beccia is an open city, there's nothing to keep invaders out. It wouldn't be hard just to storm it; they wouldn't need to destroy supplies." Sometimes when things had been slow going on our travels, Alric would teach me things about strategy. It was something we could work on that didn't involve me firing off spells. He'd explained about starving a castle or compound out…but there was no way that would be needed with an open town. And Beccia had few defenses. Unless the entire mass of thieves and thugs decided to join in and try to fight to save it. But they were probably going to be the first ones to run away.

"Things might have changed since you've been gone." Mathilda turned and went back into the cottage. We followed her in. "How long since you first left for Kenith-worth?"

I put my sword down on the sofa then plopped down next to it. "That's a good question. It seems like it's been years; what is today's date?" I ran my fingers through my hair. We'd left Beccia for Kenithworth to look for Alric, not realizing he was with us, disguised as Carlon. Then the mayor of Kenithworth had sent his syclarion henchmen after us at a dig we'd been hired for. One that resulted in me finding the emerald dragon relic.

"It's the eighteenth of Farith."

My heart started racing, but not at her words. The mayor. He'd been heading toward Beccia as Flarinen and his knights dragged Alric and me back to the hidden elven enclave. He and his army of syclarions. I didn't know if he was working with Nivinal or had his own nasty agenda. But he knew far too much about the relics, and my involve-ment in finding them, than was healthy.

"We have to go help Beccia." I bounced to my feet and

dropped back into the sofa as the lack of sleep hit me—even though I'd had a nap earlier. Most likely, Mathilda had already slipped a sleep spell on me.

"You have to rest. And I need to see what I can find out about these goings on. Usually someone in the woods has an idea of big things coming our way. Yet, I've heard nothing." She waved her hand in the direction of the hall and was already heading out the door. "I'll investigate and we'll leave in a few hours."

The faeries looked up to follow her, but I shook my head. "I think it'd be better if we stayed out of her way. Stay out here and keep an eye on the cottage. Wake me if anything happens." I looked up to the constructs watching from the rafters. "And you two keep an eye on the faeries." I went to pick up my sword, but it vanished. Hopefully, it went back in the bedroom. Most likely, it went back to wherever it took off to when it disappeared.

I hadn't seen it much during our wanderings, not even when the wolves first stalked us. Not that it would have saved me had the faeries not convinced them to leave us alone, but it could have slowed my demise. Maybe it preferred two-legged enemies. Unfortunately, wherever it had taken off to, my sword was nowhere in sight as I fell into bed. Again.

My dreams were chaotic, vivid, and vanished the minute I opened my eyes. I was left with just a vague feeling of unease. Which could have been caused from way more things going on right now than just a dream.

Mathilda was back and bustling around the cottage. The sun was up, but the faeries and constructs were gone.

"I take it we're going?" My emphasis was on 'we're', I was going whether she did or not. Beccia wasn't where I'd grown up, but I'd spent most of the life I could recall there. And I had friends there. I wasn't going to abandon Foxy and his dryad wife Amara.

"Yes. There has been some sort of change to Beccia,

something other than being under attack. The syclarions started moving in a few weeks ago, but just appeared as travelers. Then a few days ago, an attack on The Hill came. Three mages were killed, but they pushed the syclarions back out of the city. Then something odd changed about Beccia." She shook her head. "My sources don't speak the way you or I do, so details were missing."

"Where are the faeries and the constructs?" I was really hoping I could get in a quick shower before we left to go defend a city. But I needed to know where the hooligans were.

"They went to go do recon of a sort. The faeries were driving me crazy with questions, so I sent them to make sure the way out of here was secure. I sent your flying construct friends to watch them. They'll join us on the way."

"Do you think I have time?" I pointed toward her shower room.

"By all means. Who knows what we'll find in the city?"

After my shower and Mathilda's methodical locking and spelling of the cottage—no one was getting inside there without her—we were on the trail. After the first few minutes my flying friends appeared.

"Is good. Beccia bad. But trail good." Garbage had resumed her in-charge position.

"You went to the city?" I looked to Mathilda but the scowl on her face indicated she wasn't happy with that either.

"Is trail," Leaf said with far too smug a look. They knew Mathilda hadn't intended for them to go that far, but they'd done it anyway.

"Fine. So what did you see?" They shouldn't have risked going all the way there. If it was the Mayor of Kenithworth and his syclarions—they knew I traveled with faeries. I wasn't being overly self-centered; I knew he'd wanted me to dig for him for a reason.

"Green!" Crusty had been flying upside down as we

talked but finally turned right side up. "Green." She threw out her tiny arms and spun until she almost dropped to the ground.

Beccia was a lot of things, and while there were a lot of trees outside of it, there weren't many within the city itself. Certainly not enough to warrant just seeing only green.

"Green what?" Mathilda kept us moving at a good clip, but she wanted to know what the faeries had seen as well.

"Green." The three girls said at the same instant, backed up by some fly-by gronking from Bunky and Irving.

"Yeah, that's about all we'll get. Hate to say it, but I'm afraid we'll find out what it is when we get there."

Mathilda opened her mouth to try again, saw the look on my face, and shut it. With a nod, she increased our pace even more.

I'd been surprised at how close I'd walked to Beccia during my month of travels. Maybe while I had been wandering I was naturally homing in on my favorite bar, the Shimmering Dewdrop. Or the girls had been subtly nudging me that way. Even though the faeries had been living wild for hundreds of years, mine had definitely gotten a taste for city life. At least a taste for life with more bars.

The path was silent—too silent. No people, but no animals either. If we'd left closer to when the farmers had run through here, I'd think it was a reaction to that noise and ruckus. But we were far enough behind that it shouldn't have been an issue.

"You know, if we had traveled in your house, we'd have a place to hide if things go bad."

"My cottage doesn't move well," she said and ignored my snort. "It really doesn't. When I sent you and the faeries off fifteen years ago, I'd only made it a quarter of a mile away. I was using a disguise spell so you couldn't see me. It would be too awkward to walk it to Beccia from here."

There went that plan, such as it was. The path wasn't bad, I just hated going into what could be a battle without enough defenses. My sword was at my side in its scabbard. But who knew how long it was planning on staying. I hadn't tried any magic since I'd run away from the Spheres, and had no idea if it was even working.

A stabbing cold sensation on my left cheek brought me out of my mood. I rubbed my cheek but the feeling stayed. The sapphire manticore relic trapped inside of me was a defender. It did so via freezing things—starting with my face. I dropped my hand to the hilt of my sword and tried to look deeper into the forest around us. I didn't see anything moving, but I thought I felt the dirt beneath us move. "Hold up." I grabbed Mathilda's shoulder as visions of those tiny monsters, the rakasa, ran through my head. I'd really hoped that the basilisk had finally destroyed them, but I knew my luck wasn't that good.

Mathilda didn't question me but froze immediately. The faeries and the constructs overshot us, but Bunky gronked softly and they flew back. I felt silly standing there with nothing but the wind gently flowing around to show for my concern. Better safe than sorry though.

"I think we're fine. I thought I felt something under-ground." I patted my cheek. There was a glamour spell hiding the small, blue manticore tattoo-like mark, but I was sure Mathilda saw through it. "The relic is acting up. It senses something."

"You were thinking of the ground creatures." She closed her eyes and tilted her head, as if listening. Then opened her eyes and shook her head. "Nothing underneath."

We'd just started walking again when the three faeries burst into war cries. They grabbed the tiny black bags they carried and pulled out their war sticks but with whatever was coming, they didn't have time for their feathers.

"What is it?" I yelled to be heard, as their voices grew louder. Bunky and Irving flew in a wider circle around us, as if looking for the source of the faeries' agitation.

"Do you sense anything?" My magic senses weren't

great even when used regularly, but Mathilda was a powerful spell user.

"No. And I should. Something is blocking whatever is coming."

I pointed to the yelling and circling faeries. "Then what are they sensing?"

"Faeries don't do magic; they *are* magic. Whatever is coming is blocking us, but it can't block them."

A screech louder and more horrific than the faeries slammed into us a second before a dozen long flying shapes came from the trees. Sceanra anam. Flying snakes from the distant past that had come back to destroy the future. Wonderful.

Bunky and Irving flew to meet them. Chimeras were the enemies of the sceanra anam and a fleet of Bunky's chimera friends had fought back a massive attack at the elven enclave. Unfortunately, we didn't have a fleet.

But the faeries had also taken down their share of the toothy flying monsters in the past, so hopefully we were okay. What was I thinking? Mathilda could fry them all with a single spell.

"You want a shot at them?" I'd turned to watch the forest, so I wasn't facing Mathilda. But her silence surprised me. The flyers were engaged, but already a few of the sceanra anam were going around our faeries and constructs. And a quick glance backwards told me Mathilda was frozen in place.

CHAPTER SIX

———◆———

S HE REMAINED STANDING. ONE HAND raised as if
casting a spell, the other holding her staff up. But not
even a blink of her eyes to show she was alive.

"Crap!" I yelled as two of the sceanra anam got past our
flyers and headed my way. I took a step backwards to keep
me closer to Mathilda. She hadn't fallen over, and I was
hoping if something really bad had happened to her, she
wouldn't be upright. Not that being under attack, over-
matched, and losing a major magic user wasn't bad.

I had my sword out and awkwardly sliced at one of the
monsters. The move was enough to make the sceanra anam
pull back, but didn't even come close to hitting it. Thanks
to Alric and my friends, I could actually use my sword. But
it would be hard to tell right now, the angle it had come in
at was awkward to say the least. Luckily, I swung short and
was able to pull back for the second one who was coming
in fast.

Everything felt like it slowed down. The sceanra anam
dove toward my face. I knew I wasn't going to hit this one
either, but there was no way I'd trust my magic right now.

The relic inside of me had a different opinion. My face
felt like it cracked open and a shard of ice shot out. The
sceanra anam zigged to avoid the magic ice and my sword
sliced it in half. I dropped to one knee as pain from the
ice hit me. There was no time to stay down. More of the
sceanra anam were coming out of the forest. The last time

there was a group of sceanra anam, both the wild faeries and a flight of chimera had come to help. A quick glance around the skies told me that wasn't happening this time.

My faeries and constructs were holding on, but there were already too many of the sceanra anam. Mathilda was still frozen. I was out of options.

My magic was questionable at best, but after the Spheres, I had no idea what it would do. My best spell was push; however, shoving the sceanra anam onto someone else wasn't a good idea.

I kept batting them aside, using my sword more like a club than a blade at this point, while I tried to modify the spell. Maybe I could push them so far up they couldn't come back. A drunken alchemist had once cornered me in the Shimmering Dewdrop. He'd claimed that the breathable air only went up so far.

Time to test that. I took a deep breath, reaching out to sense the sceanra anam in the area with my magic, and at the same time I tapped into whatever odd awareness was in the manticore relic. Then I aimed my spell. I pushed every sceanra anam I could sense as high as the spell would go.

At first, my own flyers appeared to be going with them and I cut the spell off. Then I realized they were doing it on their own.

"Let them go! Come back to me." I hoped I'd yelled loud enough but I was tracking the spell, the manticore, and my rapidly shrinking victims—I couldn't track much else.

Bunky and Irving got the faeries to turn back, and I kept pushing. I stopped a good two minutes after I couldn't see the sceanra anam anymore.

I had no idea when I'd crumpled to the ground.

I was shoving myself up when Bunky and the rest came down. The constructs flew to me, the faeries flew to Mathilda. She still hadn't moved.

My legs were shaky as I got to my feet. At some point I'd

dropped my sword, but I managed to gather it and myself and stagger to her. The faeries were circling her, but not landing.

"No is home." Crusty looked confused as she waved a tiny hand in front of Mathilda's locked open eyes.

"Broken." Leaf nodded.

"Sceanra anam! Everyone duck!" Mathilda suddenly yelled, causing all three faeries to tumble backwards in mid-air, including Crusty who managed to slam back into me. I went down, Bunky and Irving went into defense mode, and Mathilda blinked her eyes as she realized the flying snakes were gone. "What happened? Did I just have a waking nightmare?"

I got back up again and dusted off my pants. "No, they were here. But you were frozen. It looked like you were reaching for a spell, then nothing." My sword hadn't vanished yet, so I put it in the sheath.

She ran her hand over her forehead. "That's not good. Not good at all. Well, neither is good. That those things were here, or that I froze. Something triggered it, but we don't have time to find out what." She started walking down the path, then turned slightly when I jogged to catch up to her. The flyers stayed closer to us now. "But how did you get rid of them?" I quickly explained, along with the admission that I wasn't sure if what I'd tried even worked. Like her situation of freezing, it was something we could figure out later.

"We have to assume that whoever is behind the attack on Beccia is also behind those creatures. Do you know who is controlling them?"

"No. But they had appeared before on their own." There was always a chance that they'd just been passing through. Even I didn't believe we'd be that lucky.

Neither did she. "They would have someone behind them or many someone's. Sceanra anam are fierce killers, but they aren't great thinkers. Someone is pulling their strings." She picked up the pace. I was starting to recognize the area as we came out of the mountains. The hills were softly rolling and filled with meadows. In the distance I could see crumbling elven building remains sticking out of the deep grass.

We were at the south end. The digger council had never authorized digs out this way as most of the elven buildings appeared to be smaller homes. Over the past few months I'd dreamed about returning to Beccia and my normal life. It wasn't much, a shabby little town that had only gained stature because of the relatively new digger trade. But it was home.

Rushing to the rescue was not how I wanted to return. At least not without an army of elven knights at my back.

We would be seeing the outskirts of the town as we rounded a final hill, so I mentally prepared myself. Whatever happened, we could fix it.

I was not prepared for the massive wall of green as we rounded the hill.

Seriously. The girls had been right—just green. A giant hedge, at least three stories high, and so thick I couldn't see through it, surrounded the city. At least what I could see on this side.

We stopped. The flyers had seen it before but seemed to be enjoying watching our reactions. I'm sure I looked as stunned as she did.

"Was that caused by whoever attacked it?" I wasn't sure if I was ready to get closer to it. As I watched, vines from within the hedge undulated along the top as if daring someone to try and pass through.

"I have no idea. I must admit, I don't think I've ever seen such a thing. And I've seen about everything there is to see." Mathilda lifted her staff and muttered a soft spell. A golden light came from the staff and bounced off the green wall. "Very good thing that I didn't try a harder spell. In fact, this beastie might be what shut me down when the sceanra anam attacked. Don't use magic, my dear. It didn't get you before. Possibly because of that relic inside you, but this close it would be too risky."

"So, no idea if it's good or bad?" There were some serious magic users in Beccia, but most of them were on the wrong side of the legal system. I really couldn't see any of the mage crime lords doing this. And the ones who lived on The Hill were rarely in residence. If this was an attack on the city, it was an odd one.

Mathilda walked closer but didn't touch anything, then came back. "Those farmers said they were attacked because someone was trying to destroy supplies. I'd say this is some sort of defense."

"Aside from no one that I know of being able to do that, couldn't things like the sceanra anam just fly over?"

"No fly. Get zapped." Crusty threw out her arms and shook to demonstrate. "I try."

"Told not to," Garbage said with a shake of her head.

"So flyers get zapped? Who could have done this?"

Mathilda didn't answer at first but moved back to the hedge. "I might freeze up again. If so, just move me somewhere safe." She closed her eyes and sent another spell. I felt the tendrils of it move out; it was slowly flowing toward the plant wall. Not an aggressive spell, but stronger than the golden one she'd sent before.

She didn't freeze this time, but she did rock back and land on her butt. Her eyes flew open. "It's a dryad defensive spell, but the likes of which I've never heard of before. All of that came from a single tree and an extremely annoyed dryad. The people inside are prisoners as much as they can't get out any more than we can get in."

There was only one dryad I knew living in Beccia. Dryads needed to be near their trees, so cities and towns weren't good for them. But Amara had been blackmailed to help Glorinal and Jovan try to destroy Foxy, Beccia, and pretty much the world as we knew it. But true love won,

Foxy and Amara fell in love for real, and he found a way to bring a seedling of her former tree to town. I had a feeling I was seeing the fruits of that labor before us.

"I do know a dryad living there, and she does have her tree with her. But she'd only react like this if…something happened to Foxy." My gut tightened. Amara was extremely passionate, but Foxy kept her in check. Who knew what she would do if he was injured, or worse? "We have to get in there."

"I got zap again!" Crusty started to fly to the hedge. Knowing her, she liked getting fried by whatever came out of the hedge and attacked flyers.

"No! Crusty, we need to stick together. I might need you to try and fly over in a bit, but plans first, then zaps. Okay?"

She sighed and drifted back down with a nod.

"What is your plan?" Mathilda looked more tired than she had before casting the second spell.

"I'm trying to figure that out. Are you feeling okay?"

She shook herself, then spun on the hedge and shouted a sharp word. The greenery pulled back into itself. The color returned to her cheeks.

"I am now. Somehow your dryad friend has managed to make her plants pull in a magic user's life force when a spell is cast. I didn't notice it the first time. She is a very powerful mage."

I thought of the Amara I'd known. Pretty, flighty, emotional. Powerful magic user wasn't in that line-up. Then again, love and fear can do amazing things.

"There's no way around the hedge; we have to find a way to reach Amara." I moved a few steps closer to the hedge. Without magic, it was far too solid to work our way through. I stepped away from it when I began to feel it looking back at me…and the branches near me were waving in a wind that was nowhere else.

Mathilda was studying the hedge as well, from a safer

distance. "There's no way either of us should try to use magic. I'm not sure what our options are."

"We help!" Leaf had been dancing with the moving hedge branches, but flew back to us.

I shook my head. "Crusty got zapped by that thing when she tried before."

Crusty nodded and silently reenacted her zapping.

"Fly faster than before. Find tree lady," Garbage said. She flew straight up until she was level with the top of the hedge. She kept closing one eye and tilting her head back and forth. Then she held out her left arm as if sizing up dimensions.

"If they're willing to try?" Mathilda shrugged. She knew, even better than I did, how tough the faeries were.

I looked at the three faery faces. "Okay, but you need to find Amara immediately. Tell her we can help but we need to get inside the city. And you need to avoid being seen by any syclarions that might still be there."

"We help!" Leaf gleefully repeated. I knew that's what they would tell Amara, if they found her.

I motioned for the faeries to come in closer—it helped with their focus sometimes if I was only inches from their faces. "Let's break this down. Fly directly to the Shimmering Dewdrop, only speak to Amara, and tell her, 'Taryn outside hedge'."

They stared at me blankly and Crusty chewed on a twig.

"How about, 'Taryn outside green thing'. And you each get your own ale once we get inside and have found Foxy." They brightened up at that.

"Taryn outside green thing!" Mostly in unison, Crusty still had the twig in her mouth.

I looked to Mathilda and she nodded. That was the best we could do.

"Now stay focused and fly fast. Go!" The three faeries took off toward the hedge, but so did Bunky and Irving. I had no idea what would happen to magical constructs if they were attacked by whatever spell had zapped Crusty. And I didn't think we wanted to find out.

"Bunky and Irving! Get back here." I was certain they heard me, but neither of them even twitched as they flew over the hedge. Two bolts of green lightning flew out of the hedge and struck both of them. Fortunately, both constructs were flung back to our side and tumbled to the ground behind us. Both shook themselves and stayed on the ground. But they seemed to be functioning.

The faeries paused, but I yelled for them to keep going. They were almost past the hedge, when three more green lines shot out of the hedge and hit each faery. They started shaking in mid-air. Garbage tried to keep going, but she could barely move.

"Come back! All of you!" I looked to Mathilda.

"Faeries! Attend me now!" She didn't use magic, but there was a command in her voice that got them to come back. The green force vanished once they were headed back our way.

Crusty took that to mean she could try again and did a back flip and shot out over the hedge. She got a bit further than Garbage had before, but got zapped hard enough to send her flying right at me.

I caught her and used my thumb and forefinger to pinch out the burning fabric on her overalls. Her tiny flower petal cap was nothing more than a fried cinder. Her eyes were closed and she was limp.

CHAPTER SEVEN

—◆—

"D O AGAIN?" HER EYES POPPED open and she looked ready to spring out of my hand. I tightened my fingers around her.

"No."

Garbage and Leaf had tumbled to land near Bunky and Irving. They were frazzled, but not as crispy as Crusty. They also didn't look like they wanted to do it again—unlike Crusty.

"That was a failure," Mathilda said. "I'd say your dryad friend was definitely trying to defend against those flying syclarions. Only the top caste syclarions can do it, but she must have had a run in with them. I've never heard of this kind of power in any dryad."

"Amara is passionate. But regardless of the defenses, we have to get inside there."

"Meows." Crusty muttered from inside my fingers. I wasn't sure what the odd sound was directed at, so I released the fingers a bit to see her better.

"What did you mean, sweetie?"

"Meows. We need kittahs to go through."

Maybe the multiple zaps had rattled her brain worse than she looked. That was a complete sentence, something the faeries rarely did.

"Yes, kittens," Garbage said as she flew up to us. "They work."

"How are cats going to help us get through that?" I

pointed to the hedge just in time to see three cats push their way out of the plants. The magic didn't affect them that I could see, just the denseness of the shrubbery. Once they'd cleared the hedge, I realized the three looked familiar. Many months ago, Alric and I had caught the faeries running a cat-racing operation for money.

They'd corrupted enough of the local wild faeries to join in and from what I'd seen the races were well attended and profitable. Until Alric and I shut them down anyways.

The largest was a blond, longhaired cat with a dark mask and feet and startling blue eyes, the second was a tiny calico, with an orange fur Mohawk, and the third was a long, sleek gray one with short fur. They stopped in front of Mathilda expectantly.

She looked surprised, but bent down to provide the required scratches. "These are your friends?"

"These were their money makers," I responded. "The girls ran an illegal cat racing operation in Beccia for a while. How did they cross the hedge with no problem?" The question of why they'd come out was clear. After they'd received their scratches, they went to stand by the faeries. The girls didn't look surprised, so they must have mentally called them.

"The cats aren't combatants. It's tricky to make a spell that can tell the difference."

Garbage and the other two faeries were busy getting reunited with their cats. Bunky and Irving held back but looked a bit put out.

Garbage turned to Bunky. "We ride in. You wait. Guard."

That was a level of insight I'd rarely seen from my perpetually cranky orange faery. She knew the constructs felt left out.

With a head bob and a gronk, Bunky and Irving lifted up into the air and started patrolling the area around us.

Garbage climbed onboard the back of the calico, moving forward until her tiny legs were at the cat's neck. "Is

Goblin cat, mine." She proudly patted the side of the cat's head and wrapped her hands into the fur on the back of her neck.

Leaf bounded over to the longhaired cat and quickly dug into the fur. "Fluffy Nuggets is mine." The cat's purr was so loud I think they probably heard it on the other side of the hedge.

Crusty gave a high-pitched squeal and ran to the slinky gray cat. She reminded me of Queen Mungoosey, the leader of the faeries and the only cat faery I'd heard of. But the look in those green eyes was far less sane. "Is Nutsy! My Nutsy!" Crusty buried her face in the short fur and the cat, Nutsy, did an odd little dance. The crazy was strong with those two.

All three looked to me. "Now, girls, where are you going?"

"Shimmering Dewdrop!" shouted Garbage and Leaf.

"Ale!" shouted Crusty.

"Who do you talk to?"

"Tree lady!"

"Ale!"

I glared at Crusty but she ignored it. "What do you say?"

"Taryn outside green thing!"

"Ale!"

Two out of three would have to be enough. Judging from the look of maniacal glee on both Crusty and her feline steed's face, I'd be lucky if they even made it to the same block as the Shimmering Dewdrop.

"Stay out of sight, but go quickly." Having never raced cats myself, I had no idea how the faeries got them started.

"Go!" Garbage yelled and wheeled her calico toward the hedge. The tiny cat was far faster than I would have expected and quickly vanished into the greenery. Leaf and her cat weren't far behind. Crusty and Nutsy tried to go in sideways, but eventually turned and made it in.

"So, cat racing?" Mathilda folded gracefully to the

ground into a seated position. There was no way to know how long it would take and while sitting on a path wasn't a great choice, there weren't a lot of options.

"Yes. I have no idea how long they'd been doing it by the time we broke them up, but it looked like a pretty established operation."

Mathilda nodded. "It's good they had a hobby, I suppose."

We sat in companionable silence for a bit. Finally I brought up something that had bothered me once I knew she was Siabiane's sister. "Why didn't you go with Siabiane when they hid? Were you trapped outside of the enclave?" When I'd seen her in the past, Siabiane had mentioned Mathilda, but she clearly hadn't been in the enclave.

"I wasn't trapped outside, I chose not to go. I thought it was a stupid idea. I also didn't think they'd keep it up for almost a thousand years. It was an over-reaction to a horrific attack on a people who thought they were invincible."

"I was there for the beginning, it was terrifying, and I'm not an elf." I rubbed my arms at the memory of seeing Lorcan die at the hands of his brother.

"I saw what happened to the rest of the world without the elves' influence. It was also horrific. The elves had been a power to keep the rest of the species in line. With them gone?" She shook her head. "And it wasn't as if they vanished immediately. The war with the Dark lasted over a year. No one won, even though the Dark was stopped in their grab for power. The final battle was more destructive than anyone would have guessed. The Dark hid in the southern lands, and the rest of the elves locked themselves in enclaves."

I couldn't help myself; as tragic as it was, made even more so by having gone into the past, I wanted to ask more questions. But before I could pull them together, the hedge started moving.

I'll admit it, I screamed. And jumped to my feet, stumbled back a few feet, and fell on my rear.

Bunky and Irving dropped lower and took positions between us and the moving greenery.

Mathilda rose slowly, but was using her staff to lean on, not to set a spell up.

"Taryn?" A year ago I would have been worried about a piece of hedge calling my name, now it was just a little odd. It helped that the voice sounded like Amara.

"I'm here, Amara. I've brought help, but we can't get in." I wasn't sure where to direct my comment, so I aimed it where the shrubs were moving the most. There wasn't an open pathway, but they seemed to be thinner in one area.

"It's a trap, Amara!" The voice that shouted out behind us was also familiar. "Taryn was spelled and kidnapped and there's a magic user with her."

I spun. "Alric?" He was wearing solid black as usual, but he also had a black mask pulled up to cover most of his face. But there was no way those green eyes could belong to anyone else. My heart jumped to my throat. Damn I'd missed him. "I'm not spelled, and Mathilda is a friend." I didn't move closer, although I really wanted to run to him.

Bunky and Irving were torn between greeting what appeared to be Alric and protecting us. Bunky had a fondness for Alric, but he also clearly thought I was in danger.

"Why weren't you two together?" Our hidden dryad was still speaking through her hedge, but the part that had been moving forward stilled at Alric's words.

"Alric and Amara, it's me. I wasn't kidnapped, nor am I spelled." I waved to Bunky and Irving. "Would they put up with me if I was under a spell? Would the faeries? Amara knows I sent them to her." I turned to the hedge. "Where are they, by the way?"

"Drinking. I'll agree she's not under a spell." A pause. "And neither is Alric. Have your friends come out where I can sense them better."

Alric dropped his mask, but still looked suspiciously at

Mathilda. Slowly, Covey, Padraig, and Lorcan came forward. Nasif, Dueble, Flarinen, and Kelm were missing.

"Where are the others?" I didn't think they'd be hiding, not since Amara made it clear she could tell if they were.

Lorcan watched me closely for a few seconds before smiling and coming over. "I sent the knights back to the king and queen; they'll need to rally the troops soon, I fear. Nasif and Dueble can help them in other ways." He hugged me tightly, then stepped back and turned to Mathilda. "I am sorry I failed to recognize you while we were hiding in the woods. Siabiane will be sorry she missed seeing you." He went to Mathilda and engulfed her in a warm embrace.

Alric ran forward and swung me in the air. "We thought you'd been taken!" He gave me a quick, yet passionate kiss. It was odd, being right in the middle of everyone, but I'd missed him too much to complain.

"I left the extra faeries with you. They were supposed to tell you I was okay."

"They told us you had a spell and needed to leave. Then they left. But I think they're around here somewhere. I thought I saw one or two a few days ago." His face stilled. "So you left on your own? Why?"

"I—" My attempt at an explanation got cut off as Covey ran forward and hugged me out of Alric's arms.

"Don't you ever do that to me again!" The relief, worry, and concern in her eyes almost made me break down and tell them the truth. But I couldn't. Not yet, and certainly not here.

"I'm not sure what's been happening with you people since you left, but Taryn offered her help and holding this open isn't easy," Amara's disembodied voice said. The hedge shifted a bit more and a thin trail appeared.

"I am glad to meet you, Taryn has told me of you," Mathilda said and flashed a smile to Alric. "But I agree we don't want to be on this side of the fair dryad's hedge." With a nod to the constructs, who surprisingly flew down right behind her, Mathilda and Lorcan disappeared into the breach in the green.

Padraig stopped to give me a quick hug, and then followed Mathilda, with Covey, Alric, and me right behind.

Once he'd gotten me back from Covey's uncharacteristic hug, Alric wouldn't let go. He kept his arm around me until the passage grew too thin, then dropped down to hold my hand. I couldn't believe how good it felt just to be near him again.

The hedge didn't open directly through, I felt us going along the center and the plants closing in after we passed. I really hoped Amara hadn't regressed and switched to the other side. This hedge could kill people and their bodies would be left unfound for months. It was sad that my first thought usually went to something trying to kill me.

Before my brain could move into a full panic, the hedge opened before us. Amara wasn't in sight, but I recognized where we were. The Shimmering Dewdrop was just three blocks away. Looking at the hedge from the inside was far more claustrophobic than the outside. Maybe it was because we'd just spent five minutes walking through it.

"Amara?" I felt stupid talking to thin air, but I didn't know if she was hiding somewhere. There were a number of large Gapen trees nearby and she could be in any of them.

"I'm in the pub. Just come through the back; the front is boarded up." The disembodied voice came from the hedge behind us.

That didn't bode well. We started walking toward the pub, or rather to the back alley that ran behind the pub. Some of the places that I knew were untouched, but more than a few looked boarded up. Slim Jenkins' pub was nothing more than cinders. Which was actually an improvement.

Amara's original tree had been magically destroyed to ensure she would help Jovan, an evil elf mage of the Dark who was now very dead. The manner in which it had been done left a tiny viable portion to resurrect itself. Foxy had taken that and planted it behind the pub. Even though it had been just under a year since that had happened, the tree before us looked massive enough to have been around since before the time of the elves. Thin tendrils reached out over the surrounding buildings and connected it to the hedge. We'd walked right under them and I hadn't even noticed them.

The door to the back of the pub creaked open and a moment later Alric had been torn from my side and tackled.

CHAPTER EIGHT

—◆—

THE DARK FORM THAT HAD taken him out was Dogmaela, a full-blooded troll. She'd taken a shine to Alric when he first came to the pub a year ago, and I was sure that once he could breathe again, he'd return the hug.

She finally pulled back, released him, and stood him back on his feet. "Good to see you."

I hid my smile. Most trolls spoke their own pidgin, understandable but sometimes as heavy as the faeries. Amara had clearly been working with Dogmaela on elocution.

"Come in quickly; there are still spies," Amara said. This time she wasn't speaking through the hedge, her slim form was in the doorway. She watched the alley closely.

Alric led our friends inside. Bunky and Irving heard something and flew ahead. I heard it too a moment later— drunken faery singing. I theorized if we could find a way to make their singing into a mass-produced weapon, we could destroy anyone who came against us.

The pub appeared intact, but only a few regulars were inside and the front door and windows were boarded up. The faeries and constructs were at the bar itself, with each faery staggering around in their own ale bottle. I thought about saying something, but shook my head and turned away instead.

"You have to help me save Foxy. No one else thinks he's still alive, but I know he is. We have to save him." Amara had always been slender, but she was heading toward skeletal now. Even her long green hair looked thin and lifeless.

"What happened?" Alric dropped his pack near a large table by the fire. The cats looked up as one from their spots near the fire, then shrugged, and went back to bathing.

Amara crumpled onto the nearest chair and dropped her head in her hands. Dogmaela brought her a mug of tea. "Everything. A few months ago, a mayor from a neighboring town started spending money in Beccia. He wanted to launch his own dig site, hire his own diggers, and spend lots of money. The Antiquities Committee said no and a few lower level mages from The Hill tried to force him to leave." She took a long sip of tea. "That didn't work. The mayor brought in his army, almost all syclarions and many were flyers." She nodded to make sure we knew how rare they were.

"Beccians aren't fighters. But my Foxy is. He organized the resistance. They were winning too, pushing the syclarions back. Then they grabbed him and the strongest ones with him and the resistance broke. The mayor's people started to march through here, occupying the place. It was a few days before I knew they'd taken Foxy, I'd thought he'd been doing recon work." She pointed back outside where the hedge was. "My tree and I didn't take it well."

"But wouldn't that have trapped them in here with you?" Alric nodded his thanks as Dogmaela made the rounds with ale.

"My tree really was unhappy. He was able to emit a smell that syclarions can't stand. It was a defense mechanism, and he used all of it. But they left. Then we made the hedge. That was five days ago."

Padraig, Lorcan, and Mathilda came and took up seats after introducing themselves to Amara. She and Covey nodded to each other even though Covey rarely came here.

"So there are a lot of elves just roaming around now?" Amara still looked frail, but she was looking less fragile than when we first came in. She was watching our elven companions closely. Jovan and Glorinal had also been elves, and they had almost killed all of us.

"Yes, and we keep finding more. But these are good ones; the ones who fought Jovan and Glorinal." I gave Amara a brief rundown of what had been happening outside of Beccia.

She calmed down a bit. "You knew this mayor? What town was it? Kenithworth?"

I took a long sip of my ale first. "Yes. He'd hired us to work for him on a dig site. But he already knew about our ruins here, and me. I think he's after the same relics that we are."

"We have to focus in two directions," Alric said. "I can go where Foxy and the resistance were last seen. Is it inside your hedge?" At Amara's glum nod he continued. "The rest of you try and figure out why the mayor was so focused on Beccia."

"Agreed. None of the scrolls indicate the diamond sphinx is within a hundred miles of here. And the basilisk was never rumored to be here either, nor the manticore." Lorcan helped himself to some tea after sneaking his ale to the faeries.

"Could he have come here for something else?" I looked around at my friends. I had feared that he'd traveled to Beccia to find leverage against me. When I'd run into him, we'd only found the first two relics. That the third, the emerald dragon, had been found on his dig site probably didn't sit well with him. That it had come with Alric and me, along with a group of heavily armed elven knights, most likely made him exceptionally pissed.

"We never knew, beyond him wanting full access to dig." Amara tilted her head. "But he didn't want to dig in the ruins, at least not the established ones. He wanted to go deeper into the forest. Out by the wild ruins."

I shared a look with Alric. Jovan had set up a staging area

out that way, but as far as I knew he'd never done any digging. "There might be something else out there as well."

Padraig looked concerned. "As Lorcan said, there shouldn't be any relics near here. Not anymore." He turned to me. "Since you've been gone, Lorcan and I have narrowed down the location of the diamond sphinx."

I looked to the few regulars still in the bar. Amara wouldn't say anything, and I knew Dogmaela wouldn't. But I had no idea who the rest were. Even if they had no clue as to what the relics were, the word 'diamond' would catch a person's ear.

Padraig smiled and snapped his fingers. A slight glow briefly flared into existence over the four drinking shapes, then faded back into hiding. "I spelled them when we came in. They can't hear anything. They'll be happy to sit and drink until I release them."

"Can you teach me that spell?" I ignored Alric scowling out of the corner of my eye. He was my official magic teacher, but I wasn't sure how it was going to work now that we were together. Besides, he'd never even told me such a spell existed. There were times that could have been damn handy.

"It's a difficult spell, but I'm sure we can work on it after the current crisis is over." His smile was gorgeous. Padraig was over a thousand years old, one of the elves from before the Breaking. He'd been attacked right before the war began and was put into a magical coma to heal for about five hundred years. In the last year he'd lost his wife and two close friends when Nivinal, disguised as Alric, attacked his research location. Padraig had been seriously injured. The entire side of his face was burnt badly.

He used a glamour to hide it, but one of my weird new abilities appeared to be seeing through glamours. Nevertheless, his face looked whole and unblemished right now.

I glanced toward Amara but she was sipping her tea and ignoring the mountain of food Dogmaela was piling next to her. I leaned in closer to Lorcan and dropped my voice.

"I can't see through Padraig's glamour."

Lorcan peered closely at his friend's face. "It's not there anymore."

Padraig shook his head and raised his hand to his cheek. He pulled it back as if it hurt, then cautiously put it back. "It's healed?"

Mathilda had been watching him carefully. "I'm sure you don't recall me, Padraig, I was an infrequent visitor to the palace. But I am Mathilda. You saved me from a rampaging garlon beast a long time ago. I never forgot, even though I didn't have a chance to thank you at the time. I can't bring your loved ones back, but I can remove the marks on your skin and the physical pain. I could sense that my sister had tried but wasn't able to remove them so I thought to assist. However, I should have asked before I cast the spell—I do apologize."

All of us probably had the same look—shock. The best mages in the enclave had tried to heal him and couldn't. Yet, Mathilda had done it without anyone—even Padraig—being aware.

Padraig had a look of awe as he rubbed his face. His long black hair was now on both sides of his head. Alric was insanely good looking, even taking into consideration my bias, but Padraig was like an elven prince of old. A stunned prince.

Mathilda frowned and dropped her voice. "Unless you wanted to keep them?"

I knew where she was going. His scars were a reminder of who he lost. He might feel he needed to keep them.

He was silent for a moment and closed his eyes. Then he smiled and opened them. "My wife would say I was foolish to turn down such a gracious offer. And I always listened to her. Healing this will not make me forget her, or the others. I appreciate it. And I do recall you. Siabiane's older and feistier sister. Well met, Mathilda, and thank you."

"Now back to our problem," Covey said. "Foxy has been kidnapped and the mayor of Kenithworth is trying to take over a small digger town. Yet you say none of the relics are here. Why is he here?" She was up on her feet and I could see her slipping into lecturer mode. Before this adventure began Covey had been an elven researcher at the University. The pacing and the fierce challenge in her face showed what she'd been like. She turned to Amara. "You say you know he was taken and not killed?"

Amara slowly nodded. "I can't explain how, but when my tree and I sent forth the hedge to surround us, I felt him. He is alive and within my plant ring."

"Which means that some of the enemy are still here as well," Alric said.

"Or they left him trapped somewhere," Padraig added. "How far is this hedge of yours, Amara?"

"It would be easier to show you." She got up and went to the space behind the bar. She came out with an old, and very beat up, map of Beccia. "This area is how far." She took a stick, dipped it in charcoal and drew.

Covey let out a whistle. "That is extremely impressive. You've even included some of the ruins."

Lorcan was silent, but he was watching Amara, not the map. "I am not trying to be rude, but how are you doing this? I felt the power of your tree when we came in. But by Taryn's reckoning, that tree is barely a year old. It looks like it's thousands of years old and the amount of power to do what you two have done is unheard of." He peered closely at Amara but she wouldn't meet his eyes. "You're not just a dryad, are you?" There was a deep sadness in his voice.

"I am a dryad. That is my tree. Foxy is my mate and I will do anything to save him." She'd kept her head down but looked up defiantly at the last bit. She had tears in her eyes. Green tears.

The only two who seemed to have a clue were Lorcan and Amara. Then Mathilda gasped and nodded.

"The last tree goddess?" Her words meant nothing to me, but did to pretty much everyone else. Even Covey rocked back on her heels.

"Someone fill me in? There are tree goddesses?" I wasn't a religious person, but I would have thought I'd have heard of a tree goddess pantheon.

"There were." Mathilda came up and enveloped Amara in a hug. "They died out when the Ancients were lost. But one survived, didn't she?" She was crooning soothing words and Amara started shaking with her sobs.

Amara finally pulled back and wiped her face. "I was known as Amariathia. I was the youngest, and the last made when the world was new. My sisters…they died when the Ancients were destroyed. I didn't know what happened for weeks. I had no one. Jovan found me and made me his slave for centuries. I am alone except for Foxy."

CHAPTER NINE

SHE WAS SO SAD, BROKEN, and dejected standing there, it was hard to believe we were in the presence of an actual goddess.

"Could anyone else have known who you were? Jovan wasn't working alone." An ugly thought started crawling around my head.

"No one." But she shook her head and shrugged. "I don't know. Jovan kept me mostly drugged. He stopped the drugs when he sent me here. Do you think that was why they took Foxy?"

"We know the mayor was here for something. I only met him once, but he might have had many agendas. If he had any information that there was a deity in town he might have added her to his list." I wouldn't put it past him.

Covey nodded. "I'd say he didn't know it was her for certain, at least not until he grabbed Foxy and the hedge appeared."

"I caused this? Because of what I am, Foxy was taken?" A new round of tears slid down Amara's face.

"No, child," Lorcan said. "The people we're fighting are the ones to blame, not you. And you are not alone. Between all of us, you have a group of staunch defenders."

Dogmaela had been standing back, but stepped forward. "No one hurt you or Foxy. You are family." The way she was clenching and unclenching her massive fists, I was really hoping I got to be around when she found the mayor.

I had no idea how someone should address a goddess. I also had way too many questions, but figured now wasn't the time. Since my friends seemed to be aware of the tree goddesses, I could just bug one of them about it later. Amara looked like she just wanted things to go back as they were. Something I could totally get behind.

"Lots of words." Garbage flew over to our table. She was only a little wobbly; given how long they'd been in here with their own ales; I was a little surprised she could fly. "What do now? We fight?"

Ah, that would explain a bit. The faeries loved their ale, but Garbage loved fighting better. Since we'd fled the Spheres, she hadn't had anything to fight.

Leaf and Crusty both ran across the floor, looping around each other as they went.

"No fighting yet, we're trying to figure things out." I bent down and helped Leaf and Crusty up to the top of the table. At the rate they were sliding back down as they tried to climb the leg of the table, we'd be waiting forever. Both of them stumbled to Amara.

"Knew you tree lady." Crusty planted a slobbery kiss on Amara's arm and Leaf just looked up adoringly.

"You three knew she was a tree goddess?" I'd figured they'd always called her a tree lady because she was a dryad.

"Is yes. Nice tree lady." Leaf flopped down on the table-top.

"Why didn't you tell me?" I directed the question to Garbage. She still wanted a fight, but at least she was closer to sober than the other two.

"You no ask," Garbage said as if that was a stupid question. "We fight? Things bad, we get fight."

"We will need to fight, little one, we all will," Lorcan said. "But first we have to plan. That being said, maybe you should call in the rest of your faeries?"

Being on my own for a month had rattled me more than I thought; I'd not even noticed that the other twenty tamed faeries were missing.

Covey must have seen it on my face. "They left us after conveying your message, or rather a gross misinterpretation of your message. I figured they'd gone to find your faeries. They weren't clear about them being with you either."

Garbage was spoiling for a fight, so since nothing else was around now, she'd chew out her faery lieutenants. "I fix." The look on her tiny orange face was grim as she rose in the air. She was out a tiny hole in the wooden boards covering the windows before we could stop her.

"That might not have been the best idea if there are enemies and spies in town. She's too noticeable." I didn't want to compound things by going out after her, but I wasn't happy.

"We get!" Crusty shouted from her now prone position on the table. Next to an equally prone Leaf. At least I didn't have to worry about those two going out.

Alric shook his head and went back to looking at Amara's map. "There's nothing we can do about her now; she is tiny, so hopefully no one will notice."

"But how will they get in past the hedge?" Amara finally stopped crying. "I can't open it again for a while. That took too much out of my tree and me."

As if they'd been listening to Amara, the faeries' cats rose from the fire and jogged to the back door.

"I think they have a plan, or they needed to go to the bathroom at the same time." Mathilda rose from her chair, went to the back door, and opened it. "The hedge let the cats pass without your assistance, correct?"

Amara nodded. "It's designed to let animals go through unmolested. But while three faeries on three cats weren't noticeable, I'm afraid the spell will trigger if they try to get more faeries on each cat. Or if they go back and forth multiple times."

Mathilda's laugh cut her off. "I think the faeries have that covered as well. Garbage was always the mastermind of the three."

It was hard to see from inside the pub, but it appeared that a fleet of cats was running down the back alley. Heading toward the hedge.

"Who knew cat racing would come in handy some day?" I shook my head at the inventiveness of the faeries.

"We did!" Leaf was flat on her back but was waving both hands in the air. "Kittahs good!"

Mathilda shut the door and we went back to planning. Leaf and Crusty just stayed on the table giggling to themselves.

Amara was pointing out on the map the area Foxy and the other missing resistance fighters had been when they vanished. It was on the far end of her hedged-in zone. And while I wouldn't know until I saw it, the area looked close to the ruins where Jovan had set up shop.

"What was there in the past?" I asked any of the attending elves. Alric had never reacted much to that area, but we'd been fighting for our lives at the time we'd gone through it.

Lorcan tipped his head and started measuring out space. "That is a good question. It's hard to tell now, even for me. But there were no proper buildings out that way. The woods there are dark and the trees fierce. It was never worth it to build."

"And no one digs there for those same reasons." I looked around the room. "Could it be spelled? Something left over from the Ancients?" I knew it could just be a really bad location, but it seemed like people went out of their way to avoid it. Over the past year and a half, I'd learned to question everything. Preferably before it bit me in the behind.

Alric frowned. "I never sensed anything." He rubbed his arm. "But we can't ignore that there may be something there."

Amara started to say something, then screamed in pain

and tumbled to the ground. A loud booming sound came from outside. Everyone else was around Amara, so I ran to the least boarded window and shoved aside the curtains.

I could just see the hedge down the road, a tiny bit, no more than a sliver. It vanished for a split second, and then slammed back into reality. In perfect time with another scream from Amara.

"Something is happening to the hedge!" I yelled back to the others.

"No. My. Tree." Amara got out as another scream burst forth.

Alric beat Padraig and me out the back door. Sure enough, the tree was under attack. By an army of tiny, sword-wielding squirrels.

Damn it. Our only faeries were too drunk to stand, and I had no idea how long it would take Garbage and the others to get through—especially if the hedge was twitching in and out of reality. A year ago the faeries had an ongoing battle with a clan of possessed squirrels. The squirrels had vanished after the battle for the glass gargoyle. Or so we'd thought. Judging by the hundred plus that were swarming the tree; they'd either been hiding this entire time, or been recruited back. And they brought friends.

Alric, Padraig, and I ran to the tree. They both had their swords, but mine had failed to appear. I did have a nice dagger though.

Fighting so many opponents who were much smaller than you—and, judging by their red eyes, possessed besides—wasn't easy. Most of them were now focusing on us instead of Amara's tree, but that wouldn't last for long.

We were holding them off the tree, but all of us were showing fatigue, even though it had been just a few minutes. Something else was affecting us. Because I had a dagger instead of a sword, I had to be much closer to the creatures than the other two. One squirrel got a slice in. It was weird fighting rodents armed with actual steel, but in this case I was grateful. The scratch hurt, but I'd hate to think what those teeth or claws would do. I bashed the offending squirrel away from me and the tree with the flat of my dagger.

Neither Alric nor Padraig were doing magic. At first I thought it was because they were confident of their fighting, but then I noticed them both slowing down. Not only were the squirrels possessed and armed—they were magic carriers. Not magic users, but someone had placed tiny chains with magic-dampening crystals on about a third of the squirrels. Damn it. If cats could go back and forth through the hedge, then insane attack squirrels could as well. Our enemies had sent them through to bring down the hedge.

"They're magicked."

"I know. We can't keep fighting."

Padraig's comment was cut off as a wave of noise came funneling down the alley. The sound was a massive onslaught of faeries, far more than the group of twenty we'd been expecting. They were all riding cats. Some were in war feathers, some in leaves, and some in overalls. Each one had a war blade, and none of them appeared happy to see the squirrels.

Judging by the insane screeching coming from the squirrels, the feeling was mutual.

I really had no idea why the faeries hadn't flown once they'd cleared the hedge, but the addition of the cats did make an impressive entrance.

"We might want to get out of the way." I jumped out from the two massive roots I'd been fighting from and ran to the pub door. Alric and Padraig joined me just as the cat and faery wave swept past us.

The crash of the two groups was impressive, and even more so when half of the faeries jumped off their cats and flew to attack the squirrels in the tree.

Within three minutes, most of the squirrels were dead

and the few survivors had scurried off.

Garbage flipped in the air and shouted a war cry that was echoed by the faeries surrounding us.

"We win!"

"That was impressive, sweetie. But who are your extra friends?" Getting the additional twenty faeries back was a good idea; I wasn't sure about increasing the flock.

"Is more friends! Just help now. Back later. Now they and extra meows go back." Garbage raised her staff and the leaf-clad faeries remounted their cats, bowed to Garbage, and then rode off toward the hedge.

So much had happened in the past few days, I was ready to go play faery and drink until I passed out.

I turned to Padraig and Alric but they had climbed up a bit to inspect the tree and didn't seem concerned about Garbage's apparently increasing political power in the faery realm. Both were just standing there with their heads tipped.

"I think it will be fine." Padraig finally broke the silence and reverently patted the tree before he and Alric climbed down.

"Bodies need go." Garbage scowled at the dead squirrels as if the least they could have done was die somewhere else. She raised her arm and the remaining faeries starting swirling around where the bodies were.

"Wait!" Alric held up his hand and ripped the magic command chain off the nearest squirrel. "We might be able to find out who sent them."

Garbage nodded once he stepped back again and the faeries whirled until they became a blur. When they stopped the squirrel bodies were gone.

CHAPTER TEN

ALRIC LOOKED AT THE SMALL chain and jewel in his hand. "This is far more powerful than I'd expected, and at least a third of the squirrels had them on. Not only could they have severely damaged Amara and her tree, they could have taken out half of Beccia in a few hours."

"It's not in great shape already," Padraig said and nodded down the alley to where the rest of the town could be seen.

He was right. Beccia had never been a glamorous place, or even an okay place. It probably looked tired and worn the moment it was built. However, the town had taken some serious hits as of late, and it showed. Not all of the damage from the battle of the glass gargoyle had been repaired, and since then evil elves, rakasa, and sceanra anam had played with it. Now the mayor of Kenithworth and his syclarions had taken a bite and were looking for more.

Covey stuck her head out of the pub doorway. "Whatever you did, it worked. Amara says her tree will recover and the hedge stands. Plus, we think we have a way to track Foxy."

We trooped back inside the pub, Alric still focusing on the small squirrel bauble.

The faeries flew in over our heads and went right for the bar. Twenty-three cats in a wild variety of colors and sizes were piled up near the fire. I really hoped that we weren't going to have them with us the entire time now. I liked cats, I really did. But taking care of that many would be problematic and expensive.

Mathilda and Amara were looking at Amara's map, but looked up as we came in.

"Thank you for saving us." Amara shook her head. "But I don't understand. The squirrels of Beccia love my tree. Why would they attack it?"

Alric looked up from his study of the small chain. "They didn't. These weren't your local squirrels. These were trained, spelled, and yes, possessed. I'd say our friend the mayor has many allies on his side, some possibly from inside Beccia." He looked to me.

I had the same thought. Okay, after he pointed me toward it, but I still had it. Back when we'd first run into squirrels like this, they'd been controlled by a few of the crime lords of Beccia. The extremely heavy magic-using crime lords. "Cirocco or Largen?"

"Or both," he said. "Amara, have you heard anything? Are they out of jail?"

Both had been locked up after the glass gargoyle incident but so had Grimwold and I knew he'd gotten out a few months ago. Cirocco's prime henchman had been last seen running away in Kenithworth. He could be working with the mayor now for all we knew.

"Possibly? I don't really pay attention to that." She dropped her focus back to the map.

"Let's assume one or both are helping the mayor. We need to be careful moving around out there." Alric looked down at the map. "How did you narrow down where Foxy is on just a map? When we go out we need to be targeted on him and avoid being seen."

Mathilda patted Amara's shoulder. "Our dryad and I cast a spell. Well, I did, but I used her love of Foxy to make it work. He's here, but not here." Her smile dropped. "I can't explain it, but he's right here, and there are more people with him." She tapped a section of the map near the old ruins. "But yet, when I try to scry, I only see the trees, not him, nor any buildings."

I hadn't noticed the small scrying bowl behind her. Scrying was a dicey form of old magic, often not showing anything beyond your reflection gazing into a bowl of water. Yet, I knew if anyone could make it work, it would be Mathilda.

"But if there are no buildings there, where is he?" Amara looked ready to weep again. For a goddess, she cried a lot. Then again, she was the only goddess I knew, so maybe this was normal for them.

"If they were underground, there would be some evidence," Covey was now scrutinizing the map. Actually, she was glaring at it. If it had been an errant University student, it would have given her an answer immediately.

Underground. When I'd been on the run from the evil syclarion who'd been planning world domination, and who turned out was my newest patron in disguise, I'd fallen into an aqueduct. They ran deep under the ruins but, due to expense, had never been examined. From time to time, relics that seemed to be from there showed up—usually on the black market. My friend Harlan had a collection of gold-copper squares that I was pretty sure were the remains of a sarcophagus I'd been trapped in inside that aqueduct.

"What if they were underneath? Way underneath?" I briefly retold my tale, with a few muttered cheers from Leaf from her prone location on the table near the map. She'd been with me on that adventure and had gone for help when I became trapped.

"Elven aqueducts?"

Lorcan shook his head. He'd been mostly silent the last hour, but I knew he was thinking. "Not ours. They were made by the Ancients. When we first moved into this area, after they'd vanished, we tried to utilize them. But they were too damaged and were beyond our abilities to repair. I hadn't thought of them since before the Breaking."

"Could whoever took Foxy and the others be keeping them there?" Covey rocked back a bit, but glared at the map.

"That would mean there was an opening near there. Where I went in was partially intact, that's why I ended up on that wild ride. I have no idea how far it went before I got stuck."

"I didn't get a chance to go back after I rescued you, but from the stale air I'd say most of the passages were long closed." Alric had been studying the squirrel chain, but slipped it into his pocket. "We need to go when it's night to avoid being seen crossing the city; we have to assume there are spies in town. But that's going to make it even more difficult to find an entrance."

"We find." I would have expected Garbage to be drinking with the rest of the faeries, but she flew over and landed next to Crusty and Leaf. She pulled them to their feet. They both wobbled, but mostly stood up. "Foxy friend."

I was again surprised at the changes in my orange faery. I wasn't going to complain though. "You could help find the entrance? At night?"

Crusty nodded and tapped her nose. Or rather, she tried to and ended up slapping herself in the face instead.

"Smell. Better at night." Leaf yawned but seemed to be shaking her drunk off.

I peered out the back door. It was late afternoon. It wouldn't be dark enough to hide us for a few hours.

"I think we should get what rest we can, then head out at dusk." Alric was already moving furniture around to make places to lie down.

Amara brought blankets from behind the bar. "You should be fine. No one is going outside at night anymore. It was too dangerous when that mayor person was here. I've not told anyone that I made the hedge, so they are sure the mayor is up to something."

"What about them?" I hooked a thumb at the four old

regulars sitting in their own world and not even noticing us.

Amara smiled. "They probably won't notice. But you'll need food for such a journey. I'll feed them too. They will rest well afterwards." She winked and turned to go to the kitchen, but stopped and ran back to give me a hug. "Thank you for coming back. Foxy knew you'd save us." Then she ran into the kitchen with Dogmaela following.

The good news was that Amara was an amazing cook. Mathilda's food had been very good, but prior to that I'd been eating berries, travel bread, and jerky for almost a month. A real meal sounded wonderful. The bad news was the wave of guilt at her parting words that slammed into me. Foxy had more faith in me than I deserved. Yes, I had been fighting to gather the relics over the past few months. And been taken prisoner by elves. And gone to Null, fallen into the past, and a few other things. Still. I'd never thought that maybe my friends back here needed help. When I thought of them it was for my own purposes—I missed them for me. I wasn't thinking that they might be in trouble as well.

Yet Foxy had been sure I'd save them.

I wiped away a stray tear before anyone noticed; maybe Amara was contagious. "Garbage? Do you want all of your people here to go, or just a few?" I'd gone over to pick up some ale for us and noticed the extra faeries were getting rather drunk. The little black and white one, Penqow, was no longer talking in words, but speaking in belches.

Garbage was on the table with the map. She didn't fly over, but she shook her head. "No. They disobey. They stay." She was pissed about the faeries leaving Alric and the others. I couldn't blame her. A year ago I'd say the faeries were far more annoyance than help. That had changed. Not that I thought Alric and the rest needed help, but it might have been helpful to have had the faeries with them. Not to mention if they'd been more clear in the message they told Alric when I left.

"Okay, then you, Leaf, and Crusty need to stay sober."

"Tea?" Crusty hadn't really been paying attention, or so I thought. However, she grabbed that idea quickly. We'd found out completely by accident that tea made the girls hyper. Like fly so fast no one could see them until they smashed into a tree fast.

"No." I didn't try to hide my shudder. The first time Garbage had tea she'd carved a hole in Covey's kitchen window and hunted down a bird to feed Harlan. Harlan was a chataling, a bipedal feline species. Having the bird flapping around Covey's home wasn't an experience any of the three of us were going to forget for a long time.

The girls looked disappointed but sat down to make their own plans.

"Are you sure you're up to this?" Alric came up to me and rubbed my arms.

There were so many mixed emotions on his handsome face I wasn't sure where to start. Concern, compassion, but also hurt. I knew he wasn't going to question why I'd taken off on my own and left him—yet. We were in crisis mode. But he'd gone the past month thinking that I'd been kidnapped. To find out I'd left on my own was a painful surprise that had been clear on his face.

"I am so sorry," I said.

"Not now. But if you're not up for this, you should stay here."

I pulled back. It wasn't compassion from him, but pure calculating planning. He was trying to decide if I would be a help or a hindrance on this mission. "Foxy is my friend, more so than any of yours. I'm not leaving him down there any longer than we have to." Maybe some emotional distance between us would help. I knew leaving would cause him pain, but it was better than me changing into whatever I'd become at the Spheres and accidently stomp-ing on him or one of the others. I may have made that decision rashly, but I would do it again. "Besides, I've been in those damn aqueducts longer than anyone, even you." I didn't want to fight, but this wasn't how I'd envisioned our reunion.

"Here comes Amara with food," Covey said far too cheerfully.

I looked around and pretty much everyone except for the faeries was looking at Alric and me in that 'we're not really looking at you, but we're listening' way. Both Alric and I took a step away from each other and the tension dropped.

I sat between Covey and Mathilda as Amara brought enough food for a hundred people. We finalized the plans as we ate, then bedded down on the pub floor for a few hours. That Alric and I were as far away from each other as possible wasn't a good sign.

I hadn't even had time to dream when I was rudely awakened by three beings stabbing me in the gut. Garbage, Leaf, and Crusty were awake and extremely sober. And far too energetic. I squinted at them, but they just looked to be normal energetic, not tea-driven insanity energetic. If the rest of the faeries were staying here, I needed to warn Amara about not giving them tea. Chocolate was also risky, but it just made them mellow, so I wasn't as worried about that.

It was when all three turned to me and put their fingers over their mouths that I got worried. That and the sound of heavily clawed feet walking in front of the pub.

CHAPTER ELEVEN

———◆———

THE PUB WAS MOSTLY DARK, with only a light from the kitchen breaking the gloom. Foxy always left one glow on, and it was nice to know Amara was doing the same. It was enough to see the faeries' faces, especially when they came right up to my nose. But I couldn't see much else.

The scrabbling footsteps outside continued. There was more than one syclarion out there, and they were walking slowly, as if they were looking for something.

I closed my eyes and focused my energy on my sword. Alric and Padraig could call their spirit swords to them whenever they wanted. Mine seemed to have a mind of its own and came, and went, when it felt like it. But if a bunch of syclarions were about to burst in, I really needed my sword to want to be here.

I grabbed Garbage and brought her to my mouth as I whispered. "Can you tell the others? Start with Alric and Padraig."

"Others do. And spies sent." Garbage's grin was terrifying at this distance.

Swearing came from outside and the footsteps stopped. "Damn it, it's just some of those stray cats."

I wasn't surprised to hear the low guttural voice of a syclarion. An echo of more swearing voices told me there were at least six out there.

"Keep searching. We don't have much time and the cats

must have triggered the alarm." They slowly moved off. I knew syclarions could move fast when they wanted to, so the slow walking was deliberate. Obviously not all of them had been chased off during Amara's purge, or they'd managed to sneak in while the hedge was having problems. The attack on Amara's tree might not have been expected to succeed, but just to drop the hedge long enough to get the syclarions back into town. Minutes later, the footsteps had gone and all of my friends sat up.

"I have spelled the windows now, so no light will escape," Lorcan said as he magically lit the glows in the room. Foxy used to only have cheap candles, but he'd been improving his clientele in the past year. Probably Amara had a big influence on that change. As his wife, this pub was hers too. I briefly wondered if he knew he was married to a tree goddess.

"Meows say eight," Leaf said as she flew up from conversing with two of the cats. "Bad smell."

"This doesn't change anything, except that we have to be more careful." Padraig held up his hand before Alric could speak. "No, you're not doing this alone now. The plan hasn't changed."

"How do you know that was what I was going to say?" Alric didn't even pretend to look surprised, regardless of his words. "It's a logical idea though. One person can get through unseen better than a mass of people. I can get in, get Foxy and the others out, and be back in an hour."

"No." I stepped forward before anyone else could speak. It wasn't just whatever was falling apart between Alric and me. It was that I knew we needed to do this as a group. I'd no idea why, I just knew it.

"I agree with Taryn," Mathilda said. She shot me a questioning smile. "There is more here than we see. I'm feeling that, and somehow so is Taryn." She pointed to Alric, Padraig, Covey, and me. "You four need to go. Lorcan and I will stay and protect Amara and her tree."

"And us!" Garbage had her war feathers on and the other two were donning theirs.

"Yes, and you three. The rest of the faeries, the constructs, and the cats will help us protect the tree." Mathilda might be new to everyone but myself and the faeries, but her wisdom held true. Everyone nodded. Even Alric, although he was the last and didn't look happy.

It only took a few minutes to make sure everyone was armed and ready to slip out the back door and down the alley behind the pub. The town had large lanterns on the major roads, and this street was usually well lit. There were a few working, but mostly they just created tiny pools of light separated by massive amounts of darkness.

"Keep Taryn in the middle of us. Her eyesight is the weakest in the dark," Alric said.

Covey shot me a look but I shrugged. It was rude, but it was also accurate. The two elves had excellent night vision and, while Covey's wasn't as good as theirs, as a trellian hers was better than mine.

The roads were empty, but we stayed close to the buildings. Clearly, there were people we'd rather not meet out here. Even the faeries were silent as we quickly made our way to the edge of town. Alric was in his element sneaking around and I felt a bit of pride. That feeling crumbled when I remembered what was going on between us right now.

Crusty flew to my shoulder and patted my head. "Is okay. Good." Her voice was barely a whisper and considering that neither of the sharp-eared elves acted as if they had heard her, I doubted she gave us away to anyone.

"Thank you." I kept my voice as low as she had. It was a little odd being comforted by the craziest faery, but it felt good too. The middle of a rescue wasn't where Alric and I needed to sort this out. But the time would come. Hopefully, not until I found a way to tell him and the others why I'd left. Padraig and Lorcan were patient. Covey wasn't but she'd said she'd wait. Those three didn't appear mad at me.

I hadn't appreciated the weak light from the scattered lanterns until it was gone. The forest surrounding the ruins was darker than the pits of the abyss.

Padraig lit a clearthin, a modified glow that shed a little light but was invisible to anyone beyond its short range. He also took my hand and silently guided me through. We had to slow down; I was sure that was mostly for me. Alric was dropping to his knee from time to time, checking the dirt. After his third time, he got up, dusted his knee off, and bowed to Garbage. The great tracker had admitted defeat.

Garbage didn't say anything, but flew high in the air above us, beyond the range of the clearthin glow. The other two stayed with us but the way they looked up I figured they had no trouble seeing her. She finally came shooting down, tore through our location, went about fifteen feet ahead, then dropped out of sight. Leaf and Crusty both flew after her while waving for us to follow.

Alric didn't even look back as he led us after the faeries. Padraig held my hand, half pulling me along after Covey.

Even if it had been full daylight I probably wouldn't have seen the crack in the ground. The girls were flying in and out of what looked like where the forest floor met up with a massive log. When we moved closer, the glow made it a little easier to see. There was a wide gash in the ground and the tree trunk covered up most of it. I didn't know if this was the only entrance to the aqueducts over on this side, but it had clearly been used recently.

Alric got down and peered into the hole. He slid through, and then vanished. I held my breath until he appeared a moment later. "It's a way in. Come down."

He vanished again, leaving the three of us to climb in after him. I needed to make things right between us before I thought about welcoming that monster I'd become back into my life and just letting whatever it was deal with Alric directly.

Padraig's dim glow bobbed along with us into the small space. The way opened up and started a sharp decline within a few feet.

The first and only time that I'd visited these aqueducts—the section a few miles away, under the regular dig sites—I'd fallen in. The ground beneath me had given way and I really didn't have a chance to notice the entrance.

Padraig lit another clearthin glow so we could see better, but since we weren't sure who was down here with Foxy, we couldn't run regular glows. Alric was scouting ahead in the pitch dark. The petty side of me, who was upset about his growing coldness, hoped he'd at least stub a toe. Of course, being the stoic one, he most likely wouldn't react even if he did.

The way appeared to be made of dirt at first, but that was just a few centuries worth of the stuff drifting in from the entrance. Once we got a bit further in, the path cleared and the smooth stone walls became visible. I reached out to touch them and was flung about five feet back on my ass. Luckily, the way was wide enough that I had a few feet before I'd hit the far wall. My left cheek flared with a cold stab, and a roar of jumbled voices smashed into my skull.

Alric was at my side right away, but his concern quickly cooled once he took in the fact I was intact and uninjured. He'd forgotten he was upset with me for a moment. Point for me—he still cared. Point against me—that reaction to the wall had hurt like hell.

"What happened?" He helped me to my feet but dropped my hand immediately.

Padraig and Covey closed in as well, the floating clearthin glows giving an odd orangish appearance to everything.

"I have no idea." I rubbed my cheek, which was now almost feeling normal. "All I did was touch the wall. It tried to slam me into the other side."

Padraig came closer and tilted my face toward the two

clearthin glows. "You have a bruise on your cheek, did you actually hit the wall?"

"No."

"That's where the manticore is though." Alric had leaned forward as well.

I stepped back from them. "I'm okay. I just won't touch the walls. We need to get Foxy out, remember?" That was the problem with hanging out with smart and curious people—they were always being curious. I wasn't happy about what had just happened any more than I was happy about what had happened at the Spheres. But shoving things aside for the immediate moment seemed the best course of action. I ignored the tiny voice that pointed out the Spheres had been over a month ago and I was still shoving those events aside.

Alric shot me a concerned look but said nothing as he resumed leading. Covey and Padraig both dropped behind me, which made me feel nice and safe. And like I was a little old lady they were afraid was going to totter over at any moment.

The path was extremely dry, which was good considering what we were walking down. The part I'd been trapped in before hadn't been completely filled with water, but there had been enough to almost kill me.

We'd walked in silence for another five minutes when voices echoed down the dry aqueduct. Alric held up his hand to stop, and Padraig's glows dropped even lower and became dimmer.

The faeries were flying back to us, keeping just above our heads, and flying silently. I didn't see them until the glows reflected off their wings.

Garbage was coming in for a landing, so I held out my hand for her. She scowled around, but it was in general, not at any of us. "They have. Locked. We get." She was tossing around her war stick as she spoke and I almost got stabbed with it as I grabbed her.

"No. You need to stay with us." I looked to the other two faeries. "Everyone needs to stay with us. No one goes off on their own." I didn't look to Alric but my comment was aimed at him as well.

"How many others did you see?" Alric's tone was far less cold than it had been with me.

"This." Garbage flashed her tiny fingers. At least ten but it was hard to tell beyond that. I knew she could count, she was just upset about not being able to go war faery on the enemy.

"Were they all syclarions? Or Beccians?" We'd heard the syclarions last night, but the fact that no one was on guard was a bit odd for them.

Garbage scowled. "Two bad, rest from town." She'd been hoping that if we thought there was a huge group of bad guys down there we'd be more likely to let them go down on their own. She was so smart sometimes and so clueless other times.

"I can do it alone, less risk to everyone." Alric's glance in my direction was too fast for me to guess what he meant. Beyond that it was aimed at me.

"No," all three of the non-flying beings of our group said. The faeries were now muttering among themselves.

"Let's keep going. Ladies, would you be our gallant scouts?" Padraig was laying on the charm, but it worked. "We can't have you fight until we are sure our friends are safe. Then we will charge forth together."

Leaf and Garbage beamed proudly. Crusty was chasing one of the feathers that was on her back. As long as Garbage agreed, we were fine.

"We do." Garbage raised her war stick and they flew back down the corridor.

"So we're just walking up and freeing our people?" Covey looked between Padraig and Alric. "Don't you elves have a plan? What if the rest of them come back before we're done?"

"You just stated our plan." Padraig held up his hand. "We can get them out and flee. I have left spell markers on the path behind us. If anyone comes this way, I will feel it. Besides, if Alric doesn't get to fight someone soon, he's going to explode." He raised an eyebrow in Alric's direction.

A flash of anger crossed Alric's face, but he shook it off. "You're right and I'm sorry. But if you wouldn't mind letting me go in first, I'd appreciate it." He didn't wait but turned and continued down the aqueduct.

The people we were sneaking up on weren't afraid of anyone finding them. At least that was my opinion based on the amount of noise they were making. Flickers of light coming from around the bend could be seen on the far wall. Even Alric signaled to pause.

"We can't send them back down so soon. They die, we die. You heard her."

I was expecting the dulcet tones of syclarions, but it didn't make me any happier to hear them.

"They ain't getting the job done fast enough. There are troops up top now. Not our guys."

"Why didn't you say so? The hedge dropped."

"Just for a bit. They have to be that damn Kenithworth idiot's army. We need the stuff now."

"Get them ready to dig then."

Two shadows crossed in front of the light as they went further down.

Alric took a breath, unsheathed his sword, and ran forward. Even though he'd agreed we'd go together, this was as close as he was willing to get to that. Padraig swore as he freed his sword and we ran after Alric.

The room was a massive cavern; judging by the way the walls were hacked apart it hadn't started this big. The faeries were hovering high against the ceiling, barely visible until they dropped down. Of course, the little maniacs had their war sticks out swinging wildly.

The two syclarion guards in odd livery stood before us. A giant cage held a bunch of people, including Foxy.

"Taryn! Watch out, they have something down below!" His yell ended in a grunt as the guard closest to him used a staff to ram him in the gut through the bars of the cage.

Alric and the faeries attacked the two guards. Padraig, Covey, and I turned toward the dark hole Foxy had pointed to.

CHAPTER TWELVE

THERE WAS A TRAIL LEADING to the hole from the cage, and heavy-duty digger equipment scattered nearby. Two odd flat boats were off to the side and looked like they hadn't been used for a few centuries. There were also what looked like bones of a person. They were dry and brittle, but the placement had to be deliberate. That it died in the motion of crawling away from the hole couldn't be good.

A blast of flame came out of the hole along with a rusty sounding roar. The ground shook as the head of a dragon appeared. The prisoners fled as far back in their cage as they could, dragging the injured Foxy with them.

The head was definitely a dragon, but the bits of shine coming through the muck on it told me it wasn't living. "It's a construct!"

"That can still snap a head off!" Foxy was in pain, but, as always, was watching out for me. "An' don't use magic! It'll strike back on ye!"

The dragon construct turned to us, effectively getting between the three of us and the others.

I wasn't about to go up against a thing whose head was taller than me while I was armed only with a dagger. Padraig however, had no problem and charged forward with his sword. Covey moved forward at the same time and even had her own sword out. Had the dragon construct been fully functioning they might have been in trouble, as it opened its mouth for more flame. A wisp of smoke came out.

"Told you it was too soon; it's out of fire!" The largest of the syclarions yelled at his partner just before Alric's sword ran him through. The second one didn't get a chance to respond as the faeries swarmed down and tagged him with their war sticks. The sticks were tiny and the movement of them was almost delicate. That just made it even more disturbing when the syclarion screamed in pain. Three more attacks and he crumbled to the ground. Alric finished him off with his sword.

The dragon hadn't come further out of the hole and, in fact, seemed to be slowing down in its movements.

"Foxy, what is this thing?" I didn't look back to him. Even though the dragon construct was slowing, there was a chance it could recover.

"They used it to make us keep digging; it's a magical beast their boss lady fixed up. It's supposed to be an Ancient."

I waited for the rest of his comment. "An ancient what?"

"An *Ancient*." One of the other Beccians got out before Foxy could. "It's a metal beast made to look like the dead people that lived here…only they weren't people!"

I turned back to my three friends. I would have thought that if the Ancients were actually dragons, someone would have figured that out in over two thousand years. Granted, there hadn't been a lot to examine. Someone should have noticed. Dragon bones would be hard to hide and so would huge buildings.

Unfortunately, my three braniac friends looked as surprised as I felt.

"Who claimed this was a representation of an Ancient?" Alric looked personally offended. Padraig and Covey looked confused.

"Some lady," Foxy said. He had recovered enough to try and stretch one arm through the bars to the dead guard that the faeries had struck down. There were keys on the man's belt.

Since the other three were busy muttering how impossible things were, and studying the slowly moving dragon head, I jogged over to the dead guard, grabbed the keys, and freed the prisoners. They all looked roughed up, with Foxy looking the worst. Not that it stopped him from swinging me up in a massive and painful hug.

Foxy was at least seven feet tall, with long floppy ears, and wicked-looking tusks that stuck up from his lower jaw. I'd never figured out exactly what cross breed he was. After over fifteen years of friendship, it seemed impolite to ask.

But whatever he was, I was glad to see him. And he was seconds away from crushing my ribs.

"Down!" I managed to squeak out as I pounded on his broad back.

He dropped me to my feet as the other townsfolk made their way past us.

"We need to get out of here," one of the Beccians said. "Once that beast winds down and the guards don't send the signal, the trap will close." Everyone looked to the dragon head.

"But isn't that construct the trap? If you didn't obey it would burn you?"

"Nay, lass," Foxy said. "They have something else as well. Not sure what it be, but they were too confident of it to have been false."

The Beccians started going back up the way we'd come in. The aqueduct continued down a steep slope past this place, but looked even more foreboding than the hole the dragon head came out of.

"Does this dragon go all the way down?" Covey was already moving toward the hole to view for herself. None of my friends looked like they'd heard Foxy or the others.

I walked toward them. "Guys? Threat? Coming as soon as that thing stops moving?"

Foxy was staying with me but the Beccians were almost

out of sight as they were swallowed by the darkness up the aqueduct. They weren't running, but they were moving quickly.

"Maybe we can restart it." Alric was just as inquisitive as the other two and he was leaning way too far over the edge of the hole to look at the dragon.

Padraig peered down with Covey. "Fascinating. It does look like a full construct. The engraving down the neck is definitely Ancient."

"You're going to die!" Foxy's barroom bellow might not have been the best idea if those two guards had backup anywhere down here, but it got my friends to look back at Foxy and me.

Padraig swore and turned back toward the dragon. "If we can send the right code, reset this thing, it will stop whatever might happen. Ancients' representation or not, this is a singular example of their work—we have to study it."

"We can fight off whatever they send at us." Alric went back to leaning over the hole.

Covey didn't get a chance to rationalize their insanity before screams and a roaring sound filled the cavern.

My sword finally decided to show up and popped into my hand. Its scabbard was on the ground at my feet. I'd just gotten it belted around my waist when the Beccians rounded the corner. And so did the roaring sound—a massive wall of water.

"Water!" Leaf yelled, just in case any of us had suddenly been struck both blind and deaf. The faeries had been hanging around the top of the cavern after vanquishing their foe but now came down to the dragon.

"Good friend." Crusty dropped down and patted the dragon.

I had no idea if it was what she did or something triggered by the water, but the dragon slid back down into its hole just as the water caught us. The huge hole the dragon had slid down filled with water and slowed the flood from getting us, but not enough. The Beccians ran past us and further down the dark aqueduct. We followed, but we were picked up by the water after a few steps.

Tumbling down the aqueduct in a massive copper-gold sarcophagus hadn't been fun. But it was far better than the same ride while swimming. Or drowning in my case. I'd always been terrified of water, or at least had been after my parents had been killed while boating. It was one of the main reasons I'd never gone back to my hometown after I recovered and Mathilda ditched the faeries and me. It was across the sea.

The waves were slamming me about and I was saying good-bye to everything I knew, when two hands grabbed me and pulled me out of the water and into a boat. It had been Alric and Covey who grabbed me. I had no idea how they'd gotten to the boat in time and I didn't care. Three of the Beccians were with us, and the rest were with Padraig and Foxy in the second boat. Old or not, the boats were staying afloat.

The current slowed the farther the water got from its release point. But it was still forceful enough to kill most of us if we hadn't had the boats.

Actually, it might still be enough to kill us even with the boats.

The faeries were having a great time. They were flying just above the front of the wave, bouncing along the spray being thrown in the air.

The aqueduct was dark. Padraig had reactivated his two clearthin glows, but nothing more. They were hovering above us.

"Where will this put us out?" I yelled to Alric over the water. The nice solid walls surrounding us were doing a great job magnifying the sound of the crashing water.

"No idea." Alric nodded. "You might want to sit on the bottom of the boat. No idea if this will get worse."

I'd been so excited at not drowning; I was crouched on

one of the boat seats. I quickly dropped to the bottom where the others were.

"It is fascinating that this water continues to runs through here." Not being able to be heard well wasn't going to stop Covey from making observations.

She had a damn good point. There was no doubt the aqueduct system was made well, but it was over two thousand years old. The reason there was this much water now was because whoever was behind that dig in the cavern had blocked the water far further up to release as a final solution if their workers failed.

As if my thinking of it made it happen a new type of roaring filled the area. Padraig's glows darted out ahead, just in time to see the water drop off into nothingness.

CHAPTER THIRTEEN

———◆———

I HUNG ONTO EVERYONE AROUND me; Alric, Covey, total strangers, and we ducked as low as we could. The cliff was probably not nearly as high as it felt, because if it had actually been that tall we would have been smashed to bits.

Instead, we were tossed about and the boat felt ready to flip, but the waters calmed down quickly. We were in a small pool with an extremely low arch at the end where the water was flowing out. The area was small enough that the dim glows lit the entire area. Enough to show there was no way out but that arch.

"Girls." I held up my hand to get the faeries' attention. "How do we get out of here?" We obviously couldn't go back the way we came, but we also couldn't fit the boats through that tiny tunnel.

"Weee gooo that way." Garbage spun slowly and finally pointed to the tunnel.

I turned to Alric and nodded to Padraig in the next boat. "Any other ideas?" I was not getting out of this boat until we were on dry land.

Alric looked down at my clenched hands and then to the walls around us. "I think they're right. These were made for water to go through, not people. Unlike the ones in the enclave, there's no access for us."

"We'll have to swim," Covey said calmly. Her people, the trellians, were desert dwellers, but once she'd learned to swim, she loved it. She'd initially decided to learn to help me get over my fear. I was still terrified of water and she swam like someone born to it.

"I can't swim," one of the Beccians said. A second nodded.

"Okay, so you two and Taryn can't swim. Can everyone else?" Padraig looked around the group. Everyone nodded, even Foxy. Just myself and the two Beccians couldn't swim.

"If we break up one of the boats they can use some of the wood to keep them afloat and get through." Covey started looking for ways to rip the boat apart even before that idea was agreed on. I smacked her hand as she pulled on a piece of the side.

"Taryn, all you have to do is kick," Alric said. "We'll stay near you and the other two. You'll be okay."

Crusty dropped down and patted my head. "Is squirrelable." The way she was nodding, I assumed that was good.

"I thought squirrels were bad?"

"No, no. Ones in mountains good. Play. Squirrelable is good."

Ahhh. Many times while we had been hiding in the mountains, the girls would take off for a few hours. They came back with nothing, so I figured they'd been out drinking. Instead they were making friends with the local squirrel population. And probably also drinking.

"Okay, so then how is this going to be squirrelable? I can't swim."

"Easy." Leaf made a show of holding her nose and diving into the water. I would have been more impressed if I hadn't known they could hold their breath in a bottle of ale for hours. She burst out of the water, spun, and dove back in.

Foxy and two of the Beccians jumped in and started swimming toward the tunnel.

"I'll try." The first man who'd said he didn't swim held out his hand, and Covey slapped a piece of the boat in it. It was a seat, so not crucial, but I didn't think it was a good thing to be ripping apart a boat I was in. He wasn't a young man but slid into the water after the others and started kicking toward the tunnel. The other non-swimmer was even older and he silently held out his hand, took the offered wood, and kicked his way to the rest. Soon only Alric, Covey, and I were in the boats. Padraig had gone ahead with the others in case there was something dangerous at the other end.

My fear was that there was more water. Like a waterfall, with emphasis on fall.

"Taryn, after everything that's happened to you in the past year, you're afraid of this?" Alric went into the water but hung onto the side of the boat. Covey was holding the third seat.

"We have you." She sounded more encouraging than Alric. Then she jumped into the water as well. The boats were just bumping about and eventually I'd have to get out of this one.

I went in. Images of water, boats, and drowning, slammed into me. They used to hit every time I got near any body of water larger than a bathtub, but they'd faded over the years. This was the first one in a while, and it didn't seem as strong. Maybe after fifteen years, the fear was fading.

I took the offered wooden seat and awkwardly held it in the water like it was a pillow and I was about to smack something with it.

Alric swam a bit ahead but didn't go through. Covey gave my legs a push with her own. "Kicking works better if you move."

"I'm trying to remind myself to breathe." The fact was, I wasn't as freaked out about this as I would have thought. Kicking did get me moving in the right direction and I didn't have to go far. Alric nodded at my progress then went through the tunnel. Maybe after this settled down I could actually go back to see my home village.

That thought was torn from my mind as Covey gave me a final shove, I entered the tunnel with my piece of wood, and the world vanished from beneath me.

There was a waterfall. Probably at least twenty feet high. The fact that I hadn't heard from any of my friends told me they'd died horribly and I was going to be next. I hung onto my wooden seat and closed my mouth and eyes as the fall continued.

I slammed into the water, found I was still kicking, and bounced to the surface.

To find my soggy companions, with the exception of Covey, standing on an odd beach in the cavern, wringing out their clothing. The water was stiller here, but continued to flow from a grate at the far end of the pool. There was some light coming from a tunnel behind them, and if I wasn't imagining things, it looked like forest beyond that.

"You can get out of the water, you know." Covey came up next to me as I tread water.

It took my brain a few seconds to get the rest of me to move. Covey pulled me up on the solid ground, then pried the piece of wood away from me.

"Where are we?"

Alric had watched me as I came out of the water, and I thought I saw him step forward. Instead he shook his head and stayed where he was. "I checked and it looks like we're outside the hedge. We'll have to close this side so people can't try and get into Beccia this way."

"How can anyone get in this way? That thing is…huge." As I spoke I actually turned around toward the waterfall. It was more like two feet rather than twenty. My fear of water was still alive and kicking apparently. "Never mind."

We squished and dripped our way to the cavern mouth and outside. The sun was just starting to come up; we'd only been in there a few hours. Like that waterfall, it had felt a lot longer. The woods around us looked amazing in the early morning light, green and golden. Especially after facing what I thought was going to be a watery death. That was until I looked behind us and saw the hedge. We were on the outside of it.

"We fix!" Garbage flew into the hedge before I could say anything. Directly into it. Leaf and Crusty followed behind.

I waited for them to be flung back in our direction, but nothing.

"How did they do that?" Padraig was watching the hedge for tiny returning bodies as well.

I shook my head silently. They'd gone through without even the cats to help them.

A few moments later a small gap in the hedge appeared. Followed by Amara. "Is my Foxy—" The rest of her words were cut off as Foxy ran forward, grabbed her, and tossed her into the air.

"My love! You saved me!"

Technically it was my friends and I, but Amara told us where to find him. And I really didn't care as long as they were happy.

"We probably want to get the hedge closed as soon as possible," Alric said as he scanned the woods around us.

"But I can take it down now," Amara said from her vantage point in Foxy's arms. "My Foxy is back."

"No!" All four of us yelled in unison. The other Beccians looked at us oddly.

"You can't drop the hedge. There are others out here, probably far more than you chased out when they grabbed Foxy," I said. "They destroyed the Halin communal farm a few days ago."

"Destroyed it to starve us out," one of the Beccians said. "I agree, we can't let this mayor person, or the lady bossing around those guards, take over our city. But I have a family to feed. The hedge could hurt us as well."

"This isn't the place for discussion," Padraig held up his hands as more of the Beccians started to speak. "Let's get back into the relative safety of the hedge first. We can meet at the Shimmering Dewdrop and we'll tell you what we know about who you're facing. Maybe in six hours?" He nodded when they didn't look convinced. "You've been missing for five days; don't you think your families might want to see you?" The Beccians finally muttered agreements and walked through the hedge, moving faster as they went to find their families. The way he took command was masterful. Padraig had never been to Beccia before this trip. He'd never met the mayor of Kenithworth and none of us knew who this woman was that had kidnapped Foxy and the rest.

And there was no way anyone could tell that from looking at his calm, elegant face. If you put a crown on his head, people would follow him anywhere.

I shuddered. It was a damn good thing he was on our side. When I'd first met Padraig, he'd been mad with grief, not only at the murder of his wife and friends, but at the supposed betrayal by Alric. The last few months had been a lot of change for him, and I had a feeling he was returning to the type of leader he'd been before the Breaking.

The hedge closed tight right behind us. Amara didn't care if it was up or not—she had her Foxy back, but she was willing to leave it up if we felt it needed to stay up. I had no idea how one would raise something like the hedge, let alone how much magic would be needed to keep it up and working. Then again, a tree goddess probably had unlimited magic. At least for things such as plants.

We went in the back door of the Shimmering Dewdrop to be met by Dogmaela holding a cudgel. One she fortunately dropped once she saw Amara and Foxy.

"Thank all! I've kept an eye on the food, mistress, as you asked." She stood back to let us troop in. Amara gave Foxy a long kiss then followed Dogmaela into the kitchen.

Lorcan and Mathilda were engaged in some heated debate and barely looked up to nod at our soggy entrance.

The extra faeries and cats were missing however.

I went closer to the fire as Foxy added some more logs. He even set up the second fireplace, the one he only used when things were really cold. "Where did the other faeries go?" The three who had been with us had taken off once they'd gotten Amara to open the hedge. But all of them missing was concerning.

"Hmmm?" Lorcan finally completely pulled away from the discussion. "They went scouting. When Garbage and the others came to get Amara, they were given their marching orders."

Mathilda laughed. "You have been good for our little Garbage Blossom, or bad depending on how you view it. She was a tiny, orange general as she bossed them around. Only she, Leaf, and Crusty were to keep to the skies. The rest were told to mount their cat steeds and sent on recon missions."

"Sort of scary actually," Lorcan said. "If those little ones get their collective selves together, there could be a faery uprising. And they'd probably win." He didn't seem concerned however.

"All we'd have to do is give them ale and chocolate and that would stop them." If I was any closer to the fire, I'd burst into flame. Covey and Padraig had gone into two back rooms to change. I was going to, but even wet, that fire just felt too good. Alric seemed impervious to both the cold and the wet as he went to where Lorcan and Mathilda were standing over a large map.

I leaned that direction. It didn't look familiar and it was a new addition since we'd left. But to get a good look I'd have to move from the fire. Wasn't going to happen.

"We have more of a problem than we thought," Lorcan said. "I'll wait to explain until everyone is changed and we've eaten. Amara has been cooking since you left and I fear not paying attention to such a serious breakfast would be a major mistake."

Alric scowled at the map. I knew that if it were up to him, he'd hear it now. The rest of us, and breakfast, be damned. He really was regressing back to his lone wolf state, and that wasn't good.

Covey and Padraig came out of the two tiny rooms, so I grabbed my pack from the corner of the room and went in one to change.

Once changed, but still cold, I went back to the front. Amara, Dogmaela, and Lehua, a half-giant barmaid, brought out platters of food.

I had a feeling Amara might be from the tree goddess culinary team. She had enough food to feed at least fifty Foxys. The rest of us sat down at two tables to tuck in. Alric stayed in front of the map looking soggy and annoyed. But the annoyance was directed to the map. He had the look people get when they're trying to recall something, but it stayed just out of reach.

"When he was young, and just learning magic, he used to do this all of the time," Padraig said without even looking up from the massive amount of food piled on his plate. "Gets in his own world, too busy to eat. He once passed out at his desk and smeared love bane over the side of his face. Took a week for women to stop running from him. I would have thought he'd outgrown that."

Alric looked up with a glare, but quickly became sheepish and he ran his hand through his drying hair. "You're right, I was too focused." He looked toward me and I thought he was going to say more, but he stayed silent as he came to the table and let Dogmaela pile food on a plate the size of a shield for him.

"You're so tense I'm surprised you haven't snapped in half." Covey had already wolfed down half of her food and a pot of tea. "You were bad when Taryn left us, but I swear you're worse now."

That was Covey: call things as they were regardless of whether folks wanted to hear it or not.

I'd expected Alric to lash out and deny it. I knew he'd been colder to me after the initial reunion, but clearly others were seeing it too. Instead of a quick snarky or offended response, he looked thoughtful. Of course, his mouth was also full.

He finally swallowed and nodded. "You're right. I don't know what it is, but I've just felt like there are ants crawling under my skin. It hit when we came to Beccia. I feel like I need to do something, but don't know what." He shook his head. "I apologize."

"Well, maybe there is something to that, lad." Lorcan had finished his plate and was sipping tea. For a slender old man, he could pack food away. "There's a reason the mayor wanted to come here. I do believe part of it was unfounded optimism that some of the relics would be here. But he's looking for something else too. The map I have has some information, but not enough. It does look like the syclarions had been in the process of building something underground when whatever destroyed the Ancients happened."

CHAPTER FOURTEEN

THAT WAS A NEW AND unwelcome revelation. "So, *did* the syclarions destroy the Ancients?" I thought Lorcan and Padraig had pretty much decided that the weapon hadn't belonged to our scaly friends.

"Not that we have evidence of. It doesn't appear that they completed whatever they were doing when the end of the battle came. But the research does indicate they were locked in a long term battle when the Ancients vanished." He took another long sip of tea, finally noticing that no one was eating. "Go on, finish your food. After that I'll show you what the map indicates."

Amara came out of her kitchen just as we finished and were trying to push away from the table. "Do you need more?"

The sound that came from us was a combination of a groan and no. Thank you was added belatedly.

"I believe you have successfully fed us; gracious thanks to the leaves, trunk, and roots." Mathilda did an odd move with her fingers, like a blessing, and then gave a half bow.

Amara's mouth dropped into an 'O' and tears started. She bowed back, then ran forward to hug Mathilda. "You know of the old ways. Thank you." She reached up and placed a kiss on Mathilda's brow. "Thank you all." Then the last tree goddess ran back into the kitchen. I swore she was glowing a bit as she vanished.

Mathilda met our questioning looks. "The thank you

offering for the tree goddesses. I have a plethora of eccentric knowledge. I have to say I never would have thought to have used that in my life though."

We circled the map, which gave me my first full look at it. Maps were great, and finding a way to stop the end of the world was too. But so was no longer being cold, wet, and hungry. Now I could focus.

"Wait, what happened to the wagon and your books and scrolls?" I tried not to think about the other thing they carried, the chest from the Dark. A neat little wooden box that hid spell books and other nasties that had belonged to the elves who tried to destroy their own people. And came way too close to succeeding.

Lorcan held out three small black bags, the ones the faeries used to store things. "Here. Well, not the wagons. Your trek through the mountains was too adventuresome for those. We left them in the woods two weeks ago and stabled the horses in a town." He waggled the bags in the air. "Here are our books and scrolls. The faeries gave me these when I was distraught at having to pick and choose what to bring."

It seemed that the faeries gave everyone access to their bags except me. I was going to have to have a talk with them when they got back. Maybe if I could put my stupid sword inside one it would stay put. I glared at it. The dang thing had shown up not when there was a fight, but when I was being drowned. And it was lingering now. Mocking me. I turned back to Lorcan as he pulled out a dozen dusty books from the first bag, then a mass of scrolls from the second. The third he tucked back into his cloak.

I raised my eyebrow in question.

"A certain chest."

"Ah." It was a good thing the chest with the items from the followers of the Dark had its own bag. I didn't know if it could contaminate other items, but better not to take that chance. I, personally, would have liked to have seen that third bag and its contents dropped into the pit that dragon construct had come from.

Which reminded me. I turned to Covey, Padraig, and Alric. "Oh, shouldn't we tell them about the dragon?"

Lorcan had been arranging his book and scroll collection for whatever presentation he'd created and Mathilda was examining each item, but both looked up in shock when I said 'dragon'.

"There was a dragon?" He looked to each of us. "That really should have been addressed right off."

"A dragon *construct*," Alric said. "Supposedly whoever was behind grabbing Foxy claimed it was a construct from the Ancients. One that was a representation of what they really looked like. I doubt that last part, but it was an impressive construct."

Padraig nodded. "With Ancient inscriptions engraved into it. I couldn't read enough to determine if they were spells or not. Considering that it was moving on its own, we can presume they are."

Lorcan studied the map and his scrolls, then us. "This is important, but it can wait. Perhaps we should go see the construct now."

"There won't be much to see," Padraig said. "The cavern filled with water and, judging by the amount we faced, I'd say it will stay filled for some time. The normal flow of the aqueducts has been altered by someone looking for something down there. They were using Foxy and his companions as slave labor. Since they were still at it, I'd say they haven't found what they were looking for. Not to mention the hole the dragon construct came out of was completely flooded."

"I'm assuming it will drain out eventually." Alric looked down as if he'd just realized he was still in damp clothing. "I'll be right back." He grabbed his pack and went into one of the rooms.

I took the time to study the map further as the others

discussed a future trip to visit the dragon. Although it had moved forward, it never came out of the hole. Why the Ancients would put a guardian construct in their aqueduct was a question we'd probably never be able to answer. The syclarions were dragon-like enough that something of that sort wouldn't scare them, but there was a good chance it did more than scare when it had full power.

The map was an old one, and that wasn't just a guess on my end because of the curling at the edges. The buildings were fewer. The area where my house was showed nothing but trees and farmland. Considering my house was at least fifty years old, that put this map up there in age.

Interestingly, it also had outlines of the ruins, and areas of the ruins that I knew hadn't been dug up during my time—nor prior. If this map was, say, eighty years or older, then that put it before the current era of elven ruin digging. The big explosion of elven lore that fueled the expansion of Beccia. But the ruins weren't investigated much prior to that, so why were they outlined on this map?

"Where did this map come from?" I kept looking at it, but Lorcan broke off his other conversation.

"Foxy had it. Amara showed it to me while you were gone."

Covey nodded. "I've been in Beccia for thirty years, but Foxy was here way before me." She looked around at the pub and for once didn't look like she wanted to go wash her hands. "This pub has been here over a hundred years."

As she spoke I noticed the tiny sign for the Shimmering Dewdrop on the map. That was another change, there was only it, and two other pubs on this street, now there were over ten.

Foxy had been in the kitchen since we'd come back, but the repetition of his name must have caught his attention. He came out with a smile and went for the bar. "Ale anyone?" He looked around, noticing Bunky and Irving dormant in the rafters. The constructs did need down time to recover their energy, and until we'd found Mathilda, they hadn't shut off once in the month we'd been on the road. They'd earned some serious recharging time. "Will they be okay up there? And the faeries still be out?"

He didn't even wait for our response, just started pulling out ale bottles and some of his non-alcoholic apple cider. Covey didn't drink much.

"Bunky and Irving are fine. The faeries are doing a recon of the town; hopefully they'll remember what they see long enough to tell us when they get back." I thought about taking one of the ciders, but grabbed an ale instead. "How long ago did you get that map?"

Foxy peered over from the bar and scratched his left ear. "When I first came down here." He dried his hands on his apron and walked over to the table. "Well, after I'd built this place at any rate. So maybe about a hundred and ten years ago?"

"Did they dig in the ruins then?" I tapped the odd markings that looked suspiciously like dig outlines.

Foxy had been grinning at the tiny icon of his beloved pub, but his grin dropped when he looked over to where I was pointing. "Naw, there weren't any interest then. That area was dangerous. Traps and what not. No one went there. Never thought about it until now. I haven't seen this map in forty or more years. That Amara of mine is a wonder; she finds the oddest things."

I looked at him closely, but something told me he wasn't aware of exactly how much of a wonder his dryad wife was. Most people had never even heard of tree goddesses, let alone know that one was around and cooking for people in a seedy pub. Some people might freak out finding out they were married to a deity—knowing Foxy, he'd just shrug it off.

"Then who outlined those ruins, and why?" Alric said what I was thinking and he looked up with a small smile. It felt weird between us, but now that he was aware of what he'd been doing in his reactions to me, he was dealing with it. Considering that our score was my one time vanishing on him versus his two times vanishing on me, he really had no room to complain.

Covey scowled at the map. I'd told her a dozen times on this trip alone that scowling at inanimate objects didn't do anything. She claimed that she wasn't scowling, she was deep thinking. Looked a lot like scowling to me.

"This hasn't been modified?" She looked ready to climb on the table and get a closer look.

Foxy's ears flapped as he shook his head. He peered over her shoulder in case the map had changed. "Not that I can tell. Looked like that when I got it. Never thought about them markings much."

I looked up to everyone. "These are the exact locations of the major digs." I moved my finger. "But this area is untouched. Including the section drawn heavier than the rest."

"She's right." Alric and I knew these ruins the best of anyone in this group. I found myself wishing Harlan were here right now though. His knowledge eclipsed mine, and Alric's was limited to what he found skulking about as a spy.

"How does this relate to whatever the mayor and his syclarions are doing though?" Padraig and Lorcan were longtime friends, very long time. But I'd heard enough of them debating while we were on the road to know Padraig wasn't just asking a question.

"You caught me," Lorcan said. "That was the right question. As interesting and possibly relevant as those ruin markings are, this is what caught my eye." On possibly the furthest area of the map from the ruins, way out in the dark woods was a tiny mark.

The shape was roughly a diamond, but I couldn't make out the figure inside because the entire thing was smaller than the nail on my pinky toe.

"If I may," Lorcan said as he held out a small magnifying glass.

"Thank you." I took it, but already had a feeling I knew what was in there. Yup, a lion with the head of a person, a sphinx. When I touched the spot the manticore inside me flared a blast of coldness against my cheek, and Irving woke up and bleated.

CHAPTER FIFTEEN

I RVING'S BLEATS GREW LOUDER AND the icy pain in my cheek felt like my face was going to crack in two. Dropping the magnifying glass helped my pain, but I rocked back and crashed into the chair behind me. Alric ran forward and grabbed my arm, but he flinched. He didn't release me, but looked like he wanted to.

"Are you okay? Your cheek is glowing." Once he realized that I'd landed safely into the chair, he released my arm. The look that briefly flashed across his face was anger, but it passed quickly, and he didn't look like he knew where it came from any more than I did.

I rubbed my face as everyone crowded closer. "I have no idea. But something about that map spot triggered both Irving and me. Maybe that's where the diamond sphinx really is?" Lorcan and Padraig had been sure they had an idea of where the last piece of the relic weapon was. And it wasn't this far south.

"I don't think so," Padraig said as he glanced over to the map. "It might have started there, but indications show it's in the Clarthy district up north. Somewhere. Or it should be."

"But just the location, current or not, on a map shouldn't have triggered a response in either Taryn or the gargoyle." Covey went back to glaring at the map.

"Irving, the gargoyle's name is Irving." It felt odd saying that I'd named him, but after all, I'd named Bunky. Irving had stopped bleating and drifted down to land on the table near my chair. Bunky woke up and came down as well.

"The relics in both of you are so sensitive that they reacted to the map's symbol." Lorcan shook his head. "I don't think that's good. The chimera relic augments the other relics. But aside from that, none of them should impact each other. I wish I could see what those two relics are doing inside you both."

Irving came closer to me. "I can't tell you what mine is doing, but Irving's went far inside him after we left you." I let that hang there. I couldn't keep pushing off talking about our leaving.

Mathilda looked at me encouragingly, and I swore that behind her a small, white fur-covered head popped up, nodded, and then vanished. *That* I wasn't going to talk about. But I had little choice about the rest.

As quickly and precisely as possible, I explained what happened at the Spheres. I kept emotion out of it, including my decision to leave.

I'd kept my head down as I spoke, since seeing their faces as I disclosed my monstrous leanings was going to make it harder.

"The manticore left you when this happened?" Padraig's voice was unemotional, but when I looked up there was enough hurt and confusion on Alric's and Covey's faces for an entire room.

I ignored them and focused on Padraig. "It did. Then it came back when I changed back to normal. I really don't know what spell or curse I fell into, but the thing I turned into was huge. You ran from me." That part was hard. I knew once they realized I was that beast they'd briefly seen, things would change.

I wasn't expecting blank looks from everyone around me.

Lorcan shook his head slowly. "None of us saw you change, or this being you became, or at least we don't recall it. There was a lot of fog, and the spell of Nivinal's was affecting us. But something else could have stopped us from remembering it." He shook his head and waved his hand, a move I knew meant he'd be working on this new problem on his own. "If the manticore came out of you, it viewed you as being dead. Obviously, you weren't dead, but who you had been was indirectly dead because of the metamorphosis. Very interesting."

Mathilda had already heard the tale, so she was fine. Padraig and Lorcan were looking at it as an academic exercise. Alric and Covey were looking perplexed, confused, and hurt.

"I left you to protect you. Don't you understand? That thing I became...I didn't really have control over it. I felt powerful, but also so distant from everything and everyone. I could have hurt you and not even noticed." A thought hit me. "Not exactly the same, but it was as if the times we've tried dragon bane on me were multiplied by a hundred. Destroying the enemy was too easy, and I wasn't sure I could tell the difference between friend and foe." The first few times I'd reacted to dragon bane, there had been some changes to my body. Mostly around my mouth and hands. Not unlike teeth becoming larger and hands turning to claws, like what had happened during the recent change.

"I don't sense any odd spells on you," Padraig said. "Have you had any issues since you left us?"

"No. But no massively powerful mage has been trying to kill me and my friends since then either."

Lorcan came closer and held out his hand over my head. Finally he shook his head. "I don't sense anything either. You could have the right of it, in that a spell was flung at you. But I've never heard of such a type. Transformative spells take a lot of magic. You might have that kind of power buried in there, but you certainly don't have the training. And I can't imagine that our enemy would have benefitted from having you transform into something that changed the battle against him."

I started to nod but stopped. "But he was happy about it at first. When I crashed into the Sphere that he had tried to destroy, he gloated." Everything had happened so quickly, but the look on Nivinal's face was etched in my memory.

"It doesn't make sense," Alric said. "He was winning. He would have defeated us." The sour look on his face said how much admitting that cost him.

Before I could say anything else, an explosion came from out front.

Foxy immediately ran into the kitchen and carried Amara behind the bar. She vanished into a cupboard before my eyes. "Stay safe, love." He grabbed a pike that had blended in so well that it looked like it was part of the bar itself, turned and nodded. "Your friends be coming back for more."

There was a suspicious lack of yelling in the street, most likely because Beccia had been under duress for a while, and the population took not getting involved to an entirely new level.

Foxy, Padraig, and Alric went to the front door, with Dogmaela standing a few feet behind. Like Foxy, she held a pike, but hers was a few feet longer. The rest of us stayed behind her. So far my sword hadn't left me—hopefully it would stay that way.

Foxy opened the door with less caution than I would have given the fact things had exploded. Smoke and dust were drifting by, but that was all I could see. The four ahead of me must not have seen anything either, as they stepped forward into the street. I followed, with Bunky and Irving buzzing along behind me.

"Stay down; we don't know what's out there." Unlike the faeries, the two constructs usually obeyed me. Not this time though. Both gronked and shot out over my head.

Covey came up behind me as I stepped out the door, with Lorcan and Mathilda, the only smart ones, staying in the pub. "So much for that. Maybe they'll find something."

Another explosion, further away this time but strong enough to rattle the windows in the buildings around us, cut off my response.

This time the smoke was coming from the far end of the extremely straight road. The first smoke was directly across from us, but a few streets over. It was almost dissipated by now; at least enough so that it didn't look like anything was on fire.

Still no response, that I could see, from the rest of Beccia.

"Foxy? Did everyone leave town?" As if that called them, a group of twenty or so men and women of various species turned to come down the street. They were coming from the opposite end from the recent explosion, but they had an almost mob walk to them. I doubted the syclarions working for the mayor of Kenithworth would bother disguising themselves as a bunch of merchants, but I wasn't going to count on it.

Bunky and Irving had vanished, but they came swooping back down the road—directly from the location of the nearest explosion. Since the rest of my group was watching the approaching Beccians, I paid attention to my constructs.

Bunky dove close to me and dropped a piece of fabric at my feet before circling above us again. I picked it up, flipping it over to see that it was actually a piece of burnt, and familiar, wallpaper. My kitchen wallpaper. When we'd taken off for Kenithworth all those months ago, I'd set as many protection spells around my house as I could. The house wasn't much, but it had been mine. Judging from the condition of the paper, there wasn't much left. A lump grew in my throat, but it wasn't something I could deal with right now.

The location where the second explosion had been was almost exactly where my house would be. There were other houses in that area, but I doubted if more than one had faded wallpaper with yellow flowers on a sickly green background in their kitchen.

"They blew up my house?" I wasn't sure if I wanted to see it or not. Like the first explosion, the smoke was fading. So there was no fire, just an explosion.

Covey looked away from the approaching Beccians. "Why would someone blow up your house?"

"No idea," I said, then shoved the piece of wallpaper into my cloak pocket.

"Foxmorton, what's going on?" The crowd of Beccians were upon us, but they stayed a safe distance back. The leaders were the people we'd rescued from the aqueducts.

"You'd be guessing as good as I," Foxy said. "Anyone see what's been exploding?"

Foxy hadn't seen my wallpaper, and I wasn't bringing it up with this crowd. None of them were brandishing weapons, but they were all armed. I didn't want them to connect any of us to the explosions.

Padraig had been silent and had his head tilted. He was looking at things with something more than just his eyes. "Both have been near the hedge, this side of it. They're coming from town or just outside of it."

Alric dropped to his knee and put the palm of his right hand flat on the ground and closed his eyes. He opened them with a shake. "There will be more. There's a pressure building, but I can't get a feel where it's coming from."

"Now see here. We don't like being trapped. If you're doing this to get us to side with you folks about that ring of greenery, that—" the Beccian's comment was cut short by yet a third explosion. The biggest one yet.

My friends managed to stay upright as the ground rolled under our feet. A few of the Beccians tumbled.

A second, smaller jolt almost sent me to the ground as well, but Covey caught my arm. Once she was sure I had my feet, she tore off in the direction of the newest black plume. Unfortunately, it was in the direction of where we came back through after the aqueduct adventure. Covey was out of sight almost immediately. When she wanted to, she could probably outrun anyone in this town.

Amara slowly came out of the pub, her steps growing stronger as she saw the smoke. Her bright green eyes flashed in anger.

I'd heard that phrase before, but never seen it. Even without knowing she was a long lost goddess, I wouldn't want to be on the other side of that look.

"I decide when it comes down, not you!" Unlike some mages, apparently tree goddesses didn't need spell words or movements to cast something. Her eyes did flash to a blinding white for a split-second though. And even from this distance, it was clear the hedge had grown taller. A rumbling crossed under us, but unlike the prior jolts, this one seemed more natural.

"Roots?" I hadn't meant to say that out loud as it sounded stupid even as I thought it.

Amara flashed a small smile. "Aye. Someone is trying to destroy my hedge, which tells me it is still needed." With a quick glance to the stunned Beccians, she scurried over and ducked under Foxy's arm.

"Now see here, that's what we were coming to talk to your man about." The forefront Beccian nodded to Padraig, but a worried look crossing his face took out much of the force of his words.

"And we would have discussed it, had the situation not changed. I'd say that's a bigger worry." Padraig pointed back to the smoking hedge.

"Aye, the town has enough supplies to hold out longer. But we might not survive whatever is attacking us." Foxy shifted the pike to his other hand to keep his arm around Amara, but he didn't put it down.

I studied the Beccians as they muttered among themselves. They were all from this part of town. "Where are the town guards? The private guards from The Hill?"

I knew the rich population who lived up on The Hill wouldn't be out and about if the city was under attack. But they had small standing troops in their compounds. And, although mostly corrupt and incompetent, the city did have its own guards.

Foxy shook his head. "The Hill folks either fled or locked themselves up as soon as that Kenithworth mayor started pushing people around. Especially after our own mayor and the town counsel died sudden like, of poisoning. The city guards went to Kenithworth's side at that point. They should be on the other side of the hedge with the rest." Foxy wasn't shocked by the behavior of either the rich or the guards. None of the Beccians around us looked like they felt any differently.

I looked up to see Covey jogging back to us. Her face was grim and she held something out away from her. "The ground where we came through the hedge is blackened, but the explosion appears to have actually been on the outside of the hedge. But unless we go outside the hedge there's no way to know for sure." She held up what she carried, a twisted arm the size of a child's. It had been ripped from its owner; but those long clawed fingers didn't belong to any child. "I found this in the hedge. I think it had been trying to come through and the plants destroyed it. The rakasa are back."

CHAPTER SIXTEEN

———◆———

SOMEWHERE IN THE BACK OF my mind a tiny voice had mentioned the monstrous little creatures as soon as we heard the first explosion. I'd squished that thought too soon apparently. "I thought we destroyed them out at the Spheres?" At least I knew that the basilisk had taken out a hell of a lot of them.

"For a species that had supposedly been destroyed centuries ago, they seem to be far more populous than would be expected." Lorcan looked around as he and Mathilda came out of the pub.

"But could the hedge have really tried to eat it?" I looked over to Amara. Her smile didn't admit to anything, but it didn't deny it either. Note made—do not piss off the tree goddess.

"The hedge was attacked," she finally said with a shrug of her thin shoulders. "I told it to defend itself. And it will continue to do so."

A hedge that ate its enemies. Could be good. Was definitely scary.

The leader of the Beccian group looked back to his companions and finally nodded. He was a bit paler than he'd been and not near as determined in his stance. "I think you might be right. Can always ransack the abandoned rich homes if need be. Maybe the ones outside will go away after a bit." The more he spoke, the more he looked like he was far more afraid of Amara than whoever was blowing things up.

Padraig drew himself up, even flicked back his long hair to show his ears and remind them he was an elf, still a rare sight in Beccia. Harlan needed to take acting lessons from him. "It is agreed then. It would be best if everyone returned to their homes for now. We will make sure the town is secure and the hedge will keep it that way." He turned to Alric and me and held his arms out. "How can we fail with the protectors of Beccia on our side?"

I knew that I hadn't told him about how the people had viewed Alric and me after both the glass gargoyle incident and the mess with Glorinal and Jovan. A smirk from Covey told me who had.

It was as if the Beccians hadn't even seen Alric and I until Padraig mentioned us. Their smiles grew, and they gave a few cheers, then turned and trudged back to their homes. Or to a pub.

"We'd been with them since the aqueduct. What changed?" I was glad they were leaving, but I really didn't want a return of the general population thinking we were going to save them.

"They weren't thinking of who you were then." Padraig's smile dropped. "This will keep them out of our way and hopefully help rally them if we need to gather to fight."

My sigh at his comment was far too loud in the new silence of the street. "I keep waiting for another explosion."

Amara peeked out from her Foxy embrace. "There shouldn't be. At least not on this side. They had actually managed to get some exploding spells through my hedge. They were trying to blow it up, but the spells passed through. I put an end to that."

I didn't know if it was all of us knowing she was a tree goddess, or Mathilda's thanks in the old way, but Amara seemed stronger than I'd ever seen her. She was also definitely glowing.

I waved her over as if I needed to show her something.

All of my friends knew what she was except Foxy, and I thought she might want to keep it that way. Besides, we were standing in the middle of the street.

Foxy was discussing some plan with Alric and Padraig so he wasn't paying attention when she came over to me.

"You might want to watch the glow." I kept my voice low and watched over her head to make sure Foxy was engaged. "It's going to cause attention."

At first she looked confused, and then looked down at her softly glowing skin. "Oh no." A second later the glow was gone. "It's been so long since others knew what I was…I'll have to watch out for this. Foxy can't know." She looked at me with huge pleading eyes.

I agreed on that. Most likely Foxy would take it in stride, but on the offhand chance he didn't, it was better he didn't have a clue.

"So just having others know who you are makes you glow?" Yes, there were other more urgent issues right now, but this could be important. Having a goddess on our side might help, but it would be good to know her limitations.

"In a manner of speaking. Deities need recognition, love, worship, whatever you want to call it, to build our strength."

That explained a lot about some of the religious zealots I'd seen over the years. I doubted their gods and goddesses were out stomping around though.

"What is that?" Covey's eyes were better than mine, but even I saw the plume of dust coming our way.

Followed by faeries yelling. "Seriously? They are cat racing now? With what's going on?" I'd punish them but in the time I'd known them I'd never found anything that stuck.

"No, is training." Garbage had silently flown over us. "Training good." She looked far too smug as she folded her arms and watched the herd of cats and faeries, with Crusty and Leaf flying over them, tearing right for us.

"We might want to move, not sure how good they are at stopping." I pulled Amara to the side with Covey and me. The rest of our group jogged to the other side of the street just as the racing cats tore by. I thought I saw pieces of metal, either being held by the faeries or on the cats. But they'd been moving too fast and they kicked up a lot of dust.

The cats ran around the bend a block down and vanished down an alley. Garbage, Crusty, and Leaf stayed near us though.

"What was on them?"

If Garbage got any prouder her wings were going to pop off. "Practice with armor. Meows good."

Armor? I started to ask, then shook my head and just smiled instead. This might be one of those better-not-to-know situations.

The wallpaper in my pocket rustled and reminded me of another probably better not to know situation. Somewhere in the back of my mind, I'd held on to the thought that once we found and destroyed these relics, I'd be able to go back to my little house, my pub, and just relax. I knew the odds weren't in my favor, but I needed to know if my house was standing.

I pulled out the piece of wallpaper and held it up. "I know we have a lot of bigger things going on, but I'd like to go see if anything of my house still stands." The faeries dropped down when they saw the paper, and Garbage tried to rip it out of my hand. I shoved it back in my cloak pocket. It might be all I had left.

"No boom. Not time." Garbage looked up and glared in the general direction of the house, but she and the others stayed with me.

"My house was *supposed* to boom at some point?" That, and the fact the faeries knew about it, was almost more upsetting than the fact it might have already done so.

"Maybe...not good." Leaf also glared down the road.

"Boom!" That was Crusty's contribution and she was looking at the Shimmering Dewdrop instead of the direction where the house was.

"I'll go with you," Alric said. "Padraig wants to get some more information before we do anything. And it's more his and Lorcan's area than mine." Alric was no slouch when it came to academia and research, but he really was a more physical guy. That had been extremely noticeable the last few hours.

I was happy at the first part, a bit annoyed at the second. I logically knew that my house wasn't as important as what we were doing. Emotionally it was a different matter. One I'd have liked Alric to pick up on. The distance between us kept growing and I wasn't sure how to fix it. However, I'd like him along even if his motivation wasn't as emotional as I'd hoped.

"I'm going to keep the girls and the constructs with me, unless you need them?" I asked Covey. I knew she'd be staying behind to search through the dusty scrolls.

"I think we're good," she said and looked around. "What about the extras and the cats?"

"They come back, stay." Garbage really needed something more impressive than beat-up overalls and flower petal caps if she was going to be a general.

Covey nodded and waved us off as she and the rest made their way back into the pub.

Alric started before me, but I quickly caught up. If he thought I wasn't going to talk during this, he had another think coming. I gave him two minutes of silence, and then I jumped in.

"This is going to get old, you know. We can't just ignore it." We were far enough away from the pub that I knew our friends wouldn't hear, even if they were outside.

Alric kept walking.

"Damn it, we need to talk." I grabbed his arm and turned him my direction. "Yes, I shouldn't have left. But you've ditched me too. And I had a damn good reason."

He first looked ready to keep walking, then, instead, grabbed me and kissed me. At first it was an angry kiss, not meant to hurt me, but just angry at himself. Then it softened and he pulled back, tilted his forehead to mine, and caressed my cheek. "I know. You did have a good reason. I disagree with it for a number of reasons, but it was valid." His right arm gave a twitch and he shook it off.

"What's wrong?" I pulled back his sleeve. The geas mark on his inner wrist was glowing faintly. Considering how much glamour was on it, no one should see anything at all. He'd been marked by an old mystic elf when we'd inadvertently gone back in time a thousand years. "How long as it been doing this?"

"It started when we got to Beccia. I think my current mood—I wouldn't call it that, but I know you would—is more because of this and the way I feel, than what happened when you left. I've just felt on edge since we got here." He flexed his fingers.

I looked around the deserted street. The faeries and constructs had gone ahead, and no one else was around, but I kept my voice low. "Do you think it's sensing something?" The mark on his arm was a geas supposedly passed down through his family and reactivated by an old witch at the ball we'd attended in the distant past. It would make Alric kill the person or persons behind the destruction of the missing Ancients. Since it was doubtful they were around after twenty-five hundred years—and as far as Lorcan could tell even Nivinal wasn't that old—we hadn't worried about the geas.

Alric pulled the sleeve down over the mark and shook his head. "I've no idea. I just feel a general annoyance, not as if I need to kill someone. Maybe the geas is picking up on other things. We didn't even think of how it might react to the relics. Someone used them to destroy the Ancients and they could cause the geas to act up." He nodded to me then started walking again.

"We probably need to tell Lorcan and Padraig."

"Agreed. When we get back." He wrapped his arm around my shoulder. "We need to see about your house. I do understand you taking off, but if you ever scare me like that again, I'm going to find new ways to get the faeries to sing at you…all the time."

I slipped my arm around his waist and settled into walking next to him. It felt good to be back. "Fine, next time I turn into something monster-like I'll tell you it's me. Just promise you won't slay me by accident."

"Agree—" Alric froze as we came around the corner to the block with my house. I hadn't been looking that way but I found myself standing there slack jawed once I turned as well.

CHAPTER SEVENTEEN

I'D BEEN BRACING MYSELF FOR my house being demolished. Or for it being seriously damaged in some way. I was not prepared for it to be floating five feet in the air. Mostly intact, but with a few blown out sections near the back kitchen wall.

"How…why…and *how*?" I barely felt Alric pull his arm away as he took a few steps closer and I stayed rooted to my spot. The faeries and the constructs were buzzing around as if a house floating in the air was an interesting, but not that uncommon, occurrence.

The houses on either side were untouched. I assumed my neighbors had fled at some point. I didn't think even Beccians could be so jaded that they wouldn't come out to see a floating house.

"This wasn't just an explosion; someone was looking for something." Alric waved his hand under the front door. "Interesting. The spell got cut off. Probably when Amara increased the strength of the hedge. This reinforces that whoever was sending those explosions was outside of the hedge."

I slowly walked forward. I had to admit it was damn good to see the place. I just wished it wasn't hovering there like that. "Can we get it down without destroying it? And if the spell was cut off, shouldn't it have let go?" I touched a wall. I'd expected it to at least feel wobbly. It was just hanging there, sort of like Crusty would do those times she forgot how to land. But it was solid. Just as if it were five feet lower and snuggled on the ground. I gave it a push. Nothing.

Alric walked around the entire house, pausing every once in a while, but staying silent. After a few feet the faeries decided it was a game and started bobbing along behind him. Bunky and Irving stayed near me.

"That was an impressive spell." He finally came completely around. "The damage to the kitchen was because they used too much force when they punched through. They locked the house in place so they could do something, but there's no evidence that they were ever on this side of the hedge."

"And…can we get it down?" I finally repeated when he seemed lost in his own thoughts. He also looked like he was seriously thinking of going a few houses down to where the hedge was. I wanted my house grounded first. It wasn't lost on me that this mage had specifically gone after my house when there were three houses closer to the hedge. Had causing mayhem by explosions and flying houses been their agenda, they could have picked another one closer. Which meant I was the target. Again.

Alric nodded slowly. "Yes. I'd rather leave it there until we can figure out what they were looking for, but the longer we do that the more likely people will notice. Your immediate neighbors are under a light sleep spell, but it's been cut off as well, so they will be waking soon."

The faeries buzzed closely around him as he raised his hands. The house didn't move at first, but then started wobbling and lowering. Alric's spell caught it, not helped by the faeries who were now flying under it. They shot out just as it dropped the final few inches to the ground.

"Home!" Crusty yelled, and then flew for the door. It was ajar a good five inches. And she still managed to smack into the door itself. "Whoops!" She laughed maniacally, peeled herself off the door, and flew in.

I let everyone go before me, even the constructs. This house wasn't much, but it represented my old life. The one I really wanted back. Seeing it was hard; going into it, and knowing I couldn't come back yet, was going to be even worse.

Life was easier when all I cared about was my digger work and the pub.

The inside wasn't as bad as I feared. The spells I'd put on it when we left had held until this airborne attack. That could have been why the back wall of the kitchen blew off. The spells had been centered there. Good to know I'd gotten my money's worth.

The house itself was, surprisingly, in good shape. The furniture was intact, if a bit more clustered to one side than it had been. A few knick-knacks were tumbled about. All in all, everything was good.

Even my bedroom was unmolested, just tossed about. I bent to pick up two small elven statues, mementos of my first find when I'd begun as a digger and my patron had felt generous. They were lying on the floor near my bed, along with a third item that had rolled underneath.

My hand tingled as it closed in on the small glass object under my bed. I pulled my hand and the bauble back fast in case it was a bomb. It wasn't a bomb, but I still screamed.

It was the glass gargoyle.

Alric came running in and started swearing as much as I was in my head. I really wanted to fling it across the room, but I knew that wasn't a good idea.

Bunky and Irving came flying in at the noise and Irving came right up to the glass gargoyle in my hand and nudged it. Siabiane had made him to look like the glass gargoyle relic. He turned to Bunky and the faeries and made a gronking sound.

"He say not same," Leaf translated.

Alric held out his hand and I gave it to him. The flare from his geas was visible under the sleeve of his black shirt.

"That can't be good," I said. "Neither your geas lighting up nor the fact that the gargoyle back, but according to Irving, it's not the same."

Alric switched the hand holding the small glass gargoyle and the flare from his right arm died down, but I could see a tiny bit of light peeking out from his sleeve. "The second one came into being when I took the first one into the other dimension and destroyed it. If this is not that one, then something must have destroyed the second one and this is a third incarnation." He peered at it closely, but not so close that Irving couldn't hover over it. It was difficult to tell with metal constructs, but Irving did not seem happy.

"So, maybe Nivinal has been destroyed? He had that thing. But why did it come back here? How is it coming back? And if they can all come back—how are we going to destroy them?" He and I walked out to my living room and sat. I almost felt like I should be offering tea to Alric.

"I don't think we can count on him being out of the picture until we see his dead body, but he could have come under attack and the gargoyle was destroyed in the fight. As for why it keeps coming back to you, I don't know." He held up his hand. "Yes, you weren't here, but this place is imbued with your essence. You weren't living here when the second one came to you, it found you in your old apartment. As for destroying the weapon? The relics are each different. The rest we should be able to destroy, once we find a way. The gargoyle's domain is time and space. It's just reinventing itself each time it is destroyed."

I really didn't like his emphasis on 'should be'. According to the brains of our operation, if we could get the pieces together, we could destroy them.

"The question is how did whoever attacked Beccia, specifically your house, know it was here?" The glow from his sleeve was gone, but I noticed that he wasn't touching the relic with that hand.

"And what are we going to do with it?" The words were barely out of my mouth when Irving gronked, dove for us, and swallowed the gargoyle relic.

He'd struck with enough force to knock Alric back, but it was because he was focusing on eating the relic rather than trying not to hurt anyone. He flew as high as he could in the house and gronked a few more times.

"He say sorry," Leaf translated again.

"Irving, you can't keep eating the relics. Eventually something bad will happen." I wasn't sure what. Somehow he'd not suffered any side effects from the basilisk, and that was the most overtly dangerous of the bunch. Each of the relics controlled a different aspect of the weapon used against the Ancients. The gargoyle was time and space. The chimera was an augmenter; it reinforced the others and made them stronger. The dragon was greed, although Lorcan said it wasn't really greed but an urge to possess. It called people to it. The manticore was protection. The basilisk was aggression.

"Just what does the sphinx do?" Irving was showing no sign of dropping lower, so maybe if we ignored him for a bit he might relax enough to come closer. Not that we could do much. Once he'd done whatever he did to the basilisk, I hadn't been able to even see the thing in his mouth anymore. I needed to find Siabiane and find out just what she'd built into Irving. He wasn't that much larger than the relics he kept swallowing.

Alric had been watching Irving as well, but shook his head and turned back to me. "Padraig and Lorcan aren't sure, and they've been able to figure out a lot more of these scrolls than I have. Padraig doesn't think there's a pattern to the order that they've been found, but Lorcan does. He believes these things are following a pattern of their own. Which would make the sphinx an anchor of some sort for the others."

"Is right. Come back," Garbage dropped down to hover

in front of us. "But no boom this time." She shivered and rubbed her tiny arms. I tended to forget that the faeries insisted they had been around since the time of the Ancients. If they were to be believed, they had been companions of the Ancients, and been at a huge loss when the Ancients vanished. As much as they liked booms, the ending of their companions was one boom they didn't want to return.

"Could the relics be reappearing to fix what happened?" The thought sounded stupid to me. The faeries each had the same look—something bad happened, it was going to happen again, but we might be able to change the result. Of course trying to get them to say that wasn't going to happen. I just had a feeling. The kind you get when someone walks over your grave.

"It's hard to say. There are many prophecies, both before and after the vanishing of the Ancients. I don't believe in them myself, but there are those who do."

Irving was showing no sign of coming near us; most likely the gargoyle relic was in his mouth and hadn't had a chance to go wherever the basilisk went. "Could we just feed them to Irving? The relics, I mean. He's locked away that basilisk inside him somewhere. If he does the same thing with the gargoyle, that's two that no one can touch."

Alric studied Irving, then shook his head. "We're not sure where they go in there, and if they exist on some level in this plane, they can be used. Nivinal has been waiting a very long time to get this weapon together—he won't let a construct stop him. It's not optimal that they are in Irving, but for now I say leave them there and tell no one outside of our group." He nodded to Bunky and the girls. "And you have to protect him at all costs. But he can't eat any other relics."

Irving gronked again.

"He say still sorry." Leaf was really getting into her translator role.

"We watch." Garbage was back into general mode. Crusty wasn't paying attention but was spinning in a circle, humming to herself.

Finally she stopped. "Need drink!" Just like that the three faeries tore out the door with Irving following. Bunky bobbed to Alric and me, gronked, and followed.

"He said he'll guard them." Alric got off my sofa and we went for the door. He could understand Bunky; it seemed a number of people could, but I couldn't. Judging from Leaf's need to translate, no one but the faeries and Bunky could understand Irving. Probably Siabiane could as well since she created him.

I looked at my battered house as we stood outside of it. A tiny part of me knew I might not ever be coming back. I squished that thought into a ball. "Can we protect it? Even with the holes?"

Alric had already been looking beyond the houses to the hedge, but stepped back and rubbed my shoulder. "I can repair the back wall so it is sound. The spell will be triggered to you alone, but the house will appear intact if anyone even notices it. For the most part it will just not be apparent to most people that there is anything there." He waved his hand and a soft glow settled over my house. I knew it was there, but it was already not there as well.

I kissed his cheek. "Thank you."

"You will come back some day, I feel it." He squeezed my hand.

It wasn't until we were almost to the hedge that I realized he said me and not us.

CHAPTER EIGHTEEN

I WANTED TO ASK HIM WHAT he'd meant, but things were still delicate between us. I'd wait until things settled down.

The hedge where he stood looked burnt, but it was already healing itself. If we had arrived fifteen minutes later, all signs of the explosion would have been gone. Amara was going to have to watch how much power she gave the giant plant wall, and what she used. Dryads weren't common in this part of the kingdom, but there would be talk of this hedge. Scholars who knew what a normal dryad could or couldn't do would realize something was different about her.

If she wanted to be outed as a goddess, that would be one thing. But she had been hiding for over two thousand years and didn't want Foxy to know what she was. She was going to have to lay low after this if she wanted to keep her secrets.

"They almost made it through the hedge," Alric said as he touched the leaves. "I know how strong this was even before she reinforced it; it would have taken a serious magic user to have gotten this far."

"Nivinal?" I looked around for a place to get sick as my gut heaved just mentioning his name. He knew what I'd become when I'd changed during the fight against him, or at least had been expecting it. He was also responsible for hundreds of deaths. That was just in the current time. Who knew what he'd done during the Breaking as the leader of the Dark.

Alric placed both hands on the hedge and closed his eyes. Finally he pulled back. "I don't think so. We had enough exposure to his magic to know what it feels like, and this isn't it."

I wasn't sure if that was better or worse. That it wasn't he or that there was someone else out there with that kind of power who was also attacking us.

We poked around the hedge area a bit more. Well, Alric did. I mostly watched. I'd missed him when I'd taken off. I believed it was for the best, and I was willing to avoid him and the others as long as necessary, but I'd missed him. Things were still strained between us, kisses or no. I knew that final battle against Nivinal had taken a lot of out him. We'd been losing the fight before I turned into whatever it was I'd become. Hopefully we could get back to where we were.

"What was that sigh for?"

I'd drifted off in my thoughts and hadn't noticed that Alric had stopped investigating the hedge and was right in front of me. I hadn't realized that I'd sighed out loud either. "I missed you." I briefly thought about playing off the sigh, but it wasn't worth it. I agreed with what I'd done, but I also missed him.

He gave me a quick kiss, and then rubbed my arms. "You really have no idea what you became? We do need to figure out how Nivinal cast a spell on you for that trans-formation—and why."

"I have no idea. I was huge; the Spheres only came to my shoulder. I was...scaly...but not like a syclarion. Well, sort of. I think. My hands had claws and although I was on two legs, I really felt like I might like running on all four." I'd been working hard for the past month to forget all of this, so recalling it now was harder than I'd expected. "And I had a tail."

Alric had a non-judgmental expression, but his left eyebrow did quirk up at that. "Wings?"

"No," I said. "Well, maybe? I don't think so, but I really can't be certain. I didn't fly, nor notice them if they were there. I noticed the manticore on the ground where I'd fallen, then I just started going after the stone zombies and Nivinal. After the spell he cast had been broken, he'd been stripped from his projected image, and those things he called out of the ground were destroyed, I collapsed. Came to with the manticore back inside me and all of you unconscious." My voice dropped. "I thought I'd killed you. The thought was only for a second. But it was there."

"But you didn't; you saved us. I don't know that Nivinal spelled you, but someone did. It could have even been placed on you when we were in the past, or in Null." He ran his hand through his hair. "There are too many places. But whoever did it, they were good. I can't feel a trace of it now."

"You don't think it was *just* me? Something, maybe, I am?" There was my terror in its glory. A spell that strong would be awful. However, in the past month I'd gone through far worse scenarios in my head.

"I've never heard of a dryad-human-syclarion breed combination before. And if you were part syclarion we would have noticed long before now. Someone hit you with a spell."

A quick blur of white out of the corner of my eye caught my attention. It was darting in and out of the hedge, but as soon as I focused on it, it stopped. "Did you see anything over there?" I waved where I'd seen the unfortunately familiar small being. I hadn't mentioned seeing the minkie before. Since no one, including the faeries and the constructs, had seen it, I figured it was in my head. Or maybe a side effect from whatever spell had turned me into a monster. I was ignoring the fact that I'd seen it months before that happened.

"I didn't see anything. What did you see?"

"Nothing. I thought I saw—"

"What is that?" Alric looked just past me, a bit further down the hedge.

I turned and there was the damn minkie. He was sitting up in the hedge looking quite smug. If small, mythological beings could look smug, that is.

"You see it?"

"The tall white bird? Yeah. I've never seen anything like it."

"Wait, bird?" I squinted at the minkie. Nope, still a small furry member of some twisted rodent line. "It's got fur."

"Fur? No, feathers. Long, silky feathers."

Alric reached out to try and stop me as I took a few steps closer to it, but I dodged around him. "You don't really look like this do you? Or what he sees?" Someone else at least seeing something was an improvement. But it would be nice if the creature looked the same to both of us. Would help make our story more believable if we told others.

The minkie nodded and did a shimmy. For a second I saw what Alric must see. About twice as tall as before, a white bird appeared. Long iridescent feathers curled around it. Then it went back to the way I knew it.

"It just flashed into something small and furry. You've seen it before, haven't you?" Alric didn't sound concerned, which was a plus.

The minkie looked even smugger, nodded to both of us, then vanished. I turned back to Alric with a sigh. "Yes. I think it might be the minkie the girls sing about. Or at least *a* minkie. I first saw it before Flarinen and Lorcan found us in the wagons back in the slot canyon. But the girls denied seeing it after I'd seen them with it. I mean really denied. Then those gloughstrikes hit and I had other things to worry about. I saw it a few more times, popping up in odd places. No one else saw it though. He caused the fog after my attack, might have been why none of you recall seeing me, and led me out of there. The faeries and constructs followed me, but I don't think they saw him then either."

Alric walked over to the place in the hedge where we'd seen it. I knew the little troublemaker was gone, but Alric was most likely trying to pick up magic residue. He came back shaking his head.

"I wish I could tell more, but whatever the thing is, it's elemental magic. Like the faeries. Essentially, they are magic, they don't do magic. Makes it almost impossible to tell anything more. The faeries denied seeing it?"

"Yes, that was when they told you to watch me because I'd hit my head." We started walking along the hedge but not back toward the pub.

"Maybe if we get them drunk enough we can at least find out what they think it is. At this point there's no way to be sure what side anything or anyone is on." He reached out and took my hand. Things were still weird, but at least we were on the right path. Providing that neither of us took off without warning the other again. I looked over to Alric as he watched the hedge. I wasn't sure he wasn't a flight risk.

"I want to circle this portion at least, see where they attacked the entrance to the aqueducts. Since the explosion near your house was with a purpose beyond simple destruction, I think we have to presume the others might have had other reasons as well."

I shrugged. I should have known this wasn't just a nice walk with the love of my life.

The hedge near the entrance we'd used to get into the aqueduct looked fine, but I knew the hedge had been healing itself thanks to its power increase from Amara. The woods looked okay too, which was good and bad. Amara's healing would have been for her hedge only, so if the woods weren't damaged, then whoever attacked the entrance had serious skill as well as power.

The entrance to the aqueduct was slightly smoking. It hadn't been a big entrance to start with, and now little remained. Alric dropped my hand and got down on his knees to pull out some of the rubble. I started to help.

"Keep an eye out. We know there were at least a few enemies in town last night; they might still be around." He pulled a final piece out then managed to slide into the hole. He crawled out a lot less gracefully a moment later. "They did the damage from the inside. There's no way through from this end any more, which isn't good for them either. That could be how they were getting people in."

"The construct?" The digger side of me had kicked in about the massive dragon head once I was sure I wasn't heading for a watery grave. I knew there would be no way Covey and Padraig wouldn't want a full investigation done. But I thought we had time. It was clearly designed to survive water, since it was built in an aqueduct. I had my doubts about surviving explosions.

"There's no way to get to it from this end. We can't see the third explosion site since that was outside the hedge, but I'd bet it was to block the entrance where we came out of the water. They were more concerned about us being down there than with their own people being able to sabotage things inside Beccia." He piled the debris back over the mouth of the aqueduct, even adding more to it until there was no way anyone who didn't know exactly what was under there could find it. Then we headed back toward the pub.

"Thank goodness you two are back! The faeries wouldn't tell us anything." Covey was standing by the back door and waved us in. The noise almost sounded like the pub was fully running. A peek into the main room told me it was. We could have just come in the front door since Foxy had it wide open.

"Everyone is back in that room," she said as she pointed

to what I'd always assumed was a closet. Alric pushed the door open to reveal a nicely appointed room with a few gambling tables in it. A room I'd never seen, and that looked like it hadn't been used since before I was born.

"What is this?" My question was directed to anyone since Foxy was out in the main pub and Amara was most likely cooking like a fiend.

"Ah, welcome back," Lorcan said from a table where he and Mathilda were discussing a pair of scrolls. "This is Foxy's gambling den. Apparently, gambling was briefly outlawed in Beccia sixty or so years ago. Foxy made extra funds by letting them run games out of his pub. Since then he'd been using it for storage."

The thing even had a small bar of its own. One that was almost completely covered by a mass of faeries. Including my three, who obviously had come immediately here after they left us at my house. Bunky and Irving were also lounging on the bar, watching over the tiny drunkards.
"Where are the cats?" I didn't really care specifically; my experience with cats in general was that they were almost as good at taking care of themselves as faeries. I just didn't want any surprises.

"Meows not needed now," Garbage's tone was that of the imperious general she'd been acting like. Her semi-prone position on the bar didn't support that image. "Come back in need."

I had no idea what the cats were needed for, but I wasn't going to ask. I shook my head and walked over to the scrolls.

"How is your house? The faeries wouldn't say anything except boom." Covey walked over to where Padraig had taken over another table with books and scrolls.

"It's more or less intact. Whoever was causing those attacks wasn't just trying to bring down the hedge." I glanced over to Irving. He seemed calm; most likely the glass gargoyle was now in whatever pit the basilisk was.

"They went after my house because a certain relic had appeared there."

Covey was across the room and in my face in a second. "The sphinx? You have the diamond sphinx?" She looked ready to pick me up and start shaking me to find it.

I pushed her back a bit. "No. The glass gargoyle reappeared. Irving said it's not the same as before."

"No same, no same, is a game!" The faeries sang. Luckily, they got distracted after two rounds.

That got everyone to crowd in around us.

Alric held up his hand as the questions started flying. "I held it. It is *the* relic, but as it did when I destroyed it, it recreated itself. I think it's homing in to Taryn. She's been on the move, so it appeared in her home. I don't think Nivinal is dead, but hopefully he took a serious hit when something destroyed the glass gargoyle."

Covey responded first. "Where—"

"Irving ate it. He's promised not to eat any more relics though. Right, Irving?" I nodded to my gargoyle construct.

He gronked in answer.

"He say promise!" Leaf shouted out from the bottom of a pile of faeries. "Is good!"

Lorcan moved over to the bar. "There's no way to get it out? I understand about the basilisk. Until we find a way to neutralize it, that thing needs to stay secured. But we could study the glass gargoyle."

Irving looked ready to take to the air and Bunky moved in front of him. I stepped forward too. "No. Whatever Siabiane designed him for—and who knows with her, maybe it was this—there is a way for him to completely hide them inside of himself."

"Knowing my sister, you're right," Mathilda said. "She always was a crafty one." She came closer to Irving but he didn't fly away. "However, you'd do best to hold to your promise. No more eating relics. Unless Taryn tells you to."

Irving gronked and Bunky settled down.

"Why would I tell him to do that?" I didn't like the idea he had two in him, I wasn't going to add more. We might not know how to get them out, but I had no doubt that Nivinal could find a way to tear Irving apart and get them.

Mathilda shrugged. "I've no idea. But there could be a time and it's always good to have an out."

CHAPTER NINETEEN

I'D BEEN OPTIMISTIC WITH THE research going on that something had been resolved. Yes, we were safe in here for now. But sitting in this enclosed town we were also a giant target for Nivinal. And whoever else was out there. Amara was a goddess, but I didn't know how much offensive magic a tree goddess would have. I'd think her powers would be like a dryad's, to a tenth degree. We needed to find the diamond sphinx, find a way to assemble and then destroy the relic weapon, all without dying.

Sadly, the academics were moving slower than Alric and I had and our news was more shattering than theirs.

"It's not good that they were able to send such a heavy spell through Amara's hedge. That thing blocks magic as well as people," Padraig said. He scowled at a scroll directly in front of him. Covey was rubbing off on him.

"Is there anything there?" I walked closer to his table. The others were breaking down into smaller conversations about the hedge, the gargoyle, and Irving eating the gargoyle. I'd been traveling with Padraig long enough that I knew when he was on the edge of something. Alric was more a jump in and sort it out later type; Padraig was cautious in his fights—whether they be physical, magical, or academic. I knew that look.

"I'm not sure." He moved to the side a bit so I could see it.

This scroll was more of a picture story than just words.

Which, since my ability to read elven or Ancient seemed to be weak under the best circumstances, was a good thing. The upper left corner seemed to start the tale, and it was definitely a story. Huge beings, dragons if the stylized drawing was accurate, roamed. Well, they really just seemed to be living a life. Then they started dying. Other beings were attacking them. The dragons fought back. Then there was nothing.

The detail on the prior panels had been vivid. Mountains, buildings, more massive buildings, and very small trees. But in the second to the last panel there was nothing. In the last there was a single drawing of an elf on a plain.

"Well, that's cheery. So, you *do* think the Ancients were actually dragons?" I just had a problem with that. The biggest was personal. I wanted to like the Ancients, they'd been part of the myths I recalled as a child. The elves hadn't been what I had expected. I was going to be really pissed if the Ancients were somehow a giant version of the syclarions. I shuddered.

Padraig caught it. And he was far better at extrapolating my thoughts than I believed. "I don't think they were the same species as the syclarions. As much as the latter would like to have others associate them with dragons, they aren't." He shook his head at the scroll. "But this, along with a few other references I've found, and what we found in the aqueducts? I don't know. This scroll wasn't attributed to the Ancients in prior studies. The script is an old elven one from the south. It was thought to be a story, nothing more. I don't believe that now."

I looked over the panels again. There were one or two words I could sort of make out; lost and hope. Neither were helpful.

"I don't know that we can spend time trying to solve the Ancients' mystery, not with the relics out and a new mage hunting us." Alric had been looking at the books that Padraig had on his table, but put them down with a shake of his head. "We can't stay here."

I'd been thinking the same, but I was glad he was the one who said it.

"We can't leave them defenseless either. Why would this place have come under attack if not for the relics?" Mathilda rolled up her own scroll as she spoke.

"The mayor wanted something here. If you now think there was something going on with the aqueducts before the final battle between the syclarions and the Ancients, so does he. We have to go back in." I hated when my mouth said what was in my head without clearing it through me first.

It made sense, he was after something here, and according to Lorcan the final piece wasn't speculated to be anywhere near here. But I really didn't want to go back into those dark, damp, passages of doom.

"I knew you were a bright one," Mathilda said.

Covey nodded. "I agree, we need to go back down there." She was clearly a fan of further research, but she'd wanted to see more of the aqueducts. Traitor. Someone raised in a desert really shouldn't be a fan of masses of water.

"If we can find out what is the focus of the attack on this town, and remove it, at least Beccia will be safer." Lorcan adjusted his robes. He'd been an advisor to elven kings and queens for centuries and was stepping back into that role. He might not be able to guide his own people currently, but he wasn't going to ignore the other species now that the elves were part of the outside world again. Even a shabby little town like Beccia didn't deserve to be destroyed. And as we'd seen from the few defenders who'd come out at the explosions, there was really no one else to save it.

More scrolls were brought out, including that odd one that Foxy had. The others were looking at older ones, but Foxy's was more interesting to me. As long as the icon of the diamond sphinx didn't react to me again. It clearly hadn't been done on the best paper to start with. Besides, the odd layout lines of digs that hadn't even been thought of even now, there were a lot of dark splotchy age spots.

"Is no." Crusty had managed to come off the bar and silently land behind my hand without me noticing. She was barely standing. "Go backwards." She tried spinning her arms in front of her face to pantomime backwards, but just ended up crashing to the tabletop.

"Sweetie? What's backwards?" I picked her up by the back of her overalls. Her legs flopped when I tried to stand her up, so I sat her down in my hand.

"That. Wardsback." She slid into a prone position.

I gently put her back on the table and looked at the scroll. I turned it upside down, but I had no idea how it could be backwards.

Upside down did nothing but make my head hurt. I looked to the others lost in their own studies, to ask if they had a clue, when I saw the tarnished mirror hanging over the bar.

I rolled up the scroll and walked behind the bar. No one else was really paying attention. Advantage of hanging out with so many academics, they each had their own dozen theories to work on, so they were too busy to notice you doing something odd.

Unrolling the scroll, keeping it held up to the mirror, and trying to see what was reflected was awkward at best. A soft gronking came from behind me. Bunky and Irving had joined me and both opened their mouths. It took me a second to realize they were offering to hold up the scroll.

I secured one corner with each of them and stepped forward. Nope, looked the same, only reversed.

"Not wards enough!" Crusty was prone on the table but somehow she was watching me. Of course, her yelling caught the attention of the other faeries who were on the bar right near me.

"No, more wards!" That was Leaf, also prone from the

bar.

I panicked as they struggled to crawl to their feet. I really didn't need that much assistance. Or rather that *kind* of assistance.

"Bunky and Irving? Hold on a second." I took the scroll back, flipped it upside down, and placed the ends back in the constructs' waiting mouths.

I wasn't sure what I'd been expecting, but the outline of a chest under the ruins was not it.

The chest covered two dig sites, at least the way they were divided now. I had no idea what it was marking sixty years ago. There was a symbol on the chest, but it wasn't the diamond sphinx nor any other symbol I recognized.

"Is found! Lost!" Garbage had wobbled to the edge of the bar and was peering proudly at the mirror reflection.

"What was lost, sweetie?"

"That. Maker. Good not good but lost. Need." She jabbed her finger at me on the last bit, then smiled and flopped over.

I sighed. She wasn't unconscious, but the faeries had been drinking hard when they came back. Trying to get her to explain more was pointless.

"What did you find?" Covey asked as she came around the bar. Thanks to Garbage and the other jabbering faeries, I now had everyone looking at me.

"I'm not sure." I stepped back to let Covey in between the scroll and the mirror. If everyone wanted to see it they were going to have to take turns, the bar wasn't that big.

"It's a hidden map. Usually those have coded messages, but I don't see anything." Lorcan managed to navigate from his table through the chairs and around to me and the scroll without taking his eyes off of it once. Yet another scary elf trick. "Oops, yes there is. But it's almost impossible to read. It's very old."

"But that map isn't more than a hundred years old," Alric said as he moved in closer. "I recognize the style."

Since I was standing there, pretty much no one other than Lorcan and Covey were getting a close look.

"The Beccian who did it drew over an Ancient scroll. What idiot would do that?" The tone of Covey's voice did not bode well for whoever desecrated it if she ever found a way back in time to find them.

"But they wouldn't have seen it. You can't see anything until you flip it upside-down and hold it to a mirror." I wasn't going to fight her about it.

"Wardsback!" Most of the faeries were out, but the few that were conscious yelled out.

"No, I think the map maker knew," Lorcan said. "See here, the lines crossed exactly where the center of the chest is? I'd say they somehow knew exactly what was on this paper when they used it."

"The elves were in their cozy holes back then, so who else would have known what was here and hidden an Ancient scroll in a survey map?" I aimed my look at Mathilda. Yes, she was an elf, but not one who'd been in an enclave at the time.

"It wasn't me." She scurried up for a closer look, and then shook her head. "Thought I'd make sure, the memory does play tricks. But, no, that's not my writing."

"May I?" Lorcan asked. I was in the spot closest to the scroll, but he looked like he'd noticed something, so I moved. "Oh dear, oh my."

After a few minutes of him muttering to himself even Padraig was ready to yell. "You really shouldn't do that." His voice was calmer than his face.

"What?" Lorcan looked up with a start. "Forgive me; this traveling with a group is still new to me. I believe I know who hid this. He didn't mark it to damage it, but he needed to hide it in plain sight for some reason."

He'd started to turn back to the scroll when Covey grabbed his shoulder. "Who is it?"

"Again, my apologies. I believe it was our very own

Nasif who did it. He and Dueble did roam around for quite a few years. They must have found themselves in this desolate place and, for some reason Nasif didn't feel safe taking the scroll with him."

"Or he had it with him and had disguised it already, when he lost it." Alric took my place as I moved out completely from behind the bar.

"So what exactly does the chest mean? The faeries said it was good we found it and something about a maker?" The girls were completely passed out now.

"I'm not sure, but this is a most awkward way to view this. No offense, gallant constructs." Lorcan looked around the room and nodded to a clear table. "Let's move it there. I can set a mirror spell easy enough."

I hadn't even thought of trying to use a spell. I was just glad I'd figured out 'wardsback'.

I went to the back of the bar and took the scroll from Bunky and Irving. They might have let one of the others do it, but I could tell that both were wary after the way everyone reacted to Irving eating another relic.

Once we got it rolled out and the ends held down, Lorcan muttered a few words and the image changed from the old version of Beccia to the original scroll. Even better than viewing it in the mirror, this way the original was much easier to read. I could actually see the words in the corner now, but even if they had been a language I knew, it would be difficult to read them.

Judging from the concentrated scowls on the faces around me, the others weren't able to read it well either.

I gave up. "Maybe if we take it to Nasif, since he already translated it? And then we'd find out why he hid it." Made sense to me. Sometimes my overly bright friends thought too much about things.

"We could, but I think this is related to whatever the mayor is looking for. We can't leave Beccia unguarded with whatever it is still here." Padraig looked up briefly, then back to the scroll.

Faeries and alcohol, academics and mysteries. I was surrounded by obsessive personalities.

"Okay, so this chest belonged to the Ancients?" I briefly thought of the other chest in our lives, the one that belonged to the followers of the Dark and was full of gruesome books on how to kill people and take over worlds. I shuddered. Hopefully we didn't have another one like it on our hands.

CHAPTER TWENTY

"I BELIEVE SO," PADRAIG SHOOK HIS head. "It is somehow related to the relics." He tapped a corner of the words. "I just can't figure how it's related nor why we never saw any other reference to it."

"That would be a good question for Nasif," Lorcan said. "I think we underestimated him and Dueble roaming around for almost a thousand years—and just what they were doing during that time. But right now we need to figure out where it is and how to get it."

"Unless the map is way off, this shows it covering two dig sites." I shook my head. "How are we going to dig up something that big, and what are we going to do with it?" I had hoped that maybe the spell on the scroll would make things more clear, and narrow down the location. Nope.

"I think I see what was done." Alric had been holding back, but he'd been studying the map. "There's a trick, one that elven map makers used to do with hidden locations." He looked up and his grin got wider as he took in Lorcan and Padraig's looks. "See? There are things to know outside of your studies. I learned it when I became obsessed with maps as a kid and was working out how to run away." He took the map and turned it toward himself. Then muttered a few spell words.

Lorcan's spell held, but now a new one was laid over it. The lines from the spell outline bounced around each other and finally converged in one spot.

"Is that my old dig site with Qianru?" Just how much had that crazy old lady known? Of course, she'd gone down to the south to rally the elves in her hometown, so I couldn't ask her. I was in shock that my dippy patroness was actually an agent for her people in the southern lands. She'd known where the chimeras were going to come out of the ground and now, it appeared, where an Ancient chest was.

"It looks like," Alric said. "It's in the far corner, nothing but trees there now. She most likely didn't know it was there, or you'd still be digging for it."

"It's outside of the hedge." Covey had been glaring at the map but finally came up for air. "The mayor, and whoever else is out there, must not know exactly where it is, but they know something is down there." She pointed to another area on the map. "As near as I can estimate, this is where the dragon construct was, where that woman they mentioned had prisoners digging. I questioned Foxy, but they were told nothing, other than to dig where they were told. They'd dig, be pulled back, a troop of syclarions would investigate, and then they'd dig again. They were headed this direction." She pointed to my dig site.

"We need to find it first," Alric said.

From the look on his face, I half expected him to run out the door that second.

"We need to work out a plan," Lorcan said. "We will draw attention as soon as we are out there. The people working against us are going the long way for a reason— she doesn't know exactly where it is. But she must have some information that's leading her. And we have to believe the mayor is working on his own agenda toward it as well."

"I'd really like to know what it does." I looked around at my friends. They were just ready to grab it, whatever *it* was. I was less optimistic. "What is a chest going to do? More importantly, what was it designed to do? The girls said maker, but maker of what?"

"I think it helped keep the relics hidden before they

were put together as the weapon." Mathilda had been quietly working on the corner of the map with the words.

"Could it call the relics to it?" I wasn't getting it. "I don't see what a chest that held the relics could do."

Padraig didn't look up from the scroll; he had that calculating something look. "The relics can be sensed; they seem to respond to each other, so on some level they must be felt by beings stronger in magic than those of today. The chest would have blocked that. If the Ancients could have sensed the relics, they might have stopped their destruction."

"Nasif believed the weapon wasn't supposed to be used against the Ancients, but in an attack against the syclarions." I wasn't sure if I agreed with him or not.

"True, but we've got many theories and no way of finding the truth at this point," Mathilda said. "Even if, hypothetically, this wasn't to be used against the Ancients, there were also plenty of powerful syclarion mages at the time. The chest could have blocked them from sensing the relics as well."

Alric shook his head. "It has to have some power beyond that. I've met the mayor of Kenithworth and he wouldn't be going through all of this simply for something that might have stored a bunch of relics."

Padraig nodded. "I agree. I haven't met him, but this is a lot of time and money for an academic exercise. And we're not sure who is working with him. Some of us might have done it just to find the answers, but not someone whose motive is power."

I pulled back as they kept debating. I needed to look at this as a dig. Just a normal dig. I'd been digging these ruins for over fifteen years. I knew them far better than Nivinal, whoever this woman was, or the mayor and his mage flunkies—even the ones who were from Beccia. Folks from the Hill were patrons, they didn't dig themselves.

"We have to do it at night." I studied the map. "And one

of Alric's hidey holes is close by the spot so we can use that as a staging area. Since my house has survived, I can get my supplies. And I'm pretty sure Alric can break into Harlan's place to get his." I looked up to find everyone looking at me. "What? This is what I do, people. I'm afraid it might take a while to get to it, and we don't want to tip off the mayor. Just because he, or whoever he is working with, closed off that section of the aqueduct, that doesn't mean that they're not still digging."

"I can take care of getting Harlan's supplies," Covey said. She was the first to respond; everyone else was processing. "I've had reason to break into his place before."

Alric nodded and the first serious smile I'd seen in a while appeared. "I can go with Taryn and see what we can get from her place. She's right, my cave is here." He tapped a spot next to the intersection of the lines and the supposed location of the chest.

"It's settled then. Since we only have two real experts on digging through the ruins, I think Taryn and Alric should lead. Covey and I will be back up," Padraig said.

Lorcan looked ready to argue, then shook his head. "Agreed. We can't all be out there, and this way Mathilda and I can work on getting a better idea of where the sphinx is before we leave this town."

"And make sure that Amara and Foxy are ready for us to take off quickly." Alric gathered his belongings back into his pack.

"Us too!" Garbage yelled. She, like the rest of her bunch, was still prone.

"How about you stay here and help Lorcan and Mathilda." I looked beseechingly toward Mathilda.

"Oh, please do. I shall need of you to help me." She turned back to me once Garbage waved and flopped back down. "I will go a different direction when we depart and will meet you on the trail north to the sphinx. I can follow the faeries now that we have reconnected, but I need to get my house."

I didn't blame her, having a traveling house along would make trail life much better. I'd have to figure out a way to ride in it from time to time.

"We can meet here." Padraig pointed to a location on the map that was closest to the hedge. "I'll have Amara and Foxy go with us there so that she can let us out."

Covey nodded, slipped her own pack over her shoulders, and left. Alric had gathered my pack, and Foxy's scroll, and opened the door.

"They go!" I'd thought Garbage had passed back out again, but as she yelled, Bunky and Irving followed us out the door. Bunky even made a dive for Alric's head but didn't seem upset when Alric ducked. It was an old game they used to play.

"Shouldn't they stay?" I watched the two constructs bob in the air.

Alric looked back through the door to where the faeries were stirring. "I'd rather have the constructs over the faeries. This way, if we need to get word back quickly, we can."

There were a few more people roaming around the streets than before, not at like Beccia normally, but definitely more than earlier. We were also going a different route to my house than before. Like the Shimmering Dewdrop, all of the pubs now appeared open.

We were both quiet on the way toward my house this time, but, unlike last time, I was okay with it. I was already focusing on the best way to approach the dig once the sun went down. Night digs were not my favorite, but I had done them before. Knowing Alric's sneaky ways, he was probably an expert at them. I'd have to talk to Padraig about those clearthin glows.

The house looked as we'd left it, and I heard the spells around it pop as I walked up the lawn. The door wasn't locked, but with a spell on it, it probably didn't need to be. I'd just crossed into the living room when a wave of cold air hit me.

"Please do come in and close the door, or I will kill him." The voice came from a shadow in the corner of my living room. My front door shut on Alric's face without me having to do anything.

CHAPTER TWENTY—ONE

ALRIC WAS YELLING AND POUNDING on the door. Bunky and Irving were most likely the source of the additional thunks against it. Normally, a verbal threat by an unknown source would have been met with skepticism, but there was something oddly familiar and terrifying about that voice. They were telling the truth. I wouldn't have opened the door for anything.

"Who are you?" I flexed my hand for the largest push spell I could think of. Yes, I knew deadlier spells, but fear was trying to take over my brain. Part of me recognized that I didn't know this person—the other part was shaking in terror.

"I am Edana. I am also your best hope and your worst enemy. I know that you and your friends are looking for the relics. I can give you the life you want, with the man of your dreams, peace, if you just give me the diamond sphinx." As the person spoke, their voice became more feminine, and images invaded my mind. Even knowing it was a spell didn't make the emotional and mental impact any less. A nice home, my friends coming to visit from the homes nearby, Alric holding me in his arms each night.

"Now, if you don't, I can make things so much worse." The images this time were enough to drop me hunched over to the floor. My friends were dead or dying. Alric was being slowly tortured.

The pressure in my head suddenly stopped.

"I know you don't have it yet, but I also know that you might be the one to find it. I don't know who you are, or what you are, and I don't care. I killed my son to get the chimera. I have no problem doing the same to you and your friends."

I was just rising to my feet when the shadowed form vanished and my front door blew in.

"What just happened?" Alric had his sword in one hand and his dagger in the other. Bunky and Irving were tearing around my house but kept looping over the corner where my attacker had been. Or rather, her image.

I rubbed my arms at the cold that lingered from what she'd sent me in that spell. "I'm not sure. But I think I met Nivinal's mom, she called herself Edana. She has the chimera now." I briefly explained her demands, without going into the details because they were still too fresh in my mind to say out loud.

Alric was silent for a few moments after I finished. Then pulled me into his arms. The feeling was almost too similar to what the spell had felt like, but I ignored that. "Why those two? You're certain she didn't want the rest? Just the sphinx?"

He had me bundled tightly to his chest, so I just nodded. He held me away from him so he could see me. "Are you okay? I know you're our only official digger, but I can do this without you."

I pushed at his chest. "No way, who knows what you'll mess up." I smiled. I couldn't think about whoever that woman was. I had a job and we were getting that damn chest, and then getting out of here. "Let's get my tools; we have a chest to find." I paused halfway to my back rooms. "Could you tell the others? They need to know, but I don't want to recount it again."

"I will." He walked over to the corner where the shadow had been, held out a hand, then pulled it back as if burnt. "It's the same magic tinge that I felt near the hedge and

the first time we were here. She was looking for the gargoyle, or you, before."

"I hate to say me, but since she didn't even bring up
the gargoyle, I'd say that wasn't her goal." I started sorting through my digger supplies. Then I shook my head,
grabbed them all, and dumped them in a huge pack I had.
I had no idea what we'd need, and I also had no idea when
we'd be back here. Not to mention, even spelled my house
seemed to be a target for dangerous folks.

Alric and the constructs were investigating the corner
where the woman's image had been. He turned and shook
his head. "Whoever she is, she's skilled. The residue I sensed
is already gone."

"Great, so Nivinal is dead but we've got someone worse."
I started to struggle with my new pack and my old pack.
Alric took the new one out of my hands and put it on his
back. Show off.

"We've definitely got someone different. And she didn't
give you much of an option, but this was the first time an
offer of something in exchange for a relic has been made."

As we left my house, the constructs did one more flyby
of every room, and Alric re-set the spell. "I'm setting it to
both of us this time. Not that it worked against her."

The walk to where we were meeting Covey and Padraig
was short, but both Bunky and Irving kept buzzing around
anything even remotely suspicious. By the time we reached
the hedge I was about to jump out of my skin.

Covey was there with an additional pack almost as large
as the one Alric was carrying for me. I knew that paranoid Harlan would have kept his prize digger tools hidden
somewhere, but judging by the fact that Covey looked
like she'd been sitting for a while; I'd say she didn't have a
problem finding them.

"You two look far more upset than you should be for
making a quick trip." She stood and looked us both up and
down. "Are you two still fighting?"

"We're not fighting, and we weren't earlier." Alric kept talking over Covey's snort at that. "There was a guest waiting for us at Taryn's home. It appears there is someone more dangerous than Nivinal—his mother, Edana. Or that was the name she gave us. I've never heard of her."

"The good news is she claimed to have killed him to get the chimera, so maybe he really is out of the picture?" Even I had a problem thinking that was good news, but it had to be better than both of them being alive. I might have defeated Nivinal's spell image when I'd transformed, but there was no guarantee I could do that to him in person—with or without changing into something big and scaly.

"How in the hell did she get through the hedge? We need to go back and warn Amara." Covey had her packs on her back in a second.

"She was only there as a spell image, like mother like son I guess. But she is so powerful that I probably would have given her anything she asked for." An unwelcome thought hit me. Granted, spell images could come from anywhere if the mage throwing it was strong enough. But I had a bad feeling she wasn't far. "She's probably the one helping the mayor. Or rather, he's helping her. He might not even realize he's doing it."

Padraig came jogging up at that moment; Amara and Foxy were a bit behind. He shook his head. "There's no way those looks can be good. Taryn, your distress can be felt by any strong mage in the area. Or could, it's fading."

I looked to Alric, but he shrugged. "I never felt it beyond an initial stab of terror when that door slammed. I could tell something was wrong, but no distress."

"What happened?" Padraig put one hand on the hedge, checking to see if that was the source.

"Taryn was attacked in her house by the spell image of Nivinal's mother. He might be dead," Covey said. "And they don't want to give more details."

"I can't." I looked to Alric.

He squeezed my shoulder. "Just say Nivinal might really be dead, his mother is worse than he was, she has the chimera, wants the sphinx, and scared the hell out of Taryn."

"Good enough for me; we can discuss it later." Padraig fixed one of his glorious smiles on me. Seriously, someone needed to build a new elven kingdom so he could rule it. He knew whatever happened was big, but he trusted both Alric and I enough not to push it.

Without a word, he set up eight clearthin glows around us.

"Is everything okay?" Amara asked as she and Foxy joined us.

This wasn't the time to discuss this, and since there wasn't a way that hedge was going to stop spell images, nothing that she could do right now.

"More information about those who are trying to get the relics, I'm afraid. We need to find this chest, and then leave here," Padraig said with a nod toward the hedge.

Amara's sharp green eyes took in all of us, and her look said she'd pry the information out of us later—most likely with some amazing food. That was fine with me; I'd be in a much better condition to talk about it when we were back and safe in the pub. "I will have to close the hedge after you leave; more information usually means more attacks, and I will not abide by that. But the hedge will now recognize you on this trip, all of you." She waved to Bunky and Irving bobbing in the air above us. "It will let you come back one time even without my presence. I would make it permanent, but it would weaken the spell." She waved her hand and a pathway through the hedge opened. "Good luck, and quick travels."

Padraig gave a small bow, then led us through the hedge, the clearthin glows strung along the length of us with one ahead and one behind. Going through the hedge didn't feel as closed in as the first time we went through, most likely because I didn't feel like it was thinking of eating me. Now that it recognized us as friends, it wasn't as scary.

I followed Padraig, Covey followed me, and Alric brought up the rear. A quick glance back showed the hedge closing behind Alric. Bunky and Irving kept low over our heads.

We came out of the hedge just past the prime dig spots and only a short walk from Qianru's site. She was going to be furious with herself when this was over and she found out this chest had been on her plot. I wasn't exactly sure why a chest that might have been used by the creator of the relics was going to be helpful. Then again, with my luck, it was an evil relic itself, bent on world destruction.

CHAPTER TWENTY—TWO

EVEN IN THE DIM LIGHT of the drifting clearthin glows the dig site looked a bit sad after not having anyone working it for so long. Usually, if someone abandoned a site it was declared free to anyone after a few months. It said a lot about the fear of Qianru and her money that no one had attempted to dig here.

That and this wasn't a valued site.

As Padraig and Alric conferred about setting up camp, two of the clearthin glows bobbed along with me as I looked around to see if anything besides overgrowth had changed. Covey stood in the middle and scowled. She enjoyed the outcome of digs, but not really the process itself.

Bunky and Irving flew along with me and the glows. The company was nice, but the fact they were both in guard mode was getting old. I appreciated their diligence—I did seem to need to have people keeping an eye on me a lot these days. Nevertheless, I was done with it right now.

"Would you two go watch from the woods? If someone is coming our way, come back and warn us." I pointed toward the area where I knew Alric's cave hideout was. "And circle there too—we'll be using that area as well." Neither of the constructs needed help seeing in the dark. This would keep them busy and leave me alone.

Bunky flew down level with my head and gronked seriously.

"He wants to make sure you're going to be safe," Alric said as he broke off from his conversation with Padraig.

I slipped on a pair of thin gloves that I'd tossed in my digger pack and petted Bunky. For some reason, touching Bunky with bare skin launched a flood of images to invade my brain. "I'll be fine. And you and Irving will make sure things are safe for us."

He gronked again, even I didn't need translation to know that was an affirmative, and then he and Irving flew into the treetops.

The dig site looked about as it had before Qianru and I had started. I'd never gotten a good explanation of exactly how she knew the chimeras would be coming out when they did. All of the holes caused by the escape of the chimera constructs and the sceanra anam had closed up within a day of the creatures leaving.

"So how did those creatures come out of the ground after thousands of years?" I poked at the dirt, but it was as smooth as if it had never been disturbed.

Covey came over. "That's where the sceanra anam came from, right?" She shook her head. "There's almost no information on them. The elves had fables and stories, but nothing officially recorded."

Padraig joined us. He left Alric to stage our dig area. Probably a good idea, as he knew as much or more as me about relic hunting. His way might be a bit quicker than standard digger protocol anyway.

"They were nothing more than children's tales, but they clearly were based on stories from the Ancients." He dropped down next to me to poke at the dirt himself. "The sceanra anam are elemental magic, like the faeries. They followed the chimeras into dormancy is my guess. Supposedly a nasty mage from the time of the Ancients created them—the faeries and the chimera constructs were their enemies."

"So they were made after the chimeras? Were the faeries

made?" That was a disturbing thought.

He let some dirt run through his fingers, then shook his head. "I believe the chimeras were created after the sceanra anam—to fight them. And no, the faeries came about the same way any of us did—unassisted. As a species, they've been around since the Ancients' time."

"According to the girls—*they* were around since before then, way before then in fact." I wasn't sure how I felt about my little flying wackos being the oldest creatures on the planet. It really said something about the way this world came about. Might be a good question for Amara. As a goddess, she should have some insight regarding how the world came into being.

Padraig looked thoughtful at that, and then shrugged. "It's hard to say. Elemental creatures function differently than us mortals. But however long they've been around, it is interesting that the chimeras went into dormancy, the sceanra anam did as well, but the faeries did not."

"I think this is going to be the best spot to start. Do we want to move most of our supplies into my cave first?" Alric had gone into a clump of young gapen trees. He'd been right; with the tree and other plant growth there, the site had never been torn up by diggers.

Covey added a few items to his 'use now' collection; I just brought out my favorite pick axe and trowel set.

"Unless you want anything else?" Alric had grabbed the packs and looked toward Padraig who was standing near the sceanra anam hatching locations. Advantage of hanging out with someone perpetually sneaky, they were always prepared if things went bad fast. If we were discovered, only having a few things to take with us out of the area would be to our advantage.

"No, go ahead. I'll use what you've taken out." Padraig gave one last look to the spot, then shook his head and joined us.

Alric nodded and left with the packs, but Padraig was

definitely doing some serious thinking.

"What's wrong?" Covey asked as she worked her way through the tools before settling on a larger trowel.

"Just thinking of Taryn's question. What caused them to come out of the ground? And why did they come out when they did? I do wish I'd paid more attention to Qianru, but to be honest, she might not have had much background on what she was looking for. It does appear that Jovan was using her to deflect attention from himself, and he might have had resources far beyond the rest of us."

"If I had to guess, and you know my guesses are based on research, I'd say the activation of the glass gargoyle triggered it," Covey said. "We've seen that something is calling things into play. Jovan must have known the gargoyle was the first piece. He came north afterwards."

"We have a problem," Alric said. He spoke before he came into the clearing, but was dragging something behind him.

It was a body. A dead-for-a-long-time body. There wasn't much left of it; animals, as well as time, hadn't been nice to it. However, the stature and clothing looked familiar.

"Is that Largen?" I had little love for the woman; magic wielding evil crime lords really didn't make me feel warm and fuzzy.

"I cast a spell; yes, it's her. She's been dead since a week or so after we were taken by Flarinen."

"Wait, so the one that's been working with the mayor for the past few months has been a fake?" Not that it improved things much in my mind. Of course, it took a serious magic user to hold a glamour together well enough to appear as another person, so we might have gone from bad to worse.

"Yes, and I have no idea why." Alric released the body. "Largen was as corrupt as they came. Yet someone out there has been mimicking her for the past few months."

I rubbed my eyes. The last thing we needed was yet another weird mystery tied into these relics. Who could possibly care if it was a corrupt crime lord involved or someone else?

"Alric, when I first found you, Cirocco had a bounty out for you. I never knew what you'd done to piss off him or Largen so bad." It was a jump and the events seemed like lifetimes ago. But my life had turned when Alric somehow pissed off two of the biggest crime lords in Beccia.

He'd been looking back at the body, probably to ready a spell to cover it, but turned back to me. "I'd been trying to track down the glass gargoyle." He nodded his chin toward Padraig. "He and some of our other alchemists were certain it had been found. Cirocco had some valuable elven relics…and both he and Largen were looking for a specific one. Something they were working on with someone from out of town," he swore under his breath. "Probably the mayor of Kenithworth."

"I know who those two are, but not much else," Covey said.

"They are/were both mages," Alric explained to Padraig. "Cirocco more so than Largen, but both strong enough to be dangerous. If they really were working with the mayor of Kenithworth, it explains how he knew of Taryn and her finds. But I'm not sure why whoever killed Largen wanted to keep the ruse up."

Covey narrowed her eyes. "But Cirocco is a dwoller. It's hard to fool them when it comes to things like the scent of blood. He'd realize Largen wasn't really herself."

"Unless there's yet another player who is stronger," Padraig said. He'd been watching us; obviously he'd never met Cirocco or Largen any more than he'd met the mayor of Kenithworth. However, he knew magic. "There are spells that can transform everything. Even the psychic feel of a person."

Alric's swearing resumed. "When they duplicated me in the enclave, when they attacked you. It was me in every sense to you, wasn't it?"

"That was what destroyed me. Everything was you,"

Padraig said.

"But didn't we decide it had been Nivinal? And he's dead, we hope, now." I wasn't sure how worried we should be if his mother didn't actually kill him.

Padraig sighed and ran his hand threw his hair. "We weren't certain. Nivinal had been our grand inquisitor since the enclave had been created. Obviously he was part of the Dark, but less obvious was his involvement in the attack on my study. The inquisitor had been in court that day. When I'd realized that it hadn't been Alric who attacked me, and that Nivinal wasn't who we thought, I did some checking."

"But he could have sent a projection?" I wanted him to have been that bastard in that scenario, and I wanted him dead.

Alric shook his head this time. "It wouldn't have worked in court, not with that many mages in the place."

"So the attack was orchestrated by someone else who had that kind of power, and who was inside the enclave." Covey put the pieces together.

I really didn't like her thinking.

"I believe so. There is another hidden member of the Dark, someone stronger than the knights." Alric finished his spell and the body of Largen vanished. "And they are here in Beccia."

CHAPTER TWENTY—THREE

———◆———

"AND THEY ARE WORKING IN disguise to fool some Beccian crime lords by pretending to be one of them." I shook my head. Maybe it was better not knowing the answers. Neither Largen nor Cirocco had been upstanding members of the Beccian community, but they also weren't the type to want to rule the world. They just wanted their half to be exceptionally comfortable. Still, no one would lament Largen's passing, except maybe the minions that were on her payroll.

"Or someone else," Alric said. "I stalked both of them for a few weeks before they put that bounty on me and I never noticed anything about them and what they were doing." He was clearly pissed about that.

"This is an issue, I will admit. But I think at this point we need to stick to the plan, get what we came for and get out of town," Padraig said.

"That would be just fine, except that we don't want you to leave just yet." The voice came from behind me.

Bunky and Irving gronked in warning just as I heard a rapid-fire short crossbows lock in place behind me. "Go warn the others! Fly!" I knew my little mental trick only worked with the faeries, but I sent as strong of a mental image as I could of us being under attack and to warn the others as I could muster.

Bunky was the closest to us, he gave another gronk, and then spun around and flew off with Irving right on his tail.

"Well, that wasn't a great idea. But we'll be gone before anyone gets out here."

I turned around slowly. I was pretty sure I recognized that voice. Unlike most of his kind, Cirocco didn't have the dwoller lisp. But he was just as nasty as the rest of his people. And I had no doubt that his fangs could inflict the same damage. Dwollers were a mostly nocturnal species; tall, gaunt, pale, and fanged were their calling cards. They also fed off blood, and not always of animals. Most were at least partly mad, and while Cirocco wasn't—he was still deadly.

Cirocco's man was right behind me, his crossbow pointed at my gut. Even if my friends got away, I was a goner. Considering how close he was, even a spell might not work. If there was ever a time I needed to turn into something huge and scaly, with a tough hide, this was it.

Nothing. Of course, I had no idea if the spell that triggered it was even still inside me.

"Cirocco, you're being fooled." Alric's voice was as calm as if they'd run into each other at a pub. "Largen isn't who you think."

"Alric, how in the hell are you still alive? I didn't even recognize you." Cirocco didn't look surprised at Alric being an elf, but it hadn't been a secret after the incident with the obsidian chimera.

"I'd say the same about you, the alive part anyway. You keep working with these damn syclarions and you're going to find yourself in an alley in pieces." Alric looked far more relaxed than anyone else did, including Cirocco. He had some sort of plan to get us free. I just wished I knew what it was.

"I had no idea Thaddeus was a syclarion, and to be honest, as long as it makes me money, I don't care what they are."

He had two more men beside the archer with him, ones I recognized as his enforcers. Only the archer was actively holding a weapon. Still aimed at my gut. If Alric could take the archer out, we might make it out of here alive.

"Even if they're stealing from you and picking you off one at a time?" Alric gestured and Largen's mangled body reappeared. "If you and she were working toward something, or working for someone, she's been replaced. Months ago. And I'm pretty sure you didn't give her, or whoever killed her, your watch."

Watches weren't common in Beccia and the few people who had them were the rich, powerful, and usually criminal. I hadn't noticed the gold chain when Alric first dragged in the body, but I did now.

Cirocco started swearing and moved toward the body.

"Not until he drops his weapon and backs away." Alric's sword had appeared in his hand and against the archer's throat so quickly that I didn't even see him move.

"Do it," Cirocco said. His eyes stayed on the body, focused on the chain that led into a pocket.

The archer lowered his weapon and took two steps back. Not near far enough in my mind, but I took three steps away as well. I might have also stepped partially behind Alric.

Alric lowered his sword, but didn't sheathe it. "Be my guest. Not only has the person you've been working with the past few months been an impostor, but they are most likely a high-ranking mage who stole from you, slaughtered Largen, and will kill you too the moment you stop being useful."

Cirocco pulled the watch out of Largen's pocket, jerked free the chain, and handed it to one of his men. "Have it cleaned." He turned back to Alric. "I am not working for anyone, they are working for me."

Alric rocked back on one heel and smirked.

"If you have something to say, do so."

"Do you want your men here? Are you sure?"

Cirocco's eyes narrowed.

I was trying to figure out Alric's plan. Maybe it was to trick Cirocco into sending away his people so we could overpower him. I kept my laugh inside my head. Right, even with Padraig and Covey included, Cirocco would destroy us. Just might take him a little longer. I had never been a huge fan of any of the crime lords, even though I sometimes ran bounties for them when it was that or me and the faeries being on the street. But Cirocco was more dangerous than the rest combined.

And right now he looked like he was making sure we remembered that.

"Go back to camp. Get someone working on that watch," he said. "But say nothing. Don't let anyone else see it, and tell no one what you've heard or seen here."

His people faded into the trees silently. Which left him and Alric in the most epic stare down I had ever seen.

"You are being manipulated. I wasn't sure if you were aware of it or if you were being duped." Alric sheathed his sword, then folded his arms and smiled. "Your reaction tells me you had no clue. Someone has been manipulating the Beccian underworld for at least the past two years, possibly longer."

"No one is manipulating me." Cirocco's words were solid but there was a tiny crack in his façade.

"This would be easier if I show you." Alric spread his hands wide and a series of images appeared. At first I thought they were from him, and then I realized they were coming from the body before us.

Cirocco went from pissed to concerned to scared and back to pissed in the time it took for Covey and Padraig to step forward.

"How isss this true? How issss it no one noticed?" His control was vanishing. The dwoller lisp was coming into play and a redness was filling his eyes. Alric might have convinced Cirocco he'd been had, but there was a good chance we were going to die anyway. Rampaging dwollers had been known to kill dozens.

I wasn't the only one who feared that. Padraig was next to me with his spirit sword in one hand and the other curved for a spell. Covey's fingers were longer and claw-like and were clenching and unclenching. My sword finally decided to drop in again. But it was on the ground in front of me, and I wasn't going to break this tableau to get it.

"Back off, fang thing!" Garbage yelled as she led a flight of faeries into the clearing. The clearthin glows picked them up as they passed through but it was hard to tell their numbers.

"No! Taryn, have them stay back," Alric held up his hand but didn't turn away from Cirocco. He had his sword back in his other hand, but didn't seem near as disturbed as he should be, being that close to a potentially rampaging dwoller.

I was disturbed enough for both of us.

The faeries looked to me, even Garbage. That was new. "Stay back. Alric's got this under control." I worked to keep my voice from ascending into a freaked-out screech.

She gave an intense nod, and then all of them hovered above us. Now that they were closer, it was clearly just our twenty-three; she hadn't pulled in the wild faeries. Bunky and Irving stayed up there with them.

Cirocco watched us, then took a deep breath and shook himself. The wild animal on the edge look was gone, and while it was disturbing to watch, I was glad the red fled from his eyes. "What you just showed me was troubling. Even more upsetting was that the creature behind this left it there to be discovered. I have to believe he or she delib-erately attached my watch to the body as well."

"I'm not sure what you and the rest of the criminal ele-ment thought you were working toward, but the people behind this are trying to destroy this world. That bit you saw was their idea of perfection."

A tiny part of me wanted to see what could raise such a

snarl on Cirocco's face. The more rational side of me said I could wait and get a summary from Alric. I had no idea why Alric was telling Cirocco all of this; it had saved us from a messy fight, but there was something more.

"We were misled. Thaddeus recruited us not long before your lady found the glass gargoyle. We'd been looking for it since he claimed it could make us more rich and powerful than our imaginations. But then you destroyed him." He shrugged and seemed to relax. "Then Largen brought in Rosicathin, the mayor of Kenithworth, to come meet with us. When those damn elves—no offense—moved in, he rallied us to join forces with him. Largen and he have been leading this entire attack."

"Is there another woman on your side? A powerful one?" I'd gladly let Alric take the lead on this, but something the people who had been holding Foxy said stuck with me. Not to mention my recent visitor.

"No, in fact there is another group working against us. They seem to be led by a woman, but no one has actually seen her."

"So, if someone replaced Largen, and the woman is on the other side…who is acting as Largen now?" Covey loved puzzles but she didn't look happy about this one. Having all the bad guys on the same team made it easier to keep track of them.

"Someone who will be dead once I get back to my camp, I assure you." He smiled more to show his elongated fangs than out of any warmth. We might have just solved a problem that he didn't know he had, but we were not friends. "I don't know what you're doing here, and honestly, I don't care at this point. I will not tell them where you are, but I have a feeling things will be getting ugly around here soon." With a nod to Alric, Cirocco turned and vanished into the forest.

The faeries swarmed the dead body, but pulled back quickly and waved their hands in front of their faces. "Is boom." Garbage kept them flying backwards, but not tak-ing their eyes off the body.

"Bad boom," the faeries yelled out. Even Bunky and Irving flew out of the range of the clearthin glows.

"Guys, I think they really mean explode this time."

CHAPTER TWENTY—FOUR

I GRABBED COVEY AND PADRAIG—ALRIC WAS out of reach—and started pulling backwards. Alric threw a spell bubble toward the body, one open at the back so it gave the rest of us more protection.

And not a moment too soon. The body, and a few good-sized trees over it, exploded.

Alric's spell held. Those bubbles were hard to create, and often unstable. I needed either him or Padraig to show me how they could make them strong enough to hold off explosions.

He dropped it once the debris stopped raining down.

"So much for us being sneaky," I said as I shook my head. Whatever spell had blown up that body had been far too loud for anyone to have missed it. Hell, the elves in their enclave probably heard it.

"I blocked the sound," Padraig said. "He handled the parts; I trapped everything else. No one would have heard it, but strong magic users might have felt it. We need to move quickly." He and Covey went toward the area of the explosion, leaving the faeries, constructs, and me to hang back.

"But we don't know…" I dropped those words when I saw them shoving trees and dirt out of the way. "You deliberately put the body where the chest supposedly is?"

Alric looked over his shoulder and shot me a smile. "Yes, but I really didn't think it would blow up that quickly.

There were some odd spells on it, that's why I hid it the first time. I think whoever planted the watch on it was trying to take out Cirocco."

"The watch was a trigger." Covey continued to move plants and dirt away, but her tools were set aside. So much for anything close to a proper dig. Of course, I usually didn't blow up potential ruins either.

"So they *were* trying to destroy Cirocco?" I started elbowing my way into the dig area.

"Or they just figured anyone would pull the watch. But I don't understand what that spell was doing," Covey was digging with her bare hands since the claws were still in place.

"I think Alric should share that when we're back at the pub. We shouldn't speak of whatever it was out here." Padraig stood aside to let me in to dig. I noticed he and the constructs were watching the area around us, and that there were more clearthin glows than before. He was more worried about some powerful magic users having felt the muffled explosion than he'd let on.

I looked at the hole we were digging in. Even with four of the glows hovering over it, it wasn't easy to see. "There's no way we're finishing this tonight. I mean, it's great that Alric used an exploding body to speed things along. But this chest has been down there for a fair amount of time. Digging isn't fast, folks." There was a larger clump of dirt so I shifted my small shovel under it. And hit something.

"I might have spoken too soon." I tapped the lump a bit and more dirt dislodged itself. I reached in and started brushing. Tarnished bands, the type on an old wooden sea chest, glinted faintly in the weird orange glow from the clearthins. "It's a chest." This was good and bad. Good in that hopefully we could get back behind the hedge and be on our way; bad in that it was so close to the surface, I really had a hard time believing it was what they thought it was.

It took four of us over an hour to pull it free. Using magic around relics was a bad idea, so we had to take turns digging around the sides of it. It might not have been very deep, but that thing was embedded well. The faeries had grown bored when there were no more booms, so they flew back to the pub. Bunky and Irving kept up their patrol of the skies.

I finally worked enough of it free to see most of it. It was about two feet wide by three feet high and had that rounded top that sea chests have. It was also heavier than it looked, especially if it was actually empty. "It's free, but it's too heavy for me to get out alone." I could probably lift it, but there wasn't a lot of room in the hole. Alric jumped down on the other side and with the other two pulling, he and I pushed it up and out.

I had been hoping that once out of the hole it would suddenly appear impressive. No such luck. It looked like a thousand year old sea chest buried in the ground for a long time.

"It's very heavy to be empty." Covey's words echoed my earlier thoughts.

Padraig kept looking at it—all of it. The sides, the lock, the metal bands. He finally shook his head. "I'm not sure what, if anything, is inside, but we shouldn't open it out here."

"Take it back to the pub?" I rubbed my arms and looked around the dark ruins. I knew Cirocco said he wasn't going to tell the others about us being out here. But I didn't trust that; and if he found us, someone else could too.

"No, if this is a trap, we don't want to hurt anyone else," Alric picked up the chest and turned toward the back of the site. "My cave isn't large, but if things go bad, hopefully it will contain any explosion." He didn't wait for agreement, but he did look back briefly to make sure we were following.

Covey, Padraig, and I quickly gathered the tools we'd

brought out and followed the clearthins into a grove of trees. I'd been to this cave of his, albeit briefly. But it looked far more ominous in the dark—especially with the weird orange tint from the glows.

Bunky and Irving hovered right outside the entrance. I wasn't sure if it was to keep an eye out for us, or they really didn't like the look of Alric's cave.

There was a battered heavy wooden table in the middle of the cave and Alric had set the chest on it. He was already working on picking the lock as we came in.

"Good to see you've kept the skills up over the years." Padraig shook his head and waved another glow toward Alric. "He was the master lock-pick of the enclave. Nothing was safe around him when he was growing up."

"I think at some point, once everything has settled down, I need to hear many more tales of his childhood." I grinned at the brief flash of concern on Alric's face as he looked up.

"That, my lovely lady, is a deal. We can fill many evenings discussing this hooligan's exploits. Always did wonder who taught him to pick locks though."

"Lorcan," Alric said. Then he pulled back from the chest, rubbing his arm. Right where the geas mark lay. "In case we were questioning that this chest is somehow related to the relics and whatever happened to the Ancients, I think we're sure now. My geas mark tried to rip off my arm as soon as I cleared the lock." The glow from under his sleeve was already fading, but that had to be uncomfortable at the least.

I started to move toward the chest, and then held back. I had no idea if that chest could do anything, but visions of the Dark chest flashed through my mind. My hands had been stuck to it magically and it almost killed me. Not something I wanted to replicate.

Padraig patted my shoulder and walked forward. With a nod toward Alric, he lifted the lid. Then he started patting

the obviously empty inside walls. "Nothing. But it definitely feels like—" His words were cut off as a light came
from the chest and slammed him against the cave wall.

I ran to help him. I wasn't happy he got flung, but I was
glad that for once it wasn't me.

Alric leaned over from the side. "There are scrolls in
there now." He reached in with his non-geas marked arm
and pulled out a large collection of scrolls.

Padraig got to his feet and slowly came back. The chest
didn't respond. "That was too heavy for just scrolls, and
they weren't there when I looked inside."

Covey was already pawing around in it, but I didn't want
to touch it. I did lean forward to confirm its empty status.
The scrolls in Alric's hand looked solid, but I also believed
Padraig.

Irving came flying into the cave with Bunky gronking
behind him. They circled the chest, then Irving opened
his jaws and something dropped into the chest. The glass
gargoyle. He choked, almost like a cat coughing up a fur
ball. The golden basilisk was being stubborn. Irving finally
shook his head, closed his mouth, and he and Bunky
zipped back out of the cave.

We peered into the chest. The gargoyle just sat there. I
slammed the chest shut. I thought I felt some weird images
begin to form in my head, but I didn't hold on to the chest
long enough to find out.

"Why did your construct do that? And why not the second one?" Covey kept looking at the chest, but I noticed
her hands stayed firmly locked behind her back.

"I have no idea on either count. It did look like he was
trying to get the basilisk out; it must've put up a fight."
Hopefully, being in the chest would keep the gargoyle hidden and away from trouble.

Alric tucked the scrolls he'd kept under his arm, then
moved his hands over the chest and I saw a soft light settle
on it. "Until we can get in a spell-safe environment, this

thing should stay closed." He reached in his pocket and pulled out one of the faeries' tiny black bags. "And hidden. Agreed?"

We nodded. Alric put the spell-bubble-enclosed chest into the bag. He took out another one and tucked the scrolls into it. Both went inside his pocket.

"Just how many of those do you have?" And the rest of that question; why didn't the faeries let me have any?

"A few. You just have to ask them for a bag at the right time. I think they have a never-ending supply."

I grumbled a bit as we left the cave. I should have asked during the month we were on the run. Even Garbage seemed to feel bad about what had happened to me; they might have given me one out of sympathy.

It was still night, and the clearthins followed us out of the cave and bobbed along over our heads. Irving seemed to be extremely focused on one bobbing near me.

"Don't eat it, Irving. Bunky, tell him he can't eat the lights." Irving's eyes were growing larger and he was moving closer as I spoke. He didn't seem to react to what I said, but a soft gronk from Bunky got him to pull back.

Great, this construct was becoming an eater. A former neighbor of mine had a goat she kept in her apartment and took out for daily walks. Damn thing ate everything it could reach.

We were silent as we approached the hedge. We'd found the chest, but no answers to what it was, aside from the fact Irving threw up the gargoyle in it. The revelations of Largen and Cirocco were both bigger issues in my mind right now.

True to what Amara said, the hedge opened at Padraig's touch. The path was narrow, but the clearthin lights strung themselves out along the length of us.

Beccia had a few more lights than outside of the hedge, but not much. I hadn't noticed it before, but it looked like every other glow lantern was dark. There might actually be someone in town who was trying to ration things for a long siege—that spoke of planning, which most Beccians weren't keen on.

It was late enough that the drunks had mostly gone home, or at least stumbled to a safe spot to crash until their legs started working again. Foxy's front door was shut, so we went along the alley. The damage to Amara's tree was barely visible in the glows along the alleyway; it would probably be completely healed by tomorrow.

"Did you ever get a chance to find out about the strange amulets that were possessing those squirrels?" I hadn't heard anything from Alric about it, but we'd also been busy.

He shook his head, but his hand dropped to a pouch he carried under his cloak. He might have changed clothes, but he was keeping that dead amulet with him. "Just that they were created by a powerful mage who is paranoid. The squirrels who'd been trying to get the glass gargoyle last year were possessed, but I never saw any amulets on them. The one I have is magically advanced and complicated."

The door to the pub was unlocked, but Dogmaela was dozing right next to it with a heavy cudgel in her hand. She grunted, nodded, and closed her eyes when she realized it was us.

Lorcan was sitting at the main bar with a circle of faeries watching him. Well, listening to him with actual focused interest as Lorcan spun some tale. But as I watched, they slowly laid down and fell asleep. No ale needed. I was certain Lorcan had slipped a spell into his story, but as long as he taught me how to do it at some point, I'd never tell. Bunky and Irving flew around the bar, before settling in on the rafters.

"Ah! Our wanderers have returned early!" Lorcan smiled and nodded to the faeries. "I was just telling the girls a bedtime story. A tale of great hardship and the lengths a young elf went to in order to escape his confines."

I thought that sounded interesting. Alric turned red.

Padraig looked from one to the other and smiled. "Ahh, he did tell me that you taught him lock picking."

Lorcan laughed. "I was at my wits' end. There is nothing worse than a bright, and very bored, child."

Alric stalked over to claim a seat by the dying fire. The rest of us sat at the bar.

"Can we hear the story, too?" I looked around. "And did Mathilda leave already?" I knew she was going to get her house, but I was surprised she left this early.

"She was wiser than I. She had a feeling your trip would be quick and left for her house less than fifteen minutes ago. Amara escorted her and should be back soon." Lorcan looked at Alric. "Maybe another time for the stories though. I take it the trip was a success? I admit, I expected it to take longer."

Padraig and Covey filled him in. I stayed at the bar, adding a word here or there, but mostly watching Alric. It was more than just annoyance at having his childhood become fodder for bedtime stories. The edgy anger that had been hovering around him was back.

And he was rubbing the arm where the geas was as he stared into the fire.

I finally joined him. Aside from a brief half smile when I sat down, he didn't respond. "Maybe you shouldn't have the chest on you. It's setting off the geas."

"No, it's not." He looked down. He'd obviously been rubbing his arm without thought. "Damn it. Yes, it is. I'm doing it again, aren't I?"

"If you mean being a jerk, yeah, kind of. Having that thing flaring up all the time can't be good for you."

He ran his fingers through his hair. There were times I missed the black color he'd dyed it when we first met. But the way the firelight lingered on the blond was pretty impressive. "We should give these to Lorcan anyway." He got up, held out a hand to help me up, then we went back to the bar.

"Excellent timing," Padraig said. "I know opening the chest right now wouldn't be a good idea, but having Lorcan look at the scrolls might be."

Alric nodded then pulled out both small bags and put them on the bar. "I shouldn't be carrying anything associated with the relics." As he spoke he pulled back the sleeve of his shirt and picked up both bags in the hand with the geas. The geas mark flared.

Lorcan took the bags from him and turned his arm to study the geas. He finally let go and shook his head. "We have to find a way to diffuse this mark. I'm afraid I know of nothing to get rid of it completely. Heaven help you if the destroyers of the Ancients are still alive somewhere. You will be completely at the mercy of this mark. But we should be able to make it less reactive with some work." He opened the first bag and withdrew the scrolls.

Padraig hovered over him. "Those weren't in the chest when we first opened it. Nothing was."

"Interesting," Lorcan unrolled one and peered at it. "Definitely Ancient, but a very old dialect even for them. I will leave them to you for now." He handed the scrolls and the bag to Padraig. "Although, don't you want some sleep? We will be heading north for the sphinx; but being as none of us have slept, we should wait until the day after tomorrow. We will also need to find horses, at the least."

They left the spell bubble that Alric had created on the chest, and Lorcan did a quick external examination. He finally shook his head and put it back in the faery bag. "I'm afraid that until we don't have to worry about destroying homes or businesses, we should keep this secured." He tucked the bag into a pocket inside his robes. "Impressive spell bubble by the way, Alric. That one and the one they told me you flung when the body exploded. Siabiane would be proud."

Alric gave a crooked grin. "Thank you. I didn't realize

you knew she'd taught them to me."

"I knew everything," Lorcan said, but then his smile fell. "Or I thought I did. Many of us thought we did, we were wrong." His face looked like he'd aged a thousand years right before my eyes.

I faked a yawn and stretch that really wasn't much of a fake. "I think I'm going to sleep in one of the drunk rooms." I picked up my pack and headed back. Lorcan had held up pretty well over the last few months with everything that had happened to him and his people. What he needed now was rest.

CHAPTER TWENTY–FIVE

I WANTED TO ALSO GIVE ALRIC some space. It was good he knew he was being a jerk, but it wasn't really his fault. If we could just keep the relics and their associated items away from him, he'd be okay. Right after we hunted down the diamond sphinx. I wanted to ask where exactly we were heading, but it really didn't matter. The furthest true north from here I'd ever been was less than a day's ride, so knowing where we were going would have little meaning to me.

One thing about Amara being Foxy's wife; the Shimmering Dewdrop was the cleanest seedy pub in the land. The drunk room was two hard bunks, but they had blankets and pillows. Nothing fancy nor expensive, but good and clean.

I had just settled in when the door opened and Covey came in. "Sorry, I'm not a certain elf. Lorcan went to sleep in the other room but Alric and Padraig are still talking. Amara's back and has joined in, but Foxy tumbled off to bed." She dropped her stuff on the second cot. "We need sleep, I know. But are you okay?"

I rolled up on one elbow. "I will be. We have enough things to worry about besides me worrying that I'm losing Alric." Saying the words out loud was far more painful than just thinking them.

She sat at the edge of her bed. "He was terrified when we came to and you were gone. Padraig almost had to spell

him to calm him down. He might not be the most romantic of souls, but he does love you."

"I know." My smile fell. "Or I did know. That geas and
these relics are driving him crazy and that's driving me
crazy. I didn't mean to upset any of you when I left, but I'd
do it again in the same circumstances. I thought it was the
only way to save you. Covey, it was like I went berserk."
She, of all people, should understand that.

"I can't help you with your magic, or whatever spell
turned you into that creature, but I can help with that.
It might be better not to know what you changed into.
Part of my problem was the history of my people and
our berserker era. I knew exactly what I had become. But
meditation did help me, so it might help you. I don't know
that you'll change again, especially if it was something that
Nivinal did, but it can't hurt to be ready."

We spent the next fifteen minutes with her trying to
teach me meditation techniques, and me trying to stay
awake. She finally gave up. "Go to sleep. From what I saw
of our trip, we'll be on the road for at least a week, we can
work on it then."

My period of dreams seemed to come and go. I hadn't
dreamt much before this stuff with the relics started, but
after that it became a dream-free-for-all. Then the dreams
vanished when I was on the road with the faeries. Now
they were back again.

This time I was looking down a well. Inside of it were all
of my friends, looking up at me in anger, fear, and hope-
lessness. I slowly dumped dirt on them until I couldn't see
them anymore. I felt and saw myself doing it, but I had no
control over my motions. I screamed in my head to stop,
but my arms just kept on shoveling.

I didn't scream myself awake, but I was sobbing. I needed
to find out what was causing these horrible dreams and

find a spell to block it.

I tried rolling over and going back to sleep, but the curtains were thin, and while I'd only gotten a few hours of sleep, it was clear the sun was up and had been for an hour or so.

Covey was asleep and softly snoring. I gathered my things and went out to the front. Foxy and Amara had a pair of bathrooms, and they'd shown us before that one had a secret passageway to a large shower.

Dogmaela was sleeping near the back door. I doubted this was her regular home, but she'd probably moved in when Foxy went missing and wasn't going to leave until everything settled down.

I had a quick shower, changed, and came back out to the pub proper to find a full breakfast, along with a massive pot of tea, waiting for me. At least I assumed it was for me. No one else was around.

Amara popped her head out of the kitchen. "Dig in. You'll be having a long day of it, and who knows when you'll get another real meal. I will be putting together road food, but still…" She rolled her eyes, nodded her head, and darted back into the kitchen.

I would have pointed out that we weren't leaving until tomorrow, but her food smelled too good to walk away from for even a moment. Halfway through the meal it dawned on me she might know something that we didn't—that whole being a goddess thing.

By the time I finished eating, Covey, Padraig, and Lorcan had come out, showered, and been presented with huge piles of food and tea.

I narrowed my eyes. Alric wasn't the last one to get up unless he was seriously injured, and I knew there was no way the geas had messed him up that badly.

"How long ago did he leave?" I didn't mention Padraig, but he'd been the last one with Alric, so my comment was aimed at him.

Padraig wasn't a good liar. He looked up from his tea and glanced around. When I scowled, he swallowed. "Alric? I'm not sure. Not that long ago, I'd think."

"Does anyone think our lone-wolfing-again elf should be out on his own?" I waited until everyone looked up.

"He said he wanted to do some recon on the hill, see if there was evidence of what happened when the mayor came in and when Largen was killed," Padraig said. "He left before I went to bed, and honestly I thought he'd be back by now." He held up his hand. "But Foxy went with him."

I'd been about to jump out of my chair and run after him, but those last words settled me down. Worst-case scenario, if Alric was being really stupid, Foxy could pick him up and carry him back.

"Why did you let him go? Alric hasn't been himself lately at all." Covey got out in between bites. She looked ready to take off after him herself, but there was no way she was going to do that until she finished her food.

I wasn't afraid so much for Alric; I was afraid he was going to do something stupid, like go take on all of the bad guys at once. A thought hit me. "Amara?" I called out. I was afraid to go into the kitchen when she was working.

"Did you need more?" She popped out of the kitchen with a full bowl in her hand.

"No, but you can sense Foxy, right?" I knew she'd had some trouble when he'd been grabbed. Most likely that was because she could sense him vaguely, but whatever spell was being used to hide them blocked her from narrowing it down. Hopefully no one was blocking him this time

"Aye," she said, then closed her eyes and tilted her head. A small smile played on her face, then dropped and she opened her eyes. "They are fine, but your elf is causing him distress."

Both Padraig and I jumped to our feet.

Amara waved us down. "It's annoyance. Whatever Alric is doing, it's bothering Foxy because he thinks it's stupid."

"That's Alric," both Padraig and I said.

"Are they on the Hill?"

"No, they are near my hedge. You don't want me to let him out, do you? He is trying to find a way and I think that is contributing to Foxy's annoyance."

"No!" All of us said in unison.

"In fact, could you have your hedge smack him in the head for me?" He and Foxy probably started looking into things on the Hill, then Alric decided to make a run for it. There could be a legitimate reason for them being down there, but the fact that Foxy was annoyed told me Alric was definitely trying to get out.

Amara closed her eyes, then laughed. "I did, and he is standing down."

"We should go see what his issue is." I nodded to Padraig.

"Might as well all go. I can out run him if he tries to run, and between Lorcan and Padraig they have more spell fire power than he does." Covey had finished chasing the last bit of food around her plate.

"Yes, maybe that would be best. Foxy's annoyance is increasing." A tiny line appeared between Amara's brows.

I must have been really hungry after my shower. I finally noticed that the faeries and Bunky and Irving were missing as well. "And where did the faeries and constructs go?"

Dogmaela had come out from the kitchen and was loading up our dishes. "They are sitting in the tree." The emphasis on *the* told me she meant Amara's tree.

The pub wasn't open yet, so we'd see what they were up to once we went out the back way. If they looked iffy, I'd set them on a task of some sort. I could only worry about one troublemaker at a time.

I was the first one ready, so I went out the back. Dogmaela was right, the faeries were scattered all over the tree—and far more than my current group of twenty-three. Bunky and Irving were hovering at the top. And about thirty squirrels were also there. My sword had been sticking around as of late, so I had it out and the start of a push spell as I stepped into the alley.

"Girls? Who are your friends?" They didn't seem distressed, and a quick glance at the squirrels indicated that none of them had those odd amulets on.

"See? Is told you!" Garbage wasn't responding to me, but she was pointing. The extra faeries took to the air, buzzed near me, and vanished.

The squirrels looked at me, gave odd little bows, and scampered down the alley.

"Can someone tell me what that was about?"

"Squirrelable!" Crusty shouted. She'd used that term before when we were in the aqueducts. According to her it meant something good. She refused to explain beyond that.

"We meet. Make plans. Is good. They see you now." Garbage buzzed around proudly.

"They didn't see me before?" I had a feeling there was more to that and every little bit would help. There was a nagging suspicion that what the faeries were doing was going to be important at some point.

"Saw, but no seeee." Crusty had begun a conversation with a branch, but looked up to answer me.

"Yes. Back soon!" Garbage yelled and twenty-three faeries flew off. Bunky and Irving circled me once and then followed them.

"Where did they go?" Covey asked as she and the others came up behind me.

"I have absolutely no idea, but I don't think they are up to anything bad." Maybe that was false optimism, but I was okay with it.

Padraig led the way, which was good as I was just going to start at the Hill and work my way down until I hit the hedge. "Amara was able to give me a better idea where they are, especially after you asked her to have the hedge hit Alric."

Beccia looked almost normal. The shops were open and a fair amount of people were roaming around doing everyday things.

It took far less time than I expected to find Foxy and Alric, and it was a good thing we did, too. Foxy looked about two seconds away from throwing Alric over his shoulder. That he had his hand on him wasn't a good sign.

"I'm right, this is—" Alric cut off as he spotted us. "You can tell him, we have to get out of here. We have to take down this hedge." Alric's green eyes had too much white around them and he was shaking.

"Why?" Padraig stepped forward and motioned for Foxy to step back. "We're fine here, Alric. Why do you need to leave?"

"We have to leave." He looked quickly to all of us. "This hedge is killing us. If we can take it down, everything will be fine."

Now it was Lorcan's turn to step forward. With a frown he cast a spell at Alric. It glowed, then went black and crumbled. "He's spelled. Did that crime lord you met up with touch him? He is a dwoller mage, right?"

"Yes, he is, but I don't think he touched him." Padraig looked to Alric, but whatever Lorcan's spell had done had mostly shut him down. He was standing, his eyes wide, but he didn't look like he was aware of what was going on.

"He did though. When they were having their pissing contest," Covey said. "Cirocco tapped Alric's shoulder. Why? Did he have to touch him to spell him?"

I was with Covey on this one. Cirocco was a serious mage, and he shouldn't have to touch anyone.

"For this one he did." Lorcan stepped forward and tapped Alric's shoulder. Another spell was cast and this time Alric crumpled to the ground.

I ran forward and pulled his head into my lap. "Is he

okay?" His eyes were shut, but his chest was moving.

"He will be." Lorcan stepped back looking fatigued. "That was a nasty spell. If Alric didn't have strong magic himself, the hedge would be down and he would probably have joined Cirocco and whoever else is out there."

I looked down at him. His face wasn't settled as if in sleep, but more as if he was fighting something off. Like he was having a nightmare. "He will wake up, right?"

"Yes, this is part of his own magic; my spell had to work through his defenses, and then fight off that dwoller's magical attack. Nasty spell, and definitely one only used by their kind. It's how they hunt."

"I thought Cirocco was being too agreeable," Covey said. "He must have planned this."

"Or he just couldn't stand that Alric bested him again," I said. Alric was slowly stirring. His eyes fluttered open but it took almost a full minute for him to register who I was.

"How in the hell did I get here?" He looked up to Foxy. "You and I were going to the Hill to look for evidence. Beyond that, I don't recall a thing." He shuddered. "Yes, I do. A hole. I was in a hole and there was no way out."

He didn't mention me, or look my way, but the connection to my dream was too close.

"Thank you." He patted my leg then rolled to his feet. "That asshole spelled me, didn't he?"

"You started acting weird once we got to the Hill. Stormed through a few abandoned houses, and then said the hedge was the problem." Foxy shook his head. "You was a stubborn one for certain. Even claimed I'd made the hedge attack you. Was this close to dragging you back." Foxy held his fingers about three inches apart.

"There was something on the other side of the hedge I needed to see." He walked a few feet over and stopped. "Right here." He started shaking and collapsed again.

"Is this part of his defenses?" I really didn't think it looked effective if it was.

Lorcan was beside him in a moment then glared at the hedge. "No. But we need that hedge open."

Amara was much better at sensing what was going on than we thought, or she'd improved in the past fifteen minutes. Or she had a way to spy through her hedge. A corridor appeared right where Alric had stopped.

Alric was unconscious. "Foxy and Lorcan, stay here and keep him safe." I nodded to Padraig and Covey. "Let's go see what Cirocco was really up to." I was the first one through, so I got to scream first. It was perfectly justified when faced with a semi-decapitated dwoller laying in front of the hedge.

Padraig and Covey were right behind me.

It was Cirocco for certain, but while he looked like he might have been lying there for a while, the partial decapitation was fairly recent, judging by the pale dwoller blood oozing out. His hands were clenched, and a piece of paper was clutched in one.

I didn't want to move closer, but I also needed to know what that was. I moved toward the body.

"Let me, it might be spelled." Padraig stepped forward. He kept one hand held over the body and reached forward with the second to free the paper. Then he dropped a spell bubble over the body.

"There are too many spells here. I can't be certain that this man actually cast the spell on Alric. Or if he did, it might have been something different. But somehow the spell on Alric was tied to him, so now that he's dead, Alric should recover."

I pulled out my sword, looking around the empty landscape. "The killer is still here?"

CHAPTER TWENTY–SIX

COVEY TILTED HER HEAD, AND then shook it. "Not that I can tell. His body is bringing me close to ber-serker, so my senses are extremely up right now. But he was lying here for a while before he was finally killed."

Padraig leaned closer to the body. "Someone knew of the tie Cirocco had placed between him and Alric, and they were torturing Cirocco to get the hedge down."

"As good a reason as any to keep it up then," Alric said as he came through the hedge, looking no worse for his adventure into being spelled. Lorcan, Foxy, and even Amara followed.

I did a double take at that, she hadn't been there a moment ago. I guessed that goddesses could move fast if they needed to "What did the paper say?"

Padraig let go of his spell over the body and tried to unfold the crumpled paper. It took a while. "He was hang-ing on to this with all of his might." Finally he gave up and held it to Alric. "It says for you, and won't open no matter how hard I try."

Alric had been more than his share of annoying lately, but I was disturbed at how easily he'd been taken over. And knocked out twice. I wasn't sure if he should be opening anything from anyone at this point. Of course, before I could try and talk some logic into his hard elven head, he'd ripped open the note. Then flipped it over, said a few soft swear words, and flipped it back.

"It's from Cirocco all right, but it just says 'run'. And even that didn't appear at first."

Lorcan leaned over but pulled back when Alric went to hand the paper to him. "Better you keep a hand on it, my boy. It's spelled, and a lot of power went into it. Do you have another one of the faery bags?"

"One left." Alric shook his head and didn't make a move for his pocket. "But do we need to save it? I think I can remember this message." His hand shook as a jolt arced from the paper to his skin. "Damn it, it's changing. 'You stupid elf, get yourself and your people out of here.' Seriously? It even sounds like Cirocco in my head."

I looked down at the body. I'd done jobs for Cirocco, Alric being one of them, but never liked the man. That might change if he actually died trying to help us. It was debatable that was what was going on, but I had hope.

"I hate to agree with such a vile person," Amara said. "But I do think you should leave sooner than later."

Padraig nodded. "And I think we can safely assume that whoever replaced Largen is aware that we know she was replaced and she was involved with killing Cirocco. We need to get horses and leave by nightfall."

"Couldn't we leave before dark?" I wasn't a huge fan of horseback travel, nor traveling at night.

Alric pulled out his last faery bag, folded the note into it with a few spell words of blocking, and then put it back in his cloak pocket. "The darkness will help. The syclarions function about as well as humans do in the dark, which will be an advantage for us." He grinned at me. "I promise not to let you get lost. We'll get a clearthin glow working for you."

I folded my arms and shot him a scowl, but it was good to hear him being a smartass again.

Padraig nodded to Lorcan. "Do you want to, or me?" He held one hand over Cirocco's body.

"Go ahead, my boy. Just make sure all trace is gone."

Padraig nodded and Cirocco's body vanished. As well as a good foot of ground underneath it. "Got it all." He and Lorcan turned back toward the hedge.

Once we were back on the Beccian side of the hedge, Amara closed the corridor up tight. The greenery also grew a foot taller and was either moving further into the village or had gotten thicker.

She saw me looking at it. "I don't like them targeting my hedge. I will keep it up as long as needed. Some might follow you once they know you are on the road, but I fear the rest might not until they realize what they are after is with you. This is my town now."

Alric and Padraig broke off down a side street as soon as we hit the road with the pub on it. They would get horses for the trip.

"I'm going to swing by my house and grab extra supplies," Covey said. "Do you want to come with?"

I looked to the others who were continuing on to the pub. There really wasn't much I needed to do there; my pack wasn't big enough to take much time getting together. Besides, maybe I could borrow some items from Covey. I might have some stuff I could use back at my house, but that last visit had left me not feeling like I wanted to go back any time soon.

"Yeah." The route to her house made me think of Harlan. "I wonder if the rest of them are okay?" We'd separated to try and gather as much support for whatever was going to happen with these relics as possible. Harlan and his newest ladylove, Orenda, had gone up to the land of her isolated people. He'd had some faeries assigned to him, and none had come back that I knew of. But there were some nasty things loose in the world.

Not to mention, I wasn't sure how a bunch of extremely xenophobic and isolated elves were going to react to him—or what he and Orenda were going to tell them.

"I was thinking of the old cat as well," Covey said. She

didn't agree with some of his tactics, and they often argued about interpretations of finds, but they were mostly friends. "We could check and see if the direction we're heading is close to where Orenda's enclave is."

I grinned. "My thoughts completely." Harlan and Covey were my two oldest friends, aside from the faeries. He drove me crazy a lot of the time, but it would be good to at least check in on him.

As far as I knew, Covey hadn't been back home since the night we'd joined Locksead and his crew to go look for relics outside of Kenithworth.

I was pretty sure she hadn't left the door open.

Covey saw it the same time I did, but her reaction was far faster. I was still pulling out my sword, useless if the house had been broken into months ago, and she was already at the front door.

Covey was inside yelling and kicking furniture. On closer examination, she wasn't kicking furniture but small, red-capped beings who were lounging on her furniture. The house looked far neater than mine usually did, and there were lace doilies covering every even remotely flat service.

Every space that didn't have a brownie on it at any rate.

I understood her annoyance, having your house broken into and doilied within an inch of its structural life would be hard for anyone. Not to mention that the brownies we'd run into before had been working for the bad guys— or at least trying to. As a species they had decided to try and help the rakasa regain power. That many of them were eaten by said rakasa hadn't slowed them down.

These weren't moving. The ones Covey kicked flew in the air briefly, then crashed to the ground and stayed still. The ones she hadn't booted yet were equally still. "Are they dead?" Fifty or so dead brownies in a house was grounds for saving what you could and burning the house to the ground in my book.

"What?" Covey stopped her rampage of kicking the

small squatters and looked around. "I didn't kill them—these things are almost as indestructible as faeries." She picked one off her doily encrusted sofa by the arm and shook it.

The little creature opened one eye, shook his head, and then closed the eye. "Not time, woman."

Yes, Covey was a woman. But no woman, especially a trellian academic, would enjoy being disregarded in that manner. She threw him against the wall.

"All of you, get out of my house now, and take your doilies with you!"

I personally would want to know why in the hell they'd taken over her house and why they appeared to be hibernating. I couldn't blame her for just wanting them out though.

She stalked through the kitchen and into the two bedrooms and bathroom. "They are everywhere. My house looks fine, but these…things…are all over."

I knew that look; she was going to make me help her remove the brownies and doilies. If there were about fifty in this room alone, I shuddered at the estimated full body count. I sheathed my sword and rubbed my hands together. "I have a plan."

She'd been standing in the kitchen, but she was in my face and grabbing my hands in half a second. "No magic."

"My magic isn't that bad, you know." I scowled at her. "I was actually thinking that some faeries might get them moving." I said faeries loud enough that if they had been faking they would have reacted. Faeries and brownies really didn't like each other. And that was before Garbage kidnapped and harassed one when she thought they'd been involved in taking Leaf and Crusty.

None of the brownies moved, even the one who'd taken a full face-plant into the wall. Covey looked around. I was sure she was weighing the damage the faeries could bring against the annoyance of these brownies. Not to mention, who knew what they'd been doing in her house while she was gone.

"Fine, call your little hellions. But they are only to remove the brownies and their weird doilies, nothing else."

I smiled and sent a mental call for the girls. Normally I'd add mental bottles of ale to get them to respond. Even though they knew I probably didn't have any on hand, they couldn't take that chance and usually responded. This time, I just used the image of Covey's front room filled with passed out brownies.

Our mental communication only worked one way, so I was never sure if they received my call until they showed up.

Luckily we still had the front door open as the faeries came in fast and with war feathers on. The door would not have fared well.

"We take!" Garbage's yell could have woken the dead, and it worked on the brownies. Being kicked around did nothing; a war cry from the faeries got all of the brownies to their feet in seconds.

"This our place! Leader took it!" A slightly larger brownie yelled from atop a doily on the table next to Covey's favorite chair.

Garbage was in his face in a second, waving her war stick under his nose. "This place protected by us. Your leader cried here. I make him cry. I make YOU cry."

The brownies had recovered quickly from their hibernation, or long nap, or whatever they had been doing. Maybe a little too quickly. When Garbage yelled her last line, all of the faeries—far more than my twenty-three again—yelled and charged the brownies.

To a man, the brownies screamed and passed out.

The faeries yelled again, but this time in victory. Garbage turned to lead her flock out, but Covey and I beat them to the door and slammed it shut.

"I wanted you to chase them out, not knock them back

out. They are in the same state as when we started. You need to go pick them up and dump them outside, some-where near The Hill would be good," I said and then shook my finger. "And no rivers or lakes. Somewhere inside the hedge." I didn't really care if the brownies were outside the hedge, I just didn't want the faeries going back and forth.

Garbage rattled her war stick at me, but the rest of her band stayed back. She finally folded her arms and sighed. "They hibernating. Easy to knock out when deep sleep. Stupid." She looked over her shoulder at the collapsed brownies. "Easy kill too."

"No killing. Just take them out, and their weird doilies too." I had no idea why they had doilies, and I didn't want to know. I figured Covey was going to lose her temper if they weren't removed soon though. She was a neat freak, but she was not a doily person.

Garbage looked to Covey, probably hoping that she'd be more inclined for bloody mayhem. Covey shook her head. "All of them please. They are in every room."

"Is fine." Garbage turned and yelled to the troop in native faery. Pairs of faeries joined up to each grab half a brownie and a doily.

I opened the door and they started hauling them out.

Covey waited until the brownie-dump operation was under way before she stalked into her kitchen. I knew we would probably have more food than we could carry with Amara stocking us, but she was looking for knives not food. She handed one to me and stepped in close. "There is something other than a brownie in the back bedroom. I just heard some thumps from what must be my closet."

I knew Covey's hearing was far better than mine was, but to be able to discern that out here, with the faeries chattering as they worked, was impressive.

"I have a sword, you know." I patted my sheath…only to find it empty. "Damn it."

"It vanished as we came in here. It wouldn't work in a

small space anyway; that thing is not only ostentatious, it's too big. Now, come on." Armed with kitchen knives, she led the way down the hall. Why anyone would hide in here with a bunch of passed-out brownies was beyond me.

The faeries had removed the brownies and accompanying doilies from her bedroom, but there was a noticeable rattling sound coming from the wardrobe in the back. Covey nodded for me to stand to the side, as she stepped forward to open the door.

I held my knife, seriously thinking maybe two would have been a better idea, and jumped back with a squeak as a body tumbled at my feet. A suspiciously familiar body.

CHAPTER TWENTY—SEVEN

IT WAS GRIMWOLD, SIDEKICK TO the late Cirocco, and a failed master criminal. He was dressed in a deranged version of the brownies' uniform, down to the red cap and a fake white beard. Well, theirs were real, his was hanging off in shreds.

"Mmmph!"

Covey removed his gag, but made no move toward the bonds tying his hands and feet together.

"They attacked me! I was doing nothing, and they attacked me. I've been in here for hours!"

His whining was already annoying me, and I wanted to put the gag back in his mouth.

"You're in my house, dressed like a giant, insane, brownie," Covey said as she toyed with the edge of her knife. "And somehow you were doing nothing, and they just grabbed you and shoved you into my closet. Dressed like them." She leaned lower to be closer to his face. "I've never liked you."

He tried to pull back but there was nowhere to go. "I might have dressed as them in an attempt to gain some solidarity. My magic seems to have stalled for the moment, and I am on the outs with my former employer—"

"Which one? They're both dead, unless you picked up someone new to latch on to." I would feel sorry for him, but he was just such a slime that I couldn't.

"Cirocco and Largen? Both? You two are far more

vicious than either of them gave you credit."

"I'd like to say we had a part, but Largen has been dead for months and Cirocco got killed a few hours ago by unknown persons."

He forgot he was tied up so his sudden instinct to jump to his feet had comical results. Covey pulled back a bit at the attempt though.

"Largen can't have been dead that long! I just talked to her a few days ago. She sent me here." He looked around. "Well, not here, per se. But inside that damn hedge. I was supposed to try and grab Foxmorton's dryad and get that thing taken down."

"How did you get inside the hedge?"

"Not saying anything else until you release me."

I shrugged and nodded to Covey. "Oh, she'll release you if you don't talk, but you probably won't like it. Let me make a guess, you came in through the aqueducts?"

The stillness of his face told me I was right.

"That way's destroyed now. By your own people, it looks like." Or the other group that was out there. I wasn't completely certain there were two groups. At least not anymore. They might have started as two, but I had a bad feeling Nivinal's mommy was calling the shots out there now.

"They left me? And Cirocco's really dead?" He deflated for a moment then shook himself out of it. "What is needed to gain my freedom? Obviously, you have me at a disadvantage."

I had to admit that was a quick recovery, especially for him.

"Tell me why you are in my house, dressed like a brownie, in the middle of a brownie slumber party, for starters. We don't have much time, but let's start there."

His sigh could have woken the dead. He waggled his feet, might have been moving his hands as well, he was lying back on them, so I couldn't see. "I don't suppose you could untie me first?"

"No, and you're stalling." Covey fussed with her knife some more. I thought about doing the same but, even with my knife training from Orenda, I'd probably end up cutting myself.

"I followed the brownies in. They had a way through the hedge, one I believe is gone now since they couldn't get back out. I disguised myself as them and they let me follow them in. Like I said, I was told to grab Foxmorton's mate since he was out of the picture. They don't know how she's doing it, but the folks on the other side know the dryad is making that hedge." He coughed. "Could I at least get some water? I was in there for hours."

Covey started to shake him off, and then shrugged. "Fine, but that's it."

She came back with a glass, poured some water into his mouth, and on him since she wouldn't get close, and then stood back expectantly.

"Job done!" Garbage and about half of the faeries came zooming into the room. "What this?" The tone in her voice clearly indicated she felt we'd been holding out on her. The faeries loved torturing Grimwold and had once forced him to run so far into a jungle he was lost for a few days.

"Now, now," I said, and held up my hands as she looked ready to attack and Grimwold looked ready to pass out. "He's telling us things we want to know. If he doesn't tell us what he knows, you and your entire troop of faeries can have him." Facing Garbage head on meant I could only see Grimwold out of the corner of my eye, but even I noticed his twitching.

Garbage didn't say anything but darted around me and hovered in front of Grimwold with folded arms and her crazy one-eye-closed stare. "You talk now."

"You'd better talk fast, I can't always control them." That was a laugh, I rarely could control them.

"I told you everything. I come in here, grab the dryad,

and take her back. The hedge falls. Cirocco and the others get what they want—a chest, a bunch of scrolls, and a map. Never told me what was in it, but must be a lot of gold, very valuable. Then we blow Beccia up." He froze; belatedly catching on that maybe admitting to being a part of a plan to blow up an entire town might be an issue with the residents of said town.

I gave him my own glare. "Were the brownies part of the plan?"

"I don't think so?" His voice went up at the end as he realized things weren't looking good for him getting out of here. "The mayor knew they were trying to find a way in, something about their leader following someone and finding a new home for them. When I couldn't get close to the dryad, and then you brought back Foxmorton, I decided to hide with them. Unfortunately, they have a bad bias against beings who drink. I got a bit drunk and they locked me up." He shivered. "They were planning on sleeping for a week."

"We have now?" Garbage didn't look impressed with his story, but I wasn't sure she had been listening to it.

"No, but we do need to leave him somewhere." I looked around, but I knew even if we could secure it, Covey wasn't going to lock him up in her home. "We could take him to Foxy's. He'd love to take care of him."

"No! Foxmorton will rend me limb from limb!"

"It's that or she lets the faeries have you," Covey said.

He looked from us to the gang of unstable looking faeries paying far more attention to him than anyone could ever want. Didn't even take ten seconds. "Foxmorton, please."

We left him tied up with the faeries and told them to watch but not touch unless he moved, then Covey and I went and grabbed the supplies we'd come for. Once we'd finished, and Covey had done a final check through, she darted out the front door.

She came back a minute later and parked a wheelbarrow outside the door. "Grab that old blanket I have in the closet, we can toss him in the barrow, cover him, and get him disposed of."

"I heard that!" Grimwold yelled from the back room.

"To the pub!" Covey rolled her eyes.

Loading him into the wheelbarrow was easier than I'd expected since the faeries stayed right near him the entire time.

We locked up her house and I put a spell of warding over it. It wouldn't hold nearly as well as one of Alric's, but it should keep the brownies from returning.

No one noticed as we pushed the wheelbarrow down the road and down the alley behind the pub. It was early, but there could be patrons inside, so dragging Grimwold through the back was a better idea. Neither of us trusted him so his gag had gone back on and he wasn't happy.

I was glad to see Amara's tree had finished its recovery and that there were no squirrels. I know the girls said the ones from this morning had been on our side, but after those maniacally possessed ones tried to destroy this tree, I wasn't sure if I trusted any small furry critters.

As if my thoughts brought it into being, a flash of white flittered among the branches. Could be an albino squirrel, and it was too far up there to tell, but my money was on the minkie. Of course the girls paid no attention to it.

We couldn't fit the wheelbarrow through the alley door, so Covey and I lifted Grimwold up. We kept the blanket on him and the three of us shuffled into the pub.

It looked like old times. Well, old times if you regularly came in during the daytime drinking hours. The tiny pack of daytime drinking gnomes were in place, and Foxy was regaling them with some tale. He nodded and tilted his head when he spotted Covey and me walking in a blanket-covered person.

"Foxy? Can we talk to you in the back?" I had both hands on Grimwold, so I pointed with my elbow to where the hidden bar room was.

Foxy wiped his hands on a towel, excused himself from his audience, and followed us into the room.

As I'd expected, everyone except Mathilda was there. Alric and Padraig were arguing over something on one of the more recent maps, while Lorcan was quietly working through about three books at once. Unlike the other two, he looked up when we walked in.

"Ladies, and who do we have here?" His words were pitched perfectly to get the other two to stop whatever they were arguing about.

"A friend," Covey said as she pulled off the blanket.

"Grimwold? What in the hells ye be wearing?" Foxy was the closest to us and Grimwold's outfit hadn't gotten any better looking during the awkward trip here.

"We found him and a gang of brownies in Covey's house," I said. "He was working for Cirocco and Largen."

Alric came closer and shook his head. "Were you trying to make the brownies think you were one of them? You're a bit too tall." He removed Grimwold's gag.

"I was improvising; too many things are changing around here. If you let me go—"

"He was going to grab Amara, then his bosses were planning on blowing up the town." Covey stepped back as she spoke, which was a good idea considering that as soon as the words were out, Foxy took one giant step and lifted Grimwold to the ceiling.

"Ye was going to do what?" Foxy could bellow if need be, and his face certainly looked angry enough to do so. But his quiet controlled voice was even scarier.

"I wasn't going to hurt her. I just needed to get that hedge of hers down...but she would have been safe from being blown up." His head dropped. Even he realized, yet again, he'd said the wrong thing.

Foxy shook him and made some sort of odd growl that I'd never heard before. Maybe Grimwold should have taken his chances with the faeries.

"I know how to get the diamond sphinx!" That yell got everyone's attention, and Foxy lowered Grimwold down to his eye level.

"You lie, I will smash you." Foxy put him on his feet, but not before another solid shake.

"Where is it and what is your source?" Padraig asked. He and Lorcan had held back, but the word sphinx had gotten their attention.

"I don't know where, but I know how." He tried to move an arm to point, but since he was still tied he only fell onto Foxy. "Your map there, Cirocco described it to me repeatedly before I came in here, so I could grab it. He said it's spelled." He beamed as if he'd invented cheese.

Now it was Alric's turn to glare him down. "We already knew that."

"You knew it could take you through the veil into a hidden realm and to the sphinx? Then why are you still here? Cirocco said once it's been triggered it will only work for a short time."

That we didn't know. At least I didn't know, and judging by the looks on the other's faces, they didn't either.

"The sphinx is in a *tir cudd*? One of the fabled hidden realms? How can this map take us to it?" Lorcan's voice was low and he looked like a kindly old elf. The glint in his eyes said he wasn't.

Grimwold could be pompous, but he wasn't always stupid. "I…I don't know. Cirocco knew how, but wouldn't tell anyone. Not even the mayor. It's spelled to show hidden things. If you're not seeing the way yet, maybe it's not triggered. He warned me not to use magic anywhere near it."

Lorcan turned back to the map and shook his head. "I'd say he told someone how to break it, or he wouldn't have been killed." He pointedly looked at Grimwold. "We probably want to get him out of here until we sort this out."

"There's nowhere to leave him that he won't escape." Grimwold had enough connections that I was sure he'd get out of jail in hours. Providing there was still a functioning jail and that we could get him into it.

"He be staying here," Foxy picked him up with one hand and marched for the door. "Amara and I will make sure he never escapes."

"But I can help!" Grimwold twisted in Foxy's grasp.

Alric stepped closer. "What do you know that can help?"

I figured if Grimwold knew anything else he would have yelled it out, but he just hung there. "Maybe you need another magic user? I'm sure mine will come back soon."

I felt a flare and an odd brush of magic as I'd never felt before from all three elves. Pure power flowed over me and, more importantly, Grimwold. If there was ever even the slightest doubt of the power of those three, it had just been shot to hell. Show offs.

"I think we're okay on that front. Lock him up, Foxy." Alric turned back to the map.

We crowded around the map as soon as Foxy shut the door behind him. It looked just as it had before. The marks of the chest and words in the corner were visible, but nothing else.

"What was that thing you three did? And was it a good idea considering Grimwold said no magic around the map?"

"It was a self-indulgent show of power, and we probably shouldn't have engaged, but I dislike that man immensely." Lorcan didn't even look up. "I have a feeling Cirocco just didn't want *Grimwold* using magic near it." He shook his head. "I can't feel anything else to it, no other layers. We might have to find Nasif and have him show it to us."

Covey glanced at the map, and then shook her head. "But I thought we knew where to go? You had tracked the thing down, somewhere to the north. Why do we need the map?"

I was thinking the same thing, but she beat me to it.

Padraig slid over another, smaller, and more normal looking map and tapped at some mountains at the top. "The research indicates that the diamond sphinx is in this providence in the far north. But it also states that it is hidden and only the strongest magics can find it. We'd figured that part could be addressed once we got there, but apparently Nasif had something already in this map. A *tir cudd* is as hidden as anything can get."

"I don't understand why he didn't tell us any of this?" Covey had given up looking at the magical map and was studying the mundane one. I knew we wouldn't need it now; she'd have memorized the entire thing.

"Nasif is brilliant, but he's also easily distracted. And to be honest, when he hid this map, it might have only been to hide the chest. I really feel nothing else of him from it." Lorcan shook his head.

"We have to leave soon," Alric had been standing back from the maps but I knew he'd visually take them apart later.

Lorcan sighed and rolled up the map. "Agreed. Let's get everything in the bags. I'd rather be ready to leave quickly if we need to. I'll send the faeries to warn Mathilda when we're on the move."

I would have helped with the storing of the scrolls, maps, and books, but the three of them were fast so both Covey and I stood back in case we accidently got shoved in a bag too. "One thing that's been bugging me," I said. Actually, there were a lot of things bugging me, and there had been ever since I first brought in Alric as my bounty over a year ago. "If the Ancients were gone and the syclarions diminished, how did all of the pieces of the weapon get scattered everywhere? And why is the sphinx in some sort of secret magic land and the rest weren't?"

"Ah, well, the best theory is that when the weapon was created, its maker didn't want it to be used against them, so they cast a spell to scatter it once it was used." Lorcan whipped out another map, this one from his cloak pocket. "See where all of them have been found? In a scatter pattern, but some had been moved. The sapphire manticore had been found by some ruin thieves before the Breaking, and apparently they smuggled it into the enclave without us noticing until it found you. I'll warrant that the relics had protection when they were scattered but it's broken down over the centuries. I plan on writing a paper once we've resolved this." His grin was pure crazy academician as he rolled up the map and dropped it back in his cloak pocket.

I shook my head and went with Covey to get everything else ready. We were facing forces that were trying to destroy the world as we knew it, and possibly could be able to pull it off, but he was thinking of his next academic paper. "Academics."

"That sounded like a swear word," Covey said as we gathered everything from the drunk room. Foxy must have taken over the other one for Grimwold as all of our belongings were now in this one.

"It was. Seriously, how do you not worry about what's going on? The focus is on papers?" Most of my things were together, so I finished and made sure the other bags were ready. The days were shorter this time of year, so we should be able to hit the road in a few hours. Maybe I'd sneak a nap in, or sit in the pub and pretend my life was normal again.

"Oh, we worry. We all do. But for those of us with the bent, the finding out is what is important. And once we find something new, we can't wait to share it."

I gave her a sideways look. "And gain some academic fame?"

"That never hurts." Her smile was predatory. "One of the ways to get through things like this is to talk about and visualize life after this is over. If you believe life will never be good again, even a new good, you're not going to survive anything."

I pulled back at that. Covey was one of the brightest people I knew—even hanging around these crazy elves—but she'd never been that self-aware before. "The training with the nuns?"

She laughed. "In part. I continued their training after I left them. Especially as I saw how dangerous things were getting." She paused and looked me in the eye. "Taryn, I have a feeling things are going to get a lot worse, and you're somehow in the middle whether you want to be or not. This could eat you alive."

I think it had already started. "I'll admit that I could use something. Maybe we can try the meditation again and I'll try not to fall asleep. And it would be nice to imagine a mundane existence again." All of the bags were bundled by the door.

The words had just gotten out of my mouth when the wall to the outside exploded.

CHAPTER TWENTY-EIGHT

R ATHER, IT WAS THE WALL from the room next to us that had exploded. Our section shook, and a crack formed under the small window, but it stayed in one piece.

"Grimwold." Covey and I said at the same time as we ran to the room next to ours. There was no way, even if his magic had been working right, that he would have had enough power to blow out a wall.

Foxy had beat us to the door and unlocked it as we got to him. Yup, the entire outer wall was gone. Judging from the rubble, it had been pulled out, not exploded out. We ran through the room and out to the street but there was nothing to be seen. Except one pair of full-sized footprints and a bunch of tiny ones.

I picked up a rope lying on the ground and followed it to a small hook that had wall rubble on it. "The brownies? Why in the heck would they have rescued him? And I thought they were hibernating?" I looked up and down the road again, but saw no other sign. The only footprints were the ones close to us, going through the destroyed wall; once they got to the street there was nothing to be seen.

Beccia wasn't back up to its normal self, but there were some curious folks coming out of the nearby businesses and pubs. Alric, Padraig, and Lorcan came out as well. Amara stood near the door with a pike-wielding Dog-maela right behind her.

Alric stalked around the rubble, shaking his head. "I can't tell that any magic was used. But something motivated those brownies."

The faeries had been off and about but came tearing back down the street. Considering how fast they could fly and how long it took them to get here, they must have been at the far end of town. Or very focused on something.

"We chase!" Garbage had her current band of faeries with her. They took off down the road in the direction of the vanishing footprints before I could decide if that was a good idea or not.

Padraig also looked around, and then he threw a spell at it. The rubble re-built itself into a wall and magic filled in the missing pieces.

We marched back to the pub and moved everything, including way more food than we could possibly eat, into the back room to wait until closer to dark.

"I'd say someone other than the brownies wanted to get Grimwold out," Padraig said. "Brownies aren't the strongest willed lot, and it wouldn't be that hard to take them over, particularly if they were in hibernating mode. I already warned Amara to fortify her hedge."

Alric shook his head. "We might need to re-think waiting for darkness. If they know where we're heading, it won't matter if they see us leave or not."

"True. And the longer we stay here, the more danger to Beccia's people," Covey said. "If it wasn't that difficult to manipulate magic through those brownies, then they might also try to get them past the hedge. They could use them and Grimwold to do what they want. The sooner we leave, the sooner they, hopefully, will leave the town alone."

"We find! Help!" Garbage yelled from outside the door. The faeries had developed an on-again-off-again ability to pop through solid objects. This must be one of their off times.

I opened the door and got bowled over by a gang of faeries bringing in struggling brownies. Like before, it took two faeries to one brownie, even though the brownies weren't that much larger than the faeries. Fifteen pairs of faeries came through with their brownies, then a bunch of solo faeries.

Garbage shook her head as I shut the door behind the final ones. "Not get all. They dug through plant."

"They tore through the hedge?" Considering how close Amara was to her hedge, I had trouble believing she wouldn't have noticed if it had been dug through.

"No, under, had hole. We destroy." Leaf was closer to me than Garbage and punched the brownie she was carrying when he tried to get away.

"Yes, but big one got out." Garbage scowled.

"Grimwold?" Alric came up to where the faeries were hovering with their catch. "Does anyone have a cage for these?" He waved a hand at the struggling brownies and they stopped struggling. "Their metabolism is odd, so I can knock them out for a short while, but whoever is working through them will just wake them up again. And could possibly be gathering information from what they see and hear."

There was one hanging a bit lower near me. I reached forward when something red flickered under its vest. "And that would be a yes on all of those counts." I pulled off an amulet similar to what Alric had taken off the squirrels.

I handed it to Alric; he said a few spell words and the red light dimmed. Then he said the same words toward the brownies being held. "This isn't good. We need to lock them up and get out of here, now." He put the amulet in a pocket, most likely where he was keeping the other one.

Lorcan nodded and held out a crate he'd found behind the bar. "I've spelled this to hold them, for a short while at least. You're correct; whoever is controlling them is still trying. I can feel the pulling but can't sense the source."

The faeries holding brownies dropped them into the crate and Lorcan sealed it shut.

"Didn't want to be interrupting, but is everything okay? I saw the faeries bringing in some friends?" Foxy stuck his head in.

"We need you to hide this, and keep it safe as long as possible," Padraig said and pointed to the crate. "We're not waiting for nightfall and will be leaving now. Are you and Amara ready with the distraction?"

"Distraction?" That was new to me.

"Something ye elf friend and I came up with to keep the eyes away from you all leaving out the back and out of town. Aye, Amara and Dogmaela be ready. Give us a nod and we'll start." He grabbed the crate then went back toward the door. "I can find a nice safe spot for this. Never you worry." He left, and everyone started putting on their packs. The horses that Alric and Padraig had bought were magically hidden in an abandoned stable not far off the alley, near the hedge.

"Do I want to know what the distraction is?" Part of me was curious, the other a bit concerned.

"Amara and Dogmaela are going to sing," Padraig said. "Nothing too wild, but Amara is going to put some special effort into it. Along with plants, her people can use some sound magic. They should cast a light spell that won't be picked up by any other magic users and keep everyone in town focused on them, whether they are in the pub or not."

Covey nodded. "There have been theories of the connections between plants and music, it's interesting to know that on some level they might be right."

The faeries buzzed around aimlessly after their fun of hunting the brownies. Garbage had sent the extra ones back to wherever they came from, but her faery gang still appeared out for trouble. If we were trying to be stealthy about leaving, having them on the warpath and traveling with us as we left Beccia wasn't a good idea.

"Hey, girls, I think Lorcan needed you to take a message to Mathilda; right, Lorcan?" I hoped this would work; they were getting more fidgety as I watched.

He'd been lost in his own thoughts but caught on quickly. "Ah yes. We do need to let her know of our movements. She and her cottage should be moving toward the east of us. I need you to stick together and get the message through."

"All? I send those." Garbage pointed to a clump of her faeries. Clearly, she didn't want to be left out of whatever we were doing.

"I need all of you to go; it is a very important task. Once you get to her, you must guard her and her cottage. Only all of you working together can do that." Lorcan held out a handful of sugar and the faeries swarmed him, each grabbing a piece, shoving it in their mouths, and flying back.

Garbage had taken the biggest piece, so she had to remove it before she spoke. "We do." Then she shoved it back in her mouth and flew toward the door.

I opened the door again and she favored me with a nod as if this was her decision, then led her troop back out through the pub.

"At least that's taken care of, thank you, Lorcan." Considering he was still in the 'aren't faeries cute' stage, I wasn't sure how well that was going to go. I'd just wanted them to stay clear while we were leaving, but sticking with Mathilda for a bit was a good idea too. Bunky and Irving were far better at staying inconspicuous, even if, just by existing, they were quite noticeable. I'd realized that the people of Beccia simply ignored what they didn't understand.

Maybe I should've followed their lead.

"Attention!" Foxy's voice boomed through the pub and out the open front door. He had a great voice for speaking over the din of a crowded pub, but given the time, there couldn't be more than a dozen people out there. Needless to say, they immediately went quiet.

"Today we have a treat. My lovely wife Amara will be singing a song from her homeland, accompanied by Dogmaela."

Amara's voice was clear like a stream, with Dogmaela hitting the lower notes.

"And that's our cue," Lorcan said as he led the way.

No one, aside from Foxy, even glanced at us as we skirted past the main part of the pub and out the alley door. People in the streets had stopped and were facing the pub but didn't look at us.

Bunky and Irving flew low over our heads; another advantage of them over the faeries, Bunky understood a lot more than they did. Or the faeries understood, but they just didn't care.

We got to the horses and rode to the hedge. Amara had triggered it to respond to my touch again. Alric had wanted it to be him, but she obviously didn't trust him after his earlier problem.

I got off my horse and put a hand on the greenery. Nothing happened. I glanced at the others, but they just shrugged. Lorcan gave me a nod. I put two hands on it.

It was only the last few months of freakish things happening to me that kept me from screaming as the branches reached out and engulfed me.

CHAPTER TWENTY—NINE

GREENNESS ENVELOPED ME, BUT ASIDE from the pressure from the plant surrounding me as it pulled me forward, I didn't feel pain. A vision of that severed rakasa arm we'd found made me rethink the scream, but while it was definitely pushing me forward, the hedge wasn't hurting me.

"I don't think this is what Amara meant." I kept my mouth closed after saying the words, as some leaves got a bit too close. I felt odd talking to a bunch of shrubbery, but the movement stopped. "We need a passage for us and our horses." The hedge kept pushing me forward, but now I felt an opening behind me.

"I'm sorry, Taryn; sometimes he can be too literal." The voice was Amara, but it was coming from all around me.

I tumbled out on the other side as the hedge set me free. My friends, with Alric leading my horse, followed.

I brushed off the extra plant life I'd gathered, and then got on my horse. I hadn't been thrilled about riding, but that horse looked wonderful after being pushed around by a plant. "That was…different."

"We do apologize," Amara's disembodied voice came from behind us. "Safe travels and good luck." Her last words dropped as the hedge closed behind us.

My sword reappeared in its sheath. "Good of you to show up after the threat is gone." I patted it.

"Are you okay?" Alric had been slipping back into surly

mode, a side effect from finding out Cirocco had taken him for a ride, but there was real concern in his eyes now.

"I'm fine. It didn't hurt me. To be honest, it felt more like a dog trying to get to know someone."

He nodded, but looked me over for injuries anyway. "Okay, then. Let's head toward the main road a few miles up. We can hit it earlier than that, but I'd rather we stuck to lesser known roads for a bit." Alric was definitely in his element skulking about; he was watching everything as we headed into the woods.

I really wasn't used to this part of Beccia. The outskirts to the north didn't have a lot of farms or houses and most traffic was to the west, headed toward Kenithworth. That town was to the north, but also off west quite a bit. If we were following the map, we were going straight north.

It didn't take long for night to follow, but I did feel better that we'd left when we did. In part because it meant less time riding in the pitch black. True to his word, Alric got a clearthin glow set up to follow me around, but it didn't make riding through the pitch dark woods that much better.

"How far until we camp?" There was only a slight whine in my voice, but I wasn't a horsewoman and we'd been riding for the last three hours. Any longer and my butt was going to go permanently numb.

"I would rather we go just a bit further," Lorcan said from his horse. He had one of the clearthin glows with him as well, but was using it to allow himself to read the mystery map. "Mathilda will join us tomorrow, so I'd like to time it correctly. We wouldn't want to miss her cottage."

"I don't think we can miss an entire cottage traveling along, but I need to get off soon." Covey stretched her back. "Or I can tie my horse to one of yours and I'll run alongside. My tailbone is not liking this."

"Sorry, Lorcan, this is a better place to stop," Alric said as a dozen clearthin glows flew overhead and illuminated a small clearing.

Even though we'd been on the road for a while, Alric was definitely the expert, so at his statement even Lorcan got off his horse.

Things still weren't normal between Alric and me. He was remained trapped in whatever was going on in his head. I didn't see it flare again, but I did catch him rubbing his arm in the location of the geas from time to time.

However, he clearly didn't want to talk about any of it, so I went to set up my tent.

We each had tiny, single person tents that looked like little more than thin fabric, but Amara had assured us they were extremely warm. She had a dryad friend with a magically enhanced silk pod tree who sent her reams of the fabric. I pointed out making clothing from it could be a nice side business for the pub.

"Things still off, eh?" Covey set her tent next to mine and had it up in a second. I had to refold mine three times before it finally worked.

"Yes," I said as I watched Alric set up his tent away from everyone. It should have made me feel better that he was avoiding everyone—but it didn't. "Was he like this the entire month I was gone?" He'd said it hit him when he got to Beccia, but I wasn't sure how the others felt.

"Yes and no. He was irrational when we realized you were gone, and then prickly that we were moving too slow once we tried to follow. Which asks the question of just how did you hold off a seriously motivated tracker as long as you did? We couldn't have been more than a few hours behind you when we took off, yet it wasn't until a day or so before we found you that we knew for sure we were on your trail." She grinned. "The faeries coming by and telling us that we were a bit off course didn't make Alric happy. Especially when they wouldn't stay with us and tell us what had happened to you."

"You know they just would have said I went boom."

I threw my pack in my tent. "I think it was the minkie blocking you from finding me." Alric could vouch for me if needed, but I might as well start admitting I was seeing tiny white critters. I just wouldn't mention it around the faeries.

Covey had been getting out some food and almost dropped it. "You've been hanging around the faeries too long."

I waved her off. "No, really. Alric saw it too. It's a tiny little beast that changes shape and color, and most people can't see. It also seems to have magic, and I have a feeling it was masking our trail somehow. Then it stopped right before we found Mathilda." I hadn't really thought about it, but there was a good chance that the minkie was just handing me off to her. She might have claimed never to have been aware of them—I had a feeling they were aware of her.

"I was going to ask what it looked like, but you just answered my question. How do you know it's a minkie? Especially if the girls don't see it?"

I briefly explained about the first time I saw it—when the faeries called it a minkie, then forgot.

"The critter wanted me to follow it after I'd changed. I didn't tell anyone, but it was what I followed to get us through the sands to the Spheres in the first place. So I thought it was as good as anything to follow." I shrugged. "Since it had led me away from you, I figure it might have been working to keep you off my trail."

"I don't even know what to say to that," Covey said as she ate. I was again amazed at her metabolism. We were hanging out with some fast metabolism, magic-using elves, and she ate them under the table.

"I've set up a guard shift roster," Alric said. "I don't think anyone directly followed us, but we have to assume they did, or at least were expecting us to move. Lorcan first, then Covey, Padraig, and me."

I stepped forward. "And me?"

"I didn't know if you'd be—"

I got in his face. "Do you not trust me? I'm not going to take off. I thought we settled this." Yeah, having a fight in front of our closest friends probably wasn't a good way to start a trip, but I didn't care.

"I was…" He stopped and shook his head. "You're right. I made assumptions that I shouldn't. You will be after Lorcan." He looked ready to say more, but then tilted his head and stalked off.

"Don't worry my dear," Lorcan said. "Alric has been under a lot of pressure, like us all. But even in the enclave, he was used to being on his own and worrying only about his actions. This last year has been a massive change for him. And that geas needs to be resolved. I've been looking in some of the older scrolls, the elven ones, but nothing yet."

"Thank you." I gave him a hug. He just said what I probably knew if I really thought about it—okay, not the bit about how Alric was growing up, but the rest. It helped hearing it from someone else.

Bunky and Irving had been hovering in the air, waiting. I waved them down. "Okay, guys, just like we did it before, only it's just you two since we don't have the girls." Bunky gronked at me in agreement, then he and Irving took to the sky.

I sat down next to the fire to eat my food.

"So they fly recon for you?" Padraig sat down next to me.

"Yeah, when I was out on my own, they and the faeries would scout the area we camped in. The constructs don't need regular sleep, so they were good keeping watch. I know we have people watching, but I figure a few more eyes couldn't hurt."

"Good thinking on using your resources when you left." He leaned a bit closer and dropped his voice although

Alric was at the other side of the camp. "I completely agree with your actions. You did what was best for those you cared about."

After Alric's snit fit, and even Covey getting upset, it was nice that someone understood. "Thank you. I had no control over what I became, or very little. You're an alchemist; is turning into something weird common among magic users?" A thought hit me. "Or was it something with the Spheres? Nivinal had been trying to blow that one up. My getting in the way didn't stop it."

Padraig stared into the fire as he picked at his food. "Something could have been triggered with Nivinal. I knew him when he was pretending to be the inquisitor for our enclave—a cruel man and extremely powerful. Even so, I am surprised that the Sphere shattered. Did you actually hit it when the spell flung you back?"

"Yes, I did. Wait, did I break the Sphere?" That couldn't be good for my future as a digger if it got out that I broke one of the Spheres.

He sat down his dinner. "I don't think so. Once you'd changed? Who knows? From your description you were huge. But as you, no." He shook his head. "This has to be because of Nivinal. I wish his mother hadn't killed him before I could."

The words were calm, and Padraig was usually a bastion of calm. But the raging anger at what had been done to his wife, his friends, and himself was clear on his face.

"I don't know that she did." Alric had snuck up behind us and sat down next to me. "I can't explain it, but I have an odd feeling that he's still alive."

"I wish that were true just so I could destroy him myself. Do you not believe what the voice said to Taryn?"

"That voice had seemed sure to me. I believed everything she said, including that she would have killed Alric." I shuddered.

Alric squeezed my hand. "I didn't have the same experience that Taryn did, but yes, there was a truth to Taryn's reaction. Edana killed Nivinal to get the obsidian chimera. I have no doubt on that."

"Could it have been something like the manticore? Like she only mostly killed him and his body released it?"

"I don't think so," Alric said. "The two relics are different; the chimera doesn't go inside someone on its own, it's absorbed by a mage with the proper spell. The manticore just picks a likely victim. Besides, the manticore went back into you as soon as your status changed back—that wouldn't help her gain the chimera."

"So she might have killed him, but then brought him back? Are there magic users who can do that?" That was a major game changer if true.

"Not that I know of. Even powerful healers like your friend Orenda can only bring people back that are close to death; not bring someone back who has crossed." Padraig looked down at the remains of his food. "But someone as strong as a tree goddess might be able to. And there are many theories that magic users were significantly stronger long ago."

That was something to chew over. If Nivinal *was* alive, and for the most part I trusted Alric's hunches better than my own, then his mother was either another formerly missing goddess or someone from so long ago she'd make Lorcan look like a baby. Neither of those were great options.

CHAPTER THIRTY

THERE HADN'T BEEN ANY OTHER world-chang-
ing comments by either elf, so I said good night and
went to catch a quick nap before my watch.

Amara was correct about her tents; within a few minutes
of crawling in I was toasty warm and sound asleep.

"Bad! Not finished!" That yell echoed through my vague
dreams and dragged me out of sleep. The tent was thin, so
I could make out flying shapes tearing around the camp,
their shadows visible as they passed in front of the fire. I
had only taken off my cloak and boots when I crawled in
since I knew I'd be on watch soon. I threw them back on
and crawled out of the tent.

About a dozen faeries, led by Leaf, who was yelling
about bad and unfinished, were flying everywhere. Bunky
and Irving must have heard her and came flying in from
their recon as I looked up.

"Attack! They attack!" This was from Crusty, looking
more serious than I'd ever known her to be.

"Slow down, sweetie. Tell me what's wrong." Aside from
making sure all of us were up, I couldn't tell what was
going on. The only attack we were under was from them.

Crusty flew to my outstretched hand and landed. "Boys
attack mother lady."

I didn't even know if faeries had parents, they seemed
to just be. "Wait, someone is attacking Mathilda?" We had
sent all the faeries to her.

"Yes! Mother lady! Boys not finished. Bad. Attacking."

"Can you lead us to them?" Alric came up next to me.

"Yes! We go, now!" Leaf had swung back around to us.

Padraig, Covey, and Lorcan started pulling down the tents and gathering our supplies to put back on the horses. They weren't much, but leaving them wasn't a great idea.

"Crusty, you and the rest of your faeries lead Bunky and Irving to Mathilda, defend her until we get there. Leaf can bring the rest of us in." I knew they needed to get us, and that Mathilda was a powerful magic user, but they couldn't have left that many faeries with Garbage if this many were with us.

The horses were ready and we were packed in record time. Still, Leaf and three other faeries who had stayed behind with her were about to drive me crazy with buzzing by us, yelling hurry, then flying up into the trees.

Once everyone was on their horses, Leaf flew to Alric, landed on his horse, and pointed. "That way."

We couldn't go quickly through the trees, as, of course, Leaf was just taking us the most direct route, and their ways of travel rarely involved paths or roads. After about thirty minutes of dodging low branches—Padraig had gotten the clearthin glows up, but they could only light so much—we came to a clearing with a familiar cottage in it. Padraig's army of glows flew over the cottage.

At least twelve boy faeries were hovering over and around it. The cottage was intact, but they were taking turns bashing against the shield of magic Mathilda had raised around it. Garbage and the rest of the faeries who hadn't come to get us were inside the shield. Crusty, Bunky, Irving, and their crew were nowhere in sight, and neither was Mathilda.

"Garbage! Where is Mathilda?"

Leaf and the three who had come with us flew up and started dive-bombing the boy faeries.

"We make her stay inside. Not good."

I got my answer when the door opened and Mathilda came out. She was listing as if she was drunk, and was watching the boy faeries oddly.

"My friends! Do come in, we shall dance!" She didn't even look at us; she was looking at the boy faeries.

"They love spelled her," Alric said and got off his horse. "They shouldn't be able to, since like the other faeries, they *are* magic, but they don't cast spells."

"So someone gave them a spell to cast on her." I watched as Garbage and the rest of the faeries inside the bubble flapped and pushed to get Mathilda back into the cottage. I got down off my horse as well and we walked to the boy faeries. At first they ignored us, then, as one, they turned and released some familiar nasty purple flower creatures. Gloughstrikes.

They were far faster than before, and struck everyone before we could respond. My friends crumbled to the ground as they were attacked by the gloughstrikes. I knew they were only unconscious, but who knew what would happen if I couldn't get them awake soon. I got hit twice, but felt nothing but a slight tingle. A cold tingle that came from my cheek as the manticore slapped them down with a shot of frigid air. I smashed the two that hit me. Somewhere deep inside I felt a change begin.

No. I was not going to turn into a monster again. Not for some damn flowers and overlarge faeries. I fought it down; focusing on not changing into whatever my body was trying to change me into. Once the feeling had passed, I reached out with a spell, two levels actually, a modification I'd made while on the run. First was a slowdown spell, then I smacked them with push. It took three rounds, but the gloughstrikes and the boy faeries finally vanished.

Leaf and her three faeries landed on each of my friends, one at a time, and they stirred. I walked up to the spell bubble around the cottage. "Mathilda? It's okay now. They're gone." I put one hand near the bubble. The magic bit back at me. Alric had once said that taking down another magic user's spell bubble was almost impossible if the spell caster was still alive.

"We here!" Crusty shouted as she, the constructs, and the rest of the faeries came into the clearing. From the opposite direction that we'd come. She spun around. Even our flighty one noticed something was missing. "Where they go?"

Leaf and her troop had just gotten everyone up and she flew up to Crusty. "You miss. She fix." She pointed to me as if my fixing it was the worst thing that could happen.

"Oh. Got lost." Crusty shrugged and flew right into the spell bubble, got zapped, then flung backwards. "Boom!"

"Lorcan, is there any way to get around that bubble?" I grabbed Crusty as I spoke; she was getting ready for another run. All these years I thought it had been the ale that had addled her brain; maybe it was just her love of being shocked senseless.

He shook his head and walked closer to it. "We have to get her to come out and take it down."

"Wouldn't the spell on her vanish when those faeries did?" Covey came forward a few steps but stayed a healthy distance from the bubble.

"It would have been a free-standing spell, not connected to the boy faeries." Padraig stayed back, and studied the bubble. The clearthin glows moved around the cottage as he looked for a gap.

"Garbage, go wake up Mathilda." I would have thought that would be obvious, but even generals have off days.

The faeries inside the bubble had been arguing about something in native faery, but Garbage cut them off and gave me a nod. "Do." She turned around and led her troop to the door. I expected them to do their trick of going through the door, but their tricks seemed to come and go—this time they just pounded on the door.

Mathilda slowly opened it and blinked at us. "Why are

you here in the middle of the night? And why is there a bubble around my cottage?" She shook her head but looked like she had been asleep for hours.

"You put the bubble up. You had been spelled, and a bunch of boy faeries were trying to get inside," I said. "I chased off the faeries and their weaponized flowers, and you don't seem spelled any more. You can drop the bubble."

Mathilda flicked her wrist and the bubble dropped. "I don't remember setting it up, nor a bunch of boy faeries. What kind of spell did they use?"

"A love spell was what it felt like, and you did look very much in love with the winged gentlemen callers." Lorcan came to her first and held one hand over her head. "Just making sure all vestiges are gone."

Mathilda shook her head and stepped back. "You can leave the horses tied up out back, then come inside. It'll be cozy, but no reason we can't all fit." She waved to Bunky and Irving. "You two as well. I think Lorcan and I can set up enough wards to keep us aware of any more intruders tonight." She turned to me as Alric took my horse. "And flowers as weapons? I believe some tea might be in order."

Lorcan and Covey came in as well, as Padraig and Alric took the reins of their horses.

"They fired gloughstrikes at us." I sat down and had a cup of tea in front of me almost immediately.

"Are you certain?" Mathilda had two more teacups out but sloshed a bit as she poured.

"They got all of us, far faster than they should've been able to move too," Covey said. "Well, I assume not Taryn since she saved us."

"How did they miss you?" Mathilda asked.

I rubbed the side of my face. "I think the manticore held them off. Then I used a spell to disburse the faeries and the gloughstrikes."

"Push?" Alric came into the cottage. "There are more

spells than that one, you know." He sat down on the sofa with a smile.

"I know, and I do use others, sometimes…but this one was modified." I took a long sip of my tea. "It took three tries to get rid of them. They really wanted to get in here."

"But why?" Mathilda looked a little less disheveled than she did before but was still a bit out of it. Must be a bit disconcerting to be asleep and find out you were actually awake and trying to join a bunch of male faeries.

"Did you bring your nectar with you?" I turned to the others. "The faeries had been trying to steal her nectar before."

"I did, but that seems a bit extreme."

Padraig nodded. "I agree that wouldn't have motivated anyone except perhaps those boy faeries. But if someone else was using them to get to you? They could have played off what they wanted. And someone certainly gave them access to those gloughstrikes."

"Like someone who wants to stay near Beccia but keep us thrown off," Alric said.

The faeries had come in with us, along with Bunky and Irving, but all of them sat up suddenly and looked toward the door. "We go." Garbage flew to the door with her fleet behind her. "Being called."

"Who is calling you?" I had never seen them so focused, but something was definitely reaching into their tiny heads. Maybe the same someone's who sent the boy faeries after Mathilda?

"We go." Now all of the faeries were hovering next to the door, but none were going through it. Which was a good thing if whoever was calling them was bad.

Mathilda came to the door and stood in front of it. "Who is calling you?" She folded her arms and glared at the faeries as if they'd forgotten their manners.

Garbage nodded and whispered, "Queen Mungoosey." Of course, her whisper was loud enough to be heard by people in the next county. "They stay." She pointed to Bunky and Irving who had already flown to the rafters.

Mathilda watched her for a moment more and when Garbage held fast under the scrutiny, she opened the door and they flew out. A quick glance outside and she shut it again. "I know you said their relationship with their queen had deteriorated after they broke the prophecy to save you, but hopefully this is a good sign."

I agreed, but I was also worried. The last time they had a talk with their queen, they spent the next few days getting knock-down drunk. I really didn't want to be on the road with a bunch of seriously drunk faeries.

"Back to why you were targeted, does anyone else know you have these?" Lorcan had been looking around Mathilda's bookshelves and tapped on three old books right in the middle.

"They shouldn't; most people can't even see them. And anyone questionable wouldn't be in my house."

"Aren't they just books?" I knew that was a loaded question with this academically minded bunch, but they looked normal.

"Ah, you *can* see them," Mathilda said. "To most people it would appear that Lorcan just tapped on part of the bookcase. They are books, yes, but they have great significance." She turned back to Lorcan. "You really think they were after these? How did they even know about them?"

"Did any of the boy faeries get into your house? Before, when you were on the other side of Beccia and they were looking for nectar," I said.

"No…well, yes. That night I found you, the faerie I had chased off had been in my house. Just for a short bit, but I'd left the door partially open so I could hear my teakettle. I caught him inside."

"What are they?" Alric walked over to the bookcase but didn't touch the books.

"All I see is a shelf," Covey said. "I assume that only

magic users can see these books at the moment?"

Covey was closer to her, so Mathilda nodded to her first. "Yes, the spell is a simple one, but I hadn't thought about the faeries being made of magic. I might not have added that to my spell. As for what they are, they are some of the only known historical references about when the elves first moved into the area. My homeland was the birthplace of elven kind; the migration to here was much later."

"So those might discuss the Ancients? And early elven migration?" Covey was on her feet and almost drooling. I was afraid that even if she couldn't see the books she was going to find a way to grab them.

"They most likely do cover those topics, and sadly, I think the spell on them might make them illegible for you, at least for now." She turned to us. "Actually, none of us can read them now. Siabiane and I found them when we first came here. At that time, only she and I could see them; even other magic users couldn't." She looked pointedly at Lorcan.

"You mean Siabiane had these? While in the enclave, before the Breaking?"

I'd known Lorcan for a few months and I'd never seen him so shocked and disturbed. Not even when he became a ghost at his brother's hand.

"Yes, she did. She had them sent to me a few months prior to the Breaking. After the battles, you locked yourselves up and I went on my travels. But over the past thousand or so years the spells keeping them hidden have worn thin, so more people can see them."

I looked around as they focused on the books with the same look a miner would have with a massive new find of gold. Even Covey, who couldn't see them, was drooling. "How can you all be this excited about these books if no one has been able to open them and read them since they were found? They could have a bunch of recipes, or be blank."

The looks I got ranged from compassion to crazy.

"These books are mentioned in other books, and their supposed secrets well known," Lorcan said with a shake of his head. "I was that close to them and never knew."

Alric turned away from the books. "Given what you have here, I'd assume that's what triggered the male faery invasion. But who sent them? They wouldn't have known what the books were, nor been able to control glough-strikes like that."

Padraig pulled himself away from the books and sat with his cup of tea. "We're back to the question: Are there two groups against us right now, or just the one? Working with the gloughstrikes sounds more like Nivinal...if he's not dead."

Mathilda looked over to the books, then reached into a pocket and pulled out a faery bag as she walked closer to the books. "I know we've been using these a lot as of late, but I think, given the situation, the books should go in one of these bags."

The moment she touched one of the books a spark of lightning slammed her across the room.

We ran to her, but she was knocked out cold.

"Damn it, that's what they were waiting for. She needed to break the seal." Alric ran to the books when two male faeries appeared. They grabbed the book that Mathilda had touched, and then vanished.

Mathilda blinked her eyes and we helped her to her feet. She saw the missing space and ran toward the shelf. "How could I have been so blind?" She spun around the room, saying spell words so fast I couldn't hear what they were. I probably wouldn't recognize them even if I heard them anyway.

Two spectral forms appeared, but they were fighting back. Twisting under her spell. A few more focused words and they became a little more solid. The male faeries had somehow been hiding in her cottage.

"Were they using this cottage to come through to our plane?" Lorcan walked around the creatures even as they twisted in Mathilda's spell.

"I think so, although I don't know how it works," I said. Unlike the others, I stayed back. "The girls said they're not finished so they shouldn't be here—but they can cross through at certain focus points. Someone made your cottage a point."

"That one I chased out last week," Mathilda said. She looked more like Siabiane in her fury than any other time. "I'm not sure how they got here, but unfinished things are easy to send back."

"But we could study…" Padraig's comment trailed off when Mathilda glared at him. "Agreed. Send back."

The words Mathilda said this time were short and brutal. The unfinished male faeries vanished.

CHAPTER THIRTY–ONE

"I'D SAY THAT EVEN THOUGH you were hiding as a wandering witch, someone knew who and what you are even before you ran into Taryn again." Lorcan resumed his seat. "And they knew what you had."

Mathilda grumbled as she went to refill everyone's tea, but her annoyance was clearly at herself. "I thought I'd been so clever. That's why I got custody of the books, Siabiane was too well known. Those male faeries had been hanging around, raiding my nectar stores for a few weeks. I didn't realize what they were, and even if I had, I wouldn't have thought them to be evil."

"I don't know that they are evil, or rather, that they were," I said. "One of them saved me and the girls when I somehow crashed us into Null. The faeries weren't too upset about being rescued by him, even though Garbage continued to remind everyone he was unfinished."

Lorcan nodded. "I'd say Nivinal, or someone working with him, found out about them and is luring them in from wherever they are to work for him. We assumed that they saved us against the gloughstrikes near the Spheres because of some good nature on their part. But Nivinal seemed to want Taryn at the Spheres; he might have sent them to make certain she made it."

"Should we put the remaining books in those faery bags now?" Covey stood near the books, even though she couldn't see them. "You've removed the problems in here for now, right? Maybe get them hidden before more come along?"

Mathilda shook her head. "I believe these attacks from those vile things has rattled my brains. Thank you for keeping us on track."

We gathered around her and she reached for the first book and quickly dropped it in the impossibly small faery bag. I found I was holding my breath as the second book was also picked up and stored. Mathilda tied the bag off and tucked it away in an inner pocket of her vest.

We had been a bit nervous so the sudden barrage of knocks on the door made us jump. Okay, it might have just been me who actually jumped, but it did visibly startle the others.

Mathilda went to the door, but all of us were right behind her as another volley of knocks hit. All of the magic users had one hand out, ready with a spell as she opened the door.

And we were overwhelmed by an army of dour faeries. It was just our twenty-three, and they were more subdued than dour. But I'd rarely seen them like this. They appeared to be seriously thinking. Even Crusty.

"Girls? What's wrong?" I followed them into the living room as Mathilda shut and bolted the door.

They landed on the table and politely sat. If the looks on their faces hadn't told me something was wrong, that would have. Bunky and Irving dropped down from the rafters to land on the table as well, but they stayed a respectful distance away from the faeries.

I quickly moved the tea pot off the table just in case this was a ruse to get some. We needed sleep right now, not twenty-three jacked-up faeries.

"Queen Mungoosey had words. Big words. Heavy words." Garbage nodded. "We must think."

"Do!" Leaf said.

"Think first." Garbage normally would have been yelling, but her voice was low even though she disagreed with Leaf.

"Do?" Leaf looked cowed but was still arguing. She finally sighed. "Think."

I wanted to ask them what had been said, but there was a mood surrounding them that I didn't want to disturb.

Mathilda nodded to herself and went into one of the bedrooms. She came out with a dollhouse. It wasn't near as fancy as the toy castle they used to live in at my place, but it was also large enough to hold all twenty-three faeries. "I found this in my travels a few years ago, and thought that if I ever saw you again, you might like it. It will give you room to talk tonight. I will make sure your words do not go beyond the walls of this tiny house." She tapped it as she set it on the table and a shimmer covered it.

Garbage flew up to her and gave her a kiss. "Thanks. Need thoughts and words." Then she flew down and led her faeries inside. Bunky and Irving returned to the rafters and went into their version of sleep.

"The silence was for them as well as us; I think we could all use some sleep." She pulled on a few straps off her sofa and two beds folded out. Then a third came from the chair. "Three here, and two in the extra bedroom."

Alric almost looked like he was going to go outside regardless, then shook his head and flopped down on one of the beds in the living room. "I think some sleep is a great idea."

He and I had agreed, when we first started getting involved, that intimacy would be when we were alone and not in a group. Just less weirdness for our friends when we were traveling in such close quarters. But even with the latest issues between us, I really wished we were alone. From the look on his face, Alric felt the same.

Covey and I took my old room; the two cots were small but would work. She was out almost immediately. I wasn't too far behind her.

The whistle of a teakettle is possibly the nicest sound to wake you, at least if you have to be woken up. I personally am a fan of sleeping in as long as you want. I sort of had that when I was on the run with the faeries and constructs for that month, but the girls kept such weird hours it never felt like I got enough sleep.

Covey was gone, and a quick check of the bathroom told me she was showering. Voices from the front room told me I was probably the last one up. I showered after Covey finished and joined everyone at breakfast.

The faeries' house was set further to the side, but I didn't see any faeries out and about. "Where are the girls?" I looked up. "And Bunky and Irving?"

"The girls are inside their house. I think they might have talked all night long. Whatever Queen Mungoosey had to say, it got them worked up." Mathilda handed me a plate of bacon, eggs, and toast. "As for your construct friends, you'll need to ask Padraig."

Padraig was mid-chew so I waited until he swallowed. "I asked them to do some circles outside to check for anyone else out there. I studied the map and I think, after breakfast, we should be able to solve it."

"Why not now?" Covey asked.

"Because I'll need the table and we're using it right now." He grinned. "Plus I'm mentally resolving some of the issues of deciphering it, so a little more time would be a good idea. It's a good thing we didn't go to get Nasif; I' doubt that he ever knew what he had."

"You were supposed to go to sleep," Lorcan chastised him, but his interest in what Padraig found was greater than his concern for Padraig's sleeping habits.

"I was going to, but something bothered me," Padraig said, then smiled at Mathilda. "And we'll discuss this after we've finished our lovely breakfast."

"That's my boy. Siabiane always did say you were one of her favorites."

With that added incentive, we all, including Mathilda, finished in record time. We moved our dishes off the table and Padraig unrolled the map. It had stayed in its spelled condition when we'd rolled it up. The ruins with the chest outline had still been visible. Now it looked like another layer had been put on top.

"Wait, we have to go back to Beccia?" That wasn't going to make me happy. Besides, they'd been so certain the sphinx was not there.

"No, although it does sort of look that way." Padraig placed his hands on two opposite corners, the one with the formerly hidden words and its mate. Then he said a few words to remove the warding.

At first it looked like nothing was going to happen, but Padraig just kept holding the map and smiling. Alric was looking skeptical when the map changed right before our eyes.

The levels shifted and what looked like a single vertical line led to a different section, hovering in the far corner was the same mark I'd seen before—the shape of a diamond with a sphinx inside it. I tucked my hands behind my back so I wouldn't be tempted to touch it. There wasn't a lot of room in this cottage, and slamming into a wall wouldn't be fun.

"Now here is the map that leads to the sectioned off area." Padraig moved two cups to hold down the first map, and then held what we thought was a mundane non-magical map up to it.

I was not the only one who jumped this time when the two merged.

"So that one is magical too?" I almost reached forward but held back.

"Apparently. And while this one showed where the sphinx had been, and where to find the chest, it wouldn't

have shown how to get to the area where the sphinx is."
He shook his head in admiration. "I think it is in a hidden realm as your friend Grimwold mentioned. They were called *tir cudds*, and the creators of them aren't known."

Lorcan, Alric, and Mathilda looked varying levels of shocked and interested. Covey looked as confused as I felt. Then she narrowed her eyes at the map.

"You don't mean those mythical pockets of reality where riches were stored by the Ancients? There isn't much documentation, but it was pretty much decided they were just wishful thinking by people who wanted an easy way to get rich."

"Yes and no." Lorcan pointed to part of the map right in front of the odd vertical line. "I don't believe that they were to hide riches, I believe they were created to protect things. Plants, animals, relics that might destroy the world."

Padraig shook his head. "You're right on the pieces being in order; it makes sense that whoever crafted them set the heaviest protection on the final piece."

"So how do we get into this place once we've found it?" I wasn't pleased with the distance north it looked like we'd need to go. I could be wrong, but it appeared we'd be riding for at least two weeks to get to the line, which I assumed was the demarcation for this hidden realm.

Lorcan looked up from his intense study of the hidden realm map. Padraig might have been the one to find it, but there was no way anyone other than Lorcan would be carrying it now. His focused study turned into a frown as he read a section of the map. "There has to be a sacrifice. It is the only way. We have to find out who or what before we can cast the spell to cross inside."

CHAPTER THIRTY—TWO

T HAT QUIETED EVERYONE.
      "Just what sort of sacrifice are we talking about? I am not losing someone because of this." Covey stepped back with her arms folded.

Mathilda didn't say anything, but looked exactly like Covey—no one was going down on her watch if she had anything to say about it.

Alric kept looking at the map. "If it means we can get this thing, and destroy the weapon, I will offer myself." He didn't look up at first, and when he did he carefully didn't look my way.

I kept the things I wanted to shout at him inside my head, but I was almost shaking with anger and fear.

"It might not come to something so drastic," Lorcan said. "The term sacrificed can mean many things."

"You might not be what is needed to be sacrificed," Padraig said. "The wrong sacrifice would be worse than none. Once we have gotten to the area and start the trigger spell, we can't get out."

"I know. But I stand willing to do whatever is needed." Alric had that grim, stoic, lone wolf look again.

I really needed to find out from Lorcan and Padraig just what made him that way. When I first met him I thought he was nothing more than a thief and a con man. And he was a thief and a con man. But he was doing it, every part of it, to help his people. Hard to hate someone for that, but

I could be annoyed by it in my own head. And terrified.

"Is good. Go now?" Garbage and her troop came out of the little house. They looked a bit subdued and tired; they probably had been up all night. However, they weren't as down as they had been after the brief talk with Queen Mungoosey.

"Do you know where we're going?" You never could tell with them, maybe their queen had tipped them off.

"There." Garbage pointed to the map. "Is where she say we go."

Mathilda moved closer to the table and the girls. "Queen Mungoosey told you to go to the hidden realm? Did she say why?"

Garbage shrugged, a move echoed by the rest of the faeries. "We need, we go. That all." She pointed to Padraig, Lorcan, and Alric. "You get us in."

Alric leaned closer to Garbage. "Not the others?"

"Yes, no, no." Garbage pointed to Mathilda first, then Covey and me.

"Maybe Covey and Taryn should stay back," Alric did look me in the eye this time.

"I am not missing a chance to view a *tir cudd.*" Covey didn't move, but her fingers did flex and turn a bit claw-like.

"We're not going to ruin this, you know." I wasn't happy. I'd been worried about Alric doing something glorious and stupid and now he was trying to shut me out again. Anything for his cause.

"That's not why. You might be the sacrifice. If you're not there, then you can't be pulled in." His look softened.

Covey shook her head. "I can defend myself, thank you. And if I am the sacrifice, I'll deal with that when we get there. End of discussion. I'm going." She flexed her fingers one more time, then stalked into the bedroom, and came out a moment later with her pack.

"Can Taryn and I talk outside? Alone?" Alric asked, but

he was already heading for the door.

"We have time. We should leave soon, but I want to get more of this map sorted before we get started," Lorcan said.

Mathilda and Covey shared a look, and then turned it on me. I was annoyed with Alric but I wasn't going to call him out on it—not until I heard him anyway. I shrugged and followed him out.

He'd walked away from the cottage, a little way into the woods, but his back was to me. He didn't turn until I was almost next to him.

"You can't go," he said and held up his hand to stop me from replying. "I've had the dream again—the one I had in Null. The one where you died and I couldn't save you."

He looked calmer than he had the morning after that dream back in Null, but he also looked more rattled than he had in the cottage.

"You've been hiding it." It wasn't a question, but a statement. "How long?"

"Since we found you. I had it the first night you were gone, then not again until the night we stayed at the pub. I figured it was better if only one of us was worried about it."

The pain and fear in his face drove away any annoyance or anger at his earlier behavior. I stepped forward and wrapped my arms around his waist. "I need to go." I reached up and stopped his complaint with a kiss. Once we finished I continued. "I can't explain it, but I need to be a part of this. All of this. What if I am the only way we can stop Nivinal and his people from destroying everything?"

"I'm sure we can do it without you."

"What if you can't? I have to deal with the fact that you might not survive our next fight as well. You did almost die once, you know. Orenda and I almost couldn't save you."

He kissed me again, but there was a lingering sadness. "I just don't know that I could survive losing you. I really don't. Our situation isn't great, and I've never been a romantic guy, but losing you would destroy me."

I put my head against his chest. "I feel the same way. So, let's just stick together on this. If we stay together, we can keep each other alive, right? And we don't know why the faeries said Covey and I wouldn't help get us in—it could be simply because it's somehow coded to elves and we're not."

He gave me one more kiss, and then stood back. "I hate it when you're logical. Just don't leave me. We stay together through the end."

I gave him a squeeze as we walked back to the cottage. "Deal. We stick together."

Everyone inside the cottage made a good show of not being curious about what he and I talked about.

Alric nodded to the group. "I was wrong. All of us go and get this done. Any new information?"

Padraig nodded. "It appears that part of the sphinx's ability is to call the other relics to it. As long as it's paired with the obsidian chimera and a lot of power."

Alric let out a whistle. "Now we know why Edana wants it—she already took the chimera."

"The good news is, to work with the sphinx, the chimera can't be inside someone," Mathilda said. "So that means that we have a chance to get it from her."

I shuddered at the amount of power just the projected image of that woman had. It was terrifying when we thought she was using the added strength from the chimera being inside of her; that she probably wasn't, made me want to go find a place to be ill.

The faeries had been sitting around waiting since Garbage made her pronouncement. From the looks on the tiny faces, especially their general, they were ready to go.

"Let me grab my pack," I said. By the time I came back, everyone was gone.

I refrained from shouting, but for a second I did fear that Alric had made them go without me. But only a second, and I would never admit it.

Everyone was behind the cottage loading up their horses, the faeries were buzzing around, and Bunky and Irving were hovering near Padraig.

Mathilda was watching everyone get ready, but she didn't have a horse. "Are you taking the cottage on this trip?" Didn't seem stealthy.

"Yes and no. I've found a way to keep up with you, although I'll be going a different route. Padraig and I have mapped out the general stops each night. To be honest, I was going to just have it hide once we knew where we were going, but the faeries convinced me otherwise."

I looked around at the fluttering faeries. "Which ones?"

"Oh, *our* faeries. They claimed it might be needed at some point and they thought Queen Mungoosey would like me to travel in it." She shook her head. "I think they just want to sleep inside and in their tiny house. I took a quick look, they've already decorated it."

I laughed and went to my horse. I guess as long as she didn't mind, I wasn't going to complain. Besides, having it along would mean less camping out for all of us.

Alric and Padraig took the lead after they debated the first leg. The map gave options, and of course they each had a different choice.

Alric won this round, but from the look on Padraig's face, he'd not intended to go the other way. He probably just felt Alric needed something to focus on. I wished I could figure out Alric as well as Padraig had.

The faeries did their version of recon, which was fly ahead, and then come back impatiently when we didn't move as fast as they wanted. Explaining to them the difference between flying somewhere and riding somewhere did nothing.

Except make Garbage start sizing me up for a possible pick up. I figured it out when we hit a clearing, and Garbage waved a dozen faeries my way. I scrunched low on my saddle and hung on for all I was worth as they dove low and started pulling my clothes.

"Ladies? What are you doing?" Lorcan had been studying the second map while we rode, but he looked up as they swarmed down.

"Help go faster?" Crusty looped around above me.

"I don't want to fly. Lorcan, tell them not to pick me up." I'd had two unsanctioned flying trips with those miscreants, and I didn't need a repeat performance. However, both of those times I wasn't expecting it. I was now. I knew faeries were unnaturally strong, but I didn't think even they could take my horse too, and I wasn't letting go.

"Ladies, Taryn and her horse need to stay on the ground." Lorcan had Garbage's attention but the rest were pulling on me. Even more disturbing, I swore I thought I felt my horse start to rise, just a tiny bit.

"If you take her, you'll have to wait for the rest of us," Covey rode over to my horse and put one hand on its shoulder.

Garbage buzzed around a bit, then shrugged. "Go slow, is okay. But hurry!" She chittered something to the faeries in native faery and they flew off.

Bunky dipped a bit lower and gronked at Alric.

"No, stay with us; besides, there's no telling where they're going right now." Alric seemed more relaxed than he had been. He still moved when Bunky made his obligatory dive for his head though.

It was good to hear Alric laugh as he stayed clear of the construct. I didn't even think that Bunky was really trying anymore—he just did it as their thing.

We started moving again and Alric pulled ahead. He seemed to be casually riding, but I had a feeling he knew where all of us were, exactly.

"Think we're going to be sacrifices?" Covey and I were in the rear, another argument from Alric that died with one look from Covey.

"I hope not. I don't want Alric to be right. He'll never get over it."

Covey laughed. "I have a feeling if we were; whoever asked for us would throw us back. Well, me at least." She gave her feral grin and flexed her fingers into claws again.

I dropped my voice. "Do you think we're going to do it? Get the sphinx, form the weapon, and destroy it?" I wouldn't admit it to Alric, especially when he was trying to wrap me up somewhere safe, but part of me wasn't sure about this.

"I have no idea," she said. "This is far different than either of our lives a short while ago. From an academic side? This is the most amazing thing ever. From the 'I don't want to lose my friends in some horrible world destroying battle' side? It sucks."

CHAPTER THIRTY—THREE

TRAVEL WAS SLOW, STEADY, AND boring for the next week. The faeries stayed ahead of us as they realized we weren't going to get there faster no matter what they tried. Each day Mathilda and her cottage would take off. However they traveled, it wasn't the same path as the rest of us. Unfortunately, she said it really wouldn't work having anyone other than herself inside it while it traveled. Or so she claimed.

At least Covey, Lorcan, and I slept inside most nights. Padraig and Alric stayed out near the fire.

"I just went down the road a bit and someone is definitely on the trail ahead," Alric said as he came in for breakfast on the morning of the eighth day. That was another benefit of Mathilda's cottage, good food not cooked over a fire.

"How far up?" Padraig pushed himself away from the table but kept his tea with him.

"Too close. I'm not sure how I didn't notice them on the final scouting last night. They must have been just past the point where I turned back, and kept moving later than we did." Alric didn't look up as he piled eggs and toast onto a plate, but there was a subtle jab there. He agreed with the faeries about our pace—he wanted us to ride longer each night.

Padraig and he had a long debate about it. Padraig's more conservative way of thinking was that if we tired the horses too much each day, they'd have nothing left in terms of energy if an emergency came along. He eventually won, but Alric was still a bit annoyed. A reoccurring situation these days.

"How far will we have to go off path to avoid them?" Lorcan had given over how we were getting there to Alric and Padraig. He was focused on what he was going to need to do once we got there in order to open this hidden realm. No one could completely explain to me or Covey what it was, beyond that a lot of magic would be needed to open it.

"I'd like to go on ahead on my own and check first. I pulled back once I was certain there was someone up ahead." He shrugged. "It's probably no one to worry about, they're coming south instead of following us north. But I should at least check it out."

"I'm going with you," I said as I folded my arms. I had no logical reason I should go, but I'd be damned if I would let him go into lone wolf mode again. We were a team… two teams actually. One of all of us, and one of Alric and me.

He started to shake me off, and then tilted his head. "Fine. If the rest of you don't mind, Taryn and I will be riding ahead a bit and seeing if we can find out if those coming south are a threat."

"We go too!" Crusty barreled into the side of my arm, then climbed up to my shoulder.

I looked around as Leaf came over and landed on Alric. Garbage watched and nodded.

"Why do I feel like these two are here for a reason?" I knew if it was something important Garbage would be going. But she was sending her two highest sidekicks, so it wasn't trivial.

"We love you," Crusty said as she reached over from my shoulder and tried to hug my entire neck.

Leaf just laughed and played with Alric's hair.

"I need know what go on. They tell." Garbage folded

her arms as if she always sent spies along with us.

Alric looked at me. "I'm not sure we can easily hide from them, so might as well take them along. Besides, if we need to send someone back here, we'll have two options."

I turned my head to see part of Crusty as she resumed her seat on my shoulder. "Are you going to sit there the entire time?"

"Yes." She beamed at me as she slowly moved one hand toward my hair.

"You are not to use my hair to steer me, or as a device to hang on. If you fall off, you can fly. Got that?" They'd tried steering me with my hair a few months ago. The faeries had fun. I didn't, and I wasn't going through that again.

Crusty shrugged, grinned, and pulled her arm back to hang onto my cloak.

I buckled on my sword. It had been around almost continuously recently and it might be trying to be a well-behaved weapon. I also added a brace of knives. Wouldn't hurt and I noticed Alric was stashing a fair amount of weapons on his person. It could just be him being over-prepared, or he could be more concerned about what might be out there than he was letting on.

The others had gathered around the table and were already engaging in a lively discussion about the scrolls that would hopefully get us into the hidden realm. That was another reason to go on this side trip—getting away from more scroll debates.

We got on our horses and headed through the trees. Alric usually rode off the roads and paths, but close enough that he could still see the path. With his dark horse, all black ensemble including a cape with a hood that was now up, he would be hard to spot from the road.

I had my hood up as well; since it had been growing steadily colder each day we traveled, but its deep red color really didn't make me less visible. If I was going to skulk around with Alric on a regular basis I would need to find a darker cloak.

I nudged my horse closer to Alric's as we reached a wider area. "How far up did you go this morning?" I kept my voice low, but it might have been pointless as Crusty had started to hum. Loudly.

"Crusty, shh, we need to not make noise."

"Yeah, is quiet!" Leaf yelled in Alric's ear.

"Bringing them was a mistake. I know where the others on the trail are now, they haven't moved from where I thought they were earlier. They also aren't trying to be quiet any more than our winged friends." He pulled Leaf off his shoulder. "We're close. You both need to be silent. But if someone attacks us, you two fly high and far, then go back to Mathilda's. Promise?" He watched Leaf until she nodded, then looked over to Crusty.

"Quiet." She grinned and nodded.

"This way." He put Leaf back on his shoulder and led us through some denser forest.

I dropped my horse behind him to ride single file again. He slowed then stopped, and held one hand up for me to halt. I also held my breath, but that was my doing not his. It took me a little longer to hear what he had, but I heard the noises. Someone was not only nearby, they were digging. And someone near them wasn't happy about it.

Alric slowly and gracefully got down off his horse. I got of mine slowly. Gracefully wasn't going to happen.

Even the faeries stayed quiet. Crusty had put her hands over her mouth, but her eyes were getting bigger the closer to the noise we went.

After a short while, Alric dropped down behind some bushes. We were even closer than I'd thought, the speakers were just on the other side of the plants.

"I told you we have to move on. This envoy needs to speak to the rulers immediately." The voice wasn't one I recognized and didn't sound like a syclarion—two things I was grateful for. It sounded snotty and entitled, one thing

I was not grateful for. Evil I could fight, entitled just had to be ignored.

"And I told you, *Captain*, there is definitely something here. If we leave this site half dug we are as much as giving away these treasures to the nearest ruffian!"

Alric and I both looked at each other in shock. It was Harlan.

I started to move forward, but Alric held my shoulder and shook his head. He was probably right; we needed to know what the situation was first. Harlan could be a prisoner. He and his newest ladylove, the elf Orenda, had left Alric's enclave months ago to go speak to her people about the coming troubles. She came from a group of young elves who had been separated from Alric's people after the Breaking and had been hiding in their own enclave for the past thousand years. Like Alric's people but without the elders and knowledge and documents they'd taken with them. She'd snuck out looking for the emerald dragon relic, joined a bunch of relic thieves plus Alric in disguise, and fallen in love with Harlan. He was a chataling, a species whom her people would have never seen.

Yeah, something bad could be going on.

"I cannot wait any longer, they—"

"You will wait as long as I say you will wait." Imperious and sure of herself, I knew that voice well: Orenda. When we first met her she'd sounded like that. But as the reality of the world outside of her people's enclave started settling in, most of her imperiousness had vanished. Good to know she could call it up when needed.

I was about to say we should probably go in when Crusty threw aside her hands from her mouth and yelled, "We here!" Leaf joined in and the two of them tore through the trees.

"It's done now," I said but kept my voice low. There was no way anyone was going to miss those two.

Alric frowned and shook his head. "Wait." There was

something he'd noticed that wasn't making him happy.

"Damn it! Wasn't their cage locked?" That was the captain. "Gregoli, you were to keep it locked!"

"Those aren't any of the prior ones, Captain."

"They locked up the faeries?" My voice was low, but my temper was not. When we'd split up, Garbage had called in some more faeries and sent some with Qianru and Locksead who went south to her people, and some with Harlan and Orenda. It didn't matter that I personally didn't know these faeries, nor that I had thought about locking mine up numerous times.

I did not like people who trapped faeries.

I held up my hand to Alric before he could speak. "Sorry, sneaking is over. I need to go beat up some elves." I pulled out my sword.

I thought he would stop me, but he grinned and unsheathed his sword as well. "Agreed."

He motioned for our horses to stay in place where we'd left them, and then he and I walked through the trees.

"Those are our faeries. Do you have a problem with them?" I got out before anyone could respond to our appearance.

Harlan was waist deep in a pit not too far off the road, Orenda standing between him and a tall, dark-haired elf in armor. About twenty also armored and snotty looking elves stood behind them with horses and a familiar carriage—the one Orenda and Harlan had left the enclave in.

Crusty and Leaf had swarmed Harlan first, but then the faeries in the cage sitting in front of the carriage started yelling. I hadn't seen them at first, but we all saw them now.

Crusty tore to the cage, but Leaf flew up in the Captain's face. "What. You. Do?!" She was getting really good at imitating Garbage.

The Captain pulled back at first then tried to grab her. The two guards near the cage tried to do the same to Crusty.

"Touch them and you will regret it." I raised my sword. Alric's people called the swords he and I bore spirit swords. There had been some trouble when I called mine for the first time because they are only supposed to go to special elves, and I am clearly *not* an elf. I had no idea if these elves knew of them or not, but they were still damn impressive weapons.

"I need you to unlock the cage and let our friends free," Alric said. He hadn't gone full snotty-elven-noble yet, but it was there, lurking. He'd thrown back his hood so there was no mistaking he was an elf. He wasn't flashing his high lord mark on his left cheekbone yet, but I knew that, as much as he disliked it, he would if these other elves became difficult. He preferred to keep it hidden with a glamour.

"Taryn! Alric!" Orenda ran forward and enwrapped me in a massive hug. Nice of her, but it did sort of ruin the image I was trying to project.

"Good to see you two!" Harlan waved at the dirt in front of him. "Seems odd, but I found a scroll that indicated a find of sorts here."

"Good to see both of you as well, but you let them be caged?" Crusty and Leaf were both working on the lock. One of the guards stepped forward to stop them, but I raised my hand in a ball. I personally never cast spells that way, but I knew others who did. Hopefully Orenda's people did too. "I wouldn't. We're both pretty heavy magic users and really like the faeries." He hesitated and looked to his captain. "I'd be watching me. Your captain isn't going to save you if I let this spell go."

"We didn't have a choice," Orenda answered my question about the faeries. "It was either that or they stayed with my people to be studied." She glared at the captain.

My two tiny lock picks broke open the lock, and a fleet of faeries flew out and surrounded us. The new ones carefully kept us between them and the elves. But they didn't fly away. They had promised Garbage they would keep an eye on Orenda and Harlan, and in their minds that wasn't over. Crusty and Leaf hovered between us and the elves.

I kept an eye on the elves in armor but lifted my hand to the closest new faery. "Hello there, can you come down for a moment? What's your name?"

It was a lovely purple faery with dragonfly type wings and a gorgeous smile. "Pansy Dragonfly."

"Nice to meet you," I said, still keeping my eye on the elves. "Have any of these elves hurt you or your companions? Be honest, you're safe now.

She glared at the captain and even stuck her tongue out at him, but then shook her head. "No. Trap us. But not hurt."

"That's one point in your favor," Alric stepped forward. He'd sheathed his sword. "How about we start over? I am Alric, this is Taryn, and those two are Crusty Bucket and Leaf Grub. Who are you and where are you going?"

The captain looked ready to not answer, then another glare from Orenda motivated him. It wasn't until he glared back that I saw the resemblance. Orenda had bright red hair, and lots of it, and his was almost as dark as Padraig's but their faces were similar when they glared at each other.

"I am Captain Balith of the king's guard of the land of Caeria. With me are a handpicked company of twenty royal guards sent to escort my sister Orenda and her... companion to visit with another group of elves. One that I believe you are a part of. They believe we must work together against some threat. I am here to explain why that won't happen."

"Balith, you have no call for that, and you know it." Orenda got right in her brother's face. "The king sent messages with both Harlan and me for the royals in Alric's enclave." She shook her head and looked to Alric and me. "It's probably best if you ignore Balith and his people."

Harlan had been watching the proceedings like one of

those net ball games. "Yes, well, as I was going to say, a map, which somehow disappeared while I was still in the enclave, indicated a find in this area. I do believe we have a cache of stolen relics." He held up a broken elven salt–shaker. Which was ignored.

"We are not staying here," Balith said. "I don't care if you two join us, but there are far more of us than you. And I have more than enough help to drag Orenda and Harlan back into the carriage." He was clearly not counting the faeries, or his math skills were worse than his manners.

Alric took a few steps around Harlan's pit, then nodded to Orenda. "Has he always been this big of an ass?"

She shrugged. "Yes, sadly. Not my favorite brother."

Before Balith could retort, the point of Alric's sword was under his chin. "As Taryn said, we are both magic users and could blast all of you apart without even getting close. But we do have these lovely swords. Do they mention spirit swords in your kingdom?" He added some elven words and Balith paled. He hadn't responded to the sword at his throat except to freeze. But his people obviously had memories of the spirit swords.

"She is not one of us. Only pure elven kind, the stron-gest and best of our people, can call one of those blades." His eyes narrowed. "You lie."

Alric stepped back, threw his sword, which vanished the moment that it left his hand, then called it back. "Do any of your people have mage sense? You clearly don't or you would have recognized both of our blades."

I was glad Alric didn't expect me to throw my sword. It had been behaving recently, but with my luck the thing wouldn't vanish and would just hit someone.

"I do." A smaller knight, one who looked uncomfortable in his armor, came out from the back. His eyes widened as he saw both of our swords clearly.

"It is true…how many do your people have that you can give them to outsiders?"

"You can't give someone one of these." I put mine back in its sheath. "They chose their carrier."

Harlan nodded randomly, then turned back to his hole and continued digging.

"Balith, remember the stories I told the council? The ones you didn't believe? These are two of the magic users I spoke of. Taryn sent an enemy fighter thousands of feet below ground. With just a move of her hand. Alric is an elven high lord."

A bit embellished, and Orenda hadn't actually been there when I sent Glorinal deep underground. We wouldn't mention what he came back as, or me blowing that thing up.

Balith didn't look happy, but unlike another elven knight I knew and was annoyed by, Flarinen, he was willing to back down.

"I am honored to meet you. Both. However, we can't stay here, we have a ways to go, and must be back quickly."

Orenda rolled her eyes again. I had a feeling she did it a lot with this one. "He's afraid he'll miss the tournament in three weeks."

I looked to the other knights and, aside from the mage, they looked to be of the same mindset as Balith. "Correct me if I'm wrong, but your people never really came out of their enclave until Orenda, right?" At a few nods, I continued. "So this is new. Meeting other people is new. And all you want to do is crawl back into your enclave? And you need to go to your tournament, but you are afraid to face a real threat to everyone, including your enclave? The people we're up against took down an extremely powerful shield built by elves with more power than you could imagine. *They destroyed it.* This threat is real. Quite frankly I am surprised that such a fierce fighter as Orenda came from such shoddy stock." I had no idea where that came from, and from Alric's look neither did he. But he gave a small smile and nod.

Silence filled the clearing as my words settled.

"I found something!" Harlan had been being himself and not paying attention to anything he felt didn't interest him. "A bunch of chests and trunks, a bag or two. Yup, this looks like a relic robbers haul that got stashed and forgotten. Judging by the depth and the age of the map where I found the reference, I'd say it's probably been here at least two hundred and fifty years." He finally realized that everyone was staring at him and it wasn't in admiration. "What?"

"I adore you, Harlan." I laughed and shook my head. "Come show us what you found." I ignored Balith and the other knights and walked over to the pit. The faeries followed me.

Harlan looked around, unsure if what he missed was more important than what he found. He shrugged and waved toward his find.

I'd been impressed that he'd been allowed to dig something that deep—it would have taken hours. Then I saw the sides of a box trap. Relic thieves often had to stash their finds then come back for them later, so magic devices called box traps were a big market item. The person who used them did have to dig, but once set the box trap and everything inside of it would be completely buried. But if you knew where it was and could trigger it, you could get the treasure out fairly easily

"You want us to take this with us?" Balith was not amused.

"No, no, just the important finds," Harlan said. "Most relic thieves grab what they can and run. They end up with a lot of junk. It will take me a little bit to go through it."

Balith scowled and opened his mouth to argue.

"Or we can just load all of it into the wagon and sort it out later," Orenda spoke before her brother could get a word in. "That should only take a few hours." In other words, the same amount of time as allowing Harlan to play with his toys first, but with more hassle for the knights.

Harlan had already dropped down and was fussing with a chest. I came around to where he stood to see better.

He pried the lid up while Orenda and Balith played annoy the sibling.

"Armor?" I saw dirty, but still gleaming in spots, armor piled inside. Not that exciting to me as say artwork, but you could tell about a people by the way they protected themselves.

"Oh yes, and I'd say this looks far older than elven." Harlan rubbed his paws together and started gingerly lifting out pieces. "Oh, yes. Most of this is from the Ancients' era for certain. See these markings?" He tapped one shoulder guard with a claw. "Those are Ancient." He flipped it over. "Too bad about the water damage. These must have been in heavily damp ground for a long time before they were liberated by whoever left this behind."

"Maybe the aqueducts?" Alric wasn't officially a digger, but he was a relic thief. That he did it for the good of his people didn't make him any less of a thief. And I think he'd be the first to agree.

"Under Beccia? Have you been there? Well, you were when you rescued Taryn, of course." He tilted his head. "Where are you coming from anyway?"

"Beccia," I said as I tried to reach one of the pieces without actually dropping into the hole. "And yes, we got a nice tour of the aqueducts." I would have mentioned the dragon's head, but not in front of Balith and his knights.

"Can I see that piece right there?" I was stretching my arm as far as it could go, but I was just a little short. The piece in question was smaller than most of the others and a bit darker, with etchings.

"Hmm?" Harlan noticed my reaching hand for the first time. "Of course, fellow digger after all." He handed it to me.

The metal was first bone chillingly cold, far more than

the current weather would account for. In a flash it became hot, then it flung me across the clearing and into a tree.

Luckily, I'd been slowing down in my flight, so I didn't hit the tree with full force.

"Ow." I pulled myself up into a sitting position as Alric reached me. Orenda was right behind, and Harlan scrambled out of his pit.

Balith and the knights had taken a few steps away from us.

"Are you okay?" Alric dropped down next to me.

"I think so. This little girl packs a punch though." It was a woman's shoulder piece. Lightweight, but solid and it was singing to me.

At first I thought it was the smack from hitting the tree, but nope. There was an odd and somehow familiar melody coming from it.

"Do you hear that?" Even though it had slammed me into a tree, I didn't want to let go of the piece, but I held it up toward the others.

Alric was the closest and his eyes narrowed at my words. "Hear what?" That wasn't a good sign. His hearing, and that of pretty much everyone around me including the faeries, was far better than mine.

I held the armor up to the faeries, and Leaf and Crusty flew over. "Girls, do you hear anything coming from this? Music?"

Leaf and Crusty both came to the piece and reverently touched it. They both smiled and shook their heads. "No. You do." That seemed to make Leaf far too happy. Crusty just did a few loops in the air.

"What are you hearing?" Alric watched the faeries before turning back to me.

I pulled the piece closer again. I thought about playing it off as the tree and my head, and then shrugged. "A melody. It's faint, and somehow familiar, but I don't know what it is."

Leaf and Crusty had taken the faeries and were sorting through the armor. Harlan was focused on me, so he didn't see what they were doing behind his back.

"Is this too!" Crusty chirped and she and five faeries came over and dropped a larger piece at my feet. It was also a shoulder guard, but lighter in color and far less decorated.

I was afraid to touch it.

Alric sat behind me and wrapped his arms around me to hold me down. "Now grab it."

I looked over my shoulder at him. If I flew he was probably going as well. At his nod, I picked up the piece. It was far heavier than its size indicated, and while I felt a shock run through me, and from Alric's twitch he felt it too, we didn't get flung anywhere. It was also singing to me.

CHAPTER THIRTY—FOUR

"WHY AND HOW DID THAT piece of metal send you across the way? It didn't explode." Balith didn't come any closer.

Alric released me and then helped me to my feet. "Relics and Taryn have a unique relationship; we don't question it."

I was going to hand the two pieces back to Harlan, but found I really didn't want to. It wasn't like with the emerald dragon, I didn't feel compelled. It was more as if they were comforting to me. Ancient shoulder armor as a comfort was a bit odd, but with what had been going on the last few months, I'd take whatever I could get.

"Harlan, do you mind if I keep these?" I wasn't going to explain why, especially since no one else heard the singing.

"Not at all," he said with a gracious bow. "I am not sure we could remove them from you anyway. They are glowing where you're touching them."

I looked down in surprise. He was right. It was subtle, but where my hand held them, a soft glow emitted.

As I noticed it though, the glow faded. "Thank you." I didn't have my big pack with me but I did have a good sized pouch inside my cloak so I put them in there. They were a bit bulky, but not too awkward.

"We have our own direction to go, but hopefully your king will do the right thing and join us," Alric said, as we walked back to the forest. "Oh, and Orenda, when you're there you'll meet an elf named Nasif. Can you tell him we found the scroll in Beccia? He should know what it means."

She nodded, then ran forward and gave each of us a hug. "I missed both of you, but we'll see you soon. I'm certain of that."

"Leaf? Do you want the rest of the faeries to stay with them?" I'd noticed that the ones who had been traveling with Orenda and Harlan hadn't left. Yes, Garbage had set them to their task, but Leaf was her lieutenant.

Leaf pulled the faeries into a tight circle and they all started jabbering in native faery. Finally, she and Crusty pulled back and came closer to Alric and I. "They stay. You no cage." She glared at Balith and the rest of the knights.

"I really would listen to her," I said as I added my glare to hers. "We have ways of watching you now, and if anyone does anything to these faeries—or to Harlan or Orenda— you'll find out how I managed to bury someone so far down."

Alric nodded to Harlan, who really wasn't paying much attention, and we made our way back to the horses.

Leaf and Crusty didn't ride on our shoulders on the way back, but they did stay close to us.

"So, do you really think these pieces are Ancient?" I patted my cloak where the pouch was. The pouch and cloak dampened the singing, but I heard it when I touched where they were.

"Harlan rarely is wrong. For all his blustering, he is a good digger. And the brief look I had at the markings indicate they were Ancient." He helped me up on my horse, and then went for his own. "You're not hearing actual words are you? Just the music?" He turned his horse around and mine followed.

"It's hard to explain, I heard sounds, not just the music. And I think they are words. But I can't understand them. There's something about them that is soothing though."

Hopefully he wouldn't think that was any weirder than the fact I heard something in the first place.

He shrugged. "We've established that you and the relics have an odd relationship. Those aren't relics, but they could be similar if they have magic attached to them. The way it threw you is probably a magical reaction from it. They might be responding to the manticore presence inside you. Honestly, that could be triggering these encounters."

That could be. Aside from protection, no one really knew what the manticore did. Besides taking up residence in unsuspecting people.

We both stayed in our thoughts, and even the faeries were mostly quiet as we approached the cottage. I was so lost in my own thoughts about relics, armor, and whatnot that I almost rode past Alric and right into the clearing. I somehow missed the gang of goons right in front of us, but Alric stopped me.

"Alric! Taryn! Stay back. There were ten but two are missing. Lorcan and Mathilda are barricaded in the cottage," Covey yelled from in front of the cottage door.

One of the thugs surrounding the cottage stepped forward and punched her hard enough to shut her up. She was tied up, along with Padraig. Unlike her though, he looked unconscious and had a nasty bruise already forming on his forehead. At first I didn't see Lorcan or Mathilda, but then they both briefly appeared in the window of the cottage.

The eight attacking the cottage looked like nothing more than common bandits. It was a sad state of one's life when being attacked by a bunch of bandits was a better option than what usually happened. How they got the jump on fighters like Covey and Padraig was a damn good question.

"We want your horses and your gear," the leader, or at least the largest of them, yelled toward the cottage as he kept an eye on Alric and me. "And your coin. Toss the gear and coin out soon and we won't hurt your pretty friends."

I personally didn't mind being called pretty; I'd rather it wasn't by someone who looked like he'd been beaten every day of his life with an ugly stick. Alric wasn't as fond. Actually, from the look on his face, I don't think he would have liked anything they said.

I'd figured he'd use a spell or two and clean these people out of here. But instead he slid off his horse and drew his sword. "Don't use magic, Taryn. They have a spell breaker." He pointed to the trees behind the fighters where a small spell ball blinked.

I'd heard of those. Similar to what Covey used to have in her kitchen; they could damper or mess up any spells within a set area. There went our advantage of being magic users.

"Who wants to be first?" Alric loosened his shoulders and walked forward. The grin on his face was completely inappropriate for a battle, but maybe this would help him work out some tension.

"Look, there's ten of us and two of you. Your swords might be fancy, but there's no chance for you here. Give us what we want, and we'll be on our way."

I had gotten off my horse and also drawn my sword. No magic, but I'd wager Mathilda and Lorcan were holding the cottage with magic. That spell ball's range couldn't breach into the cottage.

Leaf and Crusty flew forward but crashed to the ground after a few feet.

"Yep, don't like that much, do ya? Your friends didn't either. Too bad they got back in that triple cursed cottage before we could grab them."

"Leaf, Crusty, run back here and stay with the horses." They ran back and climbed onto the saddle of my horse, since it was the closest.

Alric had kept moving forward and the leader nodded to two of his people, a tall woman and a shorter man, who looked like maybe he was part minotaur.

He was such a strong magic user, I'd almost forgotten how well Alric fought with a sword. Unlike the two facing him all of his moves were graceful and practiced. They were also alarmingly fast. Both thugs were quickly dispatched.

He raised his bloody sword and pointed to the rest of the bandits. "I can do this for a lot longer than it would take to kill all of you, even if the rest of you come at once. Call off your two people who are pathetically trying to steal our horses but can't because magic is working back there, and leave."

"Not if we take her." The voice came from behind me a moment before I felt the sword near my neck.

I was nowhere as fast as Alric, nor did I have his skills, but anger far more reaching that just at these bandits flowed through me. I dropped down beneath the sword, spun, and ran the idiot behind me through with my sword. Then withdrew my sword from the body and spun back to the bandit leader. "Back. Off." Maybe Leaf wasn't the only one able to duplicate Garbage.

Alric had been in the act of lowering his sword when the now dead idiot grabbed me, but he smiled and raised it again. "Seriously, we have shown you we can fight; I'd listen to the pretty lady and back off. Way off."

I mimicked his stance, a calm swordswoman who knew what she was doing. But inside I was trying to figure out where I learned that move and how I did it so well.

The leader of the bandits clearly was weighing his options. Three of his people were dead, and he had nothing to show for it. Yet he was debating continuing the fight. He might look like a standard brigand, but he wasn't acting like one. A thief of opportunity would have cut his losses and run.

"We'll let you go, if you just leave," Alric said. He hadn't put away his sword, but he was relaxing.

"No, we won't." I stepped forward and took out one of

my knives. There was something wrong here. "This isn't a normal robbery, is it? You knew we were magic users. And those things are expensive as hell."

Before the bandit could respond, I threw the knife at the spell ball. It didn't hit the ball directly, but it struck the branch it was hanging from with enough force to drop it. The ball shattered as it hit the ground, and if asked I was going to state that had been my plan all along. I spun to Alric. "We can't let them go." I couldn't explain it, but there was an edgy feeling in the back of my head.

The bandits tried to run, but Alric cast a spell and five of the ones in front of us froze in place. Actually, they were moving, but it was so slow they looked frozen.

"Can you get the other two?" Alric tipped his head back toward the back of the cottage.

I wanted to get Mathilda, Lorcan, and the faeries out of the cottage, but he was right. If I didn't want these bandits free and loose, I didn't want their friends in the back running around either. Even if it was just a feeling.

The two in the back were focusing on trying to get the horses free. The animals appeared to be just tied to a post, but there was magic that kept them in place.

"Seriously? Can't even undo a few knots?" As I spoke, I cast a sleep spell, not as good as a freeze spell, but faster. It wouldn't hold more than fifteen minutes or so, but should help.

A fleet of faeries came zipping around the cottage. Alric must have told everyone they could come out. Garbage flew up and kicked both bandits. "Where put these?" As she spoke, the faery group split in half, each group surrounding one of the bandits.

"Out front with the others." I checked the spelled knots on the horses—they were still secure—and followed the faeries out front. Either they'd forgotten how to carry someone, or they were deliberately bumping them on the ground the entire way out.

Alric and Lorcan were tying up the slowly moving bandits. Mathilda was untying Covey and Padraig and trying to get him to wake up.

Covey shook off the remains of her ropes and ran for the bandit leader. She hit him hard, pounding him. "Fight back, damn you!"

"Alric put a spell on them, we can't let them go." I walked over as the faeries dropped their prey over by Alric and Lorcan.

"I want to fight him. They ambushed us." She kicked him again, but her anger was slowing.

The last of them were tied, gagged, and dragged to the far edge of the clearing.

"Why didn't we just let them go?" Lorcan looked around at us.

"There's something wrong about this Alric and I killed three of their people, there is no reason for them to think we have anything worth dying over, yet they were willing to risk it." I looked around at my friends. "So why?"

"She has a point. I was too busy trying to kill them to question it." Alric nodded to Mathilda. "No offense, but aside from it being in the middle of a clearing with no other houses around, there's nothing to indicate there are things of value."

"None taken. I think this might be a call for my magic." Mathilda nodded and stalked over to the pile of bandits. Twenty-three faeries and two constructs trailed out behind her. "We have a problem, one I'm sure you heard. Some of us want you dead, very slowly and painfully. Some of us just want to let you go. I simply want the truth. Why did you come here?"

She held up her hand and the nearest bandit rose in the air. "Now, I need to know why you were determined to get into my cottage, and what you were going to do with us."

The bandit twisted and squirmed to try and get away,

but there was nothing to push off of since he was in the air. Mathilda gave a small wave of her hand and his gag dropped.

"I don't know. He hired us, gave instructions to Jahnuis, told us it would be worth more than we'd imagine."

"What would be?" Mathilda asked, but when he didn't respond, she raised him higher.

The leader of the bandits started flopping around; clearly the freeze spell was wearing off. Covey went over and kicked him.

"The diamond, a huge diamond in the shape of a sphinx. The man that spoke to Jahnuis described you all and said we'd find it easily in your possessions."

Mathilda let him fall to the ground, and then stepped back with us. Covey stayed near the bandits in case any of them needed more kicking.

"Damn it, the mayor didn't have to go after us. They sent these idiots after us thinking they were going to get rich off the massive diamond we were just hauling around with us." Alric kept his voice low. "And whoever sent them had a lot of money, that spell breaker was top of the line, a few hundred gold easily."

"But they know we don't have it yet, correct?" Lorcan nodded to me. "Why send them to rob us of something we don't have?"

"Most likely to stop us completely." I walked over to the lead bandit and stared into his eyes. "Whether you found it or not, you were going to kill us." I really wish I knew where this knowledge came from. Kind of like that move I'd done when the guy came up behind me. The piece of armor in my cloak sang a little louder. Crap—the armor was doing it? I already had one relic messing with me; I didn't need more Ancient things joining in. The singing quieted again, just a little melody on the edge of awareness.

"We can't let them go, nor take them with us." Padraig had been quiet, but the way he was watching me said he'd noticed something odd about me.

"I get to kill the leader," Covey said as she flexed her fingers.

"Maybe leave them for Orenda's brother?" Alric said and looked to me. "We leave them here, they'll find them. They can haul them to the enclave, and let Nasif and Dueble talk to them."

"Wait, Orenda has a brother? And he's here?" Covey had unflexed her fingers and was focusing on us now.

"We would have told you when we got here, but you were busy." I looked to the pile of bandits. "Are they secure there? I'd rather continue this in comfort."

Mathilda flung another spell at them then walked toward her cottage. "Yes, and I agree. And I found this on our friend." She held up a crushed piece of paper as she walked by.

CHAPTER THIRTY—FIVE

I HADN'T SEEN HER EVEN TOUCH the bandit she had in the air, but Mathilda was a sly one. We followed her into the cottage, but the faeries and constructs didn't follow us.

"Girls? Aren't you coming in?" I held the door open, but the flyers stayed hovering near the tree line.

"Needs talks. Not happy." Garbage might not have heard all of what had happened to the faeries traveling with Orenda and Harlan, but she'd heard enough to piss her off. Not that it was difficult to do.

Bunky and Irving bobbed around, torn between which group to go with. I finally waved them on. "Stay with the girls, Bunky. You and Irving can keep an eye on them. Just come tell us if they do anything rash." I turned toward Garbage. "And that means, don't leave this clearing, got it?" There had been an itchy feeling between my shoulder blades ever since we saw the bandits. I had a feeling we might need to hit the road quickly.

"We talk," Garbage said. Which of course didn't acknowledge my comment, and she had no intention of doing so. In her mind, if the talking resulted in a good reason to leave, they'd leave. My only hope was that Bunky and Irving would warn us.

"Okay, so what's on the paper?" I settled in on the sofa next to Alric.

"I thought you were first going to tell us about seeing

Orenda's brother?" Covey wasn't going to let go of that one.

"The paper seems to be more important right now, but I agree we need to hear of your adventures." Lorcan had been trying to get a peek at the paper, but Mathilda was holding it tight.

"The paper is quick and easy. Not only did our enemies set us up to be followed by this group of bandits, they made sure all of Beccia thinks we are carrying a huge diamond." She held up the paper. "Crude drawing of us, along with the general direction we were heading. And a reward for anyone who brought back the other items with it. The finders could keep the diamond."

"That doesn't make sense." Alric scowled at the paper and Mathilda handed it to him. "Edana wants the sphinx. If she was behind this, she wouldn't be offering to let the finder keep it."

"Unless she is certain she can take it from whoever finds it. There's always a chance that if we did have it, and someone did take it from us, that they wouldn't go back for the second reward. But most thieves are too greedy—they'd go back." Padraig took the flyer from Alric and shook his head.

"Or there is a second faction besides her's," Lorcan said. "Just because those two crime lords were killed doesn't mean there couldn't be two or more groups behind what's happening. That mayor friend of yours might not be working with this woman. These relics have been appearing for over a year now. Word spreads quickly among thieves."

"So we need to modify our direction and travel faster. You win, Alric. No more time to pace ourselves," Padraig said. "Now, you found Orenda's brother?"

Everyone started gathering their things as Alric and I filled them in on Orenda, Harlan, and the knights. Mathilda was furious at them for caging the faeries.

"That was thoroughly uncalled for." She was securing

her cottage as well. She'd try to keep moving it along with us, but there was a better chance than before that she'd have to leave it behind. She shrugged off the fact that she didn't have a horse.

"That's what the girls were talking about just now." My things were packed, and aside from Mathilda, I was the last one. "So, do we leave the bandits for Balith?" I was fine if I had to kill someone to save myself or someone I cared for. But going out and slaughtering a bunch of tied-up and spelled bandits wasn't high on my okay list.

I opened the door to find the pack of faeries hovering right outside. "We no kill. Yet." Garbage was talking about the elven knights, or I assumed so. But it coincided with what was going on in my head.

She was fuming, but I was certain they'd find something to work out their frustrations on soon enough. I felt bad for the wildlife we might meet along the way.

"I think I can trigger a spell to call your friends to this clearing," Mathilda said from her open doorway after the rest of us had come out. "You mentioned that she was a healer?" At my nod, she continued. "I can set the spell to be triggered to her. Leave a note of what instructions you have, and I'll make sure to spell it for compulsion for her brother. I don't like to do that, but locking up the faeries wasn't nice." She held out a quill and paper.

Alric quickly wrote a note and handed it to her.

Mathilda said a few spell words over it, and then settled a larger spell over the bandits. "It is done. The first layer will call to your friend Orenda, and the second layer will make that brother of hers, whom I already dislike, obey. These hooligans will end up under the care of Nasif, and I added my sister too."

I chuckled. Nasif and Dueble would have been one thing, having Siabiane on them was something else. Especially with whatever spells Mathilda added to that note. Most likely neither the bandits nor the elven knights were going to have a good time of things for a while.

"We'll need to travel further in the woods; we're still a few days out from the hidden realm," Alric got on his horse and nodded to the cottage. "You might want to ride now, if we have to go too far off it could be difficult to find each other." He didn't seem concerned about her lack of a horse either. Maybe elves just called them as needed. Although I'd yet to see any of them do that. However, Mathilda seemed more connected to nature than the rest of them.

She looked up at her cottage and smiled. "I think I have at least another day's travel in here. And now that I have found Taryn again, I will be able to find you, never worry." Her smile dropped. "Just be wary on the trail. Common hooligans won't be able to follow me while this is moving, but they can follow you."

Everyone was on their horses, with the constructs and faeries circling in their eagerness to go. "Let's go. I want to get some distance between us and whoever else might be following." Alric led the group with me, Covey, Lorcan, and Padraig stringing out behind.

Even though the faeries and Bunky and Irving hadn't found signs of anyone near us, everyone stayed silent. Alric led us far deeper into the woods.

Alric was hunched down on his horse, but I knew he was watching everything around him.

The faeries and constructs were flitting around high in the trees, not dropping too low, but not flying off, either. I'd say they understood that we needed to move quickly and silently, except that would never be a consideration for faery behavior. Not for any length of time anyway. I guessed they were mulling over whatever Queen Mungoosey had told them now that we were getting closer to the hidden realm. That and Garbage was probably annoyed she hadn't been able to hunt down Balith and his knights.

We were two hours into our trip when the arrow flew

over my head. Far too close over my head. More followed but by then we were scrunching over our saddles and riding as fast as was safe.

They were coming from behind, so in my mind that was good. We could still out run them. Shooting in this dense of a forest couldn't be easy. Of course, I'd been hanging around sneaky people for the last year. Soon, a tiny voice questioned why they would be trying to come after us when the likelihood of hitting us was slim. Which meant they were trying to herd us, not hit us. I opened my mouth to share my newfound wisdom, when Alric took off to the left, cutting away from the arrows and the direction they'd been trying to push us.

Padraig brought up the rear. He waited until we'd changed to Alric's new direction, then spun and launched a volley of spell arrows.

I had been becoming a bit jaded about spells and fighting lately. But those were impressive. A bit longer than a standard arrow, their fletching looked like flame. A pair of screams told me that at least some of the group found targets.

"There are three behind us, but I can't risk another spell. They also have a spell ball with them."

Damn. Those things were expensive, and there was no way two separate troops of bandits were able to afford them. Whoever was sending the bandits our way was not only giving them directions, they were high-end outfitting them as well.

Alric was good at sliding through a forest unseen. That was a harder task with four of us trying to do the same behind him. The arrows stopped after Padraig's spell arrows hit, but there were still sounds of pursuit. We zigged again and turned back the way we came. Or so it felt to me. The forest was thinning out but Alric adjusted our direction to stay in the denser trees.

That might work great for him; I know I was having a

hard time keeping up. Padraig was awfully close to me.

"Fun! Why no arrows?" Crusty was the only faery in sight and she was flying backwards in front of me.

"Arrows are bad, sweetie. Where are the rest of the girls and Bunky and Irving?" I had been sitting up a bit more but slunk back down in case our pursuers started firing again.

"They go take care of things back there," Crusty said and pointed behind me, where whoever was following us was.

"No, we need to get them back here." I knew that under normal circumstances the faeries could hold their own. I was beginning to think there was no such thing as normal anymore. The last thing we needed was for our pursuers to hurt or grab the faeries or constructs.

"Is okay. Using golden growly thing. In friend gargoyle." Crusty stopped flying and landed right behind the horse's ears.

CHAPTER THIRTY—SIX

M Y BRAIN WAS BEING BOUNCED around by the horse or I would have immediately figured out what she was talking about. A few seconds later her meaning hit me.

The basilisk? Crap. I knew that Irving had disgorged the gargoyle into the chest, but we'd figured the basilisk was being difficult and just hadn't wanted to come out. That he was able to access it and use it as a weapon wasn't good.

Unfortunately, the sounds of pursuit were growing. Whoever our pursuers had been herding us toward must have figured out their trap was sprung and joined in the chase instead.

I hated the idea that the faeries and the constructs were off doing things with a rampaging relic bent on destruction, but right now all I could do was hang on to my horse.

Crusty was staying on top of my horse by hanging on to the forelock and mane. Her wings were tucked in behind her and her flower petal cap was long gone. She'd have an easier time of it if she just let go and flew, but judging by her grin she thought this was more fun.

Screams and thumps started coming from behind us.

"Something else is back there!" Padraig yelled.

"The faeries and constructs are using the basilisk!" I yelled back. This wasn't a good way to tell them, but my friends needed to know.

Alric was in sight, but pretty far ahead. He spun his horse

around a tree and came back as soon as the words left my mouth. I'd forgotten again how sharp elven ears were.

"We can't let them do that," he yelled as he approached.

The rest of us turned to follow him.

I used to feel guilty when my faeries did something bad—after this last year, I no longer had that issue. They were their own creatures and my control over them was non-existent. I still had a twinge at Irving's duplicity since I'd fought to let him keep his relic—I never thought he'd use it. The basilisk would turn anyone who looked at it to stone. And unlike the rest of the relics so far, it had been very active in making certain people saw it.

We finally were able to turn and follow Alric. Riderless horses passed us with bits of stones dropping off of them. At least the constructs were aiming for the riders and not the horses. Some nearby farmer was going to get a nice surprise of a dozen free horses soon.

Alric had stopped just ahead of us and we slowed to come around him. There was a circle of stone statues right in front of us. Part of the reason the horses had been saved was that many of the riders had gotten off of them. Which just made them easier targets for the basilisk.

The faeries were swarming around, yelling and waving their war sticks. Bunky was flying high. And Irving was collapsed at the bottom of a tree.

I moved to jump off my horse. How could his friends be celebrating if he was injured?

Alric held out a hand. "Wait a moment. He's re-digesting the basilisk."

Irving lifted off from the ground, wobbled a bit, and then flew up to join Bunky.

"They really let loose the basilisk?" Covey asked with a combination of fear and admiration.

Alric watched the woods around us. "I caught the tail end of it. The faeries swarmed the riders, destroyed the spell breaker, and got most of them off their horses. Bunky and Irving were circling the former riders, and Irving had his mouth open. I never saw the basilisk out, but once I knew what was in his open mouth, I didn't look at him." He shook his head as he watched our flyers looping around the trees. "And you'll be glad to know the faeries are immune to the basilisk. I saw at least three take direct hits and it didn't even slow them down." He got off his horse and walked over to the collection of stone statues.

Padraig followed but went past them and a bit further into the woods. "There are some more back here, crumbling. Somehow they got the riders but not the horses."

I was torn. On one hand the flyers saved us, but the risk they took was massive. However, watching the way Irving flew around I doubted we were getting that thing out of him unless he wanted it out. Maybe he felt that since he didn't have defensive abilities like Bunky or the faeries, the basilisk was his weapon.

"Bunky and Irving? Come down here, please." Unlike the faeries, the constructs usually listened to me. Unless the faeries told them something that went against what I said. "That was good, thank you for stopping them. But, Irving, you are guarding one of the most important pieces of a deadly weapon. You can't use it. Do you understand?" There was too much risk that the basilisk would fall out of him again and turn all of us to stone.

Both constructs looked at each other, and then turned to me with a head bob and gronk. Hopefully I got through.

"This *is* fascinating though." Lorcan had gotten off his horse and was walking around the stone people. "I didn't get a chance to see the prior victims. They truly are solid stone." He picked up a few crumbled pieces, and then dropped them. "They feel vaguely alive in a way though. Horribly fascinating."

"They must have been sent by the mayor. I can't imagine Nivinal's mother sending out common thugs to chase us." I looked at the former thugs in question from my horse.

"But the crime lords controlled these people. The mayor had only been in town a few months," Covey said, then rubbed her forehead. "And that was why Largen had been replaced, and when Cirocco found out, he was killed. Sorry, all of that horse riding has rattled my brain. Took me a bit to mentally catch up. "

"It does explain your crime lord's switch. I agree that this doesn't seem like Nivinal, and by extension, not Edana either." Padraig and Lorcan probably knew Nivinal, or rather, the Grand Inquisitor, better than anyone on our side.

"So, if there are two sides fighting over whatever they think they'll find in Beccia, can't we just wait them out? Nothing is there, right? Not anymore." I didn't want the syclarions and the scary magic users chasing after us, but it did make me nervous that they weren't.

"We have no idea how long that might take. Once they realize that what they are looking for is gone, I think they will be coming after us." Padraig gathered a few samples of the stone into a small bag.

"I think as long as Amara can keep the hedge up and the mayor and Edana out, we're safe," Alric said. "But we should keep moving. There's no way to know how many enterprising folks the mayor pulled out of town before the hedge went up, and how many more he might have following us."

"What are we going to do about them?" I pointed to the statues. The ones near the Spheres had eventually sunk into the sand, but these wouldn't do that.

Lorcan shrugged. "Not much we can do but leave them. They are dead even though the stone feels warm."

Everyone got back on their horses and Alric did a quick recon to make sure no one was lingering who hadn't been hit by the basilisk. He turned us around, pointing north but at a slightly different angle than we'd been originally heading.

The faeries and constructs dropped down a bit lower than before, first sticking closer to us, then spreading out. I knew boredom was an extremely real threat with the faeries, and we were probably going to be riding for many more hours.

"Garbage? Might I have a word with you?" I held up one hand. She came to me, but dropped on the horse instead of my hand. At least she came.

"What? We save." She folded her arms, ready to let loose her glare if I berated her for the faeries helping Irving.

"Oh, I know, and we appreciate it." I gave her my most sincere smile. "And I have a boon to ask of you. Do you think you could have your girls fly around our path, staying where you can see us, but watch the areas around where we've been and where we're going?" The faeries in the past would have been too flakey to do that. I used them as part of my bounty hunting out of desperation, but they'd always been unreliable. Things had definitely changed in the past year.

"We watch? Tell you?" She seemed to be thinking about it, but her thoughts could be somewhere else completely.

"It would be important work. You and your faeries would have to be silent and stay unseen while you are watching for others following us or lying in wait."

"Important." She puffed up her chest and nodded. "I tell them we do. Tell if things happen."

"Thank you," I said as she flew off to the other faeries. Best case, we ended up with sentries on our path ahead of and behind us. Hopefully, at the least, we kept a bunch of potentially destructive little beings from getting bored. The past week had been fine; they flew off on their own and joined us at night. But that needed to change if we were being hunted.

The rest of the day was uneventful, for which I was grateful. Mathilda met us at our stopping point within a few minutes of us getting off the horses. She must have been waiting nearby; it usually took her an hour or so to find us.

This time she found us before all of the faeries came in.

Lorcan quickly explained what had happened, with Garbage adding commentary on how the growly thing was her idea. I wasn't sure why she called it the growly thing since I'd never heard it make a sound. However, I agreed that if it did, it would probably growl.

Once Garbage decided she'd said what information that needed to be said, and the faeries had received a bunch of sugar, she flew my way.

"We find. From stone peoples. Under rock." She reached into her pocket in the front of her overalls, pulled out one of her faery bags, and from it, a crumpled piece of paper. "Here."

I took it and unrumpled it. It was the same paper about us the other group had, but with writing on the back. I read it out loud. "'They are heading north. Don't have yet. Will get other two pieces.' Then a pretty damn good description of the exact direction we were going. Garbage found this under a rock; did they think their people would find it?" I handed it to Alric.

His scowl came back after the second read. "Garbage, what type of rock was this under?"

Garbage had shoved yet another piece of sugar into her mouth but gave him a one-eyed stare.

I answered for her. "Why does the type of rock matter? The information never got to the mayor."

"Was it very round and flat? Did it feel funny when you moved it?"

The sugar in her mouth came out at the last two questions. "Yes and yes." She wiggled her fingers. "Spell-y."

Alric crumpled the paper, tossed it on the ground and threw a fire ball at it. "Damn it, not only did they give them spell breakers, they gave them a message stone. Do you know how rare those are? We had one in the enclave that we had to destroy a few years ago. Even before the Breaking, few mages could make them. The words on this page went right to the damn mage who set it up."

CHAPTER THIRTY–SEVEN

———◆———

THERE WAS NO WAY THAT was good. "Are we sure that Edana isn't involved in this? There seems to be a lot of high-end magic toys being thrown around." I wasn't sure which was worse: her being after us right now, or the mayor having that kind of magical power.

Alric ran his hand through his hair. "I have no idea what to think at this point. No one now should have the ability to make one of those."

"Could they have found an old one? Old and annoying relics seem to be popping up around here a lot." Not something I was happy about, but definitely a reality.

Padraig shook his head. "Doubtful. We had destroy the one in the enclave because it started breaking down. It was firing spells randomly and set a shop on fire."

"This is disturbing information," Mathilda said. She'd been silent when she arrived, but now seemed worried. Which we all were, but she rarely showed it. "When the surviving elves decided to hide, I took it upon myself to hunt down dangerous items. I searched for decades for any sign of those damn stones. I found nothing. I know it's a few hours ride back, and now that we're being followed we need to reach that hidden realm sooner rather than later, but we can't leave that stone out there. They were rumored to be able to do far darker things than just transmit words and images. We have to go back and get it."

"Nope. It boom," Crusty said.

The rest of the faeries had gone off to go regale each other over their battle of the day, but Crusty had stuck around. Probably looking for more sugar.

"The rock went boom? As in what, exactly?" Boom meant too many things to them for me to guess at right now.

"BOOM!" Crusty flung out her hands, shook them, and then wiggled her fingers down.

"That looks like an explosion to me," Padraig said. "How did you do it?"

I also wanted to know why. Granted, there seemed to be a 'you didn't ask so we're not telling you' situation going on with the faeries, but Garbage hadn't really seemed to have a clue what they'd found that note under.

"Zap! Boom!"

I watched Bunky and Irving flying around the faeries. The chimera constructs did have an ability for an electric discharge. I'd seen it used against rakasa and sceanra anam, but never anything else.

"Bunky? Can you come down here for a moment?"

He came down, with Irving drifting right behind him. "Did you blow up the rock that Garbage found the note under? While you guys were fighting off the people who were after us?"

He gave a hesitant head bob.

"Why?"

The series of gronks, growls, and hisses were something I'd never heard before. Nor could I understand.

Luckily, Alric could. "He said it was new, old, bad magic. Not supposed to be used here, not now."

"How did you know that, my fine construct friend?" Mathilda came forward at Alric's translation.

Bunky came closer and gronked in earnest.

"He said he can sense bad magic," Alric said, then shook his head. "That would have been good to know earlier."

"That stands with the myths of the chimera constructs,

but I honestly never thought it was literal," Lorcan said. "From what we could decipher, they were created by the Ancients as guardians, sort of magical watch-dogs, with the main purpose of destroying the sceanra anam."

"And those things are definitely bad magic," I said, then smiled at Bunky. "That was good of you to destroy it." I ignored the snorts from Alric and Padraig behind me. I really did think it was better if something that was bad magic just didn't exist anymore. "But you need to tell one of us before you do something like that again."

Bunky bobbed and gronked to Alric.

"He said his first job is to protect, but he will tell us first if it doesn't interfere with that." Alric smiled. "I can't fault him for that."

We sat up camp inside Mathilda's cottage one final time. After this she was going to have it hide, her words, then she would join us. I had no idea how to hide something that large, but I'd given up on figuring it out. The entrance to this hidden realm was closer than they'd originally thought—one of the reasons Mathilda was a bit later, she'd been recalculating its location. It was still too far to reach tonight, but the original thought had been another few days of travel.

We were settled in after dinner, with the constructs flying recon. We'd have regular watches still, but right now it was nice to just sit together.

"Can you show us those shoulder pieces? I have an odd collection of armor I've gathered over the years in my wanderings," Mathilda said.

I'd gotten so used to the soft music that I'd almost forgotten about them.

"Taryn says they sing to her." Alric shrugged when I shot him a look. Then smiled. "It's just another thing to keep in mind; you have armor sing to you." He was sitting next to me and gave the shoulder his arm had been resting on a little squeeze.

I didn't know that everyone needed to know.

I took them out of my pouch, yup, still singing. To speed things up, I passed them in opposite directions.

"Definitely from the Ancient's time. Not sure if these were the Ancients' though," Padraig said as he studied the smaller piece. "The sizing looks human."

"Humans weren't out here when the Ancients were, I thought. Couldn't they have been elves?" I asked. There really wasn't that much difference in terms of body size between the two species.

Lorcan was checking something in the bottom of the larger piece. "It could be elven, but the markings are definitely Ancient. There were a few wanderers during the time of the Ancients. Neither humans nor elves were common out here, but we were here." He fussed over where a strap would be on a normal shoulder piece. "I thought the straps had dissolved, but it looks more as if they were never made." He held the piece up where it would be on his shoulder. His eyes widened and he removed his hand. The piece stayed in place.

"It's doing that with magic?" Covey held out her hand for the smaller piece. There was no way it would fit on either Padraig or Alric, and Mathilda was still rummaging through her armor collection in the back room.

The smaller piece slid right off her shoulder. She tried twice more, and then shook her head. "Maybe they need magic to work." She handed it to me.

The piece burst into a more exuberant song when I touched it. I started to raise it to my shoulder and it jumped on from four inches away. "That can't be normal." I reached up to take it off, but Mathilda came back into the room at that point.

"Leave it on. Oh my. This is amazing." She scurried over, plucked the second piece off of Lorcan's shoulder, and held it about a foot from my other shoulder. When nothing happened, she slowly moved it closer. At four or five inches away, it jumped to me. The first piece had been gentle; this one pushed me backwards into the sofa with the force of it hitting me. Like the first one, it hung on with no problem.

"Blood magic?" Alric had leaned forward to get a better look at the armor.

"Bad blood magic?" I can't say I liked any sort of magic that had the word blood involved.

"No, no. Not bad blood magic. The armor is spelled for magic users as Covey hypothesized, and a familiar bond. Somewhere way down on your family line you were related to the owners." Mathilda beamed. "Those markings are a family line; these two pieces belonged to a joined couple." She came closer and gently pulled the smaller piece off. If felt as if it hugged me trying to stay on, but finally went with her. The larger piece came off easily, but considering that it was way too large to be fitting there at all without straps, there were still hinky things going on.

"So, there were enough humans hanging around during the time of the Ancients for a family of them to wear armor with Ancient writing? Or do we think I have elvish way back in my family?" I really wished I could read Ancient; the wording looked lovely on the smaller piece.

Mathilda shrugged, but her smile was huge. "I have no idea! Isn't it grand? Oh, Siabiane is going to need to see these."

"Any clue as to why they are singing to me?" Judging from the lack of reactions as the pieces were passed around, I figured no one else heard anything.

It said a lot that although none of them heard it, none of my friends looked surprised.

"The only thing I would guess is that it's a familial tie, as Mathilda said," Lorcan surmised. I'd handed him the smaller piece this time. "It is amazing that humans had spells strong enough to react thousands of years later. Although, if they were working and living with the Ancients, that could have been where the magic came from. Who knows what it would have done had you found this a thousand years ago."

"Is right," Crusty said, as she flew down next to Lorcan and patted the armor.

"Taryn having this is right? Is that why you and Leaf brought her the other piece?" Lorcan held out his hand and Crusty quickly grabbed the sugar in it. The rest of the faeries were having a talk in the tiny house. They'd not been happy to learn we'd have to leave it behind for this portion of the trip.

"Yes. Is her." She fluttered over to me and landed on my lap. "Good." Without further comment, she curled up on my leg like a tiny, deranged kitten and went to sleep.

CHAPTER THIRTY–EIGHT

—◆—

THE NEXT MORNING CAME QUIETLY enough, even if my sleep hadn't been. I'd tossed and turned the entire time. This time in my nightmare it was I, not my friends, who was under attack, but it was almost comical. Giant pieces of armor, elven saltshakers, and a huge sarcophagus were chasing me. First through a massive forest, then plains, and finally through a desert.

Then a giant gargoyle construct, similar to Irving only about twenty times the size and with a cruel face, started swooping down toward me. Its mouth was open and I was pretty sure it was trying to eat me.

"Ah!" I bolted upright swinging my hands around to ward off the giant creature in my dream.

"What? Are we under attack?" Unlike me, sitting in my bed trying to figure out who I was, where I was, and what was going on, Covey woke up from a sound sleep awake, aware, and with her hands already curling into claws.

"No, sorry, just a bad dream." I blinked a few times to get my bearings and swung my legs out of bed. The sounds of breakfast were coming from the front room, so even if I had been able to go back to sleep, it wouldn't have been for long. Shower and packing done, I hauled myself out to the front room.

Everyone except Alric and Padraig was there, eating and looking at the spelled map. This time they'd clustered the food to one side so that both could be done simultaneously.

"Do Alric and Padraig know that you're making plans regarding the map without them?" Hopefully food would clear the images from my mind. Although I did flinch when Irving and Bunky flew down from the rafters.

"We talked about it late last night; this is more catching the rest of you up." Lorcan pointed to the corner of the map. "Your odious friend Grimwold was right about the spell trigger. I have translated this spell completely. It will make the entrance appear, but it will only work for a few hours. We have to time it so we are far enough away that it will lead us to the correct location yet close enough to be able to work the second spell to allow us entrance." He shook his head. "It is going to be tricky."

Mathilda had been securing dishes into cabinets as we spoke but came to join us. "I was able to pick up the disturbance that must have been caused by the entrance, but only enough to tell the general direction and distance. I think once we are fully ready here, we should cast the spell." For the second time in two days, there was a crease in her forehead.

"What do we need to do?" Covey was ready for action and whatever was needed.

"I'm not sure. It appears I translated the word sacrifice incorrectly, but there is something that must come from each person." Lorcan shrugged. "It's not clear what it is. Nor is why the faeries felt you and Taryn wouldn't contribute to getting us inside. I would like at least another hour before we set this off. If we miss it, this spell won't work for another ten years. I'm afraid that was another limitation that hadn't been clear on the prior read."

"That is something good to know." I hated deadlines. "So if the only way to get the sphinx is to go inside this place, and the map is the only way inside? Could we just try the spell, fail, and leave the sphinx there?" I looked around. Yes, getting all of the relics together to be destroyed would be the best option, but if there was a simple option to make sure the weapon couldn't be assembled for a while, and possibly forgotten in that time, we should take it.

"Won't work," Alric said as he and Padraig came into the cottage. "It would be ten years for the caster or anyone connected to the spell—but another powerful mage could possibly open it before then."

"I doubled back to make sure no one was behind us," Padraig said. "We are being followed. They are a few hours away, but moving fast. I sent tracking beacons back along our path, and it's a larger group of fifty or more. The mayor of Kenithworth is leading them. The Largen copy, whoever she or he really is, is with them also. They destroyed the tracking beacons I sent back as soon as they saw them."

"We have to leave now." Alric had his pack in hand and swung toward the door. "Cast the spell."

The faeries must have been listening from inside their tiny house, as they flew out at once.

"We check path," Garbage said and led her army out of the cottage before any of us could react. Even Bunky and Irving were too fast to catch verbally.

"Not the best idea to have them out there alone, but I don't think we have a choice." Lorcan watched them vanish as we went outside. "I do admire you for dealing with them for so long. They are adorable, but quite a challenge."

I laughed. That was the understatement of the era.

Our horses were out front, saddled and ready, along with a golden shimmery palomino. I'd been right about Mathilda being able to call a horse to her. It reacted to her as if they were old friends.

Mathilda cast a series of spells on the cottage once we were saddled. "That should hold it, and keep it from unwelcome eyes." The cottage seemed to fade from view. Even though I knew it was there, my eyes couldn't focus on it.

Lorcan rode up next to Alric. They both touched the map and set the spell. I couldn't see anything, but judging by their reactions, they could. It was a good idea to have two of them involved.

Alric took the lead with Lorcan directly behind. The woods were a little thinner here, but he was still going faster than I or, judging by her constant adjusting, Covey was used to. There was little call for horses within Beccia and neither of us left town much.

However, considering who was behind us, I agreed with the increased pace. Not to mention if it was difficult to get into this thing, having more time to do it would be better.

After almost an hour and no sound of pursuit, I started to get worried. It said a lot about my current life that *not* hearing someone after me was grounds for concern.

Garbage and her entourage came flying up. "Path clear. Is bored." They swarmed Alric and Lorcan first, and then drifted along to the rest of us.

The two constructs started falling further behind us, finally dropping out of sight behind Padraig. That would be bad if they were close enough to recognize Bunky. Irving hadn't been with us when we went to Kenithworth, but Bunky had been.

"Garbage, get Bunky and Irving back here." I could have yelled but there was a stillness in the forest that disturbed me. It hadn't been silent a few moments ago.

Garbage opened her mouth to argue, but nodded instead. She sensed something as well. She motioned for two of the other faeries to join her, but left Leaf and Crusty with us.

They'd just left when my horse stumbled. Not badly, just a mis-step. But she'd been extremely sure footed up until now. Then the bushes paralleling our path started shaking and crumbled as the ground underneath them gave way.

"Rakasa!" Alric yelled from the front as three shapes exploded from the ground in front of us. He had his horse leap over them as he was only a few feet away, but Lorcan's balked.

Five more came out of the ground near us, but that was

it.

"Eight? I could kill that many on my own." Covey was not impressed and looked ready to jump off her horse and prove her statement.

"They are just trying to slow us; maybe the mayor expected more of them?" Alric stayed on the other side of the line of rakasa but didn't look concerned. "These don't look well."

I had no idea what constituted looking well for one of the small, toothy, gray-green creatures, but they did look greener than before. And they weren't attacking.

Bunky and Irving came racing back from behind us, gronking loudly. Garbage and her faeries flew faster.

"Is trap—make move now!"

Alric made to strike the head off one of the rakasa, but Garbage swooped down and blocked him. "No. Boom!"

Lorcan nudged his horse toward the rakasa in the front, but they moved out of his way. They blocked us when the rest of us tried though, so we rode into the woods to get around. They stayed on the path, their eyes dull. Alric raced through the woods with the rest of us following and the faeries and the constructs nudging us to hurry.

We'd ridden for less than a minute when the explosion happened.

The trees around us shook and a few smaller ones fell. Alric detoured around two fallen trees, glancing back to make certain we had followed.

After a half-hour he slowed the horses down.

I was shaking as much from the wild ride as the mess behind us. "Did they make the rakasa explode?" Considering the little monsters had been on the bad folks' side, that seemed a little extreme. It would have been effective had we not known to flee, however. "And why did they back off from Lorcan but not us?" I kept my voice low. Everyone was watching the woods around us, but no plants moved, and the normal bird and animal sounds were starting to come back.

"I think they didn't go after Lorcan because they didn't want the map he's carrying to explode," Padraig said. Like the rest of us, he was watching the woods carefully.

I was keeping an eye on the ground and the plant life. Maybe those ones that blew up were the last of the rakasa. But maybe they weren't. I had a bad feeling that even years from now, when this was just something we talked about in pubs on rainy days; I was still going to be disturbed when the ground shook even a little.

I finally stopped staring at the ground. "Garbage? How did you know they were going to explode?" They had been behind us, but there was no way they were far enough back to have heard anything from our followers.

Garbage scowled behind us in the general direction of the still smoking trees and path. I couldn't see anything specific, but the smoke trailing up was noticeable. There was no sign of fire, so at least the rakasa were nice enough to not burn the forest down.

"He know." She flew over to Bunky and patted him. "He save." Garbage was definitely growing in her new position as general—she usually took credit for everything whether it had anything to do with her or not. Her giving credit to Bunky was a major change.

"Thank you, Bunky. How did you know?" Padraig was closest to us and held up his hand to give Bunky some scratches.

Bunky gronked with great earnest and bobbed a few times.

"He said he could smell it, bad magic," Alric said. "Again. And again, knowing could have been helpful."

"Unless he just developed it," I said. The faeries kept developing new-old tricks. Things they said they did ages ago, and they were now doing again. Maybe the chimeras were going through the same process.

Even I understood the loud gronk that followed as an

affirmative.

Alric started slowly walking his horse in circles. At first I thought maybe he'd been hit by a spell. Then he got off his horse and stalked, there was no other word for it, between two trees. They were only about two feet apart, and they looked odd. Like no other trees I'd ever seen. Tall and slender, yet they looked solid. He turned around with a smile and a shake of his head.

"Good news: this is the entrance to the hidden realm, bad news: the mayor and his folks are very close behind us." He got back on his horse and motioned for Lorcan to ride toward the spot where he'd been standing. "I figure we have one shot before they get here."

If Lorcan was worried, he didn't show it. I really hoped that I got to be as old as him some day so I could be that calm under pressure. He started saying the spell words and a fog grew between the two trees. Then faded.

"I need more magic users to say it with me."

I rode forward but as soon as I started to say the spell words, the trees changed and their limbs appeared to move away from each other and us.

"Maybe that's what Queen Mungoosey meant, you can't help on this one." Lorcan shrugged but the other three magic users rode forward and joined in on the spell. The fog returned and a dark line running parallel to the trees appeared and held. Lorcan pulled out a small knife. "It doesn't appear that this pertains to the faeries since they are magic beings, nor the constructs, but the rest of us need to throw a few bits of hair into the passage before we cross. Part of the spell was telling the hidden realm who we were and now we have to demonstrate it." He looked at the horses. "We should probably also blindfold the horses as the passage isn't going to be like anything they are used to. Oh, and whatever you do, don't use magic inside the hidden realm. I've no idea what would happen, but it is strongly discouraged according to the map."

Once an older shirt of Padraig's had been torn into strips, and the horses' eyes covered with the strips of fabric, Lorcan handed his knife to Mathilda and she cut off a lock of her hair, tossed it at the thin dark line, then nudged her horse forward and vanished.

CHAPTER THIRTY—NINE

KNOWING WE WERE GOING THROUGH a weird portal and actually doing it were two extremely different things. We'd tied blinders on the horses, but I wished I'd asked for one as well. Even though most of my friends and their horses had gone through, the entrance still looked like nothing more than a line. One that was somehow accommodating horses loaded with full tack and equipment that was far wider than the line or even the space between the two trees.

Even Covey seemed far more interested than terrified. Maybe being an academic was similar to having a strong religious belief system—it cushioned you from fears in this world.

Alric had his horse tied behind mine and he was walking mine in. My brain tried to pull my body away as first Alric and then the front of my horse went through the impossibly narrow slot.

I held my breath as I went through, not expecting the bitter chill. There were a few moments of nothing, not unlike when I went back in time a few months ago. That got my heart racing. What if this wasn't a normal magic portal at all? What if it was a time one? I shuddered. Going back once was enough.

As soon as that thought started bouncing around my brain, my horse and I came out of the dead space. The space before me looked normal. Just a massive open plain, with little more than grasses for a long distance, which became a heavy forest a few miles away. The chilled feeling didn't fade.

Alric led us out of the way as Padraig came through. The faeries, Bunky, and Irving were right behind Padraig and the faeries were laughing as they tumbled out of the portal.

The portal that was now shutting. "Should it be doing that? Lorcan's spell will get us back out, right?" I stayed on my horse as Alric took off its blindfold, but I was ready to run back and try to hold the portal open if need be. This place was chilling more than just my skin no matter how harmless it looked.

Alric glanced up as he removed the blindfold from his horse then untied his horse from behind mine. "I wouldn't worry about it. It's safer in here with that shut. Our followers were almost upon us when we went through. I'd say less than twenty minutes behind—they were definitely using magic to increase their speed."

I opened my mouth to chastise him for not mentioning that earlier, and then shut it. He was right. It was better not knowing how close they had been to us. "If they know where we went, can't they wait for us out there until we come out?"

Alric patted my leg as if I was a skittish horse. "From the map, it doesn't look like the exit is anywhere near here, so it stands to reason it will send us out into the real world in a different spot as well." With another pat and a nod he mounted his horse.

"Is boom!" Crusty flew into my hair as she yelled.

I pulled her free after I realized she wasn't trying to get free herself.

"Sweetie? What is boom?" Booms made me nervous.

"Fixing boom. Going BOOM now!" She kissed me on the cheek and flew off after the others.

That didn't make me feel better.

As before, Alric took the lead, with Padraig bringing up

the rear. It was interesting that they didn't even communicate, but just automatically slipped into place. Even though we had an entire plain, we formed a single line, also like before, behind Alric. I stayed right behind him, with the faeries and constructs flying nearest to me. Then Mathilda, Lorcan, Covey, and Padraig. After a few moments, the faeries took off across the plain.

Since everyone else was either studying maps, scrolls, books, or lost in their own thoughts, I tried to see if I could find anything about this place that marked it as different. Aside from the chill. The sun was warm, but when I tried to find it in the sky, all I could see was a diffused glow over to the left. As if someone had a giant warehouse and a glow was lighting it from behind a curtain.

"What is it my dear?" Mathilda broke ranks and nudged her horse up alongside mine.

"Just wondering how it can look sunny, have no sun, and be so cold." It had started just as a chill, but now I was thinking of getting out my heavier cloak from my pack.

Mathilda looked up and shrugged. "We're in a hidden realm, something I'm afraid no one alive today fully understands. Even if all of the magic users with us right now were gathered together into a single being, we wouldn't have the power to create one of these. The scrolls imply they were created by the Ancients to protect favorite areas. Or used by them, but created by beings even older."

"I'm confused, is this area real or magically created?" Covey also broke the single file rank and came up on the other side of Mathilda.

Mathilda smiled. "Both. This was a real place, it still is. But it now only exists in this hidden realm. As for the lack of sun, I think it's here, but masked somehow, possibly something they were protecting here didn't like direct light. However, I'm not sure why you say it's cold—it's quite warm." Her smile dropped. "I do hope you aren't coming down with something."

"Taryn is never ill, as she will tell you, repeatedly. Hung over, yes; ill, no," Covey said.

"It's true, I can't recall being sick a day in my life. Of course, I don't recall much prior to you finding me all those years ago. But I really don't feel like I was sick before either." It was odd, never being sick. I'd never thought about it until now though. Aside from a bit of bragging when my friends got colds, that is.

Mathilda leaned over and put the back of her hand against my forehead. "I believe you are sick now. You have a fever."

I didn't think Alric was paying attention, but he turned on his horse. "How can she be sick? She was fine when we rode through."

As if Mathilda's stating it made it true, I felt my body start to collapse. I felt achy, cold, hot, sniffling, and a tickle was growing in my throat. "What is this? Am I going to die?" If this was a cold, I knew I'd never had one. This was awful and unforgettable.

"You won't die, but I've never seen a virus hit this fast or hard. Oh dear, catch her."

I was looking at Mathilda, rather the two Mathildas that had appeared when I felt the world sliding under me.

Alric got to me first, even though Covey was closer. I felt both of their hands on me as they lowered me off my horse. The rest gathered around and Mathilda and Lorcan dropped down next to me.

"What's wrong with her? She was fine." Alric looked more concerned than I'd seen for a long time—I must have looked horrible.

"She's been spelled. Damn it, the protections around this place are attacking her." Lorcan pulled out the map and was shaking his head over the words. "We did every-thing correctly, but the spell isn't recognizing you. Good thing you have a strong constitution; this could have killed someone."

"What now?" Garbage flew into view, which was a good thing because I didn't think I could move my head at this point.

"Taryn is ill and we need you to stay back," Mathilda said, as she pulled things out of her pack. Mostly herbs from what I could see. "I'll need someone to hold the water bag so I can mix these."

"No, we fix," Leaf said as she and Crusty flew into my line of sight next to Garbage. Before anyone could stop them, they and the other twenty faeries swarmed on me. Even through the aching, I felt the pairs of tiny hands grabbing on to skin, hair, and clothing.

"Is okay! One of us!" They yelled, but I had no idea at what. They were just looking upwards at the sky. They repeated it twice more and my aches subsided. By the fourth time, I felt fine, and a bit silly lying on the ground.

"Sorry, we no know." Garbage patted me on the cheek, right where the manticore was, nodded to Mathilda, and then led her flying army off across the plains again.

I was sitting up, but not ready to stand yet. The manticore was shooting off little cold rays across my face. "Can anyone see this?" I removed my hand from my cheek but from the looks I got, while I felt it, it wasn't visible.

"See what?" Alric held my other hand, studying my face.

"The manticore is sending out cold waves across my face. Could it have been making me cold?" I doubted it had been what made me sick, but the cold part I could see happening. The frigid waves subsided.

"I don't know," Lorcan said as he too studied my face. "There's almost no information about these places, and absolutely no way to know how the relic would respond. Since part of the spell to gain entrance involved establishing what creatures were coming through, it might have read you as something other than who you are because of that relic."

I rubbed the side of my face once more; it almost felt

normal. Alric got to his feet, helping me up as if I was an old lady who fell out of her moving chair.

"I'm okay."

He engulfed me in a hug. "You scared me. I've never seen you that pale."

It was a little over-kill if it had just been a cold, but since it appeared to have been a spell attacking me, or attacking the manticore, I agreed with his reaction. Besides, it felt good to be in his arms.

"I hate to break this up, but if Taryn is ready to ride, we should probably get moving." Lorcan, Padraig, and Mathilda were already back on their horses. Covey was waiting to see how I was.

I gave her a nod and Alric a quick squeeze. Maybe when this was over he and I could go somewhere nice and relaxing and sort ourselves out again.

"Come, my lady, I shall escort you to your horse." A flash of the gallant Alric that I'd seen when we were in the past appeared as he led me to my horse.

"Why so slow?" Garbage came zipping back and circled around us. "I fix. You go." She pointed to the line of trees, nodded once, and took off with her faeries, and this time the constructs as well, behind her.

"I, for one, do not wish to annoy our tiny general." Lorcan nudged his horse forward.

Alric helped me get up on mine, and it was probably a good thing. The girls might have broken whatever spell this place dropped on me, but I felt stiff. I was startled when he gave me a kiss on my hand.

"Sorry. Again." He sighed, gave me a crooked smile that could make any woman's heart melt, then went and got back on his horse.

Okay, if me getting spelled was what was needed to get us back on track, I was all for the discomfort of that spell.

The rest of the trip was quiet, aside from some muttering between Padraig and Lorcan as they debated some scroll.

About halfway to the line of trees, the sky started darkening.

"I believe we want to move faster." Lorcan looked up from his scroll with a scowl. "We should have had enough time, but Taryn collapsing put us back a bit."

Lorcan had been cryptic about this place, and finding out that we had a time limit didn't appear to be settling well with anyone.

"You didn't say it would be this tight." Even Padraig looked a bit annoyed.

"Is this a walk the horses faster, or a run situation?" Alric had resumed the lead and looked ready to run his horse regardless.

I had to say I agreed. The sky was looking less friendly by the second, and the ground seemed to be trembling.

"Does anyone else feel that? Is it an earthquake? Rakasa?" I looked around.

"Not an earthquake, nor rakasa. Run!" Lorcan flicked his reins and his horse ran ahead.

Alric called for his horse to run and the rest of ours followed. Good thing I was holding on; clearly the horse felt the others of its kind were smarter than the person sitting on it. It was right; the horses probably would have started running as soon as the sky changed.

As we ran, I looked back over my shoulder and swore. Lorcan must have seen the line of some sort of animals coming our way. Lots of animals. Big animals covering the plains. And shaking the ground.

CHAPTER FORTY

I HAD NO IDEA WHAT THEY were, nor did I care. I just really hoped they didn't like thick forests. The horses seemed to agree with my thoughts and sped up.

"Is fun!" Crusty yelled. I didn't even see them come back, but the flock plus the constructs were zipping along overhead.

"Zoom!" Leaf yelled. Bunky and Irving gronked, but they seemed to be enjoying themselves. Of course the flyers were happy; they weren't on the ground near those beasts.

The ground was shaking more, or maybe it was my imagination since it was damn hard to tell on the back of a racing horse. A quick glance back confirmed that whatever those things were, they were closer than before.

The forest was closer than the mystery beasts were, but it had been further than I'd thought. I didn't think we were going to get there before the herd of creatures caught up with us.

Then fog spread over the trees and drifted out across the plain. At first I thought it was a spell from one of my friends, but looking around it was clear they were focused on outrunning the herd.

I didn't think I liked the look of the fog. Luckily, neither did the animals charging us and the herd changed direction as easily as a flock of birds. I got a quick look at them as they turned behind us. Large horned animals, easily a good foot or two taller than our horses. With six legs.

I almost fell off my horse, but yup, six. Maybe they were somehow related to the minkies since the first time I saw one it had six legs.

We slowed our horses down once the herd changed direction.

"What were those?" Wasn't sure I really wanted to know, but stupid curiosity was sort of my thing.

"I never thought to see them." Lorcan watched the line of animals get smaller with a look of wonder and a heavy sigh. "They appear to be thrails. They once roamed the plains of our world, but they were little more than myths even in the Ancient's documents. The Ancients must have saved the last of them and placed them here."

"As long as they keep going that way, I'll like them just fine." Even Covey looked rattled after our run. "So where now? That forest?"

Alric nodded. "From what was on that map, the place Lorcan and Padraig identified is in there. And I really wouldn't use magic in there, no matter what happens."

I opened my mouth to mention that Lorcan already told us no magic in here…then shut it. I was probably the worst of all of us about impulsive use of magic. Another reminder probably wasn't a bad idea.

The fog that had been drifting along the ground was now rising higher, as if the trees ahead of us were calling it. Or creating it. I wasn't an expert on trees, but the forest we were going toward was an odd one, and not just because of the fog. I was used to the giant gapen trees with their heavy limbs and thick above ground, roots. These trees were thin and gangly, their branches reaching up in twisted formations high above us. Even from this distance, strands of moss could be seen hanging from them. As we rode closer, I saw they were also covered in short green moss. So were the rocks and assorted odd shapes covering the ground under the trees. I was even more hesitant about having to go through this place—who knew if that moss was aggressive against everything, or just things that held still too long. I made a note to not sleep in these woods if I could help it.

The faeries had largely settled down as we approached the forest. They were fine while we were being chased by those beasts, but the forest clearly made them uneasy. They kept dropping down to land on people instead of flying. They were also speaking in native faery a lot more. Bunky and Irving continued doing their normal recon, but I'd noticed that the closer we had gotten to the woods, the shorter their circles were and the more time they spent close to us. When we went into the forest, they both were flying so low they were almost bumping onto our heads. There was room, but neither construct apparently wanted to be near the twisted tree limbs above us.

As we continued deeper into the trees, I noticed that not all of what I thought were rocks were round. "I know you said this area had a heavy magic distortion, but is that making the rocks square?" Yup, not all of them, but there were definitely more than a few very square, moss-covered boulders sitting around. Most were not huge, maybe a foot or two high but in the distance I could see larger ones. Or a few of them had joined together.

Lorcan looked up from the scroll he was studying as he rode. "Actually, those are carved blocks, the remains of an ancient civilization."

I almost pulled up my horse. "Ancients? The Ancients *lived* here?" That brought a whole new level of interest to this place. I knew they'd said that the Ancients had utilized these places, but if there were ruins maybe this place wasn't too bad. Killer spells and rampaging beasts aside.

"No, at least not that we know of. These people were here even before them supposedly. The stones are all that is left, and nothing is known of their culture." He gestured to the groupings of stones that we were passing. "But don't touch them. This forest drains magic from others, but has plenty of its own. And it protects those blocks."

Okay, that just raised the interest *and* the creep factor. I wasn't sure if it was Lorcan's words or something from the forest, but an ache settled in my joints and bones. "I don't think it likes us being here." I rubbed my arms and pulled my cloak tighter. One disadvantage of riding, I couldn't cuddle into Alric for warmth.

"It doesn't," Padraig said. He'd put away the book he'd been reading while riding, and looked up at the trees in wonder. "They want to be left alone. They are old and set in their ways. The drain of magic isn't because they can use it, it's because they know it will keep most people away." Leaf and a few of the others had been riding on his shoulders. He held out a hand for her to jump down onto. None of the faeries had flown in the last half hour, pretty much as soon as we crossed into the trees.

"How are you feeling?" He rubbed her back.

"Is no good. Must be. But no good." She folded down cross-legged into his hand. He dropped a small piece of sugar next to her. She stuffed it in her mouth and grinned. "Bether." The piece took up almost her entire mouth and bulged her cheeks out. She looked like she didn't care at all.

Soon the rest of the faeries climbed up Padraig's horse. But even for sugar none of them flew.

"Garbage? *Can* you fly?" I'd assumed their staying with us was more related to whatever devious plans they'd been conversing about. But not flying for sugar was another thing entirely.

"Yes," she said as she held onto two larger chunks of sugar. Then she slumped forward. "No. Is can't."

"I wondered if they would be able to when we was discovered that the sphinx was here. I know the rumors of this place and the magic drain, and since faeries are magic, I thought this might happen to them. It shouldn't impact the constructs ability to fly however." Mathilda said. The faeries that had been riding with her scrambled back up her horse, their cheeks stuffed with sugar. "Girls, you can go back to my house. Wait for us to come back. I'm sure Bunky and Irving can help get you there."

Garbage had started chewing one of her sweets and swallowed. "Can't leave. This our time. We ready. Can fly, but won't. Miss flying though."

I narrowed my eyes and watched them. "You have something going on here and it's important." Something about the way Garbage spoke, and their recent behavior, made me wonder. "And not about the relics."

General Garbage puffed out her chest. "Yes. Is our place. War kitties come. We battle."

"Wait, you're going to fight the cats?"

She scowled at me. "No. *With* kitties. Frophacy say no fly—need kitties. Fight those." She pointed over my shoulder.

At first I thought it was the minkie playing games again, but it wasn't white. The creature she pointed to was a muddy gray-brown. The size of a small dog, but wider and heavier than the cats, it was low to the ground with a pointed face, and inch-long fangs. It snarled at us, and then scurried deeper into the woods.

"Did everyone see that? And what was it?"

Affirmatives came from my friends, but no answers.

"We fight. Those boy faeries." Garbage was still fierce, but there was a rare sadness on her face as well. "Told them not done. Now they go bad."

"Wait." I'd seen these boy faeries a few times. They looked like a combination of an elf and a giant faery. Granted, the last time they weren't helping us—but that thing looked vicious and was definitely an animal. "How can that be a boy faery?"

"Is unfinished!" The girls all joined in, but while they did raise their voices, they didn't yell. These woods subdued even Crusty.

"I get it, they aren't finished. But that wouldn't turn them into a...whatever that was." I waved in the direction the thing had gone.

Mathilda's eyes got huge, and she leaned over her horse's neck to whisper to Lorcan.

He shook his head, and then slowly stopped. "Perhaps? But they were as mythological as the sceanra anam. Who, yes I know have appeared beyond the pages of myth. But these?"

"Someone please tell me something?" The fact that Alric, Padraig, and Covey were sitting there looking concerned was freaking me out.

Mathilda spoke up first. "That creature looked like a vhin. A mythological creature of great violence. They aren't supposed to be real, but the myths said they were made from the souls of those who betrayed their kind." Everyone was looking at her except the faeries. All of them were looking down. And they looked sad. "If that is what that was, and the myths and what the faeries are saying is true—that thing was once a male faery. They supposedly betrayed faery-kind before the war where we lost the Ancients. The stories say none of the faeries had been there in that final battle—because of whatever the males did."

"Is true. They betray long ago. Stop us from helping. Sent back. Supposed to be remade. Come back too soon. Now bad." Garbage took a deep breath and her sadness was replaced with determination. "We fight."

As she spoke a fleet of cats started coming into the woods. Far more than just the twenty-three for the faeries we traveled with. As they got closer, it was clear that the cats had pieces of metal armor—the broken-up sarcophagus in many cases—and most had feather-clad faeries riding them. A group of riderless cats came toward our horses.

Garbage and her troops had changed into their war feathers while I watched the feline invasion. Then they dropped down to their waiting feline steeds.

"So where did these cats and the other faeries come from?" Covey asked as she watched them circle us. "I know you faeries seem to be able to pop around, but last I checked cats weren't magical."

This was just taking a bizarre turn, but I had a bigger concern than how they got into a sealed hidden realm. "So all the time you were cat racing, you were training to fight unfinished boy faeries?" I wasn't even sure where to start with that one.

"Cats come through house—faeries bring." Leaf nodded from atop her feline.

Mathilda laughed and shook her head. "They used the magical essence of my house to bring their troops through." She tipped her head. "But you didn't train for this fight, did you?"

"No first. When boys kept showing?" Garbage shrugged.

"Let me take a stab at it," Padraig said. "Your stories told you a big fight was coming, so you trained with the cats. The cat racing in Beccia. This isn't that fight, but you knew the boy faeries would be in these woods, didn't you?"

Leaf nodded from her cat. "Queen Mungoosey tell Garbage."

Queen Mungoosey was the leader of the faeries, a small gray cat-like faery I'd only seen briefly. She had a falling out with my girls, and their growing cohort. My three had dragged the rest of the faeries in to save us when Alric and Thaddeus ripped open our dimension with the glass gargoyle. That was against their prophecy apparently. That and their drinking and general hooliganism had distanced them from their queen.

"Queen Mungoosey told you to fight? Here?" They'd met with her a few days ago, but I'd almost forgotten how solemn they'd been when they returned.

"Yes, so can be in big battle—only way to join. Must send boy faeries back to be finished." Garbage adjusted her feathers. It looked like she had more than the rest of the faeries.

The way she said finished left no room for interpretation. She might not be happy about it, but the way to send them back was by killing them in battle. If they did that, then their queen was going to welcome them back into the fold, so to speak? Just proved that all faeries, not only mine, had their own odd way of seeing the world. It was bad timing that this was going to go on while we were skulking around a touchy and dangerous forest trying to calculate where the diamond sphinx had ended up.

I really hoped it wasn't under one of those blocks.

"Is the fight here? Can we help?" Padraig was obviously fascinated where as I was becoming more disturbed.

"Fight will come. You no help." Garbage climbed up and kissed him on the cheek. "Watch, no magic. No help." She looked over to me. "No one."

I'm not sure why she was focusing on me. I, probably more so than anyone here, knew what those faeries were capable of. Or maybe that was the reason. Obviously, the caveat of no flying in battle was meant to make this a test of skill as well as proving this group of faeries was ready to rejoin the wild ones.

"Agreed. But you won't leave once you've reunited with Queen Mungoosey, will you?" That thought worried me.

Crusty ran to my horse and quickly climbed up. "No. Never leave." She tried kissing my cheek but ended up in my ear instead. The thought was good though.

"Thank you," I said as she and Garbage both ran back to their cats.

We continued through the forest, but this time, Padraig led, and Alric dropped to the back. I knew they said that no one else from the outside should be able to get in here, so the standard security protocol being in place meant they figured there were more dangers than rampaging herds and vicious looking former faeries.

I dropped back in this new line up to ride alongside Alric. Well, where I could. The path between the trees seemed to be getting narrower and even riding single file might start proving tricky soon.

"I am sorry I was being a jerk. Again." Alric shook his head. "I hope we can get that relic out of you for good soon, but even though the geas might be forcing my reactions, I've been sloppy about letting it get to me." He reached out a hand.

I held it for a few minutes, not easy on horseback and even less so when trees kept getting in our way.

"I understand." I looked toward his arm but didn't see any glow. "Nothing now?"

"Not a thing." He held his arm up and pushed back the sleeve. The mark was completely invisible. "There's no glamour on it right now either, since we had to stop using magic."

Made sense, the geas was a thousand-year-old spell and we were in a place with no magic. "We could just stay here and you'd never have a problem with the geas again."

He shuddered and rolled his sleeve back down. "This place doesn't bother you? It looks almost normal, but just off enough to be disturbing."

"Yeah, it bothers me too. And the whole almost dying of a cold issue kind of ruined it for me as well. But it's nice to see you smile again."

"I promise, when this is done, we'll find a place just for us, have some real alone time." His smile was genuine and I loved seeing it. But I had a feeling it was going to be a long time before that happened.

"With us!" Crusty yelled from her trusty feline steed. The cats were so damn quiet that even with armor on I hadn't noticed she'd dropped back with us.

"Um, sure, sweetie. But you guys might need some time with Queen Mungoosey and the wild faeries. Celebration time." I was happy the faeries weren't planning on leaving me after they rejoined the main flock, but I really didn't want them along on a romantic trip with Alric.

"Crusty! Here!" Garbage might be only four inches high, but she could yell with the best of them. Considering that even the faeries had been keeping their voices down in this weird forest, I was surprised. Then I noticed that the faeries, along with Padraig and the others, had entered a clearing. Apparently yelling within the forest wasn't good, but yelling into it was. I shook my head as Crusty nudged her crazy gray feline and they zipped through the trees to catch up to the others.

We followed them into the clearing. Padraig and Lorcan were debating the map, the faeries had gathered into a tight group—well, as tight as a hundred and twenty or so cats could get—and Mathilda was frowning at the trees themselves.

Alric rode toward Padraig and Lorcan. I rode to Covey who looked as confused as I felt.

"What's the problem?" I looked at the faeries. "Or problems?"

She shook her head. "Not a clue. But Padraig wasn't happy to see this clearing here and neither were the faeries. This isn't on anyone's map."

"No, it's not." Mathilda walked her horse over to us and kept her voice soft. "We are being watched by something more than trees—and I don't believe it is the boy faeries either. Something has trapped us well and good."

CHAPTER FORTY–ONE

L ORCAN NUDGED HIS HORSE OVER to us. "I have to agree. This isn't on the map, so it's not a defense built in by the people who created it."

"No tell us. Not know." Garbage and her cat were suddenly in the middle of our impromptu circle. They just walked in-between the horses' legs. Those cats were too damn quiet.

"Padraig and Alric are going to continue arguing as if they have a way to figure this out. We agree that whoever or whatever triggered this is watching us," Lorcan said.

"I think we should be ready with weapons, and be prepared to run if need be." Mathilda patted her staff. I had been so used to seeing her with it that I didn't think of it as a weapon.

My sword was hanging around. Of course, if it was affected by the magic drain here, it might not be able to disappear. That and the temporary deadening of Alric's geas were about the only good things to come out of this hidden realm so far.

Padraig and Alric were making a good show of keeping up their debate. The faeries had started to break up their gathering, but Garbage must have agreed with our assessment. She went back and pulled them together into a giant collection of jabbering faeries and bored cats.

"Why don't we just walk out of the clearing if this is the trap?" I was all for us being cautious, but standing right in the middle of a known trap seemed kind of stupid.

"To what?" Covey looked up toward the trees but didn't point. The way we'd come was now blocked with trees. There was no way it was natural. For one, we just came that way, and for another, no tree could survive living that close to the others like that. I kept my head down but slowly looked around us—yup—we were surrounded.

"We figure." Again Garbage and her cat steed were right in the center of us. I'd be glad when this was over just so they couldn't keep popping in like this. Being as low and silent as they were, they were too easy to miss.

"You figure what, sweetie? Is this something to do with the boy faeries?"

"Is no, too brainy." She tapped the side of her head. "Bad."

"I know they're bad, or do you mean whoever trapped us is bad?" I might be figuring out how her brain worked. That was almost as scary as all of the other things that were going on.

"Yes, this bad. Queen Mungoosey no know." She glared around as if this entire situation was a personal affront. Obviously her queen knew everything about everything, and her not knowing about what went on in a secret pocket of reality was impossible.

"What did you figure, Garbage?" Mathilda brought us back to the current situation.

"Trees."

We looked down at her waiting for more. True, I hadn't noticed that the trees had moved in until Covey pointed it out, but we knew about them now.

"What about them?" Covey tried.

"They do this." Garbage flung her hands around her head and her cat twitched her calico ears in agreement.

Lorcan and Mathilda shared a look, then a shrug. "Could be? The map really didn't indicate anything about the trees, just that the ruin blocks needed to be avoided. But this thing was created over a thousand years ago."

I thought about the weird square rocks and the horrible way they made me feel, like when you walk into a bar and you just know you don't want to be anywhere near that toothy cherub sitting in the corner. Like they had a revulsion spell on them. "This is a really long shot, and don't ask where it came from, but could the blocks have a life of their own?" That sounded so insane, even to me that I felt like someone else said it.

Covey looked at me as if maybe she should be visiting me in an insane asylum somewhere. But Mathilda and Lorcan looked thoughtful.

I personally agreed with Covey's visual assessment. But I preferred the opportunity to not be crazy provided by the thoughtful looks from the two magic users. Besides, they were both very old and probably had seen weirder things.

"I have to say, I've never heard of rocks being sentient, but it would explain the admonishment to leave the ruin blocks alone." Mathilda looked a bit closer into the underbrush of the trees. There went my theory of this being commonplace. "The trees are moving closer, and I believe there are some blocks there as well. I know there were none near this part of the trail before we hit this clearing."

Alric and Padraig walked their horses to us and we expanded our circle to include them. Garbage jumped off her cat, scrambled up Alric's horse and climbed up Alric. "Problem. Bad rocks trap us. Need go fight." She looked up at Alric as if he would take care of everything, patted his hand, then scrambled back down, jumped on her cat and rode back to the other faeries.

"What did we miss?" Padraig watched Garbage ride off, but controlled his laugh. Garbage had been earnest in her sincerity. Riding a battle cat didn't make her any less cute, though.

"Taryn came up with an outrageous, but sadly plausible, theory," Lorcan said. He quickly outlined what I'd said, only put far more important sounding and larger words in—his version sounded much less crazy. He seemed to feel the blocks might not be the ruins of the former people who lived here—they were what those beings became. His theory was even more far-fetched than mine.

"So, what you're implying is that those square, moss-covered blocks are sentient, because they were once the species who built these hidden realms?" Covey was watching the blocks closely now.

"They might have been the creators, or some species they wanted to save. But I think we have to agree they're alive and have the ability to stalk people." Lorcan looked to the surrounding trees. "That indicates a certain level of intelligence."

"And they are moving closer." I watched as two blocks shuffled forward a few feet before stopping. A moment later the trees closest to them followed. A shiver went across my back and didn't feel like it was ever leaving. Knowing that things that shouldn't move were moving and seeing them move were extremely different things. "If we can't use magic, what is going to stop those blocks?"

"Are we worrying for nothing?" Covey asked. "Unless they can fly, how can they hurt us?" It took a lot more to upset Covey than it did me.

The faeries started taunting something inside the dense trees directly across from us. It was one of the boy faeries, in his new animal form of a vhin, who apparently had been following us. He charged forward on his heavily clawed feet. Made it right to the edge of the clearing, then touched one of the square blocks as one of the faeries zigged and he moved to follow her movement. He burst into flame, then crumbled to ash. Tree limbs reached down and brushed away the dust.

I really felt the need to be ill.

"Is that. Not good." Garbage had baited the vhin just to demonstrate what those blocks could do.

Not only were the blocks a threat, but that tree moved

to clear the ash with as much ease as any of us would have. The trees could take us out before the blocks even got involved. "How do we fight that? Girls? You said before that you could fly, but you weren't supposed to," I said. "Can you fly now?" Maybe they could get out, find help somewhere.

"Not now. Was could. Now can't." Leaf responded as Garbage continued to glare at the stone block that fried the vhin.

Crusty stood on her gray cat, jumped in the air, flapped her wings furiously, and then crashed to the ground. "Nope." She dusted herself off and climbed back on her feline steed.

Another block did its odd shuffle to move forward. A moment later the two trees closest to it moved and stretched their limbs to cover it in shadow. I looked up at the sky. That same diffused light was above us here. "When we first came in, you mentioned that maybe the diffused light was for some of the creatures who live here. What if those stone-people-things can't handle light? Every time a stone block moves, the trees move to block it from the light."

"Bad time to not be able to use magic," Covey said. "You guys could light this place up in an instant."

Which was a good reason to make this place free of magic. I looked around, maybe if we could light a fire of some sort?

The faeries were milling about on their cats, gathering in small groups to glare at the woods closing in on us.

Their bright colors made me think of something. "Mathilda, remember when that boy faery went after your nectar, and all those faeries lit up?"

"Yes. But yours didn't do it."

"But maybe they can?" I waved Garbage over. "How did those other faeries glow; remember, at the cottage?"

"They just do." She scowled but more at the situation

than at me. Or so I told myself.

"Like this?" Crusty stood on her cat again and held her breath. And glowed. She released her breath and it faded.

"Why you no tell?" Garbage was not happy.

"You no ask."

I held back my laughter at that. It was good to know they kept things from each other as well as from me.

"So, if they hold their breath, the faeries can glow? Won't that be a short glowing?" Covey asked it, but everyone was watching now.

"They stay in closed off bottles of ale for hours at a time." I shook my head as one by one various faeries tested it out. "Going without air hasn't been a problem for them yet."

Garbage glared at her faery army as they began holding their glows longer. She finally held her breath, and glowed. Her smile and nod were one of victory.

"We get them back." She rode to the rest of the faeries, and without checking with anyone, they all held their breath and scattered.

"No! We need to plan!" I knew those faeries were tough, but even they couldn't recover from being turned into ash. And the cats were mortal.

"Doing!" Garbage leapt off her cat, as did the others. The cats stayed in the clearing with their tails lashing as the faeries, running like a giant, deranged, rainbow, continued to the tree line.

Before the blocks had shuffled slowly. Now they were finding a way to roll backward even with their blocky shapes. They couldn't get away from the brightly glowing faeries fast enough. The trees tried fighting back at first, but the faeries were tiny and quicker than they were. Even so, there were a few connections of tree and faery where one of the faeries was flung back into the clearing. The faery in question shook herself off, puffed out her cheeks, and ran back into the forest.

Not all of the trees were of the moving-and-working-with-the-evil-blocks kind. A clump behind us didn't move back and the faeries in that section quickly went to either side. And there were also no blocks there. Traveling with a bunch of insanely smart folks meant they usually came up with solutions long before I did. It was nice to figure something out before they did.

The rout lasted about five minutes. With all of the blocks, and a good amount of the trees gone. The faeries came swaggering back, hopped on their waiting cats, and rode over to us. Garbage looked so proud you'd think they single-handedly saved the world.

To be honest, if we'd had to fight those blocks, it probably would have been the end of us, so their attitude wasn't too far off.

"Excellent work, ladies!" Mathilda said. "Unfortunately, I don't have any sweet treats, but I promise you each a mountain of them when we are out of here."

Once we had paid them their due acknowledgements, including Bunky and Irving, we headed back into the trees. We might have created a hundred little monsters as the forest kept popping with colors as they continued to play with their new-old trick. Even Bunky and Irving drifted higher into the trees to get away from the bright lights.

After about ten minutes, Lorcan turned back to them. Even he'd had enough; I was contemplating taking a chance with the scary stone blocks at that point. "Ladies, the boy faeries must not know how powerful you have become. You can't let them see your lights." His smile was so sincere, even I almost believed him.

Garbage had been holding her breath, but dropped it at his words. "Is right. Keep secret." One by one the other faeries stopped glowing.

Crusty flashed blue.

"Keep secret." One of the faeries closest to Crusty reached over and popped her in the head. She let go of her breath.

"Secret now," she said with a grin.

"How long until we can get this sphinx and get out of here?" I couldn't help it; even without those creepy blocks, these woods were disturbing.

"At least a day, possibly longer. Getting here was the easy part, figuring out how to locate the sphinx is the challenge." Alric was back to riding up front and even he didn't sound happy about the length of time. A day meant we'd have a night in here. I wondered how long the girls could keep their glowing up.

The forest had thinned a bit and the odd sky had started to dim when Alric and Padraig called a halt in another clearing. I looked around as they built a small fire, using only dry wood they found on the ground, but none of the trees seemed to be moving.

I really wished we could have found a way to bring Mathilda's cottage along.

"I don't think we should leave the fire burning during the night," Padraig said. "It's not safe around these trees." He was watching the branches closest to us. While the trees themselves weren't moving, the branches were waving in the wind. Except, there was no wind and they moved in different directions.

"We glow." Garbage, her army, with their cats had settled around the edges of our circle and now she dispatched about a quarter of the faeries into the trees. As they got in position, they lit up.

The clearing looked like someone was having a fancy party.

Lorcan looked around and shrugged. "I don't see why they can't. And their light should keep any of the blocks from coming back."

Bunky and Irving swooped into the clearing, made a circle, and looked ready to go out further.

"You two stay within the circle of faeries. We need you to stay close to us for protection." I tried to make it sound like we needed them to protect us, but the fact was I didn't want anyone out in that forest tonight.

CHAPTER FORTY—TWO

———◆———

THE NEXT MORNING CAME SILENTLY. I rolled over and crawled out of my tent to find everyone asleep. That wouldn't be too odd, except that the faeries were gone, and there was no guard. Padraig was drooped over awkwardly near the remains of our fire. The horses were undisturbed but they were the only thing that looked normal.

I scrambled to my feet and ran to Padraig since he was the closest. He was alive, but deeply asleep. The remains of a squished purple flower-like thing told me who'd gotten him—gloughstrikes. I couldn't use magic, the faeries were gone, and I had no other way to awaken my friends. All of them were collapsed in or near their tents.

Bunky and Irving looped through the clearing but dropped down when they saw me. Both spit out shredded gloughstrikes.

"I know I can't understand you, but do you know where the faeries are?"

The war cries that I heard not too far from me answered my question before either of them could.

I started to run toward the sounds, but both constructs followed. I stopped and held up a hand. "I need you to stay here and guard the others."

Bunky buzzed a bit and was clearly not happy.

"Please? I can't wake them, and those blocks could come back." The thought of those stone blocks working with the gloughstrikes as a hunting team flashed in my head. A chill went down my back.

He and Irving both nodded and went back to the center of our camp.

I continued running toward the war cries. After a few minutes of dodging trees that didn't appear to be moving, I came to a long clearing. I didn't see any gloughstrikes, but hopefully Bunky and Irving ate them all.

I wasn't sure what I'd been expecting, but an army of cats, armored in what appeared to be modified pieces of a sarcophagus, and being ridden by feather wearing faeries was a bit overwhelming. Impressive as hell though.

They hadn't added to their previous collection of combatants, still probably a hundred or so. Just the right amount to face off against a hundred or so boy faeries—or vhin as Mathilda had called them. If this was a test from Queen Mungoosey, she had planned it well. In the past the girls could call up thousands of their wild faery brethren. Judging by the lack of leaves on any of the ones I saw—the preferred clothing of the wild faeries—these were ones who had been corrupted by my original three.

They were holding back, watching each other, but I saw a few faeries and cats off to the side with various injuries so they must have been fighting for a while. As far as I could see there were no injured vhin. I wasn't sure if that was good or bad.

Garbage and Leaf were conferring, when a row of the vhin charged forward. Garbage yelled and all of the cats with their faery riders `ran forward as well. The claws on the vhin were long and wicked looking but the cats were steady and sure, stayed on target, and got their riders in close. At first I wasn't sure why the girls needed the cats; even if their queen forbade them from flying, they were pretty fast when they ran on the ground for only being four inches high.

Seeing them charge each other answered my question:

while on cat-back my faeries were approximately the same height as the vhin. Riding the cats leveled the playing field.

Although as skilled as my girls were with their war sticks, I wasn't sure that those and the cats' claws were comparable against the long, curved claws of the vhin.

Then I saw them in action. Garbage charged her cat forward a head in front of the rest. She swung her war blade, and her cat hunched down a bit lower, but still kept up a good speed. With a cry that should have been able to wake my friends, Garbage jumped off of her cat, leaping up toward the charging vhin. Her blade was whirling so fast that I didn't see it. I did see at least five vhin go down though. They flickered, and then vanished. Garbage bounced off another one, smacking it with her war blade as well, but using it to launch herself back onto her cat steed.

The rest of the faeries and cats had hit the vhin at that point and dozens of variations of Garbage's move could be seen. I had no idea of the rules of combat, but I knew the girls had said I couldn't help them. But I needed at least three of them to go wake the others. Each time there had been a gloughstrike attack, the faeries had helped my friends in groups of three.

I made my way over to the injured faery and cat group. I wasn't going to help them; after all, they were already out of the battle. The injuries were mostly to arms, legs, and wings.

"Girls?" I kept my voice down as I approached, mostly so I didn't disrupt the battle. "Would it be against the rules if I took you back to camp? Gloughstrikes attacked us and all of my friends are unconscious."

I didn't recognize any of the ones off to the side at first, then a familiar pink and purple faery limped over. Dingle Bottom's left arm and leg both looked crushed. "We help."

I lifted her up. "Are you going to be okay?" I knew the faeries were tough, but she looked bad.

"Yes. Sugar help?" She gave me a grin, then waved to the others. "Later. You give."

Since most of the cats off to the side were hurt too—not as bad as the faeries, which was good since they weren't as indestructible—I carried fifteen faeries with me as I walked back. Their cats trailed along behind us.

I had run out to them, but with my cargo I couldn't do that now so it was slower going back. We'd walked for a few minutes when the manticore shot out a stabbing pain and I almost stumbled. There were no threats that I could see, but a weird glow was coming from the roots of a tree a ways back from the path.

I kept going. I could come back, but right now I needed to wake my friends up.

The manticore inside my cheek had a different opinion and this time I did drop to one knee. This wasn't good: along with protecting me, the damn thing could stop me completely.

"Better follow." Dingle Bottom patted my cheek where the manticore was hidden. "Cranky."

I got back to my feet. An Ancient defensive relic having a cranky fit, sort of explained my life. "Hang on girls, let's see what's going on." I could walk toward the tree, but as soon as I tried to step away from it, my legs gave out. I hoped that Bunky and Irving were staying with our people—there was a good chance I wasn't going back to camp for a bit.

I walked quickly to the tree with the manticore sending cold stabs in time with my steps. It didn't feel like it was trying to defend me, it felt like it was trying to come out of me.

The glow within the tree roots increased as we got closer, but I had no idea what to do about it. I sat down the collection of damaged faeries, grabbed one of the roots, and tugged. "Help me pull." Dingle Bottom didn't move forward, but five of the less damaged faeries started pulling the roots.

The faeries and I were all focusing on the tree; it kept replacing each root we pulled away with two more, so not hearing the scrambling behind us wasn't shocking.

"Is bad," Dingle Bottom had stayed behind us, so I thought she was commenting on the roots. "Very bad."

I let go of the root I was holding and turned. We were surrounded by the stone blocks. They had made a circle behind us and around the tree, but they weren't moving closer.

"Girls? Can you glow even though you're hurt?" Even after fifteen years I didn't understand faery metabolism.

"Try." Dingle Bottom held her breath and a faint glow came from her. One of the others, a deep purple faery, moved toward the blocks as she held her breath, but like Dingle Bottom, she wasn't bright enough. Apparently faeries need to be in good health to glow.

The manticore in my face didn't care about the stones sneaking up on us; it wanted what was in the tree. Another stabbing movement on its part pulled me off my feet.

The blocks shuffled closer.

"How does one outsmart blocks?" I stayed on the ground; it was easier right now and brought me closer to whatever the manticore was trying to drag me to.

"Hammer. No like." Dingle Bottom nodded as if that solved everything.

"That's a good idea, but I don't have one." I wasn't going to mention that I also wasn't sure if striking one of the blocks would turn me crispy. Another few shuffles on their end, and I'd have to find out.

"Is that. Bam bam." The dark purple faery and Dingle Bottom both pointed to my cheek where the manticore relic was trying to freeze my face. "Tell it bam bam."

The stone blocks shuffled forward again.

I had no idea what it would do, but we were out of options. I focused on the manticore, and then forming a hammer of ice. Nothing. Then I threw in allowing it to get whatever it was after from the tree.

Ice leapt from my face into my hand. Not a hammer so much as a wickedly pointed heavy stick of ice. It covered my arm up to my shoulder.

One more shuffle forward from the blocks.

I jumped to my feet and brought the ice pick down on the nearest block. The shock of hitting it knocked me back into the tree, but I didn't burst into flame.

The stone block shattered as the ice cracked it open. In a few seconds there was nothing but pebbles.

The rest of the blocks moved away quickly, and my ice pick vanished.

I shook out my hand and arm to get some feeling back. Pretty much I had icy tingles everywhere the manticore had reached—but I was still alive, and so were the faeries.

The glow in the tree was stronger now, and so was the pull from the manticore. Another coating of ice enveloped my hand as I reached for one of the roots. The tree wasn't fond of the ice either and the roots pulled back.

The glow was almost unbearable once the roots fled, but when my eyes adjusted I could see that the tree had been hiding a large diamond head. I was shaking as I dragged it forward. It was massive, far too heavy for one person to carry. And it was a sphinx, not a head.

Crap. I'd found the diamond sphinx. Or rather, it had found the manticore and therefore me. They'd said the sphinx could call the other relics; well, it worked on the one I had for sure. There was no way I could lift it, let alone carry it back with the injured faeries. I was debating just covering it up and coming back with the others when two of the faeries who had been helping pull the roots stepped forward, tapped the sphinx, and then shoved it into one of their tiny bags.

Then they ran up my legs, handed me the bag, and nodded to Dingle Bottom.

"Is good. Go now." Garbage's imperiousness and command was rubbing off on all of the faeries, but I had to say that I agreed.

Bunky and Irving were in the clearing when we got back, but there were more gloughstrike bodies lying around.

"Are there more out there?" I wasn't sure what the connection was between the vhin and the gloughstrikes, but I didn't think taking out the latter would cause a problem for the battle taking place.

Both constructs nodded and I waved them on. "Go get them."

The faeries were already climbing off of me—well, the ones that could climb. The rest I gently set down. In groups of three, they ran to Alric first, then to the others. One by one my friends came to. Groggy and annoyed, but alive.

"What happened?" Alric rubbed his head. "Aside from us being attacked by those damn gloughstrikes again."

"That's it. I woke up, you guys were out, the faeries had gone into battle, and the constructs were eating gloughstrikes." As I spoke, a loud cheer came from the direction of the faery battlefield. The injured ones joined in as well. "I think they just won."

"I have to say that was an experience I would have been fine without experiencing. Every nerve feels on fire." Lorcan shook his robes and patted down his hair.

I held up the tiny faery bag. "And we found this."

"They finally gave you a faery bag?" Covey asked.

"No—well, yes, but it's what we found that's now in the bag." I was going to tell them what happened but looked around for a flat place to open the bag first. I'd been bracing myself for the massive sphinx I saw before, but when I pulled it out of the bag, it had shrunk to a size matching the other relics. I held it up for the others. "It was bigger when we first found it. My manticore buddy triggered this guy to reach out." I shuddered at how close we'd become to being ash. "We had an issue with some of the stone blocks, but we got this thing out." I stepped back after handing it to Lorcan as the others swarmed around. "Can we leave now? Please?"

They looked at the relic, but I noticed no one else tried to hold it. "I'd say yes. Let's gather our missing friends and depart." Lorcan tucked the sphinx back into its bag, and was about to add it to his growing collection of tiny faery bags, but held it out to me instead. "You found it; you should carry it for now."

Mathilda was working on the injured faeries and was creating slings to carry the injured cats on our horses. The faeries came back whooping and yelling. And eventually so did two slowly moving constructs. I had a feeling those gloughstrikes were hard to digest. Assuming that constructs digested anything.

"Were you hurt by the gloughstrikes?" I ran over to where they had landed. Garbage and Leaf ran over as well. A few gronks from both and the faeries started laughing.

"They too full. Ate too many noms." Garbage and Leaf patted them both and then ran back to their cats.

"Can you fly?" When both gronked and bobbed, I motioned toward Alric. "Stay up front near him. If you get too tired, land on us, okay?" That answered the digestion issue. I'd never seen either of them eat anything—beyond Irving and his relic obsession.

Getting through the woods and the plains to get out was even quicker than coming in. Alric kept checking the scrolls and making slight changes in direction, but it all looked the same to me. But there wasn't a pair of trees on this side to show where the passage was.

Lorcan knew where to go, however. He didn't take the scroll back from Alric, but started repeating the spell. Unlike going in, he didn't need the other elves to add their spell casting. I was going to ask, since we weren't supposed to use magic inside here, how he was able to cast a spell. Then thought better of it. I just wanted out of this place.

Again the thin line appeared, but this time it hovered in mid-air. Alric went through with Bunky and Irving, the rest of us following. Even the horses didn't have a problem entering it, although it looked the same as the one coming in had to me. I kept the faeries and cats behind me.

The passage wasn't as cold as before, but it was still unnerving. I was surprised to come out of it to see my friends standing perfectly still with their hands up, when I came out. Then I saw the mayor of Kenithworth and about fifty of his syclarion and human thugs, including Largen and Cirocco. Or rather, including whoever was pretending to be them.

CHAPTER FORTY—THREE

T HERE WERE AT LEAST FIVE archers that I could
   see, two with crossbows and three with long bows.
The faeries, still riding their cats, came through at that
moment.

"Fly away!" I yelled at them, then held up my hands, as
the closest archer looked ready to fire.

The faeries leapt off their cats and flew right for the may-
or's forces. A few arrows were let loose but they weren't
aimed and didn't come close to hitting anything. The cats
kept running and tangled themselves in the legs of horses
and fighters on the other side.

I had wanted the faeries to fly away, not charge the
enemy. They were too cocky after their victory over the
vhin.

But their chaos worked. Because they'd come through
the portal at cat level and behind us, no one had noticed
the faeries or cats until they charged. Their distraction
was enough for Alric, Padraig, and Covey to leap off their
horses and engage the enemy.

The attack brought forward the phony Largen and
Cirocco. We were right; they were serious magic users. I
felt their spells building and saw their images flicker. The
mayor was yelling at the rest of his people to fight back,
not even noticing the two changing shapes.

Mathilda and Lorcan had stayed on their horses but were
trying to send spells to attack the two mages on the other

side. If the fact we'd seen the bodies hadn't been enough to let us know these weren't the real crime lords, the ease with which they threw up a shield to block Lorcan and Mathilda's spells would have done it. The real Largen and Cirocco didn't have that kind of power.

They flickered one more time and there was no question as to who they were. Granted, I'd never seen Edana outside of a smoky shape in the corner of my house, but I recognized Nivinal. Although he was shifting between elven, syclarion, and dwoller, I knew it was him. I also knew in my gut that syclarion was the right form for him. That meant the vicious looking syclarion woman flashing next to him had to be his mother, Edana.

They were slowly pushing their way to us and I saw her reach into her cloak. Their spells grew stronger. Damn it, she might have been able to bring back her son from the dead, but she still had that chimera and was drawing strength from it, even though it wasn't inside of her.

I reached in and pulled the tiny faery bag out of my pocket. I didn't know if I had to touch the sphinx to make it work, but I clutched the bag and told it and the manticore that we needed that chimera.

A burst of light came from both the bag and my face, and the chimera flew into the air, but Edana grabbed it again. Before I could try once more, Bunky and Irving dove down. Bunky sent a heavy electrical charge at Edana, cutting through her shield. The chimera flew in the air again, and Irving ate it. Then he spun to me and opened his mouth.

"Swallow it!" It was good of him to check but the middle of a fight wasn't the best place.

He swallowed, and he and Bunky flew high over the trees. Edana dropped her shield and sent a spell arrow right toward me. I dodged but it was aiming for the tiny bag in my hand, not me. I felt something in my hand change, and then I was holding an empty bag. She'd gotten the sphinx without even opening the bag.

"We leave," Edana yelled and turned her horse around.

The mayor watched in shock. He obviously had no clue who they really were, and his great heist was falling apart. "This is my job, who do you think you are?" His voice rose at the end as the reins of his horse started to strangle him. From the movements of Edana's hand, she was behind it.

"I am the one who might let you live. I have what I came for; I will get back the rest soon enough. And if you weren't such an idiot, you'd hear armored knights riding our way." She bowed to Padraig and Alric. "Most likely elven ones."

The rest of the surviving thugs turned and followed her. The mayor rubbed his neck, but as the sound of the approaching knights grew, he took off as well.

"They got the sphinx!" I couldn't believe that I'd had it, then lost it.

"But you got the chimera, right?" Mathilda nodded. "I saw Irving. We can protect the rest of the relics with the chest."

The sound of armored knights on horseback was unique, distinctive, and extremely loud. Flarinen rode into sight first, followed by Kelm. I wasn't surprised about them, but Harlan, Orenda, Siabiane, Nasif, and Dueble were a surprise.

"Well met, Master Lorcan." Flarinen gave a stiff bow, but didn't even acknowledge the rest of us. "We have come to escort you, Alric, and Padraig back to the enclave."

"And Orenda and I are joining the rest of you," Harlan wasn't a great rider, but he managed to nudge his horse around Flarinen. Orenda and Siabiane followed, with Siabiane jumping off her horse and running to her sister.

Mathilda jumped off her horse as well and the two had a silent reunion. Well, silent to others, it was clear they were talking to each other.

"Why would we come back right now?" Alric shook his

head. "We're trying to take care of this. That's what we're out here for."

"No, you're out here to gather the relics and bring them back. You have them; bring them back to your king."

Lorcan looked at the knights. "The king and queen have given me release to resolve this my way. And this is my way. There's no reason to go back and certainly not to take the relics we have back. They have to be destroyed."

"My kingdom disagreed and gave evidence to your king," Orenda said with a tone of disgust most likely aimed at her absent brother. "They now want to examine them further. My people will be coming down along with three other enclaves."

"That won't work." Mathilda shook her head. "They have to be destroyed. Lorcan and I have come up with a plan to gather them, destroy them, and make certain enough people know they are destroyed to leave no doubt. We need a battle. Not a time for study."

"We might be able to use some of the relics, not the weapon, but some of the individual pieces." Flarinen didn't sound certain. He was repeating what his superiors had said.

"No. This has to end. I came along to see my sister, but I had no idea this was the plan of the king and queen." Siabiane was clearly furious.

"We're not going back," Alric said.

"And you're not getting the relics," Lorcan said as he pulled out the faery bags he had in his pouch. With a whistle he called Irving down. "Taryn? If you please?" He threw the bags in the air.

"Irving! Eat them! Then fly away!" I didn't think the knights would hurt the constructs, but even Flarinen would figure out what was in those bags soon enough.

Irving did as he was told and swallowed the bags, then he and Bunky tore off toward the south.

"Garbage, take the girls and stay with the constructs.

Guard them." This wasn't going to end well.

"Faeries rule, elves drool!" Garbage yelled as she flew down low over the elves. Then she and her flock followed the constructs. Their cat steeds had already slipped into the woods.

Alric got back on his horse and grinned at Flarinen, and it wasn't a nice one. "We're not going, and the relics certainly aren't going."

Siabiane and Mathilda had been talking fast and low. I doubted I could have understood them even if they spoke louder; it didn't sound like any language I knew. Siabiane turned to the knights. "I'm not going back either. I now understand their plan here, and it will end this quickly. The only relic the others have is the sphinx. We will place information in select circles that we can destroy the others without it, and with enough historical creativity behind it we can make it appear valid. A large battle must be called; we will need all of the enclaves to attend. We will get the sphinx back and destroy the weapon—and there will be no doubt." She folded her arms and managed to look down at Flarinen, even though she was standing on the ground and he sat on a horse. "This will be over."

I had no idea that was what Mathilda and Lorcan had been planning, and no matter how simple Siabiane made it sound, even I knew it wasn't going to be anything but close to impossible. But I trusted them.

From the looks on their faces, Alric and Padraig hadn't been completely involved in this plan either. But neither said anything in front of the knights.

"Someone is coming back to explain this to them. If not, there is no way the clans will support your fight." Flarinen scowled at everyone with narrowed eyes.

Padraig nodded. "He is right. This is an ambitious plan, and we need two knights to explain it to them." He looked at an even more annoyed Alric.

My head spun toward him. He was a knight? And never

told me?

Alric scowled. "I gave up that life; I never followed it."

"Yet you and I are still knights," Padraig said. "We can discuss this, but we have to go back."

Alric gave a short, tight nod, but wouldn't look my way.

After us just saying we would stick together no matter what, he was going to leave. I knew about it this time. But I was still pissed. Not to mention, the bastard never told me he was a knight.

"We will go with Siabiane and the rest." Nasif had been watching the exchange, and also looked annoyed that he hadn't been told the truth by the king and queen. Dueble just sat awkwardly atop his horse in silence.

"I've a better plan for you two," Siabiane said. "Rather, for your academic nom de plume. You need to get the word out about the five out of six majority needed to destroy the weapon. I know you can get it established quickly."

Nasif bowed from his horse. "As you wish, milady. Come on, Dueble, we've a lot of work ahead." He started to ride away.

"Nothing has been decided," Flarinen said.

Nasif looked back over his shoulder. "Yes, it has, you just haven't caught up yet." He and Dueble went the direction of the faeries, cats, and constructs.

Alric wouldn't look at me, and he seemed to be having a serious fight with himself. He finally said a few quiet words to Padraig and rode over to me.

"We won't run off, but I'd like to talk to Taryn alone." It wasn't a question, and as he rode closer he nodded to the forest behind us.

I knew I wasn't going to like what he said at all, but we did need to talk.

The others could be heard discussing the situation behind us; Flarinen's annoying tones and Lorcan and Siabiane pushing back at everything he said. Once we got far enough to not understand what they were saying, Alric stopped his horse and got down. I did the same.

"I have to go back. If I don't they won't support this. Knights can call witness and make the royals reconsider our side quickly."

"Why do you need two? Can't Padraig go on his own?" I wasn't happy about losing Padraig either; he was a good fighter and magic user. But that wasn't as emotional as Alric not being with me in what could be the final battle. Somewhere deep inside, as soon as they said he was a knight, I knew if he went back he wouldn't come back to us. We could both die in this, never being close enough to say good-bye. I rubbed my arms at the chill that thought brought.

Alric came and held me tight. "It's a knight thing. Formally, our knights work in pairs. Some, like Flarinen, are assigned whoever is available. Normally he's leading a troop so it doesn't pertain to him. But when he came after us those months ago, it did, so they matched him with Kelm for that trip. Padraig and I have to go in together."

"Why didn't you tell me you were a knight? I thought you hated them?"

"I do, on the whole. There are some good ones, more good than bad. But as a concept, and people like Flarinen who embody that concept, I don't agree with them. I trained as one when I was young. Padraig was doing it, and I wanted to be like him."

"I don't want you gone." It sounded whiny and petulant when I said it; the tone more so than the words. But I had a horrible feeling we shouldn't be separated right now. We needed to be together to see this through.

He didn't answer me, but kissed me. The intensity told me he didn't want us to be separated either. But there was enough regret there that I knew he was going through with it.

"I have to do this. I have to say their plan sounds dangerous to me. Neither Lorcan nor Mathilda had brought it up before. But we can't take the relics back to the enclave."

"I feel that if we separate now, I'll never see you again," I said. "And no, I'm not being melodramatic." I wished there was a way to make him understand the growing fear in my head. This wasn't how things were supposed to go. "I can come with you." Not my first choice, but I couldn't help it. We needed to be together on this.

He kissed me again, softly. It was a farewell kiss. "Not unless you can get that manticore out of you for good. I don't want to risk *any* of the relics with them. Besides, you will need all of them together to destroy them. There's no guarantee that Padraig and I can get the royals to agree."

He was being so logical, but it was tearing me up. "Don't. Die." I gave him one more kiss, then ran for my horse and rode back to the others.

CHAPTER FORTY—FOUR

THAT NIGHT WAS ROUGH. I kept going over the things I could have said. The things Alric should have said. Alric, Padraig, and the rest of the knights had left as soon as Alric came back into the clearing.

At one point I dreamt that I was walking through the forest, but it felt much darker than it had when we'd set up camp. An icy wind shot through me, and an unnamed terror struck my soul. I had no idea what it was, but something was following me, and even knowing it was a dream wasn't enough to stop the feeling.

I kept walking, almost unable to stop. Then I heard the chanting. It was loud, but the voices were high pitched. Their volume was due to the quantity of voices, not because they were loud on their own.

Part of me yelled to wake up, or at least turn a different direction, but my feet kept moving. The clearing ahead of me had a small fire, and shadows danced around it. They were chanting but I wasn't sure whether they were actually dancing or not.

My heart dropped. The fire was surrounded by hundreds of squirrels, all flashing the red amulets we'd found before. But what was worse were the three still forms tied to a stake at the top of the pile of wood: Crusty, Leaf, and Garbage.

I ran forward, stubbing my toe as I did so. Two things came immediately to my attention: I was barefoot and this wasn't a dream.

I must have been dreaming and walked out of the camp—a disturbing enough thought made worse by the fact that someone should have been on guard.

The stumbling into their clearing and the swearing that followed got the possessed demon squirrels' attention. Something I was pretty sure I didn't want to happen.

I glanced to the fire and my faeries, they were unconscious, but I had hope they were still alive. The flames weren't close, but I still ran toward the fire, grabbed a big fire-free stick, and used it to smack the stake with the faeries into the bushes. The demon squirrels watched it fly, but went after me instead.

I flung a push spell at them but it made no impact. I tried slowing them down, making them sleep, anything my frantic brain could think of. Of course, my sword hadn't decided to join me either.

My first night away from Alric, and I was going to be torn apart by rabid demonic squirrels with a jewelry fetish.

The initial wave of demon squirrels was almost upon me when a band of new furry beasts ran in front of them. More squirrels. These turned their backs to me and charged forward, attacking the possessed ones. The new ones didn't have the red amulets, but they were armed. I looked twice, but yes, every squirrel out there—on either side—was armed with tiny, real looking swords.

I really should be asleep for something as insane as this. A few hundred squirrels, sword fighting over me and my three faeries.

The faeries.

I skirted around the battling rodents—yes, the possessed ones had been focusing on me, but apparently the non-possessed squirrels were a more dangerous enemy to them now.

I ran to where I thought I'd flung the stake with the faeries on it. It took a few panicked moments to find the stake; the fire wasn't large enough to throw much light, but I finally spotted a tiny orange arm sticking out of a bush.

The girls were just starting to regain consciousness when I finished untying them. "Are you all right? How did they grab you?"

Garbage shook her head and looked a bit cross-eyed. "Sewer-weed. Didn't smell. Trap." She kicked my hand. "Go fight now."

I'd kept all three in my hands once I'd freed them, but she startled me when she kicked my hand so I'd opened it automatically. And she fell right out of it. I grabbed her and looked at the other two. They were even groggier than their leader. None of them would be flying for a bit.

The fight was still going on, and my new friends were falling back. "Girls, I have to find a way to help those squirrels—they are trying to save us." I wasn't sure where to put the faeries, but I had to try to help.

Garbage focused on my words, and all three noticed the squirrels for the first time.

"Need help!" Garbage yelled, but I really wasn't sure who she was yelling to. A moment later, Bunky, Irving, the remaining faeries, and a couple dozen more, many clothed in leaves, swarmed the area.

My original three were in no condition to fight, but the rest of the faeries and Bunky and Irving helped the normal sword-bearing squirrels fight off the possessed sword-bearing squirrels.

Irving would dive down low and chase them toward Bunky, who zapped them. I watched to make sure Irving wasn't going to turn them to stone, but his mouth stayed closed. Maybe he was being more cautious now that he had other relics in there as well.

"No! You go!" Garbage didn't look good, but she'd staggered to her feet and was waving off the constructs. "They want."

I looked around, not sure who *they* were, then I saw

three of the mayor's thugs come out of the woods on the far end of the clearing with a net and cage. They didn't look good; someone had beaten them badly. I was thinking there had been a recent change of leadership in the evil thug army. By someone with enough magic to trigger the demonic squirrels to act as a distraction.

They were trying to grab Irving.

I was tired, pissed, had almost no sleep, and these bastards had tried to kill my faeries to draw Irving out. So they could rip him apart and get the relics inside him.

My magic might not be working right now, but I had another option. I felt the change coming on, and this time I called it to me. "Bunky, get everyone out of here and guard Irving too." Everything hurt as I changed into whatever my other form was. The manticore dropped out of me again, but I was too busy looking at the idiots in front of me. There were still some demonic squirrels, but the good ones fled with the faeries and constructs.

The three thugs tried to run. Even though I was big, I was a lot faster than any of us thought and stomped on two of them before they knew it. The third I had to pluck out of a tree. She deserved to die just for being stupid enough to get eye level with the thing she was trying to escape from.

I focused on changing back to myself, fell over once I'd done it, and threw up into some shrubbery. The flash of cold in my cheek told me the manticore was back.

Once I'd recovered, I made my way back to camp. Covey and Lorcan were heading my way. When they saw me they both ran forward and each took a side and helped me the rest of the way to camp.

"Garbage and Bunky told us what happened. Did you actually change?" Lorcan was definitely concerned about my well-being, but a thousand questions about what had happened were hanging around him as well.

"They tried to burn the faeries to death in order to capture Irving. It sort of happened on its own." Covey led me to a large log near the fire and pushed me to sit. "We need to destroy these things now, and I think it's time they go into that chest. Those were the mayor's thugs, but we have to assume Edana knows where they are too. If she can get enough power behind the sphinx, she might pull Irving to her."

"I have to say, I agree," Lorcan said and dropped a blanket around my shoulders. "This was too well planned."

Harlan and Orenda joined us, but the sisters were missing. "Where are Siabiane and Mathilda?"

"They had both been on guard when everything happened. A spell lured them away and they had just returned when the faeries arrived here. They went looking for the magic user behind the spell. I almost feel sorry for whoever did it." Harlan shook his head. "Good to know you still get into a lot of trouble on a regular basis."

"If I hadn't been sleep-walking, they could have killed the faeries." It was a good thing I'd already thrown up, the thought of what those demon squirrels had wanted to do to my faeries made me sick. I didn't think even the faeries could come back from the dead.

The faeries and constructs were clustered in the middle of camp—well, our faeries were. The wilds had gone off again. Garbage trotted over to me, climbed up my leg, then up to my shoulder, and stared. "You save."

"Well, your squirrel friends, the other faeries, Bunky, and Irving saved you too."

She shook her head, her face uncommonly solemn. "You. Save. Me." She actually had tears in her eyes and started hugging my neck. "Thank you." She gave me a kiss on the cheek, patted the spot where the manticore was, and scampered back to her gang.

I had nothing to say. Leaf and Crusty were often demonstrative, but I'd only seen Garbage get like this once—when the other two had been cut off from her.

Mathilda and Siabiane must have come back while Garbage and I were having our moment. They were both standing across the fire and smiling.

"I told you they needed to be together," Mathilda said.

Siabiane nodded. "As usual, you were right."

The fact that they were sisters was evident a moment later as the smiles dropped.

"We couldn't catch whoever was behind the spells or the trap." Siabiane was usually the more vicious of the two, but Mathilda was showing it now. They were pissed.

"We need to get the relics into the chest," Lorcan said. "Although we will have to hide out for a bit, I'm afraid. Not more than a few weeks. We need to give Nasif and Dueble time to spread the academic ruse substantiating that the weapon can be destroyed with only five of the six relics. And let the others get the knights in place." It was reassuring that he obviously didn't doubt Alric and Padraig's ability to convince the royals to go along.

As much as I wanted these relics gone, I had to agree with him. There were many factions after the relics, and probably far more than the ones we knew about. Edana might have gathered most of them under her banner, but we needed everyone to know without a doubt that the weapon and the relics were destroyed. Once we were able to actually get the diamond sphinx back from Edana and do just that.

CHAPTER FORTY—FIVE

TWO WEEKS LATER, ALMOST TO the day, we took our positions inside the tree line that marked a wide plain. We watched as the horses and riders that we'd been hearing for ten minutes finally came forward through the hills. Alric and Padraig were at the front of the elven forces as the mass rode forward. Both were almost unrecognizable in the bright armor of the elven knights. Even when they came to a halt and removed their helmets. Their faces were so cold and stern it was still difficult to recognize them, even with the spyglass Covey had gotten for me. But my heart knew who it was. I knew I had a massive part to play in this scenario, but all I wanted to do was run to Alric.

The considerable number of knights behind them were too large to be from the Glaisdale enclave alone, and a closer look revealed that while there were a large number of knights with the same white plumes on their helmets as Alric and Padraig, there were at least five other colors. Even after a thousand years of hiding, they were prepared to fight. I'd guess over two thousand of elvenkind's best warriors were out there.

The knights parted, and the king rode forward. I almost expected to see five more kings or queens as well. After that many years, one would think the other enclaves would have started their own royal lines. Unless one knew how set in their ways elves were.

This field was now looking like a battlefield. We just

needed an enemy. There was no way to know for sure if Edana believed the rumors we planted that said we could destroy the weapon with just five relics, or if she was counting on beating us and taking all of them for herself. Either way, we were ending this now. According to the spies, a huge syclarion army was heading our way. This had to work; too many innocents had died, and they would keep dying until we stopped this.

I took a deep breath and lowered the spyglass. My terror of releasing the manticore was only getting worse. I knew why I needed to do it. However, changing was still new enough to me, that the idea of transforming in front of a few thousand warriors made me physically ill. Yes, we were hiding in the woods, and Lorcan had layered a dozen spells of hiding around us. As long as Covey and Lorcan got the manticore into the faeries' bag quickly and then into the chest, I should be able to change back without it coming back into me. And without anyone beyond us noticing.

I'd wanted to get the manticore out two weeks ago when they'd mentioned they had a plan to do it, but it had taken this long for Lorcan to create a spell that would keep it from immediately coming back into me.

I watched the waiting elves through the trees. The idea of being some weird genetic mutation was bad enough without thousands gawking at me. Not to mention that the elven knights looked on edge enough to kill first and ask questions later. I hoped they stuck to their agreement not to interfere with the destruction once we got the weapon together.

I'd thought that when a decision had been made, Alric might come back to us. Instead, five days ago, an elven knight came out to deliver the response accepting our plan and telling us the knights were already on their way. The royals and the rest of the rulers weren't happy, but they would stand by to fight.

There was nothing from Alric.

Mathilda and Siabiane stood guard over the chest with the four relics in it. Both nodded encouragingly to me.

Taking a deep breath, I removed my ancestors' armor from my shoulders. Logically, I knew my clothes were perfectly fine when I changed back, but emotionally, I wanted those two pieces safe.

The female shoulder guard always felt like it gave a brief squeeze whenever I removed it. The male one didn't, but the fact it stayed on even though it was far too big for me was enough. I handed both to Covey.

I thought I saw Alric looking for me but it could be wishful thinking. He could have at least sent a note.

This was when I should change. Everyone was distracted, which hopefully would keep any mages out there from noticing the spells covering the trees. I took a deep breath, focused, and waited. I'd only been able to change once on my own, but it had been a combination of will, focus, and need.

We had the need and I was focusing my will like crazy.

"There's not much time," Covey whispered. "You might want to hurry things along,"

"I am trying." My focus was in full force. My will to turn into whatever it was I became was shouting inside my head. And nothing.

A rustling came from the undergrowth surrounding the trees around us and broke my concentration.

Garbage, Leaf, and Crusty, all in their war feathers and proudly riding their armored feline steeds, came forward.

"Weren't you still having to attend Queen Mungoosey?" I was glad to see them, but I knew the faeries had their own agenda with an end-of-the-world scenario. They'd been called away two days ago by their queen—and I'd really thought we'd be doing this without them. Queen Mungoosey had banished them when they helped us before. Not helping us could be the cost for her taking them back.

"We done!"

"We back! Fight now!"

"You need!" As Crusty spoke, she and her sleek gray battle cat darted forward, quickly followed by the other two. All three jumped off their cats and climbed to sit on my shoulders.

Garbage reached over and patted my cheek. "Now try."

I closed my eyes and focused again on changing. I shoved the questions I had about what the faeries had been doing into a dark corner and just thought of changing.

And saw a minkie pop up in my mind. Knowing he was probably harmless wasn't helpful, but he was in my head, so I'd just have to work around him.

The familiar feeling crashed into my gut and I felt my skin and bones stretch. Unlike that first time, it didn't hurt really, more like a stretch gone a bit too long. I kept my eyes shut since if I saw my friends gaping at me, I'd lose focus.

After a few seconds of no more changes, I opened my eyes. It was a good thing that Lorcan's spell went far over the tree line. If I could see the battlefield, the people on it could have seen me. Alric briefly looked up from his discussion with Padraig. He scowled but didn't look like he could see me. Most likely he was sensing the edges of the spell. One thing about whatever I changed into, it had far better eyes than I normally had. Alric shook his head and turned back to Padraig.

The three faeries had resumed sitting on their cats and Lorcan was tightening one of their tiny bags when I looked down. Then he slipped it into a second bag and knotted the ties. Then he dropped it into the chest and nodded to me. Going back to my real form felt easier, as if I'd been holding my breath and just released it.

This time was better than the last one; I didn't fall over or throw up.

"Did we get it?" I nodded to the faeries. I couldn't feel the manticore inside me, but no one was completely certain the bags would hold it, even with Lorcan's spell.

Garbage rode her battle cat to Lorcan and slowly raised her left hand in the air. She closed her eyes and finally nodded. "Is there."

I had a feeling that she knew without doing anything, but if she wanted some pomp, I wasn't going to say no.

I put my shoulder guards back on; the rest of my mismatched armor had come back along with my clothes. I also buckled on my belt and scabbard; my sword had stayed with me constantly since the incident with the possessed squirrels.

"Now what?" Getting the manticore out of me had been such a focus that I was at a loss for the next step.

Lorcan dropped the spells he had over the woods and nodded to the battlefield. "Now we get back our world from the threat of these things." He turned to the faeries. "I assume there are more than just you three?"

Garbage smiled. "All."

We came out of the forest at the same time that a cloud came out from behind the trees. Garbage's troop still rode cats. But the cloud was a mass of faeries the likes of which I'd never seen—there were even more than had been at the battle of the glass gargoyle. Between them and a fleet of chimera constructs flying alongside, they briefly blocked the sun as they passed. They stayed in formation, but two constructs bobbed as they passed. The way the light bounced off the one, as if it was made of glass, I knew it had to be Bunky and Irving.

Padraig and Alric had been conferring with the king, and then both got off their horses. Mathilda and Siabiane moved the chest closer to the middle of the battlefield—dangerous, but they needed to be seen for this to work. Alric and Padraig were walking toward them when all hell broke loose.

Too many things happened at once. Alric looked like he'd been struck with a spell as he froze, and then dropped to one knee. His helmet was back with his horse, so I clearly saw the snarl he flashed my direction as he struggled to regain his feet.

At the same time, a roar broke out behind us as our forces were attacked by the syclarions and their allies—the same forces that we thought were at least a half day's ride away.

Siabiane and Mathilda slammed up a spell bubble shield around themselves and the chest. It took their magic out of our defense, but protecting those relics was more important. We took a gamble with this plan—and it might have failed. Edana's people were supposedly still a ways away.

Lorcan also put up a spell bubble. His was modified, not as strong as the one around the chest, so he could continue to cast spells. However, he wouldn't have done that unless he felt that Edana was nearby.

I'd expected the gathering elven leaders to go back to their troops, and all of them, including Padraig, did.

But Alric was on his feet and running for me. The snarl was still on his face but he also looked to be in massive pain.

CHAPTER FORTY—SIX

THEN I NOTICED THAT THE geas mark on his arm was glowing through his armor. Actually, it looked like it was branded onto the armor. I first thought that he was coming for someone close to me, but no one was nearby.

"Run!" Alric was almost upon me and tears were now flowing down his face. His first strike at me was wild and I was able to block it. "I can't stop this, you have to run!" He was readying another strike when Nivinal rushed out from the trees, slammed into him, and dragged him to the ground. He'd come around through the trees, intent not on winning a battle but destroying Alric.

"I told you I was going to be the one to kill you, elf." Nivinal hadn't even noticed who Alric had been fighting; he was too focused on executing Alric.

Alric rolled to his feet and immediately cast a spell bubble over him and Nivinal.

I stumbled forward to help, but images and emotions slammed me to my knees as a group of minkies appeared before me. Not just in my head; judging by the yelling, others saw them as well.

The distant past spread out before me. Another battle. Part of the vivid images matched Covey and Lorcan's theories, but a lot didn't. But I suddenly knew where and when I was. The battle had gone on for years, friends and family murdered by the syclarions—my parents both recently killed in a horrific battle in the air over the ocean not far from here. My people were losing the fight.

I was the only one who could save them; the species now known as the Ancients. The syclarions had to be destroyed so we could live. I hadn't told anyone about my weapon when I made it.

I held a staff in my hands, a totem staff. Gargoyle, chimera, dragon, manticore, basilisk, and sphinx. The me of thousands of years ago pulled the syclarions in close, against their will with the power from the dragon. They fought, but couldn't pull back. They'd murdered my people. My friends and family. The words of my spell crashed into the air and set it on fire.

First my people vanished. I'd wanted them safe, but I'd sent them out of time and place instead with my uncontrolled weapon. The syclarions were mostly dead. The survivors were far away and genetically devolving.

Then the memory shattered and I snapped back into the present battle. I threw up. I was an Ancient. A proud, grieving, powerful being who had lashed out in fear and anger. I'd pushed my people into a time void, and sent myself, amnesic and magicless, twenty-five hundred years into the future.

As if my realization had called them to me, all of the relic pieces broke free of the chest and spell bubble and dropped at my feet. The diamond sphinx hovered in the air in front of me a moment later.

The current battle in front of me raged on as more syclarions, dwollers, and Dark elves flooded the field.

Nivinal and Alric were locked in a fight in their bubble. Nivinal couldn't break the bubble because Alric would slaughter him the moment he turned away his focus.

Edana wasn't in sight, but I knew she was here. No one else would have had the sphinx. I also felt her, just like I had twenty-five hundred years ago. She and Nivinal were syclarions. Somehow she'd survived when most of her people hadn't.

A yell of pain brought my focus back to the spell bubble. Nivinal had managed to get a strike into the gap in the armor near Alric's shoulder. Alric stumbled back and the spell bubble fluctuated. He put one hand out and reinforced it. He was focusing far more on the bubble than the fight. The geas mark was still there, but it was fainter than before.

The geas that commanded him to kill the one who had destroyed the Ancients. I knew they weren't dead. I wasn't sure how I knew, but they'd been thrown out of time. They were alive—just not on this plane of existence.

Somehow I didn't think that geas really cared about the difference.

Alric was going to have to kill me.

Covey ran toward me, mowing through a group of syclarions to do it. We weren't in the center of the fighting, but that wouldn't last long once people spotted the relics.

"Are you okay?"

Her question brought a hysterical giggle from me that I quickly cut short. I'd just found out I'd sent my people into some murky time void, created the relics that murdered thousands, and the love of my life was going to have to kill me.

I was never going to be okay again.

"I can't explain," I said as I grabbed her arm. "But whatever happens, and I mean *whatever*, don't try to stop Alric. And don't let anyone else."

Covey looked over her shoulder to the spell bubble and frowned. "I don't think he's coming out."

"I'm going to change that."

Covey jumped as I called the relics together and reformed them into the staff. The diamond sphinx reflected the sun from the top. She hadn't seen them before they moved; judging by the lack of ruckus around us, no one had. At least not until now.

I'd been rash and over-emotional in my creation of the

weapon twenty-five hundred years ago. My people normally fought in their dragon forms for obvious reasons. However, a large dragon claw wouldn't have been able to wield the staff. That had been deliberate on my part. The syclarions thought us weak for our human form; twenty-five hundred years ago, I had destroyed them in it.

At Covey's wide-eyed nod of agreement of my request, I ran to the spell bubble. Alric was barely standing, and clearly losing the fight. I had a feeling that had been his plan once the geas told him I was his intended victim. He hadn't locked them in that bubble to keep me safe from Nivinal; he'd done it to keep me safe from him. Even a thousand-year old geas couldn't work from beyond the grave.

"Stand back, I'm getting you out now!"

Alric stumbled to my side of the bubble. Nivinal didn't look much better. "I will not kill you." He raised his arm with the glowing geas. "This will make it happen, and I can't. I love you." He smiled and seemed to be memorizing my face. Then he flung up his sword and blocked a weak attack from Nivinal.

"I won't let that happen. I love you too much to let this happen either." I raised the completed staff weapon over my head. I'd lost too much—I wasn't losing him too.

"No! You can't use that. You won't. Please." The love, pain, and sorrow in his bright green eyes as he spoke brought my arm down. The bubble didn't disable the geas, but it weakened it enough for him to be himself.

I glanced over the battlefield, images of the old battle intermixed with the new one. One of the minkies popped up in front of me.

"Follow heart—not fear." Cryptic little bugger. Now that I knew who I was, I knew who they were. Spirit animals of the Ancients. Edana had blocked them, the faeries, and the constructs from the final battle twenty-five hundred years ago using tricks the vhin had given her. I shifted the staff in my hand. I was far calmer and more balanced than I had been then. I could save my friends this time and only destroy our enemies.

But this staff wasn't going to be a part of it. I snapped the staff in half, then quickly changed form into my dragon shape and stomped on it with both front feet.

An enormous wave of magic slammed into the world from the destroyed weapon as one by one the relics shattered to dust. I managed to stay standing, but most people in the field went down.

Edana screamed, I knew where she was at the back of the field, and knew she would soon be upon me. Before anyone could recover, I swung my tail and shattered Alric's spell bubble. I was prepared for him to try to attack me, but not for him to not move at all.

Nivinal stumbled toward me with a snarl, but I stomped him into the ground with both magic and weight. Then I changed back to my human form and ran to Alric. The geas mark was gone. He was alive but the rattle in his chest told me that wouldn't last for long. Now that I knew who and what I was, I knew my limits; I could tell at a touch that I couldn't save him.

"Help me!" I sensed Orenda before I saw her running my way. She'd been close enough that I knew she had seen what just happened, but she didn't hesitate to run to Alric's side.

Her armor clanked as she dropped down and threw off her gauntlets. "I'll need your help." She held out her hand and I flashed back to another time of her and me saving Alric. I had more power now than before, but as much as we tried, we couldn't stop his life from slipping away.

I grabbed Alric's head as if I could bring him back by sheer will alone. "No!"

His eyes fluttered open but their light was fading. "We broke the geas. I will always love you." His eyes closed and he slipped away from us.

My sobs were echoed by Orenda's. A small hand gently pushed mine aside from his chest.

I flung open my eyes, ready to destroy anyone who got between him and me.

Amara looked down at me gently as her power flowed to Alric.

"This could kill you too." I had accepted me dying with Alric, but I didn't want my friends to as well. Pulling someone back from the dead was beyond even my power.

A goddess might be able to do it.

"No, I will live. As a mortal dryad. I freely give my power." She looked down at him and smiled. "His love and sacrifice destroyed the geas before he died. This is good."

Without another word, she took my hand, drawing in as much power as I could give. I might or might not have had dryad in my family—but my magic felt right at home with hers.

Alric spasmed, then gasped raggedly. His opened eyes were the best sight I'd ever seen. "Are we dead? I know I died."

Foxy ran to us as Amara collapsed. She looked pale, no longer glowing, but she was breathing.

"Amara brought you back." I wiped away my tears and kissed him gently.

"You saved me. I told you to let me die." His breathing was uneven and he looked like a three hundred-year-old drunken cherub could have knocked him over.

"I told you a long time ago that I wasn't good at following orders." I hiccupped and realized I was still sobbing. And that we were on the losing side of a battle. The relics were gone, but this was about more than just them, even if they were what led to it. This was the conclusion to a battle that started over twenty-five hundred years ago. With Edana's skills and power, there was a good chance she could rule things around here for a very long time, even without the relics.

That wasn't going to happen.

I motioned Covey over. "Guard him." Just because I'd chosen not to use the weapon didn't mean I was going to let the people I cared about die. The Ancients hadn't been prepared for the final battle and had been alone. We had allies this time. And I was going to see if adding an Ancient to the current mix could tip the scales.

CHAPTER FORTY—SEVEN

——◆——

COVEY NODDED AND WENT INTO berserker mode. I kissed Alric one more time, then stepped away from them and changed. Anger raged in me, but it was more focused now. The relics were no longer an issue, and I knew Edana was aware that they were gone.

As my height changed, I spotted her. She was at the far side of the battlefield and had changed into the syclarion's dragon-like form. I used to think it was fearsome—now it just pissed me off.

Unfortunately, there was that huge field of people between us. Now that my memories were back, I knew that Edana didn't care if her people were killed—as long as she got what she wanted, which was full control over everything and everyone. I wasn't going to risk others just to stop her. There had to be another way.

Alric had once asked if I'd had wings when I changed. I now knew that I did and I didn't. We could control our wings and whether they appeared or not. Whatever had forced me into changing at the Spheres hadn't been under my control, so no wings.

I remembered I had them this time. I moved even further away from my friends, most of the enemy were staying clear of me on their own.

"Stay back," I yelled, then flexed my wings into being. I gave one massive flap. Went about ten feet up, then slammed backwards into the woods behind us.

Garbage, Crusty, and Leaf flew off their battle cats and up to my face.

"Boom!" Crusty shouted then spun in a mid-air circle.

"Is good, we fly, you fly." Leaf bounced around in the air.

"Why you in trees?" Garbage narrowed her eyes as if there must be something she was missing.

My memories were coming back, but apparently physical memory took longer.

"I'm trying to fly across the field." I could tell that on some level the faeries knew this was going to happen. I'd deal with that, and anything else they might know, when we got rid of Edana and her troops. Boon companions to the Ancients, indeed.

"We help!" all three shouted and immediately a few thousand more faeries swarmed me.

Queen Mungoosey flew to my face. "Pleased we are that you have returned. We will help." She gave a regal nod and a flick of her long gray tail.

I cautiously flapped my wings again and slowly rose above the trees, surrounded by my cloud of faeries.

Yells came in full force from across both sides of the battlefield. A few archers took aim, but my hide was too thick for their arrows to pierce.

Edana hovered in the air, but stayed on her side of the field. She wasn't near as large as I was, but she'd been flying and casting spells for the past twenty-five hundred years.

At least I had the faeries.

Taking to the air was better than fighting on the ground in terms of not killing our own troops. But we could still hurt them from up here—or rather, Edana could.

More memories were flowing back. Like when my parents died. It had been an ambush over the ocean. Syclarions didn't like large bodies of water any more than we did, but Edana had sacrificed dozens of her own people in order to murder my parents.

The fleet of constructs now joined us. I might not have

dozens of my people flying alongside me like she did, but I had my friends. I banked away from the battlefield and toward the ocean. This fight was going to end today one way or another. By taking the top fighters out of the ground battle, I was hopeful my friends had a chance.

Edana chased after me and showed no hesitation when she must have realized where I was going.

"You want to die as your parents did? Or are you simply trying to run away?"

She wasn't close enough for her voice to carry but I could taste the spell that carried her words to me. As soon as I sensed the spell, I knew how to do it. Providing I survived, I wasn't going to have trouble learning magic anymore.

I didn't respond, but flapped harder. The faeries were around me, with the mass of chimeras intermingled. Bunky and Irving flew the closest to me.

I waited until I got far enough out that getting back to land would be difficult for someone who was injured. Yes, if that someone was me, this was a bad plan. I just had to make sure it wasn't me.

When I could barely see only a thin outline of land behind us, I spun. A few times actually. Navigation in this form wasn't easy. However, I made it look like I'd intended to do that and came out of it facing Edana and her flyers. They'd picked up the sceanra anam along the way, and they and the chimeras were already racing toward each other.

The faeries stayed with me, but it was me and a cloud of faeries verses Edana and twenty or so flying syclarions. I wasn't holding out a lot of hope, but I wasn't giving up either. Alric had been willing to die to save me—that needed to be addressed.

Edana was smaller than I was, but she flew as if she knew what she was doing. My memories were coming back, but still not a lot of the physical abilities. She flew in closer and let loose a fire spell.

I was shocked at how quickly the flames hit and how horrific the pain was until I was able to put them out. That was no normal fire. My hide in this form had the ability to withstand normal fire—this spell was designed for my people.

"Your parents died because of a spell like that," she yelled. "Of course we had been attacking them for hours, no land in sight, nothing but water. I doubt you'll last that long. I have no idea where you've been hiding for the last twenty-five hundred years, but you'll wish you were back there before the end."

She was busy taunting me and didn't notice the arrow of faeries that went for her back. I'd seen them kill with those war sticks of theirs and while we weren't that lucky this time, they did make her pull back in pain.

And fury. She lashed out and sent most of her attackers tumbling into the ocean. Then she spun on her own people. "You let them through!" She reached out and one of the flying syclarions burst into flames and fell into the ocean.

If I could keep her at this long enough she might work her way through all of her people.

"Your son won't be coming back this time, by the way." I was crappy at taunting and I was seriously outmatched here.

"He was weak. Like you. You shouldn't have destroyed the staff. You could have had everything." She fired another bolt, but this time I got a wing and a spell up to deflect it. Not great, still hurt, but not as bad as the first one.

Or so I thought.

My wing was beginning to go numb, and that numbness was spreading toward my heart.

"Stupid girl. I thought highly of you; you'd created a weapon unlike any other. I thought you must be brilliant. But you were just lucky." She fired another shot.

I moved and missed most of it, but was having trouble staying aloft as my entire body started going numb. I had hope that the faeries survived their fall into the ocean; I knew I wouldn't.

Push was one of my best spells before I knew who and what I was. Even though the memories of other, more complicated spells were coming back to me, that one was just waiting to be used. It was an elven spell, not one used by my people.

I flung the spell down at her as hard as I could, pushing me up as I pushed her down. It gave me more lift. I'd be able to fall a bit longer before I crashed into the ocean. But she'd managed to deflect the worst of the spell. Three of her own people were slammed into the ocean at her deflection.

Half the faeries were in the ocean, and the remaining ones went for the other syclarions. The constructs were fighting the sceanra anam, but they were being overwhelmed.

And I was growing number.

"Would you just die? You can't win, your spells are juvenile, and your body is about to give up."

As she spoke, Edana slammed me with more fire spells. I managed to block two, sent a third back at her, but the fourth hit my side. I spun, trying to put it out, but I couldn't do it. I was falling faster, and the smell of salt from the water was as unwelcome as it was strong.

I flung whatever spells I could at her, but they were weak and badly formed. I gave one last thought for Alric, the faeries, and the rest of my friends then closed my eyes as my body surrendered to the pain and I fell toward the waves.

Minkies appeared in front of me. Seriously? Last visions should be of Alric, not tiny furry, feathery creatures. Maybe I actually was dead, because just as I had my thought about the minkies, a song burst in my head.

When I'd changed this time, I hadn't had a chance to remove my armor—including the shoulder pieces. They were now wherever my clothing went when I changed. Those pieces weren't from my long ago ancestors, they were from my parents, and their strength was coming to me in the song. I'd not been able to get the full impact before because I hadn't known who I was, who they were.

In my spinning, I saw Edana smiling as she watched me crash into the ocean.

The song from my parents filled my ears, and the minkies stayed right alongside me as I hit the icy waves.

The coldness of the water shocked my body into responding and fighting off the spell. Pretty sure my parents and the minkies helped as well.

My people didn't swim, but that didn't mean that I couldn't fly out of the water. The minkies were in front of me and around me, mentally cheering me on as the song of my parents soared through my blood.

I had talons, cruel long ones. I grabbed Edana's side with them and flung her away as hard as I could. I wanted to rip her apart, but my body was fighting to recover. Flinging her away seemed like the best way to give myself a few moments of respite.

The faeries were trying to get the rest of the syclarions, but either they were a different class of magic users than most of their kind, or Edana gave them extra power. They were slowly defeating the faery horde.

"Pick on someone your own size." It was a cheesy line, but the power flowing through my veins right now was stronger than any ale. I sent the slowing spell, the push spell, and a fireball all at once. The remaining syclarions were wrapped in flames and pushed by my spells into the water where they slowly vanished under the waves. Since I was throwing them in the water, the fireball seemed a bit much, but that was one spell I'd not learned from Alric—it came from the old me.

The faeries swarmed around me, but there were so many that I couldn't pick my own out. "You need to pull your friends out of the water. Then help the constructs." The flapping of wings behind me told me my stalling time was over.

The faeries nodded and left as I spun to Edana. She was bleeding from the gash in her side, but she still flew strong. The song of my parents increased and only one minkie remained. He nodded, then vanished.

Edana and I met in the air. Her skill against my size and the spirits of my parents. At first she tried to do quick strikes, but on her third dive in I froze her with a spell. It wouldn't stop her but it allowed me to grab ahold of her. We were locked together, both of us fighting to get in the final strike.

She gave a vicious grin, and then changed into her non-flying form. Whatever spell she used was targeted against me as well. I became human and we both fell into the ocean.

I didn't release her as we hit, but swimming was not something I was good at and I needed my arms to stay afloat. I knew as soon as I let her go though, I'd lose. Syclarions were stronger than humans. And somehow she'd locked me into my human shape. With armor on.

And a sword.

I'd forgotten about it, but it had come back with my clothing when she forced the change. I pulled my sword free, and ran her through.

The shock in her eyes as the blade hit was something I hoped my parents' spirits could sense. I wasn't a violent person, not if I could help it. But she deserved to die. Too many lives had been destroyed because of her greed and need to rule.

She tried hanging onto me as she slid off my blade, but I managed to stay clear. She sunk lower in the water until I could no longer see her.

The rest of the syclarions were gone, and the faeries and constructs had turned the battle and were chasing the last of the sceanra anam.

I was in the middle of the ocean, treading water, wearing armor, and holding a sword. Changing forms right now would just make me sink faster, not to mention I was so cold there was no way I could have focused enough to switch. I'd won. I destroyed the one who'd killed my parents. Now I was going to drown.

It took my brain a few minutes of pitying itself before I was able to fight back. I got the sword back in the sheath, closed my eyes, and focused on Garbage, Leaf, and Crusty. I didn't add ale, or sugar, just how much they meant to me. And that I was in danger.

"We come!" I was shocked to hear Garbage that quickly. Even more so when I opened my eyes and saw them leading two boats that were being magically sailed against the wind and at high speed. Alric was at the bow of one.

"We save!" Crusty got to me first, followed by the other two. They started kissing my hair.

"Girls! This is great, but I'm freezing. How did you get them here so fast?"

"Went get them before you go swimming. Knew you need." If Garbage got any smugger her head would explode.

The first boat got to us before I could say more. Alric looked ready to jump into the water, but Covey pushed him back. "You are recovering from being dead. I will not allow you to undo that by diving into that water." She pushed his chest again. "We don't have another tree goddess." With that she dove into the water and came up beside me. "Looks like a certain Ancient might need some help?"

I hugged her and she hauled us both to the boat. Alric was allowed to help lift me into it and I was immediately wrapped in blankets.

I looked up at the faces in both boats. People who were

truly a family to me. I'd thought I'd lost my people, my family. I'd just found a new one. My thoughts were cut off as Alric pulled me close, held me tight, and kissed me for a very long time.

EPILOGUE

I ROLLED OVER AND WATCHED ALRIC sleep. In the past week it had become my second favorite hobby. He looked so much younger when he slept. All the worries he still carried, even though he claimed to have left them in the elven enclave, were still in his eyes.

But asleep he looked like an elven angel. *My* elven angel. The battle for the relics ended just eight days ago. Seven days ago Alric and I said goodbye to our friends and headed out deep into the forest above the enclave. He had found another one of the elven traveling houses when he'd gone back to argue the case for destroying the relics. We'd hitched it to our horses, and went into the woods. Alric claimed to just be wandering, but somehow we ended up in a perfect meadow with a stream.

Seven days of glorious peace. No relics, no faeries, not even any discussion about my being an Ancient, and him almost having to kill me.

Alric didn't open his eyes, but reached out and pulled me into his arms. "What shall we do today?"

I started to answer when the side of our traveling house shook. Then the door rattled.

Alric was on his feet with his sword in his hand before I could even process the sounds. It was a good thing we both had sleeping clothes on, or flinging open the door would have been far more interesting for anyone bothering us.

Three familiar bright zips of color flew into the house,

yelling and jabbering. I didn't get up, but I could see more hovering in the meadow. And cats. Lots of cats.

"Girls, you promised us we could have a month off," I said, then climbed out of bed and wrapped my robe around myself.

"Is bad! You come!" Garbage yelled, while flying around trying to see everything in the house at once.

Alric sighed, banished his sword, and turned. "What's bad?"

"Fighting. Bird lady under attack!" Leaf was also looking at everything. There might be something really happening, but I also figured they'd wanted an excuse to visit.

"Bird lady?" Alric only had pants on, so he reached for a shirt.

I sighed this time. Watching him without a shirt was favorite thing number three. "I'm thinking they mean Qianru?"

"Yes!" Garbage spun in a tight circle. "Let loose the kittahs of war!"

THE END

Dear Reader,

Thank you for joining Taryn, Alric, and the faeries in the final book of The Lost Ancients series. This was a great book to write and I'm so glad you joined us!

This series has ended, but in case you missed it—there are still some shenanigans to be dealt with! Stay tuned for a NEW adventure with all of the gang in 2020/21. Updates will be posted on all social media outlets—so make sure you're following me somewhere.

If you're also interested in a little bit of space opera, please check out the completed Asarlaí Wars trilogy.

Fancy some tea and adventures? You might be interested in the steampunk cozy series: The Adventures of Smith & Jones.

I really appreciate each and every one of you so please keep in touch. You can find me at www.marieandreas.com.

If you enjoyed this book (or any book for that matter ;)) please spread the word! Positive reviews are like emotional gold to any writer and mean more than you know.

Thank you again!

~

ABOUT THE AUTHOR

Marie is a multi-award winning fantasy and science fiction writer with a serious reading addiction. If she wasn't writing about all the people in her head, she'd be lurking about coffee shops annoying total strangers with her stories. So really, writing is a way of saving the masses.

Her six book fantasy series, The Lost Ancients, starts with The Glass Gargoyle. The Obsidian Chimera, The Emerald Dragon, The Sapphire Manticore, The Golden Basilisk, and The Diamond Sphinx follow and are all available.

A space opera trilogy, The Asarlaí Wars, launched with Warrior Wench, and continued with the Victorious Dead. The final book, Defiant Ruin, is available now.

A steampunk adventure, A Curious Invasion has also been released with the second book slated to come out in late 2019—The Mayhem of Mermaids.

When not saving the masses from coffee shop shenanigans, Marie likes to visit the UK and keeps hoping someone will give her a nice summer home in the Forest of Dean or in northern Wales.

Marie is also a member of SFWA (Science Fiction and Fantasy Writers of America) and RWA (Romance Writers of America).

To find out more about the books, and future series, please visit her website at www.marieandreas.com—especially if you happen to have a small cottage to give her.